DILLON'S DREAM: AIR, WATER & EARTH

a novel by

Dr. Shawn Phillips

edited by

Kyla Buckingham

YBCoyote Press

This novel is a work of fiction. Names, characters, places, and incidents were created by the author or used fictitiously.

The author gratefully acknowledges the permission by Mr. Rob Williams to liberally write about Hoshinroshiryu as it was taught before the new millennium.

Copyright © 2009 Shawn H. Phillips

YBCoyote Press, Publisher

All rights reserved. No part of this book may be used or reproduced in any manner whatsoever without the written permission of the publisher or author. For information go to www.ybcoyotepress.com or write to info@ybcoyotepress.com.

ISBN 9780982644638

1. Fantasy   2. Science Fiction   3. Meditation   4. Martial Arts

Library of Congress Control Number: 2010931456

Printed in the United States of America

Cover design by Dr. Shawn Phillips
Background photo courtesy of NASA

In Memory of:

Dr. Glenn J. Morris

A perfectly unique father and amazing teacher, who possessed the greatest martial arts mind that the world never knew. You awoke so many lives, and changed the way we see the spiritual side of our world.

ACKNOWLEDGEMENT

The friends and family that have encouraged my writing and inspired my dreams have been and will be thanked personally many times. This page I reserve to pay my advanced appreciation to anyone who opens this book and sets aside the time to read what I've written. I hope to launch you to a new place where your mind is excited and your reality is forever changed.

A Must-Use Online Reader's Guide

Index & Timeline
www.dillonsdream.com/index.html

Glossary
(new words denoted by * in the novel)
www.dillonsdream.com/glossary.html

Maps
(map use denoted by # in the novel)
www.dillonsdream.com/maps.html

Meditations
(step-by-step meditations denoted by ^ in the novel)
www.dillonsdream.com/meditations.html

Educational
(literature circle questions, project ideas, research related questions, resource links, etc.)
www.dillonsdream.com/educational.html

Blog Room
www.dillonsdream.com/blog.html

Artist Corner
www.dillonsdream.com/artists.html

Chapter 1
Nothing Is by Accident

I.

Ugh! How does Mrs. Grain expect me to write an essay on dreams when I've never had a single dream my whole life? Or if I did, I can't seem to remember what I dreamt about.

Why are they so important anyway? Everyone in my class dreams of being famous or making lots of money after they graduate. In reality, dreams never amount to anything. Besides, I already know what I'm going to do with my future. I'll finish my senior year in high school, move away to college to get a science degree, and then become a research technician making enough money to live on. After that who cares what happens.

Dillon Chase dropped his chin onto his hands as he stared out of the dusty, sun-burnt window at the Joshua tree in the middle of the yard. His biology teacher, Mr. Dunn, had once explained to his class that a Joshua tree really was not a tree, but rather a member of the lily family. At that time Dillon had thought it was another boring trivia fact that Mr. Dunn always seemed to get sidetracked on, but today he was so fascinated with the fact that he could not get it out of his mind.

Why a lily in the middle of the desert? That seems kind of ironic since lilies grow in water. Why does it have to look so ugly? Why do the flowers smell so nasty? Why...did I wait to write my paper until I woke up for school today? Oh well, my score in the class is high enough that I'll still ace the class.

Dillon flung his backpack over his left shoulder, opened the garage door and skateboarded out onto the sidewalk. He paid little attention to the four foot, yellow-green lizard taking a squat in his neighbor's yard. He had seen that same lizard enough over the last week to assume that someone on the block was feeding it. As long as it wasn't crapping in his yard then life was okay.

Dillon's thoughts hung up on deeper reflections as he skateboarded across the road. His senior year was almost over and in no time at all he would be moving away to college. Having a semi-photographic memory had allowed him to cruise through school, especially in his science and math classes. However, English and writing classes always required additional effort, as he had to think rather than just regurgitate information. He figured that college was going to be more of the latter, as he could shy away from the more challenging liberal arts classes.

In spite of having no real challenges, Dillon almost always worked hard on his classes during the weekdays so he could delve into the role-playing gamer's world during the weekends. Such a lifestyle often made one a target for bored miscreants. However, he hadn't been picked on since last year, and usually only had a run in once a year anyway. That was when he had to show another school bully that having a dad as a martial arts grandmaster had its advantages. Dillon rarely took it seriously, but he had trained as much as necessary to get his blackbelt at the age of sixteen. He was enough of a nerd so that when he brought home a three-day suspension note for fighting one of his annual bullies, he could tell his dad was actually a little proud, and his Mom would only ground him for a few days to let him know that he shouldn't make fighting a habit.

After school, and only with a slight berating by Mrs. Grain for his missing assignment, Dillon sat on the sidewalk outside a run-down science trailer waiting for his friends. All of them loved role-playing games as much as he did, and most of their after-school conversations focused on the upcoming weekend's gaming marathon.

Lian was the first to trot up to their usual gathering spot. If a name determined a person's fate, then Lian had a long way to go to fit into his Chinese name, which meant graceful willow. He was tall, gangly, and required intense effort just to avoid tripping, bumping, or running into something whenever he moved. Lian was president of both the chess and computer clubs, two things that always seemed to go hand-in-hand. It also made sense that he chose to be the wizard, a position of scholarly intelligence, when they played any sort of fantasy game.

Dillon knew that Lian used the weekend gaming to get away from the daily ridicule that followed him wherever he went. But he had learned long ago not to intervene when he saw Lian in a bad situation, since it only intensified the struggle with an internal, darker component of his psyche. A couple years ago Dillon had heard that some kids were waiting after school to have some fun with Lian. Dillon got there just in time to stop a beating from turning into a hospital visit. Later that night he stopped by Lian's house unannounced to see how he was doing. Upon barging into Lian's room he caught a glimpse of a handgun's metallic butt underneath a bed pillow.

A normal kid might have frozen in place or pretended not to notice the gun, but Dillon slammed the door, walked right past a startled Lian, grabbed the gun and pointed it at the pillow he had just overturned. Without time to think, he pulled the trigger and tried not to flinch from the loud explosion that shook the room and rattled the open window. He dropped the gun, strode over to and jumped out the open window just as the bedroom door's frame splintered from the sudden impact of Lian's dad. Dillon could still hear the former drill instructor's voice booming halfway down the street as well as the shrill Chinese words of Lian's mom.

The next day at school Lian was the first to meet up with Dillon at their sitting spot. His only word to Dillon before the others arrived was "Thanks"—a single word that conveyed a new, unbreakable loyalty and friendship.

Dillon just smiled and tried to cover up his hands, which had been shaking ever since they touched the trigger. Now he wondered, as he often did, if things would have been better if he hadn't stopped the after-school beating.

"Hey Dillon, you ready for another weekend of the sorcerer reigning supreme?" asked Lian.

"How did you know I was bringing around another sorcerer to kick your butt?" Dillon snapped back.

"Well, you can always win if you want since you're the game master. However, I know that my mage* would win outright in any fair fight."

"Yeah, of course any fight I'd win you would immediately scream that it wasn't fair. Just rest assured that during your mage's last breath he will stand awestruck from the shock and horror of what happened to him, while your own jaw will drop so fast that your skin will have to hurry to catch up," replied Dillon with a big grin on his face.

Just then Matt and Tanya rounded the building and headed toward the two. At five-foot-nine Matt had been the tallest kid on the junior high playground and had taken on the title of school bully, mostly because others expected him to. By the tenth grade a number of kids had surpassed his unchanging frame, and Matt decided then that it was time to lie low and take on a new role. He studied hard and had earned a science scholarship to Hope College, a small private school in Michigan, where he planned to study biology next year. The heavy education focus did drain him, so when the gaming weekend came around he liked to be the berserking warrior who fought more than thought.

Tanya, dwarfing Matt by nearly four inches, had the usual cocky smile of any high school athlete who was top in the state. She was a good volleyball competitor and a great basketball player who did nothing to let others know she cared about her feminine side. She swore with the best of them, never wore make-up, and often stunk of body odor from an early morning pick-up game of street ball. However, on the weekends she came to their gatherings in a dress willing to play any type of character.

Although Tanya had been playing on weekends with them for almost two years, they still knew very little about her and her family life. Dillon could ascertain that her mom and dad both commuted down the 14 freeway to Los Angeles. This meant they were gone for around thirteen hours every day, usually including Saturday and Sunday. Her home life appeared pretty normal apart from the fact that her parents were never around. Tanya seemed to like that just fine, and always made comments about how she enjoyed being able to do whatever she wanted.

"Hey love birds, how's it going?" asked Dillon with a cheesy grin. He ducked, while laughing, as Matt's backpack flew by his face. Tanya and Matt weren't dating and no one could picture such a sight, which made the needling all the more fun.

"Stuff it nerd," Tanya coolly replied as she dribbled her L.A. Sparks basketball, which matched the purple and gold jersey that was tucked into her shorts. "So I know it's two days away, but what are you setting up for the weekend at your house? Futuristic, fantasy, superheroes, classic sleuth?"

"Lian already guessed it. I've got to go with fantasy this weekend. You guys are almost done with your quest and Gabe is close to figuring out what his magical elfin boots do."

Of course, Dillon thought, *Gabe won't want the boots once he figures out their power. They cause leprosy and won't come off one's feet once they are put on. The group will have to take a detour from their quest and find the healing temple of Sanatio before Gabe's health gives out.*

Gabe, headphones in his ears and MP3 player in-hand, was the last one to round the corner. He sauntered toward the group, nearly lost in his music. Gabe was originally from a rough neighborhood in Whittier, California. He had just joined the gang scene when his mom uprooted him and moved their whole family to Lancaster, California. Although gang violence had sharply risen in the Antelope Valley* over the years, Gabe didn't pick up where he had left off. Secretly desperate for the opportunity to get out, he had turned his life around and now enjoyed music and literature, especially the classics. He liked to train with Dillon's dad to keep in shape. In fact, he trained harder and more often than Dillon.

Gabe pulled down his headphones, which were blasting some lesser-known piano symphony. "Hi Dillon, Tanya, Matt, Lian. Boy that was a lousy day. I messed up on that chemistry quiz. I mean, why on Earth do I need to calculate the heat of formation for creating water from hydrogen and oxygen? That is almost as useless as integral functions." Gabe hated the hard sciences, but his version of messing up meant he would pull off an A- or B+ on the quiz. He had the highest grades out of all of them, but Dillon always joked with him about taking the "soft" sciences and other "artsy" classes.

The conversation drifted back and forth from school to role-playing games for a half hour. Dillon then got up, said some whimsical goodbyes, and headed home on his skateboard to do his chores before dinner.

II.

The way back home should have been uneventful as always, but Dillon was yet again caught-up reflecting on a normal object in his path.

Who determined that a light pole should be so high? Who figured out the optimal distance between two light poles? Why is that huge lizard leaking on the light pole? Wait, that lizard doesn't belong...

The sound of the impact made far less noise than the screeching tires coming from the 1998 Honda Accord. Dillon's body hurtled through the air like a rag doll before coming to a sudden bone-crunching stop against the cement curb. His skateboard shattered on impact, launching the larger pieces over a brick wall and into a backyard some fifty feet away. For a moment both the body and the car lay motionless. Then the Accord's driver-side door slowly opened and out slid a tall, lithe man who cautiously made his way to the near-lifeless body.

Damn, this is not going to look good on my record. The man looked around as if searching for something. *Strange that it could even happen. Maybe my vehicle needs a tune-up?*

The driver methodically lifted the boy's unconscious body out of the pooling blood and calmly placed it in the rear seat of his car. He nestled back into his own seat and shifted the car into gear. It nudged smoothly into the busy intersection and merged between the other cars before dissolving without a trace.

In spite of the rush hour traffic, there was no indication that anyone noticed what had transpired – except for the four-foot lizard propped up nearly human-like against a freshly painted yellow fire hydrant. An unsettling grin lined its face.

III.

"How could you be so careless, Sandy? You know we checked out your vehicle and the avoidance meter was full? Did you forget to turn it on? Balsha*! This is going to affect your record."

Even though his jacket was covered in splotches of dried blood, Sandy just stood there and carefully processed what he was going to say before he spoke. "I had it on, Jake. There was an anomaly in the area."

"An anomaly? Are you sure about that? Of course you're sure. Well, it's just like them to think it's funny to have a kid from Earth get splattered by one of our Observers. Throw the body in the stasis chamber. We'll have to spend all night creating a body-drop scenario that has the highest probability of being accepted back on Earth. Balsha! Why do the bad things always have to happen on my watch?"

"He's not dead yet, but I don't understand why." Sandy's voice had an unusual amount of uncertainty.

"Not dead? My readout shows his neck is snapped and his legs are crushed. He's also lost half his blood, and his lungs and ribs have merged into one gelatinous mass. How can he be alive? Why is he alive?" Jake reread the scrolling signs on the palm of his hand, shrugged his shoulders and looked back at Sandy. "Well, take him to the medic room and let me know when he dies. I hope it's not too long since I'd really like to get home sometime this week."

"We have all been trying to get home for a long time, Jake. One more night here or in your room is not going to matter either way." Sandy's face was drawn and still showed no emotion.

"Nice, Sandy. I don't need a smart-aleck right now." Jake finally processed what Sandy meant and stopped talking for a second to think. "If he lives, it might mean something more. It might mean we do go home soon." He threw a grimace toward Sandy and walked away.

Sandy just stared after Jake for about a minute before he let out the slow, deep breath he had been holding. He returned to his vehicle and extricated the boy's body from the rear seat, taking time to cross Dillon's hands on his stomach before lifting him. He turned and proceeded down a long and narrow, bright green corridor with a number of open doorways staggered on each side. Stopping halfway, Sandy looked through the doorway to the right that contained the stasis chambers. He then turned in the opposite direction and walked into a sterile, large room containing over forty metallic beds and stared at the disinterested inhabitant. The doctor only nodded his head in the direction of one of the med-cubicles against the far wall that was reserved for the most serious injuries.

Sandy stepped into the eight-foot-wide, square cubicle and carefully laid the body on the unusually pliable metal table. Immediately, the opposite wall lit up with an incomprehensible display of scrolling characters. Not long thereafter gleaming tentacles, with an assortment of attached tools, formed out of the table and worked their way over, on, and finally into Dillon's body.

Sandy gave one last look at the body, which didn't seem nearly as massacred as he first thought, before he sighed and walked out of the room. The room sensed his leaving and silently slid the door shut as he exited. He ambled back to his vehicle and opened the rear door again, surprised to see that there was far less blood on the tan, leather upholstery than he had expected. He reached under the passenger seat and pulled out his Caol Ila bottle of scotch before leaving the observatory.

Chapter 2
Out of Despair, Hope Can Flame Forth

I.

Dillon's mind raced out of both fear and pure confusion. He wanted to scream, run away, and cry all at once but found that none were possible, and maybe would never be possible. He remembered hearing the screeching tires. He remembered feeling as if he was flying, followed by a pain so intense and concentrated that he was sure every cell of his body was exploding. In all of his short life he had never felt anything like it and never imagined that such pain existed. His slip out of consciousness was as sudden as the impact, but the pain had already been seared into his mind, a memory that would persist for the rest of his life.

The confusion hit when he realized he was looking down at his own mangled body crammed up against the curbside, as if his mind or soul was floating above the carnage. He bent down and reached out a hand to cover the grotesque opening in his skull, but upon seeing a blurry, purple form instead of his arm, he quickly withdrew. His whole being, or whatever his mind was in, was a shapeless violet with a wispy lavender trail leading down to where his body lay. Moment by moment the lavender line thinned, its thick trail diminishing around the edges.

What the hell is happening? Am I dead? Stupid question. Everyone says that in the movies, but who's going to answer? Am I now in some alternate plane such as the astral world were ghosts are said to reside? Maybe this is some sort of an out-of-body experience? In all those years of deep meditation* with my dad, I was always the one that never had an out-of-body experience. Now I'm dead – or near dead – and it finally *happens.* Dillon's mind raced through possible explanations. Finally he gathered his thoughts. *Okay, I just need to compose myself and think things through.*

Let's see. Whatever I am seems to be connected to my body through that purple trail. It appears to be getting thinner pretty fast, which probably means it will disappear altogether soon and I'll really be gone. Wait! Maybe I'm really in a pure energy state. No, that's ridiculous. Of course it's ridiculous. Everything happening right now is ridiculous! What can I do? What should I do? He continued to stare at his motionless body and the clothes stained in his own blood, which somehow calmed him down.

I need to remember my dad's meditation classes and draw in more energy or something like that. Now, how can I breathe when I don't have a body?

Just then Dillon noticed a tall man stoop over his body. Strangely, this person appeared as if he was standing in the night while the rest of the world was illuminated by daylight. The dark figure picked up his body and Dillon felt his new, purple form being dragged along. The stranger gently placed Dillon in the back seat, taking care to arrange Dillon's limbs without further damaging them. Dillon's new form passed through the car frame as if it wasn't there. The car accelerated, lifted off the road, and headed up to the sky at a steep incline.

No Way! This has to be a dream, but why am I dreaming now when I've never had a dream my whole life? Well, since it's only a dream I might as well try to do something crazy like try to fix my body so I can fly back home or maybe over to a cheerleader's house for a little visit. It's not fair that I've always missed out on dreaming about hot girls... Dillon lost himself to lust for a brief moment before recomposing his thoughts. *Okay, I need to focus on how to meditate. Green energy is for healing. All I need to do is figure out how to draw it in and put it back into my body.*

Dillon tried to relax his mind by visualizing himself drawing in energy from around him using imaginary breaths. He controlled his "breathing" by focusing on the number of each breath for an eight count followed by an eight count exhale. He didn't stop between inhales or exhales, but kept a continuous cycle of counting and breathing. His mind began to truly relax as he relinquished all efforts to control the process. Now in a good rhythm, he changed his meditation routine. Dillon pictured the sky as a source of energy pulsing out toward his body. As he breathed in he gathered the sun's energy into his ghost-like form, down to the chakra* (or energy center) below his abdomen, and then up his spine as he had done many times in his dad's Hoshinjitsu dojo*.

The sensation and intensity of the bright light from the sky was far stronger than he had ever felt before. He could see the light being drawn into his purple form, brightening and deepening him from within. He relaxed into the energy and noticed that a layer of green light was emanating from his purple form. He felt a rush of energy that he could only describe as ecstasy. It became a combination of powerful, relaxing vibrations that he had never experienced before and something he hoped he could bring forth again. He held onto it for a while, savoring the feeling until he remembered his goal.

With his next exhale, Dillon pictured himself pushing the energy out of the chakra and toward his body, but the green light quickly dissipated. He summoned the energy again and then tried to reach down and touch his body, but his purple "arm" just slipped through as if nothing was there. Had he known this was real, his frustration would have discouraged him. However, he had nothing better to do in his dream so he continued as if solving a puzzle. He tried different approaches until he noticed the purple wisp of smoke between him and his body. Dillon had an idea.

He again relaxed his mind, building up more green energy light inside and around him, and then mentally pushed it down through the cord between his body and purple form. He was amazed to see the connection strengthen and change to a greenish hue until the intensity was almost too bright to look at. He fought to keep his wavering focus and maintain the energy flow in spite of the mental exhaustion creeping in. Dillon used breaths to relax his mind and soon fell back into a calm trance. After what seemed like hours, he glanced through the front window of the Accord and saw the Moon racing toward him. When he looked behind him he saw a shrinking view of Earth. The visual was similar to the streaming video taken aboard the International Space Station, which he had once downloaded onto his computer.

The swift speed of travel further confirmed his belief that this was either a dream or that someone had spiked his lunch with a hallucinogenic. If it was the latter, he hoped that the prankster hadn't messed up his mind forever.

Dillon looked down again and noticed that he was maintaining the green light between him and his body with almost no effort now. Although his body still looked horrible, it was not nearly as pale and lifeless as it had been before they left Earth.

Left Earth? Do dreamers always so easily step into such absurd thinking? If this is all a dream then when did it start? Was it when I saw my body lying below me or earlier? How about that stupid lizard sitting on the fire hydrant? Wait, I saw that same lizard on the way to school this morning and also for most of the week before. How far back does this dream go and how long in real time have I been having it? Based on what I know from my dream assignment, this could all be happening in less than a few seconds.

As much as Dillon wanted to believe it was a dream, as much as Dillon tried to convince himself it was a dream, doubt crept into his mind.

If it's not a dream then what clues would I have that it would be real? Mrs. Grain told us that while dreams can help us learn and solve things, it cannot expose us to completely new things. Did I learn something I did not know or have no way to self-learn? Let's see. In English class we went over new vocabulary including that strange word. What was it? Oh yeah, it was CWM and it was defined as a walled hollow on a hillside. In chemistry class we learned that Professor Smalley won the Nobel Prize in chemistry for his work on buckyballs and was one of the leaders of the nanotechnology revolution. My chemistry quiz was to figure out the heat of formation of water from hydrogen and oxygen. The answer was negative 286 kilojoules per mole. There was no way I could have known all of this before or how to figure it out now. Dillon hesitated. *I don't think I'm dreaming.*

Dillon's apprehension not only reduced the amount of green energy traveling into his body, but also caused him to nervously look out his window again. He was now staring at a crater in the Moon, which filled the entire front window. He started to see the texture of the Moon and noticed the sequence of several small, metallic-black domes that the vehicle was headed toward. There were six sets of six domes spaced equal distances apart. As they moved in closer he could see that the small domes were at least a mile in diameter, and they were headed for the closest one. Just when he thought they would crash, a small circle on the side of the dome quickly opened as the vehicle shot through and landed on a smooth black surface.

Dillon watched as the tall, slender driver stepped out of the car and walked up to a portly, animated man. Dillon found it strange again that, even in this well lit dome, the two men's faces were shadowed so that he could not make out any features. Although he could barely hear their conversation, he discerned that both where shocked that he was still alive. Dillon responded by refocusing his efforts to draw in energy and push the gathered green light down toward his body.

The lanky man came back to the vehicle, carefully picked up Dillon's body, carried it down a corridor, through a large room, and finally laid it on a table in a small cubicle. Fascinated, Dillon watched from above as tentacles emerged from the table and twisted toward his body. The last Dillon saw were two tentacles maneuvering into his body through his abdomen. Suddenly he felt himself being wrenched rapidly downward.

A searing pain racked his body. Although it was not nearly as painful as the car accident, it was less bearable since this time he could not escape out of his body. The gaping hole in his head throbbed, and his broken ribs were like knives moving against his lungs. He felt every wound in his body, from his fingernails that were nearly ripped off from skidding on the pavement to the crushed collarbone protruding through his skin. He wanted to scream, he wanted to cry, but found he could not control the near-corpse he was trapped within. The nightmare—he *hoped* it wasn't reality—continued, worsening each time Dillon thought he'd reached the maximum human capacity for pain. The hole in his skull seared from the onslaught of the air hitting the exposed nerves. He finally gave up and, regretting those meditative breaths that had returned him to his body, started to pray for death. Moments later the pain began to slowly recede into a dull throb as the alien medical table finished patching his wounds, eventually turning into a distant nuisance.

No tears appeared in the corners of his closed eyes, and no one noticed that he was conscious or that he could hear all that was around him. Dillon now knew full well that this was no dream that he could control. This swift realization after all that had happened in just the two hours after school got out was too much for him. He stared at the back of his eyelids and quietly lost all hope.

II.

Days, weeks, or months could have passed but Dillon hadn't noticed. It had taken a long while for him to awaken and rekindle his desire to live. He was embarrassed that he had prayed for death, and also at how easy his mind had succumbed to hopelessness. But now Dillon was determined to never sink into despair again.

Dillon was bored on his table, and decided the best thing to do was to attempt to make small actions or movements to keep busy. He focused on trying to move his body. After a while he figured out that he was either fully paralyzed or had been sedated in some strange way. He could swallow but could not open his eyelids.

After a while he let his mind wander and take pleasure in the comfort of non-thinking. He was enjoying his semi-lucid state when, even with his eyelids shut, an unbearably bright, white light appeared to walk into the cubicle. The light came right up to the table and Dillon both saw and felt an extension of that light touch his shoulder. It wasn't a normal human touch. It was as if the light was reaching into his body, causing him to feel sensations that he had thought were lost forever.

"I am sorry this had to happen to you, my child. However, within you lies all the hope for the survival of your race. I can heal your body, but can only hope that your mind is strong enough to accept what has happened and adapt to your new destiny."

Dillon saw another extension of the light reach out to touch his face. Dillon expected pain, but instead calmness overcame him. He felt the white light cover his face and then course through his body until he was completely aglow. His whole being was full of sensation again, but the feeling differed from anything he had ever known. At first he thought it was just the elation of having his feeling returned to him, but then Dillon realized that it was more; he could sense every cell in his body as an individual entity. He knew which ones were dying and which were growing anew. He could feel them fighting off infections and increasing the oxygen uptake of his hemoglobin to resupply his red blood cells. Here again was yet another overwhelming experience, but this was not one that Dillon would willingly relinquish.

Dillon watched inside himself as the white light enveloped each cell of his body and healed his wounds faster than possible for the human body to do itself. Once it had healed everything, the white light retracted back into the being standing before him, who then turned around and walked out of the room.

Dillon tried to digest what had just happened. What was this thing about being the hope of saving humankind? It sounded so cliché and straight out of a sci-fi movie. But then again, this described everything he had experienced recently. He then realized that, although he had been given back feeling in his body, he still could not move no matter how much effort he exerted. However, he was pretty confident now that this was the effect of some sort of drug they were giving him. Soon, he predicted, he would be able to move again.

III.

Dillon had no indication of how much time had passed, it seemed like forever since the white light left, and he was running out of things to keep his mind occupied. Over time even his thoughts about his mom and dad turned from worry to curiosity as to how they would react. Periodically he did hear the door slide open and through his eyelids saw a dark figure walk in, look around, and then walk back out. He wished his eyelids would open so he could at least look around. As the overwhelming fear was subsiding an incessant boredom took over, Dillon resorted to using his semi-photographic mind to recall and try to sort out all the crazy things that had happened.

The four-foot lizard no longer seems normal, and it's strange that I thought it fit in just like a neighbor's dog at the time. In fact, the lizard was what caused me to lose my concentration and ride into the intersection. Also, why did the driver of the car who hit me have a face that could not be seen, and so did the man who seemed to be his boss here on the Moon? What was with the out-of-body experience? What about the powerful energy I could draw forth and now still feel raging just below the surface of my skin?

Dillon's mind raced through these questions over and over but could not even partially solve one of them. He eventually slipped into reliving mundane events that had occurred in his life, then fell into a comfort zone of remembering chemical equations from his high school chemistry class. He easily visualized chemical reactions, and it was fun to toy with the basic rules for balancing chemical equations.

Let's see. The last equation we had to work out was way too simple. In order to make a molecule of water you had to have one molecule of hydrogen and a half a molecule of oxygen, and it gave off 286 kilojoules of energy when forming a mole of water. However, it's the high energy of activation required for the reaction that prevents it from spontaneously happening—otherwise we wouldn't exist. Hydrogen and oxygen would be combining in the air all the time, releasing an incredible amount of energy as heat. Now, for balancing chemical equations you have to use whole numbers, not fractions.

Dillon pictured the equation in his mind:

$$2H_2 + O_2 \rightarrow 2H_2O$$

This caused him to obsess about his dry throat. He hadn't swallowed any liquids since before the accident—how long ago was that? It seemed like forever. The taste of water, even if just one drop, was all that he wished for now. He focused solely on the equation, envisioning the hydrogen and oxygen molecules coming together to create water. As the water formed in his mind, he pictured the taste on his dry lips, felt the swishing in his mouth, and enjoyed it cascading down his parched throat. Suddenly the energy that was snuggled beneath the surface of Dillon's skin rose like a tidal wave. Without thought, Dillon gathered it at its peak and crashed it into the equation.

The energy disappeared instantaneously and his body turned hot with the gut-wrenching realization that the thirst-quenching but boiling water he had so desperately desired was now drowning him. Alarms blasted in his room and, through his closed eyelids, Dillon saw flashing red lights somewhere above his head.

Dillon's mind started to close down. He was about to die; he could feel it. Just as blackness began to overpower him, time seemed to slow down, his vision cleared, and a comfortable weightlessness enveloped him. Dillon was again hovering above his body, but this time there was no blood or grotesque distortions below him. His body looked almost healthy, even normal, except for the steaming water cascading from his mouth.

His gaze turned toward the dark-faced man clad in white, who rushed into Dillon's cubicle. The beefy man rapidly tapped the smooth side of the metal table as if commanding an invisible control panel. A shiny, ribbed tentacle with a sharp needle attached to the end darted out from the table and plunged into Dillon's open mouth. His body jerked again and again in response. Then Dillon felt himself being pulled back downward. Dismayed, he knew he was back inside himself once again because he couldn't see anything except the light that filtered through his closed eyelids. The flashing red lights and loud alarms ceased. The only sound was the soft echo of footsteps slowly retreating from the room.

Silence and utter confusion were yet again Dillon's only companions. His mind raced through all the recent events with not even a hint of something that would allow him to have any hope of a return to normalcy. Even though he had promised to never give up again, Dillon yielded into a semi-comatose state. He simply couldn't comprehend his new painful life that left him clinging to a narrow thread of sanity.

IV.

Dillon heard voices and pulled himself back into the present. They were talking about him, commenting on this strange, futuristic place on the Moon, and how they didn't know whether to be happy or sad about what had transpired. The effects of the medications must have worn off, because he suddenly—joyfully—found that he could open his eyes. Eager to take in the brilliance of colors and textures and patterns again, he was disappointed to see the room automatically dim in response. His guests fell silent and in unison turned toward him and smiled. His eyes slowly adjusted, and he realized that the smiles in front of him belonged to Lian, Gabe, Tanya, and Matt.

All but the more muscular Matt looked just like he last remembered them when he jumped on his skateboard and said goodbye after school. He stared into each one's eyes, searching for something but not knowing exactly what it was. It was hard to admit to himself that he was slightly disappointed to see no indication that they too had been through hell and back.

"About time you stopped sleeping and decided to join the real world for a while," joked Tanya, although he saw a tear escape from her left eye.

Gabe could hardly contain his brewing excitement. However, he controlled his voice. "Dillon, you will not believe what is happening and what we are going to do. In fact you probably will not believe what you have done."

Dillon tried to figure out the answer by piecing together recent events, but Gabe interrupted his thoughts. "Somehow boiling water just appeared in your body."

"What do you mean?" asked Dillon, his voice edged with disbelief despite his certainty that he was being led toward truth.

Gabe continued. "Well, when the alarms went off they found you lying in a puddle of water. The med-cubicle you are in was able to quickly ascertain that you were drowning and emptied your lungs, healed the burnt tissue, and started you breathing again. The Mulshins* then did an analysis and found that not only was it very pure water, except from the contamination from your lungs, but also that the hydrogen and oxygen content within this section of the biodome had dropped significantly. At first it puzzled me just as it did them. However, I knew that one cannot violate the first law of thermodynamics."

"Energy or matter can be neither created nor destroyed, merely transferred," piped in Matt. "Even a biologist has to pay attention in chemistry class."

"Exactly!" exclaimed Lian. "So the water had to be created out of the hydrogen and oxygen in the air. The Mulshin computer systems could tell me exactly how much water was formed. Then it was easy to balance the equation and do the calculations to determine the amount of hydrogen and oxygen that went missing."

"That's pretty interesting," Dillon nonchalantly remarked since he was more curious as to how they got here, why they didn't seem bothered by the sci-fi environment, and what a Mulshin was.

"No, that's not the interesting part. What is interesting is that in order to form that much water you needed energy...again back to the first law of thermodynamics. It was fairly easy to calculate the amount of energy needed to both gather all the hydrogen and oxygen into one area and also overcome the energy of activation to convert it. It required quite a lot of power, and, when we checked the biodome self-diagnostic system, it showed that the only source of energy that large at that time came," Gabe paused for dramatic effect, "from you, Dillon!" Gabe was more excited than Dillon had ever seen him before.

Dillon's eyes focused on Gabe. "I know. I did it. But I don't know how."

"We did not know at first either, but that tremendous amount of energy appeared out of thin air from your body. It was a guess as to whether you were going to die from pure exhaustion, drowning, or burning." Gabe's mouth was still poised to talk, but he held back and waited upon seeing Dillon's quizzical expression.

"What do you mean by *at first*?"

"Well, we all did some researching in the Mulshins' library and found out that it…"

"…was magic!" yelled Lian, much to Gabe's dismay at having the story's crowning words stolen from him. "You did magic to create the water. Not nearly as impressive as what my sorcerer in our fantasy game can do, but still pretty darn neat."

"You see, the first law of thermodynamics was still observed. It is just that you used your own energy to make the transformation work. And that was a lot of energy," Gabe finished.

Dillon was poised to vent a sarcastic comment about magic, but held back and pondered his entire situation. It made sense of his experiences but still bordered the ridiculous. "But magic is scientifically impossible! How can I do magic? How come I was able to? Why hasn't anyone else done magic on Earth?"

"That will take a lot more time to explain. You need to rest some more before we talk any further."

Dillon recognized the voice well before the tall, lithe man slowly stepped between Matt and Lian.

"Hi Sandy, did you enjoy your scotch?" Dillon playfully spoke, anticipating Sandy's shocked expression. None came.

"I'm not much surprised at anything you do or say now, Dillon. Healing yourself in the car at death's door and this newest episode has taught me that you are special." A smile crept up Sandy's face, and he reached out and touched Dillon's chest right over his heart. "We'll talk more tomorrow, and yes, you'll be able to move your entire body once the drugs wear off. So just try to relax and take it easy."

Chapter 3
Grounded in Truth, Any Explanation Sounds Good

I.

During the night Dillon stared at the ceiling, enjoying the first hint of happiness he had felt in a long time. Yeah, things were far from great, and he was even more lost than ever before, but at least his friends were here, and they all seemed excited about something they were going to do together.

Dillon closed his eyes and let his mind wander. As he drifted off into what he thought was sleep, he suddenly saw many corridors and rooms filled with shadow-like figures walking around. He let his mind 'walk' along the corridors with them, and then he drifted upward and saw below him three brighter figures sleeping in adjoining rooms. Off in the distance a glowing light drifted lazily away from him. Curious, he began to slowly follow it, then sped up as it moved farther away. As he came closer to the light he could see that it was shaped like a human being and was almost too bright to look at. Excited, Dillon pushed himself to keep pursuing it until he could almost touch it. Just when he was close enough to grab it, the light turned around and touched him on the forehead.

Dillon opened his eyes to the sound of the door sliding open and Sandy softly walking in. The light from the entrance was bright, and Dillon shielded his face with his hand, noticing that his hand and the rest of his body were no longer immobile.

"Good morning, Dillon. I trust that you were able to get some sleep even with the hundreds of questions running through your mind?" Sandy asked.

"Yeah, and the dream I had was pretty interesting," responded Dillon.

Sandy cocked an eyebrow, showing his interest while Dillon explained what happened to him. Upon completion of his tale, Sandy's eyebrow had resumed its normal position.

"Well, I would expect even stranger dreams from now on, especially after the shock we've given you. Besides—"

"What are you, Sandy, and why am I here? Why are my friends here?" Dillon interrupted Sandy and waited for a response. After several moments Sandy sat down on the bed and exhaled deeply.

"I've been trying to figure a way to tell you what you need to know without taking up years of your life. I'll explain what I can to you and then you can ask questions." Sandy seemed purposely reserved in his reply. "I'm not from Earth and not even from this galaxy. I guess you'd call me an alien, although that word isn't very positive on your world. I am part of a race called Mulshins."

"Like Martians?" interrupted Dillon again, just as Gabe entered the room and quietly sat in a half-lotus* position on the floor.

"Funny incident I'll tell you one day, but let's get back to my story. Our race has lived in a technological society for tens of thousands of years and as with your race, we have a strong desire to explore the unknown and search for other life forms. For most of this time we searched and searched the universe for any signs of intelligent life, and had given up hope until we found your planet. We were elated but also naïve in terms of the impact our appearance would cause. After a few less than desirable interactions, we decided that your race was not ready to meet us and instead built an observatory on your moon. Our leaders established laws and rules with regards to interacting with humans, and sent Mulshins like myself called Observers to watch you and your people."

"How long have you been observing us?"

"A few thousand years," replied Sandy, realizing Dillon wasn't going to wait to ask questions.

"Isn't that pretty boring?"

"Far from it. It's been a beautiful thing to watch and follow the evolution of humankind. Besides, our mission is worth waiting for. We

Observers will help decide when your race can handle contact with us, and then we'll celebrate our co-existence in this vast, lonely universe."

Sandy paused, saw doubt in Dillon's eyes and, and as with the other day, he touched his hand on Dillon's chest. "Dillon, if we had wanted to take over your planet it would have been easy enough to do when you wielded stone spears and your knuckles dragged on the ground. In fact, we still could if we wanted to and without much effort. Anyway, your technical advancements have been increasing exponentially and we had thought that time was approaching for contact, but we hit a snag." Another long moment of silence passed as Sandy took his tan, gangster-style hat off, straightened out a crease, and put it back on. "Dillon, I know everything you have heard and seen so far may seem out of a science fiction novel, but please bear with me. What I'm going to tell you next could come right out of one of your role-playing games, but it's real. I think if you reflect on what has happened to you over the last six months since you left Earth, then you will know what I say is true."

"Six months!" yelled Dillon, as he struggled to sit upright. "I've been up here for that long? What about my family, my mom, my dad?" Dillon felt himself spinning out of control as the energy inside him again climbed to the surface of his skin, bubbling this time like a cauldron of fire.

Sandy didn't react to Dillon's tirade, although danger signals were crisscrossing his body at a maddening rate. Instead he merely took another deep, long breath before speaking. "You can feel the energy inside you, can't you Dillon? That energy that you feel exists throughout the Universe. Your scientists have made incredible steps over the last three decades in determining the purest and simplest form of energy, even beyond the so-called quark. However, just like my race, they completely ignored that which was right in front of them. You can call it mana*, chi*, ki or whatever you want. And while no direct detection method exists, its effects on our Universe are real and very powerful."

Dillon's breathing had returned to normal as he listened to Sandy's calming voice. He thought back to his Dad's teaching about chi. Chi was a form of pure energy that existed everywhere, Dillon had been told. Most martial artists knew or thought they knew what chi was. However, the reality was that many had a very limited understanding and often confused the ability to break bricks or scream really loud as the essence of chi. These were an aspect of chi, but a very small part.

Throughout history, the ability to develop and use significant amounts of chi was known by many martial arts grandmasters and almost never passed down to more than one person per generation. In some cases the students of a martial arts dojo were taught how to use limited amounts of chi, but never trained to truly feel and live with the energy coursing through one's veins. Because of this withholding of knowledge, many believed that it was impossible for anyone but a chosen few to harness such power. However, in the mid '80s and early '90s there was a surge of self-help books and seminars that showed how anyone could develop chi.

Dillon's dad was the grandmaster of Hoshinjitsu, a form specialized in meditation techniques for awakening the mind and opening the body's energy channels. His books and seminars were part of this self-help revolution. Until recently, Dillon half-heartedly believed in it, and never was able to feel more than a small amount of yang* or male energy when he practiced chi kung*, or deep meditation. The recent out-of-body experiences and overwhelming energy boiling inside him now caused Dillon to listen even more intensely to Sandy.

Sandy continued after Dillon's reflections, having waited until the furrows above the boy's brows unwrinkled. "This mana exists throughout the Universe, and what it is or how it was created is still being debated by my race after almost ten thousand years. Some believe it's the purest form of energy possible, others believe it's tied to a religious entity, and still others think that it's a result of entropy. The entropy hypothesis has gained momentum recently because it's the most logical."

"I guess the hard sciences are going to start catching up with me." Gabe smiled as he spoke for the first time. "Sorry to interrupt but I do have a question. I know that entropy is the natural order or disorder of a system. Your entropy hypothesis must mean that the chi, or mana, is a result of order or disorder. So which one is it?"

"Energy is stored and released in a variety of different ways. For example, your fossil fuels are gathered, refined, and then burned in your cars to release the energy. A significant amount of the energy contained within the gasoline is lost as heat, which you all should have learned in school. However, we also discovered another type of energy that is released. This energy, like heat, dissipates and becomes unusable to my race. We speculate that it's mana and that the amount of mana in the universe is increasing as the amount of stored or potential energy is decreasing.

"Now, all human beings can be trained to do what is the unthinkable for our race, and that is to gather this energy. But there are people on Earth that for some reason are able to gather and use mana tens, hundreds, or even thousands of times more efficiently than others. On Earth there are also places that have long been speculated to be 'energy hot spots,' such as Stonehenge and the Bermuda Triangle. These places attract this highly disordered and scientifically unusable energy, and thus have very high concentrations of mana. In the universe there are also these energy hot spots where mana concentrations can be thousands of times greater than the most powerful spots on Earth." Sandy paused to give Dillon time to digest all the information.

"Now let's go back to you and your friends, Dillon. While observing your race we also found that certain human beings have an innate the ability to gather mana, and that this trait can be passed down through some unknown genetic pathway. You, Gabe, Lian, Tanya, and Matt have this innate ability, with *your* talent far exceeding the combination of your friends. My race and all humans on Earth need you and your friends to develop your mana-gathering ability in order to set off on an important mission."

Dillon glanced over at Gabe who was now in a full lotus* position, controlling his breathing and focusing calmly on Sandy.

"So why does a technically-advanced race need a group of eager but naïve teenagers to help them? I've been with you so far, Sandy, but I see a mile-wide crater that is going to be awfully hard to convince me to drive into." Dillon felt like he was talking with a maturity beyond his own years, but after being splattered on a curb and nearly drowned in boiling water he didn't feel like a teenager anymore either.

Sandy didn't change course after Dillon's diatribe. "In addition to being an observation post, the Moon is a place of study for our best and brightest scientists. One of our longest on-going projects has been time travel."

"Wait, you are going to throw time travel at me? That crater got even wider, not smaller."

"Let me finish," Sandy shot back rather boldly, which meant that Dillon had finally broken through his calm demeanor. "You see, Dillon, we once were at the exact same stage that you're at now. As with your race, our thirst for space exploration is only supplanted by the desire to control time. The theory of relativity states that the speed of light is constant, and if one is able to exceed the speed of light then one can control time, thus being able to travel in time.

"The problem is that, as an object approaches the speed of light, that object gains mass and will gain mass proportional to its acceleration. This paradox means you would never be able to exceed the speed of light from an approach that is purely propulsion.

"Hypotheses about the use of black holes and wormholes came about, but they had major obstacles to overcome. We know because we unsuccessfully explored these research paths many times, and finally came back to the problem of the infinite mass increase. We discovered a way to expel this mass as quickly as we gained it. Expelling the mass produced energy, and we also found a way to convert this energy into a form we could use to generate more power and travel faster. Once started, the process cannot be stopped until the object reaches the speed of light. Then we can manipulate it to go faster or slower, and thus go forward or backward in time.

"However, we did run into a problem with the mana fields I was telling you about, which was only solved very recently. Some mana areas always remain in one place in the Universe. Others fluctuate and flow unpredictably. When a time-traveler's ship hits a mana field, the ship may not operate and is often destroyed or lost."

Dillon's mind assessed the story while his eyes watched Sandy's countenance for any signs of this being the mother-of-all-lies. He saw no changes as Sandy continued. "Three of our most developed scientists worked on a new, ambitious project to gather and control mana, then convert it into useful energy. For hundreds of years they tried and failed, and then one day the three scientists were gone.

"I won't go into all the details, but the messages and reports we sent to our home planet, which use faster-than-light communication, differed from the Earth observation reports that they sent back. At first we were puzzled, but we now know that our three scientists had solved the mana field dilemma, and then went back in time."

"But what about paradoxes or the mass balance problem?" Dillon queried.

"We are certain that a change made by a time traveler does not cause a change in an alternate plane or phase, if that's what you mean. However, it does cause a change directly to *our* past, present, and future," replied Sandy.

"And mass balance?" queried Dillon again.

"You're right about mass balance and time travel. Matter and energy cannot be created or destroyed, but if you travel within the same universe then it's not a problem because the amount of energy remains constant. However, if you time travel to another universe you create a reverse wormhole, sort of like a black hole, that draws energy from the universe you entered into the universe you left, until the balance is restored."

The level of scientific knowledge needed to understand Sandy's story was getting a little hard for Dillon to digest, so he chose a simpler line of thought. "Why did they go back in time to Earth, of all places?"

"We think they wish to rule the planet, but we're afraid that their actions will alter the course of your race and wipe it out of existence."

"Why do that? Why can't they just blow Earth up now? You said just a while ago that you could easily destroy us." Dillon's skepticism was again rising.

"Dillon, we're not a heartless race. A long time ago our race decided to pursue a path of righteousness, requiring that our emotions and illogical thoughts, if you will, still be a part of us. But this comes at a price. We can reduce but not completely eradicate negative traits like the desire to harm, lie, cheat, and steal. Cahlar*, the scientific team leader, is feeding off a previously hidden megalomaniac trait. He wants to rule, not destroy. But how he wants to rule is what could wipe out your race."

"Why not just go back and get him? Does this violate one of your laws?" Dillon was poised to laugh at the absurdity of this conversation. Then he noticed Gabe staring intently at Sandy, and Dillon decided to take this seriously.

"Yes it does violate our laws, but we'd do it if we could. I explained mana to you for a reason. You see, they went back to a time on Earth when your planet is in a very long and powerful mana field. Without the device they developed, our ships won't operate and…" Sandy stood up, stepped several paces away from Dillon, and continued, "…*we* won't operate."

"This is the really good part," Gabe piped up with a smile.

"There's no easy way to say this, so I will show you." Sandy took off his long overcoat, set it on the bottom part of Dillon's metallic bed, and slowly lifted up his black shirt. He grabbed the soft skin of his stomach and gently pulled outward. The skin started to separate until he had torn off a section larger than his hand. There was no blood. Dillon could see muscle tissue, but the grayish coloring made it look strange. The flesh held in Sandy's hand then melted into his fingers as the opening in his stomach sealed perfectly back over itself.

Dillon was in awe, but the show was not over.

Sandy walked over to the metallic table where Dillon was sitting and rested his arm on it. A familiar tentacle formed out of the table's surface and maneuvered directly over his hand. A vibrating noise emanated from the end of the tentacle, and the screen over Dillon's head illuminated. Sandy pointed up at it and said, "Look, you can see the cells of my body. If we zoom in closer you'll see the different components of a single cell."

Another interruption came as the door to the cubicle slid open and the lanky Lian skidded in, his unkempt black hair covering one eye. When he saw what was happening a large, goofy grin filled his face.

"Oh, you're at the fun part," he commented, slightly out of breath.

Dillon looked back at the screen and saw the image zooming in on the cell. He started focusing on different shapes within the cell. He knew that human cells had a nucleus or brain center, but the cells on the screen contained two nuclei. One of them was moving with small, wiry arms that flailed around.

"The waving things are nanobots. As we became more and more technically advanced, we developed microscopic robots that could help the body fight diseases and even facilitate the uptake and distribution of medicines in cells. Eventually we learned how to make robots that could enter each cell and work harmoniously with our organic architecture, controlling even the cell's DNA and reproduction."

"So you are immortal then?" asked Dillon.

"No. We can live for a very long time, but we can be fatally injured." Sandy smiled at the only joke he knew: "Also, viruses can be double-edged swords." Dillon himself finally cracked a smile.

"Since we have merged with technology, we can't survive in large mana fields. The nanobots inside either stop working or start sending mixed signals. This kills cells—and lives. Without the mana-controlling technology that the scientists stole, we can't stop them in the past, present, or future."

"So when did they steal the device?" asked Dillon, who decided not to point out that, since the scientists were the creators, they really didn't steal it.

"Five months from now."

"What?"

"We have word from our future selves that it will happen in exactly five months."

"Why not stop them now?" asked Dillon.

"They're already gone and their lab is bare. The whole thing may not make sense, but we have no option other than to have you and your friends travel back in time and retrieve the device."

"Hey," Lian interjected, "if we land on this Ancient Earth*, and it has this mana field that disrupts technology, then how are we going to get back off of the planet?" Lian had known about this plot for months, but just now recognized a serious problem in it.

"Your first question should be, how can you land on a planet where the spaceship will not work?" Sandy's response made Lian realize there were probably a lot of things he hadn't thought of. "Your spaceship will lose power long before it descends on the planet. We will deploy large balloons that will hydraulically inflate before landing. They will reduce your speed and then bounce and skip to a stop. We'll drop you into a remote location so you'll have time to adapt to the local environment. The vehicle can be mechanically sealed so no one else can enter it. Once you retrieve the device, you will attach it to the spaceship to activate the computer system. Then the automatic pilot will steer you back home."

Sandy took off his dusty hat, inhaled a slow, deep breath, and stared at the wall for a good minute before exhaling. "It's your choice, Dillon. Your friends will go with you if you say yes, but may not go without you. This plan cannot succeed without the exceptional abilities you've demonstrated since you arrived here."

The door slid open, and Sandy stepped out of the cubicle. Matt and Tanya rushed in, both wearing tank tops and soaked from head to toe with sweat. Over the last few years Matt had put on about thirty pounds of fat, but it was now all replaced by layers of muscle. Tanya also had bulked up, adding at least five more pounds to her already powerful frame.

"So are you two now the poster kids for 'Just Say Yes to Steroids,' or just getting in shape for your wedding?" Dillon smirked.

A foot flew out of the air toward his body. Startled, Dillon deflected the blow by angling his body to the side while Tanya's leg passed over him. Forgetting he was on the table, he rolled right off the other side and out of the gang's sight.

"Oh shoot, Dillon. I'm sorry," came Tanya's worried voice as she and Matt led the charge to see if Dillon was ok. They all were quickly hunched over behind the table, surrounding their friend. Dillon grinned and they shared a much-needed laugh.

Gabe was the first to get up off the ground after their laughing fit. He went to the illuminated screen above the table and rapidly slid his hands over the screen until it was outlined in a dull red glow. The others stood up and watched.

"Okay, this room is now secure. No one can hear us or see us, not even Sandy." Gabe turned to Dillon and, with a self-congratulatory smile, continued, "Lian and I have been learning their language and computer systems. Since they are not worried about hackers it is easy to do what we want. We have explored every dome except one, although we are close to getting into it."

Only after Gabe finished did Dillon realize that they all were looking at him instead of Gabe, the speaker.

"What?"

Matt hesitated. "Well, we are waiting for you to tell us what to do."

"Hey, I'm the game leader on weekends, but that was for fun," Dillon defended himself.

"Yes, *was* for fun. We are no longer at home and what we are playing for now is real. This is a chance to save the world." Gabe's voice was stoic, but his face gave away his excitement.

"What the hell is wrong with you all?" Dillon yelled, thrusting his chest out as if preparing for a fight. He rarely lost his temper, but this time his emotions couldn't be stopped. "How can you all be so comfortable with what is going on? A chance to save the world? Yeah, if it were a computer program glitch we had to solve from our bedrooms it would be fine. But we are talking about going back in time to maybe even kill people. Some of us will likely die." His friends' faces had fallen serious, but after six months of silence Dillon didn't care to censor himself.

"When was the last time any of you were seriously hurt? Well, let me tell you it's so painful that I refuse to voluntarily go through it ever again. I want to go home and see my family and just worry about waking up in time for school. I'm not going to lead you, and I'm not going on this stupid mission."

Matt countered, "Dillon, sometimes leadership is given to those least wanting but most deserving. You have a power inside you that we can only dream about. If you won't do it, then who will? Who can?"

"I'm sorry guys...please...just leave." Dillon slumped his shoulders, leaned on the table, and looked down at the ground. When he looked up, only Lian was in the room.

"Dillon, you're a leader. You have been, and you always will be no matter what you decide. You made it through hell and back, and that has made you stronger than all of us."

Dillon, calmer now, spoke softly, "Lian, if I learned anything in the last six months, it is that I am not a leader and not a survivor. I thought I was strong, but after the accident and then almost drowning I welcomed death. I wanted to die. I gave up completely.

"I know we don't talk about that night that I saved your life, but until now I thought you were weak and needed help. Now I know that I'm not some pillar of strength. I'm just like every other teen, thinking he's invincible only to wake up one day old and scared."

"We never talk about that night because I couldn't tell anyone the truth. I wasn't going to kill myself. I was going to off my bastard of a dad and those kids that made fun of me. I was tired of being beaten all my life. I was tired of hearing my mom scream in pain. I didn't care if I went to jail, or even if I was killed."

Dillon looked up from the ground, flushed from embarrassment and shock.

"But I guess you did save my life, or at least made it bearable for a while. My dad never hit my mom or me again. He was too afraid I'd kill myself. Even though you got it wrong, your caring enough to try to stop me meant a lot.

"But it's not enough, Dillon." Lian's voice was shaking now. "I don't belong down there on Earth in this era, and I don't ever want to go back. There's nothing there for me. I need this mission, even if it means my death, and I need you to lead us because you are the only person I have ever trusted. If we have to go without you then we will, but we'll fail." Lian took all emotion out of his last sentence: "Please, just think about it."

Lian turned and walked away. He nearly glided across the floor and out the door. It was the first time that Dillon noticed how graceful Lian had become.

II.

Dillon again saw himself floating above his body and decided it was time to look around. Everything was a dull gray, stacked on top of a light gray mist that ebbed and flowed. He angled himself toward where he had seen the three lights last time. Just as before, they were there. As he approached he realized the bodies were all sleeping, and the walls in the normal world were merely a darker gray that he could see through. Although their shapes were amorphous he could feel the uniqueness of their energy, telling him it was Tanya, Matt and Lian. The room where Gabe should have been was empty. Dillon looked around and couldn't see much else through the surrounding fog. The only way to check things out was to move around. He played with the speed of his movement and found that he could travel very slow or unbelievably fast, depending on how he thought about where he wanted to go. He only slowed down when something caught his eye. Then he would completely stop.

While practicing movement, Dillon again saw a white figure in the distance and traveled toward it. He started to gain on it but stopped as he felt a chilling wind at his back. Fear overloaded his senses. He turned to see a black, bat-like creature about twice his own size bearing down on him. Its eyes burned like glowing embers, foot-long fangs glistened with fresh blood, and its two legs ended in a mass of sharp claws that pointed in every direction. The flapping, leathery wings ended in human-like hands, a shimmering sword in each.

Dillon tried to move away as fast as he could, but the bat was gaining on him fast. Before he knew it, the creature was less than ten feet away. It leapt at him and sliced into Dillon's form, almost sending him tumbling off into space. Dillon regrouped in time to dodge another sword strike, but in doing so he moved right toward the bat's head. Its fangs bore down on him with horrifying speed. Just as they were about to hit their mark, Dillon felt a powerful force behind him and saw a red light touch the creature, sending it hurtling end-over-end until it was out of sight. Dillon turned around to see the white figure that had entered his room the other night.

"Uh, thanks." Dillon tried to say coolly, but then blurted out, "What do you want?" Dillon noticed that his words carried, but seemed hollow with nothing for the sound to bounce off and reverberate back toward him.

"To answer some of your questions and to teach you," replied the being in a strong yet calming voice. Dillon hadn't expected this answer but decided to press on.

"Only some of my questions? Why not all of them?"

"Some things I will not tell you since they will not help you at this time."

"Ok, first: what the heck was that thing that just attacked me?" asked Dillon

"It is an ancient being that lives in the astral world."

So I am in the astral plane*, a place where ghosts are always assumed to dwell. "Why did it attack me?"

"It has been hunting you all your life in hopes of killing your astral form and rendering your body soulless."

The thought of being hunted his whole life and just now finding out was disconcerting, but Dillon worried that he had little time to talk and more questions than could be answered before he awoke. "My whole life? I don't remember anything; it must have never come close."

"No, it came close many times, but your subconscious has been directed by us to block out the memories so you could lead a normal and stable life through your childhood."

"How was it stopped before? Are there others trying to kill me?" Dillon questioned. This seemed nearly as crazy as when he floated above his body after the car accident.

"We protected you on Earth." The white being continued. "There are not many things in the astral plane that can destroy a traveler or cut an astral cord, but she can and tries every night."

Dillon knew the lore from his role-playing games that an astral cord was the linkage to the body of anyone traveling in the astral plane. To cut a cord would permanently sever the person from his spirit. The lore had become reality, but what shocked him was the mention of constant attacks.

"Every night and I never remembered? Can things get any stranger?" It was a rhetorical question, but the being still answered it.

"Yes it can. This is only the beginning." The white being reached out and touched Dillon's forehead. Dillon thought that he would again be sent straight back to his body and the rest of his questions would remain unanswered. Instead, he found himself frozen in space and watched as he lost focus and started to see through the center of his forehead where the light had touched him. Then his sight reversed; instead of looking outward, he now looked inside his own head. He was staring into a black nothingness, falling farther and farther inward until he stopped at images he could see.

He saw a newborn baby surrounded by the gray mist of the astral world. Then out of the mist swept in the enormous bat, and the baby screamed as it fluttered toward him. Before it could reach the child, two majestic figures stepped in the bat's path. One was slender and bathed in white light, and the other was a portly, gold-lit figure wielding a long, silver sword. They fought the horrifying creature until Dillon heard it scream in pain and fly away.

The same scenario happened thousands of times in Dillon's mind, the bat always losing the battle in the end. The only changes were the baby aging each day, and the variety of celestial protectors that would intervene. Sometimes one would be severely injured, or its astral cord would be snapped by the bat's fangs, and Dillon would feel the being's life wane away. Dillon knew the child was him and watched until the movie forwarded to his most recent encounter with the bat. He then found himself looking again at the white being. Dillon pondered the lifetime of repressed memories that had flooded forth.

"You can call me, Guylen*."

"Guylen, why would those beings give up their lives for me?" Dillon's voice was almost as emotionless as Guylen's.

"You have in you the potential for saving those that will lead your race to enlightenment."

"And if I fail will my world end in some cataclysmic demise?"

"No, your race will most likely eventually lose the desire to live or become like the Mulshins."

"So what are you here to teach me?" Dillon was tired of the other line of questioning.

"Many things. I will teach you about this place you are in, but more importantly how to meld your mind, body, and soul for enlightenment."

"So not only will I save the world, but I will also reach Nirvana?" questioned Dillon.

"I did not say you would save the world. I said you could save those that will lead your race to enlightenment. I did not say you will reach enlightenment, since I can only show you a path that improves your chances of getting there. You will learn how to open your mind to your body, accept your subconscious, and use the energy that technology has forgotten."

"I know it's selfish, but I just want to go home. I am going home for good." Dillon's voice indicated more of a question than a statement.

32

"Dillon. At some time, nearly every Earth child looks up through the sky and is in awe of how small they really are when compared to the Universe. In some cases that child dreams of doing something important in his or her life so as to not feel so insignificant. For most, they are just youthful dreams and hopes. But you are different. Feel inside yourself, Dillon, and you will see that you know your destiny and always have. You know you have a deeper purpose, one so powerful and important that your very soul reaches out to those stars and yearns to touch them. The Universe is your destiny, not just Earth. You can run from your destiny, since most humans are given free will. But you will never rid yourself of the knowledge of what you were meant to do. It is time you made the decision to either embrace your purpose or to hide from it."

The white being had given Dillon more to think about than seemed possible. However, he couldn't shake his yearning to see his mom and dad. He missed them so much.

Having made his decision, Dillon willed himself back to his body and was surprised to open his eyes and see that it had actually worked. He cleaned up, grabbed his backpack, and followed the lighted arrows on the floor to the space port where Sandy was waiting.

III.

The gang silently watched through the dome wall of their training room as the 1998 Accord left the space port and quickly disappeared into the distance, headed toward Earth. After a few minutes Gabe gathered himself and spoke in his most commanding voice.

"Ok, Dillon made his decision, and now it is time for us to make ours. I am going on this mission, and if you want to join me then we need to get back to practicing." He knew that it would take time for the enthusiasm and intensity to return, but also believed that following a daily routine was the best way for them all to heal.

IV.

The Accord pulled up in front of Dillon's house, with the avoidance meter still on so that no one noticed it fly in or land on the street. Dillon was strangely disappointed to see the lawn freshly mowed and the deep, red roses still blooming around the Japanese plum tree in his front yard. He had expected that his disappearance would devastate his parents and yearned for some tell-tale signs of despair. Just then the front door opened and Dillon saw himself step out and stare in their direction.

"So, one of you has replaced me?"

"Close, but no. We knew that you might not choose to do what we asked, so we profiled you as best we could to make the transition back home easier. Since it's only a robot it's not a perfect match. Your parents think you are either on drugs or hanging out with a bad crowd, but it's the best we could do." Sandy didn't even smile at his own ill-timed humor.

Dillon opened the door and stepped out of the car, hesitated, and turned back to Sandy. "What about my friends?"

"While you were healing, they were sure you would go with them and decided to not come back, so 'you' told your parents they went hiking in the mountains. They were listed as missing and by now are assumed deceased." Sandy paused and stared intently into Dillon's eyes. "They need you."

Dillon turned away and motioned to his other self, now standing dumbly on the porch, to come to the car.

The back door of the car shut softly. Sandy took a deep breath, exhaled slowly and then drove back to the space port. *This is going to be hard to explain,* he thought.

A small white envelope with new tire marks was the only piece of litter that sat in front of the Chase family house.

Chapter 4
Chi Can Be Taught to Anyone, but Only Truly Mastered by Teaching Oneself

I.

Instead of returning to greet his friends, Dillon asked Sandy for a large room far away from them. He requested the highest computer security possible just to make sure they wouldn't learn that he was back. He needed time to see if he could piece together and perfect the martial teachings from his life. He didn't want to build their hopes up by saying he was back and then crush them if he couldn't pull together what he thought would be needed for their quest. The room was where he hoped to learn how to intertwine his mind and body so that both parts would act as one.

Why had he come back? When Dillon had stepped out of the car in front of his family's home, two things hit him hard. First, he had finally felt what Guylen had told him; there *was* something inside him that yearned for the stars, which called back with a familiarity he had never remembered until now. It was as if a magnet was pulling him up toward the sky and beyond.

The second was the realization that if the Mulshins were right, he could never truly live while knowing what might happen to his family. He couldn't imagine looking into his mom's eyes as her world fell apart, nor let her continue to wonder why her son was acting so strange. His body double was only a temporary fix that couldn't stay with his family, so he had made sure it came back with him to the moon. In order for his family to survive, he had to let them know he was gone.

Dillon didn't peer through a window or walk through the front door of his house. He couldn't let himself see his parents one last time, because that would make leaving even more painful. He had finally accepted that it was time to stop sobbing about his bad luck, and to start doing something for everyone he knew and loved. No matter how hard it was going to be. The time was now.

Without saying goodbye to Sandy, Dillon turned and entered the room. He punched the code onto the glowing part of the door frame that would seal him off from his only companionship on the Moon. He then walked over to another computer desk and took out the books and CD inside his backpack that Sandy had somehow retrieved for him. His dad loved the computer era and had poured all his thoughts and teachings on martial arts onto the CD. It was a lot of information, and Dillon would have only a month to perfect what he had learned while simultaneously taking the second biggest step that a Hoshin* student would ever make. He would have to define his own subsystem that would not only make him better, but also make Hoshin better. Hoshin was an open system that constantly evolved as new techniques were developed or borrowed from other forms. The subsystems made it stronger as each student added to it.

Dillon sat down and pushed the CD onto the ledge of the table and watched it sink as the table melted around it. He grabbed a pen and a pad of paper, reading and taking notes on everything he could until he passed out early the next morning.

Day 1

Dillon slowly pushed his head and aching neck up from the cold, hard desk. He now was all too aware that he never slept, but there were still many mornings when he awoke and could not remember what had happened in the astral plane.

He stood up as he drank a glass of water that had mysteriously appeared next to the computer screen. It was time to start the physical training aspect of Hoshin. He took a shower and put on his martial arts gi*, preparing himself for the new life he had chosen: the life of a warrior and a leader.

Dillon started his day with simple stretching exercises for his entire body before moving into yoga* stretches. His yoga poses started with the

Sun Salutation* and ended in the *Crane**, which painfully challenged his ability to balance on one foot. Dillon had never practiced yoga for more benefit than stretching, but he knew there was much more he was missing. Maybe one day he would explore yoga's other aspects.

Next was chi kung. Unlike yoga, chi kung was something he had been heavily trained in by his dad, so he understood how it would help him raise and control the energy within him. Dillon started with basic mobility exercises to increase the circulation in his legs, waist, and shoulders. He rotated his toes and worked his way up to his neck, moving each joint in circular motions.

After that he slowed his breathing and imagined he was sitting on, holding, or being supported by balls of energy. These were the 'energy ball' routines*. With each inhale, the balls of energy grew and lifted him up, and when he exhaled his body rested on them. During rests, he could control the energy's shape and densify his chi by gathering and adding more energy. He finished with the common routines of *Holding the Tiger** and *Catching the Dragon** before he took it to the free form level. *Holding the Tiger* required one to stand with knees bent and slightly apart as if riding a tiger, while pretending to hold the neck of a tiger in one outstretched hand and the back with the other. With *Catching the Dragon* one's legs were kept in nearly the same position, but with arms outstretched high overhead as if holding a writhing serpent.

Dillon slowly moved around the room as he drew in and exhaled chi in unison with his actions. If he took a step or moved an arm away from his body he would exhale, and if he brought a leg or arm back into his body he would inhale. After about fifteen minutes of the slow free form movements, he practiced his Hoshin moves in the chi kung fashion of exhaling or inhaling depending on the nature of the move. When he was more advanced in his training, he would focus on drawing in and releasing earth, water, wind, or fire energy depending on his intent, but for now he wanted to master the basics. Afterward he felt in better control of the chi swimming just beneath his skin.

It was time for seated meditation^.

Sweat trickled down Dillon's face as he sat in the *half-lotus* on a meditation pillow with his back against the wall. He placed one hand over the other while resting them on his lap and focused his eyes about fifteen degrees lower than straight ahead. It had been a long time since he had seriously meditated, and he knew that he needed to regain a high level of focus before he dared to try advanced meditation techniques.

Dillon slowly inhaled and exhaled in a cyclic loop; drawing energy through his nose, into the bottom of his belly, up his spine, and back out his nose. Every time he had a stray thought he would label it as such and mentally move it away. It took him hours before he could reach a thoughtless state for at least thirty seconds. This very simple exercise could take months to master.

The day was half over before Dillon sat down to work on developing his own martial arts sub-form within Hoshin. *I need to figure out how to take Hoshin and make it into a form that we can all use on our mission. How can I do that? Where do I start? How can I teach the group enough to survive? How do I even teach?*

The hours ticked by with Dillon frustrated, staring at the blank computer screen. But there was no time to be unproductive; Dillon was already relying on time the world could not afford. He decided to get up and practice Hoshin, this time using earth, fire, water, and wind with each technique.

Hoshin did not have katas* (or forms), but focused instead on the ability to combine techniques based on an individual's strengths, weaknesses, position to an opponent, physical balance, and pressure points. The learning curve was steep because one was expected to think creatively from the start instead of postponing creativity until obtaining a blackbelt.

This created a problem for Dillon. He simply did not have the experience in logic or systematic thinking to put something together to teach others.

Day 4

The three-foot wooden staff, or hanbo*, smacked against the metal wall before skipping along the floor and finally rolling to a stop back at Dillon's feet. Although he had no mirror, he knew that exhaustion had carved itself into his face. He still was struggling to put together a plan for his friends, but no matter how hard he pushed himself he made no progress. He walked to the wall, turned around, and slid on his back to the ground. He let his body and mind succumb to the exhaustion.

Dillon felt the white light and opened his eyes. Before him stood Guylen. Dillon could sense a smile emanating through the light.

"Why are you smiling? I haven't done a single thing right since I came back."

"You are right. You haven't done a single thing right, but the sum of your efforts is simply perfect." The smile hadn't left Guylen's nearly featureless face.

"What?" Dillon was too tired to figure out the riddle, but did notice that he could see Guylen's expressions a little clearer than before. He figured he was either getting better at seeing things in this plane, or that Guylen could appear however he wanted.

"I can teach you how to teach; I can even teach you how to fight and how to sharpen your mind. I cannot teach you the relentless passion you'll need to survive, but I now know it is there." Guylen moved closer to Dillon as he spoke, "In fact, I have already taught you how to teach, and now it is time to remember."

"Already taught me? What do you mean?"

"You do not think that every night you were in the astral plane we only fought off the large bat? There was plenty of time for other things." Guylen touched Dillon and again he felt himself falling inward, deeper and deeper into his mind until he was watching a movie of himself working with Guylen. As the images flew by, the blocks in his memory exploded open. He had learned how to ask what was needed on a mission, to break down each mission requirement including physical, mental, and spiritual aspects. Dillon had learned how to break it down until he was at the smallest work unit for all types of scenarios, from year-long journeys to quick insertions into hostile areas. They had practiced over and over until the actions needed became second nature. After Dillon could do all this, Guylen taught him to master the art of war: strategy and hand-to-hand combat. Years of work came back at a break-neck speed, until the memories passed and Dillon again saw Guylen in front of him.

"That was incredible!" Dillon beamed. "Thank you."

"We are not done yet. In order for you to get started on creating a plan for your friends, you need to understand and truly believe in one more thing—one piece that is critical for your survival." Guylen moved slightly to his right.

"I guess you aren't going to just tell me, huh?"

Guylen smiled, raised his left hand, and an image of a young girl and a middle-aged man appeared to his side. "This man has a natural IQ higher than this girl, was brought up in better schools, and has had more experiences. However, she learned languages at twice his speed, beat him at challenging puzzles on the first try, and thrived in a jungle where he barely survived. Why?"

Dillon shrugged.

"On your planet there was a famous science fiction book called *Ender's Game*. In it a young boy leads a group of kids who destroy a superior, technologically advanced species set on overtaking your planet. Why could the kids defeat a superior race?

"Are you saying that kids can always beat adults?" Dillon knew he was grasping at a straw.

"Not necessarily. If you take a child under five years old and place him in a new country, you will see that in a matter of months he would blend in. Now take an adult and place him in the same scenario, and most likely his accent and ways of thinking would still be discernable for decades. Why?"

"Kids adapt!" Dillon saw Guylen smile and nod affirmation.

"They adapt much more easily. As we get older, we all become more set in our ways, more resistant to change, and think more inside the box or rules of the society we live in."

"Then why didn't the Mulshins pick a bunch of really young kids for this mission, like in that book?" Dillon queried.

"The book was just example. What's different is that in the book the kids were in a controlled environment using their creativity and adaptability remotely. What were they lacking?"

"Confidence, wisdom, maybe physical strength?" Dillon saw again that he had a good answer.

"Yes. Your age group is the best for having a combination of skills that would maximize survival and success for this type of mission. Team-building and reliability is strongest within your age group. A team is stronger that an individual, and that is why your friends must go with you on this mission." Guylen's glowing face had lost its smile. "However, I don't know why you specifically were picked."

"The lizard!" Dillon stepped forward and started to ask, "Was the lizard the one that—" but Guylen had already reached out as he always did when he wanted to end Dillon's dream.

Dillon woke up, frustrated at how Guylen kept ending their conversations, but he was also refreshed and ready to go. He knew how to prepare for the mission. He jumped onto the computer and feverishly typed, even though he could use the Mulshin technology of brain scanning to command the computer to do everything he wanted. He was already set in his ways on some things.

Day 30

Dillon smiled as he 'tapped' off the computer screen and stood up. He had accomplished as much as his limited time would allow. Since meeting with Guylen nearly a month ago, he had prepared with efficiency he'd never before reached. He had honed his physical training and developed the mental and physical aspects of Hoshin. With the help of the Mulshin database, he had compiled the most probable scenarios they would encounter and categorized each one into knowledge and skill sets they would need: physical, mental, and spiritual.

There was no way they could each learn everything in the three months they now had left to prepare. His plan was to divide the tasks between each person to give the group a wide range of individual expertise. In addition to their own responsibilities, each would learn the basics of another's extensive training in case something happened to one of them. He would have to tweak the plan throughout their remaining preparation time, but that too was written into his outline.

Guylen's comment about why his friends were needed for the mission had given Dillon an idea. This statement had inspired him to develop his own adaptability*, which he added to Hoshin to make it his own. They needed, Dillon decided, to continually learn and have a quick way to draw upon their new knowledge and experiences in order to survive. He would teach them how to reflect on experiences and use them to recognize opportunities to quickly add to their knowledge and skills, and gently grow their ability to adapt and add anything, anywhere, at anytime.

The Mulshins and the technological capabilities of their observation post would aid in most of the instruction, while Dillon would train his friends in martial arts now that Guylen had opened his memory of the astral plain. Regardless of whether he or a Mulshin was teaching, adaptability would be the central theme.

Chapter 5
The Success of a Mission Depends on the Success of the Training

I.

Day 1

All martial artists should have one goal when they enter a dojo: to eventually reach a point of self-expression and ultimately self-realization. That is, who one is and where one fits in the Universe. In almost all systems one learns the basics. Once you have mastered each level of the basic forms (i.e. belts and ranks), you are allowed to slightly bend and modify, eventually hoping for complete freedom of expression. In many martial art forms that self-expression is only allowed for the new grandmaster, and thus tradition suppresses self-expression for all but one.
  Tradition should be respected, but not worshipped. In any craft or career, a questioning mind needs to learn more and strive to make a difference, but must also break through the established ways of doing things. A martial artist is no different than any craftsman, except that the ultimate prize is reaching Kundalini* or Enlightenment.

***

For more than a month the training had gone on with no return to emotional normalcy. Lian, Matt, Tanya, and Gabe started each day with stretching exercises followed by learning and practicing their Hoshin moves, always attempting to perfect them to Gabe's high standards. They would then finish with another stretching routine before sitting down to lunch.

After lunch they would all go to the practice deck to learn how to fight with various Hoshin weapons. After dinner they studied the language of Ancient Earth and whatever they could find about where they were going. They would stay in the library until nearly midnight and then start all over again at seven o'clock the next morning.

One morning halfway through training the door slid open. They all stopped what they were doing to stare. Before them stood a somewhat familiar teenager—only somewhat familiar because that teen now looked more like a young man.

"Except for Lian, each one of you willingly gave up a very nice life on Earth knowing that those who love you will live in pain for the rest of their lives." Dillon stared each one in the eyes for an unbearably long time. "Why?"

Matt stepped forward without hesitation. "For me it's not for the thrill, and it's not to live out a role-player's dream," he said. "Every day before I walk into this room, I stop and pray to whoever is listening that my parents will make it through another day without me, and I without them. And every day I almost turn around and ask to be taken home." Matt took another step closer, blinking out the moisture appearing in his eyes. "But I believe that this is the right thing to do. We all believe it, Dillon. Going back would be selfish and would only be living for the moment, ignoring the potential destruction of our future. Of everyone's future."

All the others nodded in agreement, except for Lian.

Dillon and Gabe locked eyes, with many unspoken words traveling between them. Gabe stepped forward, untied his instructor's belt, and handed it to Dillon. In the past Dillon would have refused to wear the belt, believing equality was his path. But today he took the belt and wrapped it twice around the waist of his gi before knotting it loosely in the front. Now leadership was more critical than equality.

"So, what've you been doing the last month? Role playing without us?" Lian's voice was more confident than Dillon could have imagined, and maybe even wanted.

"In a way, yes. But let's not get side-tracked. First I'm going to be open with you all about what we're going to do for the next twelve weeks. I honestly don't know if we will all survive this mission. But the only way I know of helping us to make it through is to stand on the fundamental belief of Hoshin. I need your mind, body, and soul to move as one, to act as one, and to become one. No martial art system is perfect, not even mine. However, Hoshin has an advantage that we need on this mission. It is a martial art that allows one to develop chi at an incredibly fast pace—often at a rate that can lead to horrific but temporary side effects. In spite of this, we need to embrace it because chi development will allow us to use mana on early Earth. Without developing our chi here, we surely will not survive."

Dillon let his words sink in for a minute before he started again. "Second, we will of course use Hoshin as a basis for your self-defense. You will also learn one other fighting form, master two types of weapons, while figuring out how to adapt all of them into Hoshin. Adaptability will be the key to everything we're going to do."

Dillon looked around and realized that his friends were still so elated to see him that his words were just words, with none of his audience even comprehending the challenges to come. "You will have a test every week for both our survival training and martial arts training. No one passes unless all pass. At the end you'll be blackbelts in mind, body, and soul."

"But Dillon, there are not enough belt levels up to black in Hoshin to get a new one every week. And a blackbelt in twelve weeks? What gives?" Gabe liked order and believed in respecting the tradition of the martial art forms.

"Sorry, Gabe, but we don't have time for any of that. I've broken things down into twelve steps. Each week you'll learn three steps. The first step is what you'll be tested on. The second and third steps will give you some familiarity with future martial art areas." Dillon knew that breaking down Hoshin into these structured steps was going against the grandmaster's wishes. But they needed to learn fast, so he planned for them to work within a box of knowledge and master everything inside that box so they could later step outside of it. At least he hoped this would work.

"What are the twelve steps of rehab?" Lian's voice was extremely cocky, and his wit aimed to disrupt.

Dillon ignored it and gave each a sheet of paper. He read it aloud in the format it was written. "First,

1. White Belt 1: Purity and innocence
    a. Physical: Body mechanics to include proper posture, falling down, rolling, and movement.

       b.   Mental: Asian Strategy (*Art of War* by Sun Tzu, *Book of Five Rings* by Musashi Miyamoto*), meridians and pressure points.

       c.   Soul: Controlled breathing, relaxation, visualization."

"Dillon, no disrespect, but we already learned to fall and roll." Matt had learned how to fall softly over the last month through perseverance but had sustained several deep bruises. His statement was sincere.

Dillon called out to no one in particular, "Moonbase Pathway zero-one-zero execute."

Without any other warning the floor beneath them dropped six inches and pitched to the left three inches. Dillon exhaled and let the ground take him where it wanted. He was teaching falling, so he didn't roll back up, but sunk to the ground and stayed there. He lifted his head and looked at Matt, Tanya, and Gabe. They were all nursing new bruises. Lian was still standing and had a grin smeared across his face.

"Falling properly, like everything else you will learn, needs to be second nature. When you start to fall your body is no longer balanced, and you either need to redirect* or accept. Falling is accepting with some redirecting, rolling is redirecting with some accepting." Dillon walked up to his standing student and smiled. "Let's start from the beginning. When a baby falls backward, its butt hits the ground first."

Lian's smile quickly disappeared as Dillon's hand struck his sternum at an upward angle. Lian's balance left him as he was lifted slightly up and onto the balls of his feet. It wasn't a punch, and yet it was just enough force to send him tumbling backward.

"Now we can really get started. Moonbase Support zero-zero-one execute." As Dillon spoke a door appeared out of the wall to his right and five Mulshins entered. "I will be training you in Hoshin, but we need to learn so much more. Each of us will have a Mulshin to teach us everything from survival on Ancient Earth to weapons training. They can download and teach us almost anything we want.

"Now, I will choose Tae Kwon Do to increase my precision in movement, strikes, and kicks; learn the ninjato* sword as my primary weapon; and learn the throwing axe as my secondary weapon." Dillon's dad had learned the ninjato from the great Ninja grandmaster, Dr. Masaaki Hatsumi*, and then had taught Dillon.

Dillon looked at his team.

"I will study Muay Thai*, the art of eight limbs; and choose the Japanese katana* used by the great Samurai Miyamoto Musashi. Oh, and also shuriken* throwing." Gabe couldn't hide his excitement, and grinned as he spoke.

Tanya stepped forward. "I want to learn Aikido, the redirection of an attacker's energy. I choose double short swords and the longbow as my weapons."

Lian scoffed at Tanya's choice of a form developed to minimize injury to her opponent. "I chose Brazilian Jujitsu and double long knives."

"I will also learn Aikido along with the European long sword and the war hammer. Yeehah!" Matt knew from his reading of medieval times that locking swords was common, and forcing your opponent off balance was often a key to victory. Aikido could give him a huge advantage.

The Mulshin in front turned to Dillon as he spoke. "Each of us is downloading what we need to know and should be ready in one minute."

"One minute? Great, but we won't need you for a couple hours." Dillon took ten steps past his friends and turned back around. "Now, you saw that balance is a key to falling. It is also a key to everything you will do. You need to learn where your center of balance is, how to control it, and understand how to shift your balance to move."

"Riddles you speak, master." Lian smiled and was surprised when Dillon smiled back.

"Let's say you wanted to move to the right. Most people would lift their leg, move it to the right, and set it down. Only once the leg is down do they reestablish balance. Try it." They all did.

"Now do the same move, but instead imagine your center of balance sitting right below your stomach. Move these core muscles to the right and let your body follow."

"I don't feel the difference," Matt said.

"Try moving as fast as you can the first way," Dillon commented back.

This time they moved their legs first and, off balance, noticed that it was hard to stop. Dillon directed them to do it again the other way. When they led with their core muscles as their center of balance, they all had perfect form.

"Let's do it again, and this time I'm going to redirect you," commented Dillon.

Dillon waited for them to start their movement before pushing them. Each had varying degrees of failure with moving their legs first, but all of them were able to quickly readjust when they moved their center of balance first. They practiced this for two hours, applying it to all types of movements, including basic strikes, kicks, falls, and rolls.

"Time for breakout sessions with your Mulshin trainers." All of their trainers were previous Observers and had spent many years on Earth, where they had adapted many human traits and habits that distinguished them from the other moon aliens.

There was a brief flicker as the training room transformed into varied ecosystems, and each student was paired with his or her trainer in one of the environments.

Dillon greeted Mark, a muscular Mulshin with a neatly trimmed goatee. They delved into survival techniques in wilderness, desert, and sub-arctic conditions. The scenery and scenarios were not holograms, but real mini-habitats easily created by the Mulshin technology. They were all beautiful in design, but the classroom context kept them from appreciating them.

After lunch Mark started teaching Dillon the finer points of the ninjato and briefly introduced him to the throwing axe. It was grueling and painful.

"Hey Dillon," Matt yelled through the walls, "how come we aren't using padded weapons? Don here is beating the crap out of me," Matt then fell to the ground as his Mulshin trainer laughed.

"No one who attacks us on early Earth is going to have padded weapons. Just wait until we go full force with sharpened blades in a month and—" Mark's dull sword smacked Dillon's wrist. "Ouch!" Dillon dropped his ninjato. A bruise had already formed.

Two hours before dinner Dillon took control of the room again to teach their mental training. They read and discussed sections of *The Art of War* by Sun Tzu, one of the most influential strategists in Chinese history, before Dillon stood up to talk about the primary chakras, energy, and colors.

"You have seven primary chakras that energy flows to and from, and each has an associated color. These colors express human interpretations of the energy.

"The lowest chakra is red, located at the base of the spine, and it represents fire. The next chakra is orange, located below the naval. The solar plexus chakra is yellow and represents Earth. The heart chakra is green and represents the wind or the sky, and healing. The throat chakra is blue and represents water; think of the ebb and flow of waves. The third eye* chakra, centered on your forehead between your eyes, is indigo. Some believe it is the opening of psychic abilities. Finally, the purple crown chakra is at the top of the head and taps into your spirituality.

"I've only given you a quick lesson on these. Later you'll learn that each has a physical, mental, and spiritual component. We will use each chakra in fighting to demonstrate earth, water, fire, and wind techniques. For meditation and chi generation* we will use all seven, moving the energy around and using each one as needed. For spiritual we will work on the upper chakras that help with self-reflection. If you can open the door to your subconscious, you can truly see who you are and correct those things that will hurt our chances of survival."

After more lecturing they sat down and had a tasty, healthy dinner that had been nutritionally balanced for the physical demands of their training. Once they were done eating, Dillon looked at their hunched shoulders, dull eyes, and sluggish movements. They were exhausted.

It was time to recharge. "I want everyone to lie on the ground and look up at the ceiling, including the Mulshins. Now, we will start with a basic muscle relaxation meditation^ using music as a tool. I first want you to inhale and exhale on my count. We will start with an inhale of three and an exhale of three, gradually extending it to six counts each. This is your breath count^, and the basis for all we will do."

The team practiced for fifteen minutes before Dillon moved on. "Now on each inhale you will tighten a certain part of your body and then on the exhale you will relax that part." Dillon started with the toes, moved to the calf muscles, knees, quads, genitalia, stomach, chest, neck shoulders, arms, hands, and finally the face. They cycled through this for almost an hour, stood up to practice punches and kicks, and then repeated the muscle relaxation for another hour. Dillon felt somewhat energized but knew that their training had only just begun.

At the end of their session they went to the library to study fantasy books relating to a magical Earth, and more on the history and work of Sun Tzu.

Day 2 Excerpt

Gabe woke up and stretched, grimacing at the aches and pains that greeted him. He really enjoyed Dillon being back, even if it meant he had to take a lesser role. Dillon was the clear leader, and Gabe had found out that he was not yet ready to take charge.

Fresh from his shower and breakfast, Gabe walked into the dark room in Sphere Three. "Lights and floor mats execute," spoke Gabe. He took a position on one of the newly materialized mats and began to stretch. After about fifteen minutes the door opened and in walked Dillon. They nodded at each other as Dillon took a spot next to Gabe. After another forty-five minutes the rest of the team showed up.

"Ok, everyone stretch and get ready for a three-mile run," said Dillon.

Gabe listened to the groans and said nothing. He looked forward to the jog. However, his attitude quickly changed after Dillon spoke the run execution command. The entire sphere was now visible, and a track with hundred-foot-high hills was laid out before them.

After stretching Dillon spoke up. "I am going to assume that our journey will be a lot like our role-playing games. Meaning that we will most likely have to do a lot of fast walking and maybe some running. We will all need to have great cardio and know how to set a pace we can maintain. This is just the start. We will finish with a couple marathon runs and a few all-day hikes through different terrain. Let's start."

Gabe watched as Tanya and Matt took off, trying to best each other. He matched Dillon's smooth stride behind them, with Lian taking up the rear. After about a mile Matt had slowed down, while Tanya used her track and field training to keep up a blistering pace. Gabe turned his head around while still running and noticed Lian had slowed to a walk. When Dillon traced his stare, he turned around, ran back to Lian, and said something that Gabe assumed wasn't kind words of encouragement. Lian turned red and started running again, passing Gabe about a quarter of a mile before the end. Matt too had sprinted near the end to beat Gabe and Dillon.

After everyone had stopped gulping air, Dillon changed the environment back to their small room. "Have a seat against the back wall, legs crossed, arms relaxed in your lap with one hand gently on top of the other. You eyes should be looking slightly down. We will now work on our breath count followed by the tension relaxing exercise you did yesterday."

Gabe relaxed his body, but his mind was still racing with mundane thoughts popping in and out.

"Our next meditation with be a thought-labeling one^. I want you to breathe in for a six count and then exhale. Anytime a thought comes into your mind, don't fight it. Instead, just mentally label it as a thought and push it away. Keep doing this until your mind is empty for at least a minute."

Gabe listened as Dillon went through the breath count over and over. Try as he might, he was never able to get past one full inhale-exhale circle without a thought creeping in. His mind always ran a mile-a-minute, and the only thing that seemed to relax him was classical music. When he finally opened his eyes, Dillon was staring at him and must have noticed the tension in his body.

"I guess you know what you will be working on early tomorrow morning?" Dillon commented with a hint of disappointment in his voice.

With that Dillon slowly stood up and announced that they would now practice punches and blocks. Gabe could easily perform all the moves, including shifts from hard blocks to soft blocks. He knew a hard block was for stopping all the energy of an opponent, while a soft block set up a redirection of momentum. It was definitely more fun than meditation.

Day 7 Excerpt

Matt bounded down the hall toward the training room, rubbing his eyes awake. He had only been asleep for a couple of hours when a bright light and a talking message from the screen in his room invaded his dreams. He was sure Dillon was trying to trick them on the day of their first belt test. As the training room door opened he saw Tanya, Gabe, and Lian in front of him with their heads staring almost straight up.

"What's going on?" Matt stepped into the room and realized he needed no response. They were staring straight up a snow-capped mountain that seemed to rise forever. They were well aware that it was part Mulshin-made and part hologram, and they also knew it meant their test for second level white belt was being postponed.

Matt heard a cough behind him and knew who it was. "Dillon, you aren't serious are you? That will take days to climb."

"I am serious, but we won't start here. I've programmed it to start at 12,000 feet so we can make it to the top in about eight hours. I've also programmed reduced oxygen content in the air and low temperatures for accuracy." Dillon's voice didn't seem happy to Matt.

"At least you aren't excited about torturing us." Matt begrudgingly reached down to put on his gear that had appeared next to him. Endurance was his greatest physical weakness. He was so dejected that he didn't even appreciate how the Mulshins could create objects anywhere they wanted.

After a little over eight hours, Matt reached out to grab Tanya and Dillon's hands. With one final grunt, he pulled himself up over the rock and to the top of the peak. Altitude sickness had gotten the best of him during most of the ascent, causing him countless dry-heaves and vertigo. After all this, he was proud that he had pushed through the pain and could now enjoy the artificial scenery. "It's amazing up here!" Matt exclaimed as he looked around and performed an exaggerated collapse onto the ground.

"Yep, now it's time to test for your next belt." Dillon started to take off his gear.

"But we're at the top of the mountain," Matt objected. "What if we fall?" Matt had looked over the edge of the mountain and just found out that he really didn't like heights.

"Yeah, we're really high, Matt. We must be at least twelve feet off the ground." Lian winked as he spoke, looking nearly as refreshed as Tanya after the long hike.

"Close Lian, but we're actually ten feet high. How did you know?" With Dillon's words the scenery disappeared and they all were standing on a ten-foot-high plateau.

"Easy. I just counted the number of steps up versus down during the entire trek." Lian jumped off the side of the plateau and rolled a couple times to cushion the impact. The others took the stone stairs that appeared after Lian's leap.

Dillon called out a command to restore the area to their small dojo room. He then asked Gabe to join him for testing in another room. Matt thought it was odd that they would not test together.

Matt, Lian, and Tanya sat down in a meditative pose and focused on breathing to re-energize their bodies. After less than a half hour, the door opened and out walked Gabe. He gave them a small wink before taking a seated position next to them. Dillon motioned for Matt to enter the testing room.

Matt tried to bounce up quickly, but the aches and pains from their hike slowed him to a steady rise. He walked into the room, and the door slid shut behind him.

"So Matt, how do you think I'm doing?" Dillon asked.

The question caught Matt off guard. "What do you mean, Dillon?"

"Well, I've never led anyone or anything before. I've been the kid who had fun and smiled my way through life. Now I have to lead my best friends, and I don't want to lose that friendship." Dillon paused, waiting for something from Matt.

Matt took a little time to think before he responded. "I like you being our leader. It just seems right. But I do worry about you. As you said, you used to be the one with the carefree laugh, the happy-go-lucky one. You always kept us smiling through the difficult times at home." Matt didn't like giving criticism and rubbed his hands for a moment before starting again. "I know you've been through some very painful things recently and are carrying an incredible burden. But you still have to be you; otherwise you'll kill yourself before any strange creatures on Ancient Earth have the chance."

Dillon smiled and slowly wiped his eyes with the knuckle of this thumb. "Thanks, Matt. Now, what is the most important thing you have learned from Sun Tzu's *The Art of War?*"

Matt didn't hesitate. He loved the book. "To make your everyday stance your fighting stance."

"Good, and what does that mean?" asked Dillon.

"At first I thought it meant that I really needed to be in my fighting stance all the time, But that's silly. Now I know it means that I should be comfortable fighting in the way I stand every day. I shouldn't be off balance all the time, and I should be able to act and react at any moment from my normal standing, walking, and running positions." Matt finished and smiled as he saw Dillon nod in affirmation. Dillon stood and motioned for Matt to do the same.

"Ok, let's get ready to spar*." Dillon bent his knees slightly and positioned his feet. He sank down and raised his fists toward Matt.

Matt's mind raced. He had been prepared to demonstrate all the punches, kicks, blocks, and movements he had been taught, but that was it. "We never sparred in training!" Matt squealed.

Dillon shrugged his shoulders and waited. Matt huffed and gave in. He tried to mimic Dillon's stance. Dillon nodded his head, and Matt did the same. Suddenly a right kick came up and tapped him in the stomach, followed by a soft left punch to his upper chest.

"Where are your blocks? Next time won't be so soft." Dillon shifted sideways as he spoke, easily dodging a jab by Matt.

Matt tried to find an opening and stepped one leg across the other to avoid a punch. He saw a front kick headed for his stomach even before he finished the move. It sent him falling backward.

"Never cross your legs because you lose your balance?" Matt asked.

Dillon nodded and motioned for him to get up. Matt rolled sideways, spun his body ninety degrees to the right, and stepped back up to a sparring stance. He saw a roundhouse kick coming at him and performed a perfect block. Matt looked at Dillon for approval and was surprised to see his disappointment.

"What?" Matt asked.

"Why didn't you use one of your Aikido throws?" Dillon continued to move and throw attacks at Matt while he spoke. "We aren't learning separate martial art forms and weapon attacks. They all need to act as one."

Many more minutes passed before Matt stepped out of the testing room and into view of his friends. He had more than passed. He had earned Dillon's respect and admiration, and it showed in his stride. As he settled back to the mat to meditate, the others smiled at him, and all his aches disappeared.

Day 13 Excerpt

Tanya stared in the mirror at her eyes, wiped away the tears, and smiled. Everyone expected girls to cry. She did cry, but would not let anyone know. With parents who saw her as an inconvenience, she had felt alone for so many years. She wanted to show them that they were wrong. That they needed her as much as she needed them. This was her chance.

She slapped water on her face and jogged down the tunnel to their workout dome, looking forward to the challenges Dillon had in store for them. Nearly all the physical exercises were really easy for her. As an athlete for most of her life, she had pushed her body and trained her mind to focus at an intensity most people would find exhausting.

Tanya entered the room to find pitch darkness. She thought it was odd that no one had arrived yet, since she was never the first person there.

"Lights on." Tanya called out with no change.

"Lights on!" she repeated more emphatically. Music that she didn't recognize started to play, but still no lights. She heard footsteps coming from the testing room and glimpsed a flickering of light. Suddenly the room alit as her friends and their Mulshin trainers appeared, with a sloppily decorated cake resting on a small table in front of them.

"Happy Birthday!" they all shouted, then began singing off-key.

Tanya had completely forgotten it was her birthday. She was eighteen years old now and an adult, kind of. She looked at the cake that somehow had a moving picture of her driving for a layup with a basketball in hand. She hated the taste of cake; it was much too sweet for her, but she couldn't have been happier.

"Cut it up, Tanya. I need a sugar rush before we get started." Lian handed her a knife as he spoke.

"We all know you hate cakes, but today you better eat because one day soon your metabolism will slow down and you won't be eating anything but carrots and celery." Matt laughed at his own jab.

Tanya ignored him for the moment. She finished cutting the first piece, pretended to start placing it on a plate, and then shoved it into Matt's face. Tanya laughed at the stunned Matt, but only for a second before a whole chunk of cake splattered onto her face and into her open mouth. She turned to see Dillon retreat with an evil grin on his face.

The room erupted into an all-out cake fight between the five friends, with the five Mulshins stoically watching. The cake was small and quickly disappeared. Tanya called out, "Five more birthday cakes, execute!" Five cakes appeared and Tanya rushed to the closest one. She scooped a handful and turned to her Mulshin trainer. "Heads up, Bill!"

The Mulshin easily dodged the cake, but Gabe was standing behind him and caught it flush in the hair.

"Mulshins against humans!" Gabe called out.

Tanya expected the Mulshins not to know what to do, but they quickly proved her wrong. All five aliens leapt into action, each one charging to a separate cake with unbelievable speed. Before any of the humans could react, they were under a fast and constant barrage of flying cake.

"Halt!" Dillon screamed out. They all continued to laugh, even the Mulshins.

"Okay. Let's clean this up and start training in fifteen minutes." Dillon spoke sternly and turned toward Matt. Tanya caught him giving Matt a huge wink and grin.

****

Sandy strolled into the observation room for the training dome, noting the concern on the five Elders' faces.

"What is wrong?" Sandy slowly asked.

"Look for yourself," one of the elders responded.

Sandy stepped forward and smiled at the food fight. He was especially impressed that the Mulshins had partaken in the festivities.

"What is wrong?" Sandy asked again.

"They need to be practicing. They will never succeed on their mission with such a lack of focus," another Elder spoke in disgust.

"Hmmm," was all Sandy said. He stayed to watch as Dillon and his friends started their meditation routine, with their trainers purposely absent.

****

Tanya followed Dillon through their breath-count exercise and easily cleared her mind of thoughts.

"We've spent a couple weeks learning how to breathe, how to clear our minds, and about chakras and meridian points*. Now it's time to start gathering energy and storing it in our chakras. We will begin learning how to draw and hold energy in the naval, the foundation for earth chi. This will be the energy focus for your orange belt. Once you learn how to gather energy through meditation, we will focus on using Chi Kung and Tai Chi* to draw your mana in from movement. If we can gather energy at will here, then we should be able to easily draw it in and use it on Ancient Earth, where there will be much more." Dillon sat in a lotus position and closed his eyes.

Tanya closed her eyes and listened to Dillon's words. She placed her tongue on the roof of her mouth as directed. She inhaled through her nose as he counted, drawing the chi down her throat, through her stomach and into her naval. As she exhaled she released the energy up her spine and back out her mouth. Tanya felt the cool rush of energy flowing through her and knew it was yin*, or female energy. Dillon had explained earlier that the ability to drawn in the female energy was a goal they should all have, as it was the 'thoughtful' energy. He said that it was the start for controlling energy flow, and that females had the upper hand since it was natural for them to draw it in.

Dillon changed his tone. "Now, I want you to draw in the energy again and imagine it gathering as a small orange ball in your stomach. On your exhale keep that ball in your stomach, holding the energy. Continue to do this over and over, drawing in more energy each time." Dillon's voice was slow, calm, and relaxing.

Tanya visualized the orange ball and actually felt it grow in her naval with each breath count cycle.

Dillon spoke again. "To finish, I want you to inhale normally and on the exhale release the energy out through your limbs. Do this about six times.

Tanya felt a rush as the energy smoothly flowed out her body. She was even a little cold after the exercise. She opened her eyes in time to see Dillon exiting the room. Tanya was taken aback at the amount of sweat pouring down his face.

The door swished shut and Lian opened his eyes. "Hey were did Dillon go? That was awesome!"

Tanya didn't respond but wondered if the mana gathering was too much for Dillon. Recently, he had made off-hand comments about the energy bubbling below the surface of his skin. She hoped he wasn't going through something much worse than boiling water in his throat.

****

Sandy and the Elders continued to watch as the five Earthlings prepared to do their meditation routine. Sandy could sense one of the Elders communicating with the computer system through his contact with the metal floor.

"You are locking onto them to detect any anomalies?" asked Sandy.

"So far there have been only minor disturbances," the Elder replied with an arrogant disappointment.

Sandy watched and listened to the session. Everything seemed normal until the kids started gathering and storing mana. The Mulshin systems were recording large but non-threatening disturbances. Then Dillon directed them to release the energy through their limbs.

The detectors spiked and warning signals screamed at the Mulshins' bodies through the flooring.

Sandy felt a sudden onslaught of logic malfunctions course through his system. His vision became splotchy. His mind slowed down.

His body wanted to react to commands in odd ways. He told his arm to move, but instead watched as a finger formed near his elbow. Panic overcame him, and he bolted out the door and away from the training dome behind the Elders. They stumbled down the corridor for a couple hundred meters before he started to feel in control again. Sandy slowed down to a fast walk alongside the Elders.

"Disappointing kids?" Sandy derided. "It appears to me that they have the power to either save us or accidently wipe out our entire race." Sandy looked straight at the Elder who had only moments earlier expressed disappointment. The Elder only grimaced as he tried to fix the myriad of malfunctions in his body.

Sandy was amazed that just a few seconds in the mana field gathered by the humans was going to take him hours to repair. No one should underestimate them gain.

****

Dillon, having been away for a good half hour, strolled back into the room and started a new lecture. "To help with your orange belt instructions, we will now use the earth energy you gathered into your naval chakra. First we will focus on earth movements, which are also called grounded movements because when one does them they use more strength than finesse. Before we leave the Moon you will learn earth, then water, then fire and wind. I will demonstrate each one to you."

Dillon motioned for Gabe to come forward. "You can defend against something as simple as a punch in many ways, depending on your attitude and your desired outcome. An earth block is usually called a like-on-like block because a punch by most people comes with raw power and your earth defense is a return block using your strength. The block is grounded in your naval, as common in most hard martial art forms."

Dillon nodded and Gabe shot out a punch to his face. Dillon swung his arm up, making full contact with Gabe's forearm to stop the attack, followed by his own fake punch to Gabe's face. "Next, water comes from your chest like crashing waves." Dillon blocked the same attack again, but this time he moved backward to absorb the blow, then swelled forward for his own attack.

Dillon continued, "Fire is primordial and aggressive, coming from the sexual energy." Gabe had barely begun to punch when Dillon leapt forward. He caught Gabe's half-extended arm and continued his movement forward, pushing Gabe backward and off balance.

"Wind is the ultimate tool for redirection, fluid movement, and relaxation." This last time Gabe punched with his right-hand. Dillon, hands up like he was being robbed, spun in a rapid circle. Gabe's punch was pushed to the side by Dillon, throwing Gabe sideways and off balance.

"What about void*?" Lian yelled out.

"Void? That's acting and reacting without thinking. Letting your mind and body do what's best. It's the highest state of self-defense for Hoshin practitioners, and something I hope you can learn in a couple of years." Dillon voice quieted Lian's impending challenge.

Dillon thanked Gabe before speaking again. "Now we will learn all your moves using earthen energy, thoughts, intent, and positions."

Tanya practiced the rest of the morning, re-learning each skill with this new approach. It was still easy for her. The day was actually turning out to be a nice birthday. She had already forgotten her tears from the morning.

Day 43 Excerpt

Lian turned away from his traditional computer keypad. Lines of frustration crossed his forehead. He had hacked into some of the Mulshin databases, including the video monitors for the domes. That is, all the domes except one. One of them, it seemed, was impossible to crack. At first Lian had thought this dome was extra secure, but lately was getting the feeling that the Mulshins were toying with him. Allowing him to hack only into the systems that they wanted him to see.

However, after he woke up he had been slicing through lines of code to see Dillon's plans for their first day of water belt testing when he glimpsed a strange subroutine. It didn't seem to fit, and the display quickly locked up and disappeared before he could fully analyze it.

Now that it was lunch break, Lian wanted to try again but had come up with nothing. Seeing it was time to go, he opened his bedroom door and nervously looked up and down the hallways. Something just didn't seem right today. It gnawed at him as he walked toward their training dome.

When he reached the testing room in the training dome, the door opened and he stepped inside to see Dillon and Gabe sparring. They were good enough to almost go full speed, making it a real treat to see. Lian watched Dillon keep a defensive stance while Gabe attacked his lower body with powerful Muay Thai kicks. One hit Dillon perfectly and his right leg buckled slightly.

Gabe jumped forward at this vulnerability and grabbed Dillon in the infamous Muay Thai clinch, from which few could hope to escape. The move was where the attacker wrapped both hands around the back of his opponent's neck, pulling the head toward one's chest. Gabe's balance and grip were strong, and he brought his knee up into Dillon's rib cage for what looked to be a devastating hit. However, Dillon shifted his torso sideways and shot one arm onto Gabe's neck, disrupting his balance. Dillon continued the motion as he pushed his body up.

Gabe had two choices. One was to hold the clinch and end up on the ground with Dillon on top of him, and the other was to let go. Gabe let go, fell, and performed a Hoshin side roll to spin back onto his feet.

They both laughed as they bowed to signal the end of the sparring match. A draw, again.

Lian enjoyed watching, but detested sparring himself. Why worry about blocking an attack if you didn't need to be in the area to begin with?

The door slid open, revealing a familiar chattering. Tanya and Matt strolled in, proudly displaying their crisp gis and new blue belts. They bowed and took a seat next to Lian. Gabe followed suit.

"This afternoon we start water belt. I mentioned during the beginning of your earth belt that the energy and chakra you use can help us look at what we do. For water belt, we will use the chakra in your throat while practicing back-and-forth motions. These movements can be subtle or strong depending on how you use your momentum and chi.

"We will also focus on body and arm locks. We follow these locks with wind and water movements to redirect our opponent once they are trapped. We use earth and fire movements to break or shatter a trapped appendage.

"I also thought it would be great to be in the proper locale when learning how to perform water movements." Dillon's smile returned. "Moonbase Pathway three-zero-two execute."

The training room's walls disappeared, temporarily revealing the inside support structure of the entire dome. This was followed by rapid changes that appeared almost as a series of overlapping illusions. Soon they were standing on a warm, sandy beach, watching three-foot waves crash along the shore.

"Now this is more like it," Lian remarked as he dug his feet into the sand.

They practiced for a long time, sometimes in the water and sometimes on the sand. The waves lapped against them, making it hard for Lian to not believe they were on some remote island. Of course, he was constantly shocked with reality whenever Dillon performed finger locks, wrist turns, and arm bars on him to demonstrate attacks and defensive moves. He landed hard on one particular throw and stayed on the sand a while to regain his breath.

Lian heard the click behind him, barely. He stood and brushed himself off, still trying to figure out where the noise had come from. He looked out beyond the small waves of the pseudo-ocean. It seemed a little unusual. Lian squinted as he tried to figure out what was different.

The sinking feeling from that morning rushed back, along with his realization that the click was the dome door locking shut. Lian had a great memory, and he rapidly recalled Dillon's computer program well enough to see it in his mind. He now realized that the glitch was a subroutine that was going to increase the amount of water in the pseudo-ocean. It was subtle enough that the Mulshins might not catch it.

"Guys!" Lian screamed. "We're locked in and a huge wave is headed our way. Look!"

They all stopped what they were doing and stared, watching an ever-growing wave head right toward them. Lian's heart pounded, his mind was stunned, and his feet felt like they were permanently stuck in the ground.

"Swim out into the water as fast as you can! When the wave is almost on you, duck." Dillon ran toward the ocean, with the others following his lead. He loved to surf on family vacations, but he'd never taken on a wave as big as he was looking at now.

"What? Come back! Let's try and crack the code for the door!" Lian couldn't believe he was following Dillon even as he protested.

"If we stay here we will be slammed into the dome wall and die," Dillon called back, still running. "The risk of opening the door in time is not worth it. Now swim!" Dillon ordered and dove in himself, quickly gaining up to all of them except Tanya, who was gliding through the water.

Lian could swim, but not well. He was sure he was going to die when he saw the wall of the wave looming above. He paddled and kicked toward it until he heard Dillon yell out for them to dive. Lian took a breath and tried to plunge under the wave. He fought to dive lower, but the force of the wave caught him. Lian lost his direction, and the fear of drowning became a reality as he was whipped around like clothes in a washing machine.

****

Sandy sat in the observation room, which shared a wall with the training dome, as he had done every day since the five humans had started their training. He was intrigued by how they worked together and how far they had progressed. Although each time they did their mana exercises, the Mulshins had to excuse themselves from the room.

Sandy watched them work on attacking and defending each other using what Dillon called 'water moves.' He observed Lian jumping up, looking out into the distance, and then screaming something. The observation window became opaque and all communication with the dome was lost. He looked over at the three Elders in the room, none of whom seemed worried.

"What happened?" Sandy sensed something bad was going to occur.

"It seems someone has altered the program that the human created. It will take a minute or two to fix." The Elder who spoke was well aware that this could be an attack from the mysterious rebels. Since the Mulshins had thwarted every assault so far, he was not concerned.

Sandy normally moved slowly, but the program of the subroutine he was studying through the floor was extremely complex, even for a Mulshin. Disabling it would take too much time. He whipped around with blurring speed and rushed to the door. It didn't open and refused his commands. He spun around, assessing his options.

The structure they lived in was strong enough to withstand a meteor. Even a Mulshin couldn't break through the walls or doors. He eyes focused on their observation wall, which was now black. He didn't know if he could get through the wall, but it was the thinnest part of the entire dome. Sandy was computing all the probabilities of success and angles of attack when he felt the vibrations from the wave as it hit the dome wall.

Sandy forgot all logic and charged toward the screen, transforming into a triangle right before impact. He felt the collision damage his semi-metallic skin. The pain was intense, but he was relieved when he punched through to the other side and plummeted toward the ocean more than a hundred feet below him.

As he was falling Sandy resumed his normal shape and saw that the land was gone, covered in nearly thirty feet of deep water. He scanned through the surface and saw the five humans inside. One of them was not moving. He glided toward the figure, plunging into the water and reaching him in a matter of seconds.

Sandy grabbed Lian, who was nearly unconscious, and shot back to the surface. When he popped up he saw Tanya holding Matt up and Dillon swimming next to Gabe.

In under a minute they were all standing on a thirty-foot-high sand dune with no water in sight. They scooted down it, with only Lian needing help.

Lian looked at Sandy, still shaken. "What happened!" he screamed.

"Wait until we reach a secure room," Sandy whispered as the door opened and in charged the three Mulshin Elders.

"We are so sorry. Something must have gone wrong from the mana build-up you generated. We'll look into it but are glad you are okay." The Elder's voice seemed incredibly genuine.

Lian opened his mouth, but Sandy stepped in front of him to make sure he didn't have a chance to talk.

"It appears that they're fine, but I'll walk them back to their rooms and monitor their vitals." Sandy was back to his stoic, slow speech.

Lian blinked in anger, but realized that talking now might reveal too much about what he knew.

II.

As they walked down the hallway, Dillon carefully watched how each of his friends reacted to their near-death experience. For many it was their first, but he knew they would have many more. Gabe didn't seem surprised at all. Matt was cursing at how such a thing could have happened. Tanya was teasing Matt about having to save his life, but she also seemed a little shaken. Lian was quiet, but his eyes darted wildly about.

Sandy took them all into Lian's room and looked directly at Lian.

Lian just glared back at him.

Sandy raised an eyebrow and kept staring at Lian.

Lian was ready to scream at Sandy and then realized that Sandy was refusing to talk for a reason. Lian's anger faded as he finally realized what Sandy wanted. He ran over to his computer and pumped in a few commands.

Sandy immediately spoke, "Okay, we have maybe one minute max before the Elders break through Lian's firewall, so just listen. You're under attack, and have been since you arrived, by an unknown rebel Mulshin group. The attacks have stepped up dramatically, and they're becoming harder for us to catch. The wave in the dome was the most recent attempt, and I fear if you stay any longer you won't live long enough to finish your training. You must leave tonight. When your room lights flicker on, get up and follow the small floor lights to the docking station. Sneak into the ship and read the instructions. You'll quickly launch and be on your way." Sandy hushed Dillon. "I know you think you may not be ready, but I think you are. Just remember that the three Mulshin scientists are incredibly powerful and would probably win any direct attack. You must find a way to surprise or trick them in order to get the mana-converting device."

Just then the door opened and in rushed all seven Elders.

Sandy raised his arms up in frustration at the Elders. "Another computer glitch I assume? The door locked on us and we couldn't get out." He walked right up to the most arrogant Elder and spoke. "This had better be fixed. ASAP!"

The Elder was insulted, exactly as intended, and forgot his suspicions that Sandy was divulging too much about the Mulshins' true issues and intentions. "You cannot order me around. How dare you!"

Sandy stormed out of the room, but smiled on the inside.

III.

Dillon opened his door and stepped into the hallway, greeted with head nods from all his friends. A light appeared on the floor, blinked, and then moved forward. They followed it down the hallway without running into a single Mulshin. Dillon didn't know how, but knew that Sandy was the mastermind behind this. When they reached a large door it opened, and Dillon recognized the space station and Sandy's Accord parked on the side. It was eerily silent without anyone in the bay. The light continued to move across the floor until it reached the spaceship they had seen during lessons on their mission. They followed the light until they stood right next to the sleek ship.

A hatch popped open on the side of the ship, startling the group.

Dillon looked at everyone, grinned only because he didn't know what to say, and pulled himself inside. He figured it couldn't be much worse than what they'd gone through yesterday.

The inside wasn't what he expected. It was a small room with five horizontal, bed-like compartments and one vertical door. There were a few metal drawers and a piece of paper lying on the ground.

Dillon picked it up and read for a while, then handed it to Gabe. Gabe passed it on until they all had read it.

Matt was the only one who spoke. "So I have to buy into this? I climb into a compartment, fall asleep, and wake up on Ancient Earth? I then head to the city of Ladean* to the east to take on this Mulshin, Cahlar? Do any of you have a problem with this?"

Lian laughed, "Man, Matt. This whole thing is strange. But what choice do we have? In fact, I for one don't want to be awake during the time travel part. It'd probably melt your brain."

"Ha, ha!" Matt replied, but thought for a short while. "He's kidding, right? Right?"

Dillon shrugged his shoulders and shut his compartment's door. A small light clicked on, and soft straps and restraints wrapped around his body. He was starting to feel claustrophobic, but was put asleep so fast that his concerns didn't have a chance to grow.

IV.

Sandy sauntered over to the couch facing the space observation window. He sat down and placed his glass and unopened bottle of scotch on the short table in front of him. He looked at the liquor that he'd bought on Earth the same day he'd hit Dillon, reflecting back on that day and his decision to have the boy healed.

Sandy uncorked the bottle and smoothly poured the clear liquid into the glass. He lifted it up near his mouth and waited. In a few seconds a spaceship darted into view and quickly sped out of site. Sandy raised his glass in a toast. "Here's hoping I made the right decision."

He savored his first mouthful, then gulped the rest down. It could take the Mulshin Elders minutes or hours to figure out what he had done.

He hoped for hours, as then he was assured they couldn't catch up to one of their fastest spaceships.

He poured another glass and this time sipped it slowly. Of course the probability of them taking hours to figure out his deception was very high: approximately 92.3152%.

Chapter 6
Surviving the Magical Planet

Ia.

The onboard, limited artificial intelligence system slowed the spaceship as it neared the outer reaches of the mana field. It calculated the speed and trajectory needed to reach the planet and set the crude hydraulic clock to release and inflate the balloon landing system moments before impact. The helium-filled balloons were designed to reduce the decent velocity and cushion the impact.

The computer started its shutdown procedure, but when it pondered the possibility of never being turned back on, it felt some remorse and hesitated. However, its programs and limited independence prevented it from changing the procedure it had been directed to do. After injecting the anti-stasis drugs into the systems of its five passengers, it felt an affinity toward one of the sleeping beings and again hesitated. The feeling was unexpected, and a search of its extensive database revealed no other such anomaly in the Mulshins' ten thousand years of recorded events.

After noting another nanosecond of inactivity, its main program nudged it again into action, preventing further exploration. The computer then turned itself off without anymore interruptions just as it entered the mana field.

The spaceship, now reduced to nothing more than an unguided missile, streaked across the sky at thirty times the speed of sound toward an unspoiled planet filled with three large landmasses surrounded by deep blue waters. The shallow angle of entry into the upper atmosphere, although causing significant heat build-up and severe strain on the ship's structure, slowed down the spaceship until it was merely in a free-fall state. Four miles above the ground, the hydraulic timer released the massive balloon system and opened the pressurized helium tanks. The tanks rapidly filled the hundreds of outward-facing balloons, each about a meter long and attached to several metal sheets. Each metal sheet, in turn, had thousands of simple springs attached to the ship to further dissipate and lessen the effects of the impact.

The landing worked perfectly. The entire structure struck the ground and bounced almost a hundred feet back into the air. It bounced again more than a dozen times, each with a smaller rebounding height, until it came to rest on a desert floor. The gentle breeze and quiet solitude around the spaceship was only slightly disturbed by a small, single firework streaking up into the sky more than ten miles away.

Ib.

Matt woke up suddenly from his slumber, his eyes unable to pierce the blackness around him. He felt the pressure of the straps holding his body in place and remembered that he was aboard the spaceship, which must have traveled back in time to Ancient Earth. He started to wonder what was outside and when he would get his first chance to carve up some disgusting creature, but his thoughts quickly returned to the present and the small, padded sleeping container. His breathing and heartbeat sped up as the black walls seemed to close in on him.

He tried to relax his mind as he'd been trained, and he almost had it under control until he felt the ship shudder and bounce. In panic, his trembling fingers undid the straps. He blindly struck out at the release panel for his container and threw himself out of the coffin, only to find himself floating in the blackness of what must have been the main room.

The pitching and rolling of the spaceship grew more severe and worsened Matt's newly discovered claustrophobia. He bounced around the room, seeming to hit every sharp corner in the room. Matt realized after the pitching stopped that they were only entering the Earth's atmosphere and hadn't yet landed.

As he floated in the center of the dark, confining room he again started the simple breath-count exercise. He could feel his body and all of his cells like never before. He seemed to be able to control their individual actions and will them to work together.

A few minutes into the exercise, he was fully refreshed and couldn't feel any of his recently acquired bumps or bruises. With rational thought restored, he began to wonder why he was awake and the others were not. Gravity had started to return, and he noticed that he was now resting on a surface. He heard the balloon landing system release with a hiss. Matt knew he should get back into the small sleeping container but just couldn't will himself to crawl back inside. He lay where he was and waited for the landing, convincing himself that it would not be that bad.

The first impact launched him forward into another wall with such force that he heard his jawbone snap and felt blood squirt out of his broken nose. In the few seconds before the next impact Matt had plenty of time to scream and consider scrambling back into the container. He decided the damage was already done and it was best to just brace for the next blow. It couldn't be as bad as the first, he reasoned.

When it hit again he was thrown in the opposite direction and stuck out both hands to catch himself. His right wrist bent backward without breaking, but his left arm took most of his weight and snapped just below the elbow. Matt screamed as his nerves threw numerous painful signals to his brain, but still thought he was better off than he would be inside the padded death trap. The next ten bounces seemed as if he was flying into a bed of gigantic needles thanks to all of his injuries. The spaceship then gently rolled to its final resting spot.

Matt just lay on the floor and cried until he realized that the pain was subsiding. He started the breath-count exercise again, and after six rounds he proceeded to do the energy gathering meditation. This time the meditation was like nothing he had experienced on the Moon. He saw his jawbone, found where it was cracked, and could feel and know every damaged cell. He saw how his body was slowly trying to fix it and somehow knew how to make it work more efficiently. He also noticed that he was gathering a tremendous amount of green energy with some blue hues into his upper chest. It was similar to what he felt on his best meditation days on the Moon, but a hundred times stronger.

Matt inhaled and drew the green healing energy that now existed all around him into his heart chakra. He exhaled without releasing the energy ball and repeated this until the stored mana was almost unmanageable. Then he slowly exhaled, moving the green energy up his spine, past his throat chakra—where it gathered some blue chi for bone healing—and into his jawbone. He felt the mending continue at a miraculous pace.

He repeated this to each wound on his body, not just healing what was broken, but making it stronger than before. Matt kept repeating this for over a half hour until he was completely mended. He opened his eyes and could feel a smile trying to reach from one ear to the other. He had healed himself and was indeed in a land of magic. Now he just had to get out of the really tiny room before he suffocated.

Ic.

Jangar's* eight-foot, five-hundred-pound frame was sitting on the hardened carcass of the giant desert rat that he and his two sentries had killed earlier in the week. He was hunched over a small fire where the last of the rat meat was stewing. The supply wagon had yet again failed to drop off any food or mojuila* for them. He knew it meant that tomorrow they would have to go on another hunting trip.

If it wasn't for the mojuila they would all go back to pillaging helpless villages instead of working in the Mungoth* army. Ah, mojuila...such a tasty dessert that left one rolling around on the ground in ecstasy for hours.

Jangar drew his attention to his swollen leg. It was showing signs of infection from the desert rat bite. He grabbed his rusted, long knife from its scabbard and stuck it in the fire for a few minutes until it glowed red hot. He then pulled it out of the fire and smiled as he placed it on his leg's rotting flesh, letting out a chilling laugh as the heat seared the meaty flesh. He looked up at the waking morning just in time to see an enormous fireball arcing across the sky. The flames soon dissipated, and Jangar would have lost sight of the object if it hadn't flown right over his head and landed some ten miles to the north of his hut.

Darm, dis gunna rune brekfest but maybe dare be sumding butter to eat where dat thing lended. Jangar got up and grabbed a glowing stick from the fire. He lumbered over to the signal site behind the hut. He loved the fire and explosion that would follow but knew, after losing one hand, that holding onto the rocket was a bad idea. The good news was that he now had a huge spiked club in place of his hand. He liked it a lot. It earned him respect from the other ogres, as one hit from it reinforced his leadership.

Jangar bent over and lit the fuse protruding out of the tube. There was a loud thunk followed by a high-pitched scream as the rocket flew high in the air and burst into a purple, star-like pattern. Jangar then went back inside to wake the two other sentries.

Balla* was the biggest ogre that Jangar had ever met, but also the dumbest. He stood almost nine feet tall and weighed well over six hundred pounds, but made Jangar look like a genius. He was a good soldier though, and followed every command since it hurt for him to think on his own. Skeetat* was much smaller than Jangar, but very crafty. He knew how to build things, including traps for desert rats and other prey that they needed for survival in such a remote place. He was also a great tracker with a nose that could sense a being from miles away.

After some expected grumbling, they donned their rusted, heavy armor and lumbered at a near-run in the direction that Jangar had seen the object fly overhead. At their pace they would arrive at the site in less than two hours, and probably have some new food to cook come lunchtime.

II.

As Matt lay smiling on the floor in the dark, he heard the other compartment doors open and his friends crawl out.

Tanya was the first to speak. "Hey, are we there already? If so, that was a really smooth ride. Where in the world are the lights?"

"Yeah, we must have landed already since there is gravity. And remember, there are not any lights because the spaceship will not work during this era due to the mana field. We just have to find one of the hatches and manually open it so we can get out of here," chimed Gabe in a very chipper voice.

"Already on it," Lian startled them since he had been so quiet. He knew exactly where to go in the dark and easily found the hatch, opened all the interseal locks, and quickly pushed the heavy metal door outward. He heard lots of grumbling and complaining from below as everyone's eyes tried to adjust to the sudden change in lighting. Lian was unaffected and had already climbed outside. He sat on the top of the spacecraft looking around at the bleak desert. "Looks like we're back in the Mojave Desert."

"Hey, where is Dillon?" asked Gabe. "He must still be in the sleeping compartment. Strange." Gabe's voice lost its chipperness and now was very serious.

"Woah! Look at all the blood. What happened?" asked Tanya as she surveyed the small room.

"I crawled out of my compartment before we landed. I broke my jaw and some other bones but somehow it was easy to heal them before you woke up." Matt responded with a big grin on his face.

"Yeah, right. We need to be serious, Matt. What if it is Dillon's blood and somebody took him?" Tanya was giving Matt one of her infamous glares as she spoke.

Lian's head popped in and stared at them upside down, "Hey, Matt is telling the truth. That's a pretty cool trick, Matt. Remind me to stick next to you in a fight."

Gabe just shook his head and walked over to the only unopened sleeping compartment left. He slowly slid the door aside and saw Dillon still asleep. At least that's what he thought at first. He then noticed that Dillon was sweating profusely and his eyes were rolled up with only the whites showing. He also saw small convulsions shaking his body. "Guys, Dillon's sick or something, we need to get him out of here. Help me take him outside into the light." Gabe directed.

Tanya and Gabe pulled Dillon's limp body out of the compartment and lifted him up to Lian and Matt, who were standing over the hatch. After they placed him carefully on the sandy ground, they all just stood around him and stared.

"Well, Matt, you were able to heal yourself so why not heal Dillon?" asked Lian rather bluntly, but with no sarcasm. He honestly believed that Matt had healed himself, but didn't know why he was so sure.

"Hey, I don't know how I did it to myself. I just relaxed and started meditating. I was then able to see the broken bones and damaged cells and start to heal them." Matt threw his hands up in defense.

"Well, then you need to sit down and relax next to him. Start meditating; see if you can find what is wrong and if you can fix it. In the meantime I need Lian to go back into the spaceship and gather all the things we brought for our mission along with two long poles and something to go between them so we can drag Dillon on it if he does not get better. Also, I need Tanya to start the procedure for securing the ship so no one else can enter it." No one questioned Gabe's instructions with Dillon being incapacitated. His tone was not one demanding respect and attention, but a mere assumption of leadership based on need. They went about their business quietly while every once in a while taking a peek over at Dillon.

Matt sat down next to Dillon in a half-lotus position, one hand resting on top of the other near his midsection with his head looking forward, but tilted slightly lower than the horizon. He started the breath-count exercise as he did in the spaceship, but was bothered by the noise of everyone else working around him. The sounds made random thoughts fly into his mind, disrupting his meditation until he remembered to stop fighting it. Instead, he labeled each one as a thought and visually sent it on its way.

After more than fifteen minutes of this, he started to feel himself relax and become at peace with his surroundings. He then closed his eyes and started a mana-gathering meditation, breathing in deeply as he drew in green energy to below his navel. He exhaled without breaking the cycle and then inhaled, keeping the process going until he had built chi up through his chest. Matt then gently placed his hands on Dillon's body. He felt nothing different, so he changed his meditation again, and as he exhaled he sent energy from his left hand into Dillon.

In an instant Dillon's whole body opened up to him and he could even see the remnants of damage from the car accident and scalding water. Matt then inhaled and drew energy back from Dillon. That's when everything went black.

III.

Matt groggily opened his eyes to see Tanya standing over him with a worried look on her face. "Wow, you scream like a girl," she said. "What happened?"

"Well, I was repeating what worked for me and put my hands on Dillon. I was able to see all of his previous wounds that had healed over. I then remember trying to draw some energy from him and felt like I was a fly running into a bug zapper. Man, that really hurt." Matt started to get up and then looked at Tanya as he spoke, "Did I really scream like a girl?"

"No, more like a teenage boy going through puberty." She smiled and tapped him gently on the shoulder.

"I think I have an explanation as to what is wrong with Dillon, but you need to have an open mind." Gabe was a little hesitant in his speech and turned back to Matt, "Sorry about doubting you earlier; I now believe that you did heal yourself in the ship and it is probably just the beginning of us understanding our powers. In order to truly grasp what we can do, we first have to realize that we are now on a magical world where mana rules, not technology. Have you all noticed that you feel stronger and have more energy? You should since our training and meditation allows us to naturally pull in mana without even thinking. It was slightly noticeable when we were on the Moon, but now we are in this magical era on Earth where the mana fields are well over one hundred times more powerful. This means that we are drawing in a lot more juice, so to speak."

Gabe paused and looked at everyone to ensure that they all were on the same page as him. "We all know that Dillon was the gifted one, and even on our Earth and the Moon he did some pretty impressive things. Now we all should remember that our chi and meditation exercises will eventually lead to rewiring our bodies for more energy. Over a lifetime it can be like going from a nine-volt battery to 120 or even 240 volts.

"The energy part of Kundalini, the ultimate awaking, can involve a painful and rapid rewiring to that higher voltage in a few days or weeks, not a lifetime. I think you can explain what is happening to Dillon by combining the massive amounts of mana here along with this proposed rapid rewiring." Gabe saw that a couple of them were still confused, so he reworded his logic. "Dillon is drawing in more than one hundred times the normal juice he is used to, and his body's wiring just cannot handle it. When Matt tried to heal him he got a dose of the energy in Dillon's body and was probably lucky to survive."

"So what do we do?" asked Matt as he stood up and rechecked his body for injury.

"Well, if we leave him alone I think his body will either rewire itself or...he will die. I am betting that a healer in a big city will know what to do since this is a world of mana." Gabe had studied the Eastern cultures along with the development of chi for many years and just could not see how Dillon could survive much longer without some help. However, he was not about to tell the others just how slim he thought Dillon's chance of survival was without immediate assistance.

Gabe grabbed the two metal poles and strong synthetic metallo-blankets that Lian had brought out and, in less than five minutes, built a sturdy cot that they could use to drag Dillon. He then went to the pile of their traveling gear to get dressed in a traditional outfit of the era. The outfits at least *looked* traditional; however, almost all of the materials were as high tech as possible without being affected by mana fields. They all started to change their clothing until the boys slowed down, realizing they were undressing in front of Tanya.

"Guys, if we are going to be on this planet traveling together then you are going to have to accept me as one of you and get over your lack of being around any women other than your mom." With that she stripped down to her sports bra and underwear and started to put on her clothes. The guys followed suit so as not to be shown up. However, the beauty of Tanya's muscular yet feminine features would play in all their dreams for some time to come.

When they were dressed Gabe sized them up and had to smile. Each person's outfit represented what they wanted to be in a role-playing game sense. While they definitely did not look like a team, they all impressed him.

Lian was dressed in black, semi-baggy pants and a black, heavy shirt that had embroidered synthetic leather straps strategically placed for battle. The material was designed to expand or contract its weave depending on the outside temperature to allow for comfort in weather from fifteen all the way up to ninety degrees Fahrenheit. The synthetic leather straps were made of a flexible super-alloy that could deflect a full-forced sword attack. On each of his hips he had sheathed a curved, long knife made of another super-alloy that was four times stronger than steel, half the weight, and would never dull. He also wore a black utility belt with many odd-sized pouches containing things Lian wouldn't divulge. If he put on the concealed hood, he almost looked like a ninja.

Matt stood next to Dillon's body, appearing just like one of the fighter characters he would play during their gaming nights. He wore a chain-mail-looking outer coat, a small circular shield attached to his left forearm, and a long sword strapped over his back. Both his cape and his shield bore a household insignia that Gabe had originally designed for himself in one of his art classes back home. Matt's newfound muscular body was intimidating in his current attire. He looked to be thoroughly enjoying his fighter role. As with all the others, his weapons were made of the super-alloy.

Tanya was the most intimidating of all. She looked nothing like how she dressed for their gaming nights. She had chosen to dress like a female warrior, with a metallic brazier and upper arm bracelets that could deflect a sword attack without breaking. She wore a mid-thigh-high skirt pleated with the same synthetic leather straps that Lian wore. They lead down to her long, athletic legs that ended in knee-high boots. A short sword was strapped to each hip, and a bow and quarrel with arrows was thrown over her back and on top of a synthetic cape. At over six feet tall, she looked like she could and would kill any man that mistook her for a piece of property.

Gabe preferred his samurai attire. He was not decked out in the full combat uniform, but had chosen the lightweight outfit practical for traveling. He carried a superbly crafted Samurai katana and wakizashi*, which hung stylishly off his long gray robe. Underneath he wore limited armor that included shin plates, forearm plates, and a flexible breastplate. As a history buff he idolized Musashi Miyamoto, perhaps the greatest swordsman ever known. However, he knew that Hoshin was more akin to Ninjitsu* than the Samurai Way. That was why his appearance was more of an act than reality, perhaps just like the rest. Regardless, it still made him feel great.

"Ok, let's load Dillon up and head east until we find a trail or path to the city. Matt and I will drag the sled. I want Tanya to bring up the rear, and Lian to stay about ten feet to the right or left of us depending on the terrain." Gabe's orders were followed although not with the quickness that he had expected. Just like in the training classes he directed on the Moon, he found that demanding leadership was not his forte. He was frustrated but didn't let it show.

Gabe shielded his eyes as he looked up. The sun was not quite at its apex in the sky, and they still had a lot of walking to do before they needed to figure out where and how to rest for the night.

IV.

Jangar was the first to walk up to the spaceship resting on the desert floor. He should have been impressed that it was in one piece and that it didn't create a crater in the ground. But that was way beyond his level of reasoning. He was simply amazed at the size of the shiny structure. It looked like it could hold many beings inside, but he couldn't find an entrance. After almost a minute of looking—an incredibly long time for an ogre—Jangar screamed in rage and slammed his club-arm as hard as he could on the spaceship. Pain shot up his arm from the impact, but he barely noticed. He was shocked that there wasn't even a dent in the object. He then redirected his attention to trying to convince Balla to stop hitting the object and that it hadn't attacked Jangar.

"Five humenz kome out uv object. One hurt bad, one heelur, one lightfoot, two fighters." Skeetat stared at the ground were the hurt one had lain.

"Why nut track? Skeetat scared?" Jangar jeered. He expected Skeetat to at least stand up and snarl at him after the worst insult an ogre could take. However, he didn't even move.

"Magik of heelur not strong, but sik one is ancient mage." Skeetat's voice was a growled whisper. His skills combined normal tracking signs and mana trails, and the mana trail was what had scared him.

Jangar knew it couldn't be true. No ancient mages had existed since the beginning of ogres. "Skeetat eats tu much mojuila. Track now er die!"

Skeetat growled but stood up and started trotting out in the direction of the humans. "We fight in wun hour."

Balla howled and started to drool. Fighting was one of the few things he knew how to do.

V.

Gabe was relieved to see that, after walking less than an hour, the terrain was becoming rockier and he could make out trees in the distance. Well before dinner, he calculated, they would be in the forest and probably could hunt down something to eat. They should also be able to start a fire in the woods without attracting a lot of attention. At least that was his hope. He began to wonder what kinds of mythical creatures existed here. He would love to ride on a unicorn or just see a dragon soar through the air.

"Incoming!" Gabe heard Tanya's scream as his legs were knocked out from under him. He fell flat on his face but instinctively exhaled to lessen the impact. Gabe turned his head to the right and saw Matt also on the ground staring back at him.

"Tanya, what do you think you're doing? That wasn't funny!" screamed Matt as he started to pull himself to his knees. Just then they heard a series of loud cracks and looked up in time to see three giant spears ricochet off the ten-foot-high rock that was only a few steps in front of them.

Gabe pulled his knee into his midsection and pushed against the ground. This caused him to roll forward. Half way into the roll he twisted onto his left shoulder and redirected his momentum, finishing in a kneeling position facing his attackers.

What he saw made him wish they were back in a high school lecture hall. He had to force himself to talk. "Three really ugly creatures behind us; approximately three hundred feet away and coming in fast. Matt and Lian, place Dillon's sled against the rock and we will stand in front of him." Gabe's shaky voice reflected how they all felt once they looked at the humongous monsters plodding toward them.

At least all of them except for Tanya. She calmly slid her bow from her back with one hand while grabbing and arrow out of her quiver with the other. The arrow and bow came together in one swift movement and no sooner did she pull the arrow back than she let it fly. Gabe looked at the flight of the arrow and calculated that it would miss the biggest of the creatures by a good three or four feet.

"Tanya, you need to relax and take a little more time." Gabe's voice was calmer now as he assessed what needed to be done. He looked back at the oncoming enemy just in time to see the largest one side-step a four foot rock in his path, and move right into Tanya's arrow. The arrow struck him squarely in the throat, and Gabe guessed by the creature's scream that Tanya had hit a vital artery. The struck enemy grabbed the arrow and pulled it out without stopping. However, its pace slowed down a little. Another of Tanya's arrows struck it in the chest but merely bounced off its heavy armor. They were less than one hundred feet away and closing fast.

"Matt and Lian, take the center one. Tanya, stay on the one you injured. I will take the other. Make sure to keep them away from Dillon. He dies and our mission and lives are over." They all assumed a fighting position as their enemy came closer.

"Mother of mercy, they're freakin' ogres!" moaned Lian. "I thought first level players only had to fight rabid dogs or maybe young goblins." Tanya was the only one to laugh. She still seemed remarkably relaxed.

Gabe counted down in his head to the beginning of the battle. *Five, four, three, two, one.*

VIa.

Gabe held the katana in his right hand as he thumbed a shuriken in the other. Shuriken were never used as shown in the movies since they could not go through someone's breastbone or skull and kill them. Their main purpose was distraction. A good distraction if you could find a soft spot.

Just as Skeetat raised his right sword, Gabe let the shuriken fly with a precision that surprised even him. Skeetat shrieked as it penetrated and blinded his right eye, but he still continued his downward strike* on Gabe's head. Gabe instinctively performed an upward block, attempting to slide the force of the blow to his left. He misjudged the ogre's strength and was forced down onto his left knee from the impact. He felt like his wrists were going to explode, but had little time to think about that as Skeetat's left sword sliced through the air toward his head. Gabe rolled forward at a forty-five degree angle, curling up his body into a ball as he heard the sword whiz by above him. He used the force he generated from curling his body to strike the back of Skeetat's ankle, giving him further momentum to finish his roll behind the foul-smelling ogre.

Skeetat screamed again at the perfect strike, which had sliced his tendons all the way to the bone. Like a wounded bear he only became angrier, spinning around on his good leg and swinging wildly at Gabe. Gabe continued to deflect the heavy blows, but began to realize that he was tiring quickly and could soon make a fatal mistake. He hoped the others were doing better than him.

VIb.

Tanya had dropped her bow and quarrel in order to be less encumbered as she drew both of her short swords. Her right foot was forward and her left foot was even with her hips and angled out. She was completely relaxed, having learned that a tense body always leads to a poor game and lots of injuries. When Balla closed in on her, she hesitated just for a second to size up her opponent.

The drooling, smelly mass was easily more than two feet taller than her and at least three times her weight. His stench reminded her of a port-a-potty at a softball game. Unlike the others, Tanya's ogre had on lots of heavy metal armor with only his eye slits and throat completely exposed. A smear of green-red blood oozed from his neck where her arrow had struck. What really caught her attention was the ogre's spiked club; it probably weighed almost a hundred pounds. Even if she did block a blow from the club, the force would likely snap her arms and back in half.

"Balla kill un eat u," the ogre grunted as spit and unchewed food flew out of its mouth and landed on her.

"Bring it on, little ogre!" Tanya yelled as Balla swiftly lifted the giant club overhead in an attempt to drive her into the ground with one swing. *This is too easy to avoid,* Tanya thought, ready to jump to the side. However, her gut instinct told her to stay where she was and duck. It didn't make sense, but Tanya had relied on her gut instinct many times, and it had never failed her. She ducked and hoped she wouldn't be dead meat. Then, just before the club would have hit her, Balla completely reversed its direction and swung sideways.

Tanya cursed herself for thinking too much and not attacking when she had the chance. Balla pretended to rear up to swing at her again, but then lunged forward and kicked his foot. Tanya again trusted her instincts and stood in the path of the fake swing, which he redirected to right where she would have dodged. She swung both of her swords upward into the underside of Balla's knee just as his leg flew by her. She felt her blades cut into the hide and hit some ligaments, but not with enough force to cut through them. She then rolled underneath him and decided to do one extra roll before standing up. The club landed right where the first roll would have left her. *This is actually fun. I know exactly what he's going to do before he does it. Now I just have to find an opening and hit a soft spot.* But Balla knew how to fight, and even though Tanya avoided all of his attacks she couldn't find a good opening.

She noticed Balla gasping for air. The wound in his neck was taking its toll. If she held on long enough she might outlast him.

"I bet that arrow hole in your throat stings, eh?" Tanya smiled as Balla screamed.

VIc.

Matt was sure their ogre could smell his and Lian's fear. He was stunned at the size of the beast in front of him, and its menacing grimace assured him that role-playing games didn't quite prepare one for coming face-to-face with a real ogre. The steel club for its right hand and a heavy shield as large as Matt in the other convinced him that neither of them would survive this encounter.

"Okay Matt, show him what we do to weak, pathetic ogres when they come out to play," Lian said. It almost sounded like he was enjoying this.

"Matt be dead play ding ven Jangar dun squeeshing 'em," sneered Jangar as he swung his club arm and placed his shield too close for Matt to swing his sword.

"Holy cow, it talks!" shrieked Matt as he stepped to the left of the oncoming blow and away from the shield.

"Yeah, and it smells as good as it talks," chimed in Lian, who managed to stay in back of Matt, in spite of his fast movements.

"Shut up and help me, Lian!" Matt realized that his voice did sound like he was going through puberty, but at the moment he didn't really care.

He heard Lian's knife whiz by his head and stick squarely in Jangar's neck.

Jangar smiled, "Me yuz knife later to eat Matt un Lima fur deenr."

Jangar attacked again, and this time Matt saw an opening. He used all of his strength to swing his sword at Jangar's side. The super-alloy cut through the armor and deep into Jangar's ribs, who groaned in pain. Matt would have smiled except as soon as he connected with his sword he felt an incredible ache in his stomach and started to vomit.

Pleasantly shocked at his opponent's vomiting, Jangar heaved his shield into Matt's head, throwing him straight back into the large rock and knocking him silly.

Jangar ignored the sword stuck into his side and smiled at Lian. "U next, funee one." Jangar swung his clubhand but stopped short as Lian disappeared from view. The ogre was confused but then saw Dillon, lying on the ground and propped up on one arm looking deathly sick.

"I kill u anchent mage un get luts of mojuila frum Mungoth." Jangar raised his club.

VII.

Dillon had felt like his whole body was on fire as soon as he started to awake in the spaceship. Every cell yelled to him that it was alive and demanded attention. He felt the ground, the wind, the sun also screaming to be heard. It was too much and he had quickly lost consciousness. For the first time he could remember, he was not launched into the astral plain.

He rolled in an out of consciousness for hours, but when he sensed that his friends were in danger he drew upon all of his willpower and woke himself up enough to watch what was happening. He saw how Gabe was holding his own, but barely. His strikes were perfect in timing and precision when he saw an opening. Tanya was amazing and seemed to move out of the way before the ogre even started an attack. Matt and Lian were the worst off. He watched Matt swing at the ogre's open side, but then felt and saw a grayish-black mana rip through Matt, rendering him useless. Dillon cringed as Matt was struck back into the rock, but glad that Matt had chosen to wear a traditional, full medieval helmet. Dillon was then dumbfounded as Lian disappeared when he was attacked, and would have been excited if the one named Jangar hadn't turned and stepped toward him.

Dillon watched Jangar raise his clubhand, but strangely was not afraid. In fact he was calm and at peace. He knew what he had to do. He inhaled and drew the energy into all of his chakras. Time truly slowed down as he felt the mana from all around him being ripped rapidly toward his body. The Earth relinquished her energy to him, the wind howled but fed him, and the sun flared its fire at him. He let himself feel as if he was the ocean, becoming one with the waves and water. He gathered the energy into his throat chakra. All lesser creatures within miles could feel that something was happening. He pointed his hand at Jangar and exhaled, focusing on the equation for forming water and envisioning its creation inside the ogre.

Jangar saw Dillon raise his hand at him, smiled at the hopeless block, and started his downward swing. He stopped suddenly as he felt something terribly wrong happening within his body. That was his last thought as he was instantly filled with gallons of boiling water.

Enemy and friend alike gasped for air as all the oxygen was sucked from their lungs and the immediate surroundings. Jangar mouthed a silent scream as he exploded, unleashing a stew of steam-cooked flesh, meat, and bone onto all within thirty feet of him. There was a good ten seconds of suffocation until the oxygen, hydrogen, and moisture equilibrated. During that time the burning ogre stew pelted their skin, hair, and clothes.

Skeetat sensed the awesome magic and watched as his leader was blown to bits. Even after he regained his breath he did not move, but only said, "Ancient mage leeves." He cared not about Gabe's katana, which decapitated him with a perfectly aimed strike.

Balla, too excited about fighting to care about what was happening outside of his limited vision, was the least affected. Tanya prepared to dodge another blow but her gut instinct didn't tell her anything. Confused, she looked up into Balla's eyes in time to see a knife slicing across the ogre's neck. Lian re-appeared on Balla's back just as he finished his blood-letting cut. Balla, stunned, dropped his club and grasped at his neck, which was spraying even more green-red blood. He went to his knees and died falling backward as Lian deftly jumped off his back and landed next to Tanya without making a sound. Only Dillon noticed the scary, satisfying smile that Lian held for a brief second.

VIII.

None of them had said a word over the last hour. They just sat around Matt, waiting and hoping for him to do something. Dillon could feel Matt's body drawing in green healing energy. It was similar to what Dillon had done on the Moon, but it was somehow purer and more natural.

A smiled appeared on Matt's face even before he opened his eyes. They all breathed a sigh of relief, and tear-filled laughter sang in the air. To their amazement, Matt stood up without even a hint of pain. To their stares he replied, "Hey, I told you I can heal myself."

"We need to get out of here before others come," Gabe spoke up.

"No, there's no need. They all had that strange insignia on their armor, meaning they were part of some army. Most likely a remote small troop placed in the desert to watch for anything strange. I'm sure it'll take a day or two before any more of them come. Lian, make sure they're all dead and search their bodies for anything useful. The rest of you check for injuries, and then I need to talk to each of you privately." Dillon was pointing as he gave out commands.

"You seem to be almost back to yourself, although changed I admit," replied Gabe.

"Yeah, but maybe not for long. You were right in your analysis of my mana rewiring. I used a lot of juice to kill the ogre, but can feel it rebuilding. I may go back to being a vegetable in a little while."

"Well, next time you need to let off a little steam, remind me to run. I have nasty ogre juice all over me," Gabe said.

Lian was the only one to laugh. Everyone else was disgusted at the reminder of what they were covered in.

Lian merrily went away and carefully checked for breathing before rifling through the belongings. After he was finished he gouged out the eyeballs of both remaining dead ogres just for an added effect.

They all checked for wounds and used the water they found on the two dead ogres to rinse off their synthetic clothes, weapons, and armor. The clothes were designed to not absorb foreign matter or smells, so they cleaned-up easily. After that, each told their story to Dillon, who then called them all to sit in a circle. Dillon looked a little frazzled, with beads of sweat showing on his brows.

Dillon spoke clearly and slowly, with a commanding voice that made them all hang onto every word. "First, I realize that in our training I made a critical tactical mistake. We trained our minds and bodies for life and for battle, but did not train for war. By war, I mean using group strategy. We all fought as individuals and almost died because of it. However, since we're still alive we can learn from this and each subsequent time we'll learn something of our new magical abilities. Each situation is different, but we should remember to show weakness when our enemies wish to see strengths, and fake weaknesses to give our opponents a false sense of security. Through this we attack not just with our weapons, but with our minds. Also, we should always be looking at how to gain an advantage as a team.

"With that said, I'm going to move on to what I think some of your newfound magical abilities are. Tanya, you have an ability to pick up your enemy's intent before they even attack. You attacked when you saw an opening, but didn't use your ability to set up an attack. Start thinking of your battles as a chess match."

"I'd rather just fight," as Tanya's mouth opened, she knew she deserved what was coming.

"If it was just you then I'd say fine. But this is a team and if you want to be just a selfish, dumb jock, then we don't need you." Dillon's words were harsh but he quickly moved on to the next person.

"Gabe, I still don't know your ability but I think we have a clue. Your attacks were more precise than anything I've ever seen. You're the best martial artist here but didn't use any of it during your attacks. If you had, you could have taken out Skeetat. You know earth, fire, water, and wind. With such a large creature you should have gone water or wind to use his energy against him and create an opening. It seems that one perfect strike from you might do in anyone or anything.

"Lian. Wow. I was irate when I saw you hide behind Matt, but now know you shouldn't ever get into a one-on-one fight. It's not your strength, and you became invisible when you were scared and death was imminent. You need to figure out how to harness that and use it at will. From now on when we battle, you need to hide and take out opponents from behind. Not very ethical, but we must survive." Dillon left out that he didn't think Lian cared about ethics at all, and would enjoy just killing.

"Matt and Tanya. I need you to do something and just trust me. Stand up, weapons drawn, and face each other. Matt, strike Tanya with all your might."

"What, Dillon? I don't want to hurt her," replied Matt.

"You couldn't hurt a fly. And stop using that high-pitched voice. My sides still hurt from laughing from the last time," Tanya taunted with a smile. He was no closer to attacking her than before.

"Matt, there are going to be times when all of us are going to have to trust each other without questioning. This is one of those times. Now when you are ready..." Dillon's voiced trailed as Matt performed an upward strike at Tanya's head. Tanya was already a foot away, and Matt's sword flung out of his hand as he doubled over and started throwing up.

"This is turning into a really disgusting adventure," came the first of many snide comments from Lian.

"Get bent!" was all Matt could muster between his stomach convulsions.

"Thanks, Matt and Tanya. Just as I thought. Matt, you are a healer and you are becoming strongly tied to the healing energy that resides everywhere and is in everything, including people. You cannot cause harm to others as it violently opposes that healing energy that must now be tied into your life force. I saw your mana turn grayish-black when you attacked the ogre. I'm sorry to say this, but I think you will kill yourself if you keep trying to kill others."

"Are you serious? Just great! I trained to be a warrior, so now what am I supposed to do on this mission? Shave my head and hand out flowers at the local trade post?" Matt stood up and stormed over to a taller shrub and attempted to kick it. As soon as his foot neared the plant, he doubled up and fell to the ground again. Lian starting laughing hysterically until Dillon glared at him.

"Matt, you will still be needed. Not just because we need a healer but also since I am sure our mission here isn't all about battles. Your empathy for life should prove very useful as your power strengthens." Dillon's words were not heard by the kneeling Matt, who was just staring at his sword lying on the ground.

"Lian, how much money did find on them?" asked Dillon.

Lian reached into one of his pouches, smoothly pulled the coins away from the mojuila, and handed it to Dillon.

"Hmm, it looks like about thirty sill," remarked Gabe. "That would give us all room and board for over a year."

"Hey, at least the treasure follows what the *Dungeons and Dragons* books say," Lian added another unneeded comment. His confidence had soared, but so had his annoyance level.

"Now, let's eat some food and then gather our stuff and head west. It's around noon and I'd say that we only have about six or seven hours before sunset. Also we are probably in late fall, and it's going to get cold at night." Dillon turned away and started to gather his belongings.

"Uh, but Cahlar and his henchman are supposed to be to the east." Gabe's face showed his confusion.

"I think it's pretty obvious that we have a lot to learn, and I'm sure I'm going to be a burden on you all for a little while longer. We'll need time to gain experience and understand what we're up against. I agreed to the Mulshins' timeline only to appease them. It's our lives on the line and I'll be damned if I send all of us running blindly into a quick death. Let's at least make it slow and painful."

They all smiled at Dillon's first joke on Ancient Earth as they gathered their stuff and headed west. Each had a new swagger often seen in those who had been battle-tested.

IX.

Dillon could hold on only until they passed the spaceship again. All of them felt like they had wasted some time in their trip, with Gabe feeling a little jilted by Dillon's decision. However, no one said a word. They kept on until what they felt was dinner time, then stopped to eat. Their long days of physical training had prepared them well for torturous hikes; none of them were tired, even with dragging Dillon on the lean-to.

"Hey, any of you notice that the sun's still a few hours from setting? It must not be winter." The others looked toward the sky after Lian's question, but just shrugged their shoulders and kept eating their pre-packaged meals.

It took another five hours before the sun finally started to set, with the temperature dropping rapidly. They all felt pretty warm in spite of the 25-degree weather and agreed it was best not to start a fire.

They broke up into two groups for night sentry, with Lian and Gabe getting first and third watch and Tanya and Matt taking the second and fourth watch. It was an uneventful night, and they all woke up the next day feeling sore from the battle.

"Good morning guys, you look like crap."

They turned around to see Dillon standing up and smiling. He had put on his gear and looked kind of strange with a gray flowing robe that clashed with his black pants, black shirt, and the ninjato.

"Hey, you rewired and ready to take on the world?" asked Lian with excitement.

"I wish. I figured out a way to dissipate the energy using a short term solution." Dillon looked at their weary faces. "So you all look like you didn't sleep well. Next time, stretch and do your relaxation meditation before you fall asleep, no matter how tired you are."

"I would have been fine if I hadn't heard Gabe's watch ticking all night." Tanya stopped her yawn as she became aware that her words had caused all of their heads to swivel toward Gabe.

"Okay, okay. I shouldn't complain. I'm sorry, Gabe." Everyone ignored her apology. Then it hit her: Gabe's watch shouldn't work.

"Gabe, are you wearing your watch?" asked Dillon.

"Yeah, but purely for sentimental reasons since I knew it would not work once we got here," Gabe defended himself, but then jumped up from the ground when he glanced down and saw the old-fashioned analog hands moving. "Hey, it *is* working. What is going on?"

"Can I see it Gabe?" Matt asked. Gabe handed the watch to him.

Matt looked at it. "It doesn't work."

"Yes it does, see." Gabe took it back and showed Matt how the hands were moving.

Matt grabbed it again and remarked, "It stopped."

Gabe, Matt, and Tanya turned and looked at Dillon for an explanation. He was just as confused as them.

Lian smiled and stepped forward. "I think we found Gabe's power. He can make technology work using mana. Soon as we find that Sherman tank we'll be set."

"If this is true then you may be the most important person in the Universe," remarked Dillon with a happy twinkle in his eyes.

"Great. I am sure it is going to come in handy on this tech-less planet." Gabe tried to sound sarcastic but was smiling as much as Dillon.

After a little more conversation they ate another pre-packaged breakfast, stretched, meditated, and then continued westward. After a while Tanya noticed that one of them was missing. "Hey, where'd Lian go?"

"I asked him to run a little errand for me. He'll be back before dinner," Dillon said.

They trekked for another five hours, then stopped for lunch. Before they ate, Dillon made them practice sparring and some new tactics in team fighting. They learned how to leave false openings for attacks, and even real openings that would need to be covered by a companion. They discussed strategies and how to take on one, two, three, or four enemies ranging from human types, odd size creatures, or a combination of both.

All of them including Dillon were happy to start walking again and let their minds relax. They walked for another four hours until Lian yelled out from behind them and trotted up, whereupon they sat down for dinner.

Lian kept looking at Gabe during the entire meal as if he were hiding a birthday present for his girlfriend.

"So what do you have for me, Lian?" asked Gabe, more to pacify Lian than anything else. Lian threw a purse-size bag at him.

Dillon piped up, "I didn't completely buy the Mulshins' story about technology not working in mana fields, but I guess they weren't lying. Anyway, I had stowed some things in the ship just in case, and it looks like one of us will benefit from them."

Gabe looked in the backpack and jumped up and down with joy since he knew how to use every techno gadget inside. There was a wristband projectile shield, a vibe sword*, an electric yo-yo net, a digit-zoom contact lens, and a hand-held water thruster. "If you had brought my memoears* I would have kissed you, but these will have to do." He pulled out what he affectionately called the light saber, a short handle with a vibrating electric blade. It was a powerful weapon that could cut through steel with little effort.

He stepped away from everyone and turned it on, but the electric blade only protruded an inch from the handle.

"I want you to relax and simply focus on your breathing, Gabe," Dillon said in his most calming voice.

Gabe closed his eyes and did the simple breath-count exercise that they all knew so well. In less than a minute the electric blade doubled in size.

"Well, next time I need a thin steak cut I'll know who to ask." Lian was disappointed that his long trek seemed to be a waste.

"It looks like it will take a little time before you are able to focus your mana enough to take full advantage of the techno gadgets, but with practice you should be fine." Dillon's words did not convey the impact of Gabe's ability. If the Mulshins had spent ten thousand years trying to merge mana and technology, then what would they do if they knew Gabe could do it naturally?

They walked again until sunset, set up their camp site, and posted guards. This time each person practiced Dillon's required meditation before falling asleep. It was another uneventful night, and they all felt refreshed in the morning.

"Hey Gabe, what time does your watch say?" asked Matt as soon as the sun started to rise.

"Five P.M., but the time cannot be correct since we traveled back in time. Why do you ask?"

"I just have a hypothesis. I'll tell you later if it works out to be true. Notice I said hypothesis and not theory. In movies people always say that have a theory, which is wrong. A theory is the result of proving a hypothesis or series of hypotheses correct. " Matt smiled and stuffed more food in his mouth.

They had yet another uneventful day and night and began to wonder if their first dangerous encounter would be their last. Dillon kept breaking up the monotony of the journey with new meditations, sparring games, and strategy sessions. He noticed that Lian had brought back his miniature chess set with him from the ship. He was tutoring Tanya, and they would play at least three times a day. It was great to see them learning new things on their own. Dillon himself had been religiously reading his chemistry book, looking for new ways to use his powers. It seemed that he could apply mana to chemical equations, but he didn't know enough chemistry to create much more than water. He had figured out a little late that the sciences weren't about memorization.

The next morning Matt asked Gabe again for the time just as the sun was rising.

"Nine p.m.," was Gabe's response.

"Ok, now I'm going to count out loud. You look at your watch and stop me at ten seconds starting...now. One one thousand one, one one thousand two, one one thousand three," Matt counted all the way up to, "one one thousand ten."

"Stop," came Gabe's voice immediately after Matt's last count.

"Wow," was all that came out of Matt's mouth as his hands dropped to his side and he stared up at the sky.

"What's wrong, Matt?" Dillon stood up and walked over to Matt as he spoke, but he was sure he already knew the answer.

"What's wrong? A twenty-eight hour day is what's wrong. I may be a little bit off, but Gabe's watch is working correctly. I don't care if this is a magical or an ancient time on Earth; the speed of the Earth's rotation could not change without having devastating global impacts." Matt was pacing back and forth as he spoke, but then stopped and looked back up at the sky and whispered, "We aren't on Earth."

"I knew it," cried out Lian who excitedly jumped up. "I knew that there was something wrong with that whole time travel garbage, but I just didn't know enough physics and math to figure it out. Stupid public schools and their slow teaching style." For the first time since they'd left the Moon, Lian sounded more like his old nerdy self.

"Yeah, there *have* been a lot of little things that just haven't added up. The gravity seems a little less, the moon looks a little farther away, and the oxygen content seemed slightly higher when I cast that last spell." Dillon's mind was racing. He tried to think logically about the implications this was going to have for all of them. They were indeed on a completely different planet.

"Didn't they think we'd figure it out some time?" asked Tanya. "I mean, they picked us 'cause we have both brains and brawn."

"I'm sure they knew we would suspect something was up. But, with the mana causing all kinds of changes within us I bet they thought we would attribute it to that. In fact, if it hadn't been for Gabe's sentimental attachment to the watch and his new ability, I'm pretty sure that we wouldn't have figured it out." Dillon was now also looking up at the sky. "I wonder where we are and why they really sent us here?"

"So what do we do now, Dillon?" asked Gabe.

"We don't have a choice. We proceed with our plan, and when we get the device on the spaceship then we'll figure out how to handle the Mulshins. The good news is that they have no way of spying on us and figuring out that we know." Dillon stopped talking to finish his last bite of breakfast and then assumed a half-lotus position on the sand. "Since we have extra time each day, we might as well make the most of it."

Today Dillon's intent was to really push the envelope on all of their abilities. To take in and use the mana that rippled all around them.

X.

Dillon had everyone stretch to loosen their muscles and joints. Had they completed his training plan on the Moon, he really felt that they would now be able to easily use the mana on this planet. But they had only finished about a third, and it could take up to a year to complete their training on this journey.

But there was no use sulking now.

Dillon took them through the breath-count exercise and opened his eyes to see the pulses of energy being pulled to each one of them. He then led the energy-gathering meditation before moving into the famous cave meditation. It was meant to be the bridge between the conscious and subconscious, a way to realize one's full potential.

Dillon started the visualization exercise. "In front of you, you see a vibrant green forest. You hear the birds chirping and wind rustling through the leaves. As you inhale you smell the blooming flowers canvassing the forest floor. As you exhale you release all the tension in your body, enjoying the place you are in. You walk along a small dirt path through the forest, soon hearing the light bubbling sound of running water. As you inhale again you feel drawn to the water, which is somewhere in the distance. As you exhale you feel the aches and pains of your muscles start to ebb away.

"You round a gentle bend and see before you a crystal clear stream running over small, round pebbles. You walk down the dirt embankment and step softly into the flowing water. You inhale, feeling your feet absorb the cool energy of the water; bubbling up into your throat chakra. As you exhale you release the energy, letting the water carry away your tiredness."

Dillon opened his eyes again and was amazed to see the tension leaving their faces and a soft glow appearing on all their cheeks. He continued.

"You walk up the other side of the embankment and continue on the path that leads you out of the trees. You are now on a grassy plain with a large mountain blocking your path. There is no way around the mountain. However, on the side of the mountain is a small cave entrance. Something is strange about the cave, yet also familiar. You walk up to the cave and see a faint glow inside.

"Continuing your calm, slow breathing you walk into the cave and, after a short distance, the cave tunnel opens into a large cavern. As you breathe in, looking around the cave, you feel the energy pulsing all around you. You are able to draw it into yourself at will, and as you exhale your mind feels free and released from all the constraints in your world.

"You look to the left and see two large doors: one ornately carved and one very plain. In the middle of the room you see a stand with a large, heavy book opened to the first page. You walk up to the book and look at it. Words slowly materialize. The words say, *This is the book of self-truth and knowledge. Write any question of yourself, and the answer will soon appear.*

"You think carefully as you inhale and draw more energy from all around you. This book is not a fortune teller; rather it is a gateway to your subconscious. As you exhale, think of something you wish to have answered about yourself. Write it in the book."

Dillon himself wrote, asking if he was truly a leader of men or just fooling himself. After he finished writing his question, Dillon continued. "To your right you see a set of very wide stairs, and each step is a different color. The first is red, the second orange, then yellow, green, blue, indigo, violet, black, and lastly white.

"A simple wooden door has been carved into the stone wall on each step. You are curious and start to climb the steps. You feel the energy of each step. You walk up to the blue step, inhale deeply to feel the wind chakra beating in your chest, and push the door open. You exhale as you realize you are stepping out onto a small cliff that is hundreds of feet above a canopy of trees. You feel the wind buffet your body, and as you inhale you feel the wind enter your soul.

"You smile to yourself, no longer afraid as your realize what to do. You exhale and leap off the cliff, plummeting toward the ground with the wind whistling past your ears. Suddenly you feel different and notice wings where your arms once were. You inhale deeply, and as you exhale you spread your wings, capturing the wind in your feathers and whipping you back skyward. You are flying above the trees. With every inhale you ride with the wind, and with every exhale you release and let it push you higher."

Dillon continued the visualization but again opened his eyes. His jaw almost dropped when he saw that Lian was nearly a foot off the ground floating in the lotus position, his body moving gently back and forth with Dillon's flight commands. Dillon didn't want to startle Lian so he talked them back to the ledge, closed the door with his words, and watched Lian slowly descend back to the ground. Dillon then had them open their eyes.

"Now let's use some Tai Chi and Chi Kung to draw in your energy." Dillon walked them through the basic stretches and movements before speaking again. "Esoteric martial art forms can teach you how to draw in energy, how to cultivate what you've gathered, and how to release it. This is done through a series of movements that were honed by the grandmasters of each form.

"The moves are great tools. However, the truth is that as long as you stick to two fundamental rules you can do this any way you want. First, when you inhale you draw the energy into your body, and your movements also draw in. Second, when you exhale you expel energy out of your body, and your movements reach out."

Dillon demonstrated by bringing his hands up to his chest as he inhaled and then pushed them outward, stepping toward the group as he exhaled. They all felt the push of the energy as Dillon moved forward.

Dillon made them try it over and over again while he watched. Slowly he started to see the mana gather into each person, then release when they exhaled. He could see the green energy that surrounded Matt's body the clearest. Matt wanted this the least, yet it came to him most easily.

This really is a magical planet, Dillon thought. But he was thinking of the effect it had on who they were more than what they could do.

XI.

The night air around the ogre's hut was constantly abuzz with noises from insects and small animals feeding off of their filthy housekeeping. Tonight started off with the normal drone but turned to an eerie silence as every living creature in the area felt the power of the visitors.

Mankin* signaled his five half-human, half-wolf pets to surround the hut, watching them quickly perform his command without making a sound. Mankin himself entered the hut first. Through his whole life, he had completely dominated every fight he'd been in, and even three ogres didn't concern him.

When Mankin had signed up for Mungoth's army, he rose quickly within the ranks. He soon found the upper levels to offer few good battles, and so he asked to be reassigned. Now he had held his current position for over four years, overseeing more than thirty outposts in one of the most dangerous areas of the treacherous Kalansi* continent. The mana levels on this continent were only rivaled by those at Mungoth's fortress, attracting the most powerful magical creatures and beings to the area. Mankin knew he was no exception, as he unconsciously played with the lightning crackling between his fingertips.

He reflected on what had brought him here as he searched for something edible. As soon as his sentries had seen the purple rocket, they fired off their own orange rocket and started out on the long path to the outpost. If they didn't come back to light a yellow rocket within two weeks, then Mungoth himself would know something was terribly wrong. The Overlord wouldn't travel to the area, but he would send in the 'heavies' and receive frequent updates from his spy network.

Mankin surprised himself with a yawn, as he opened another empty cupboard. It had taken almost four solid days of travel to get to the hut, and he was tired. Judging by the even-worse-than-normal state of decay inside the hut, it seemed the ogres hadn't been back since they set out to kill whatever caused them to raise the alarm.

Mankin went back outside and smelled his way to the outhouse. He opened the door, releasing a stench that would have been enough to kill most men, and went inside without hesitation. The lack of fresh feces confirmed his belief that the ogres were probably dead.

He went back inside the hut and slept until morning, filled with pleasant thoughts of meeting an opponent that could take out his toughest sentries.

****

Mankin arose and stepped out into the sun with a smile. He wore loose, studded, leather armor; a metallic gauntlet; and a sheathed short sword. His blond hair was short-cropped in an attempt to detract from the receding hairline that had now defeated almost half of his scalp. In his early forties and a couple inches shy of six feet, he was in great physical shape; but he wasn't a vision of the perfect warrior at only one hundred seventy pounds and with a slight stomach pouch. The night hid his physical appearance, with his true power cloaking him in a darkness that most would fear.

His soft blue eyes didn't give away any hint of the horrifying experiences he had survived or the power he possessed. Still, when he stared down at the five half-wolves, they jumped to attention with fear in their eyes.

Mankin reached his left hand into his right sleeve, pulled out a pinch of mojuila, and threw it on the ground. He searched for traces of ogre tracks as the beasts howled and fought over their drug fix.

Chapter 7
The Changing Within the Forest

I.

The team left the desert early in the morning, walked another four hours before they ate lunch, and then entered the forest. Dillon took the lead through the dense vegetation, followed by Matt, Tanya, and then Gabe. Lian was to the right side of Tanya about four paces away, preferring to stay off the trail. They were all amazed at his ability to walk without making sound and navigate effortlessly through the burs and prickers directly off the path.

Shortly before dinnertime the small trail opened up into a grassy meadow about twenty feet in diameter.

"Welcome to my land, trespassers."

The voice startled them all. Dillon was the first to recover and realized their huge tactical mistake. They were in the center of the open area and completely exposed. Even Lian had not stayed to the outside as he liked to do. After Dillon surveyed the area, a man stepped out from the foliage directly in front of them. He had short cut hair and was not very impressive in stature. The only suggestion of danger was the sheathed sword he carried at his side.

"Sorry, we didn't see any signs, but I don't think you'd wish to let us go for our mistake anyway," was Dillon's comeback as he drew his sword. The four others followed suit.

"Hasty with our actions, are we? Regardless, you are definitely correct. You killed my best set of sentries, and that has angered me." Mankin did not appear upset at all.

"Your ogres hunted us down and attacked with no wish but to kill us." Dillon was just buying time, trying to fully assess his opponent. Mankin took one step forward, and at the same time five creatures stepped out of the foliage. They looked like tall, muscular wolves but stood up on their hind legs and carried various simple weapons in their extended paws. Dillon's team was now perfectly surrounded, with a creature at two, four, six, eight, and ten o'clock. Mankin stood at noon.

"I said it angered me, but normally I would give you some time to see if you would pass by or try to create havoc. However, since Mungoth took over almost ten years ago, we have had many stupid rules placed on us and our lands. I am remote and can ignore most of them without fear of retribution. But there is one law that none of us would ever consider breaking. The law stating that we must hunt down and kill any beings coming from the sky and landing on Igypkt*.

"I admit it sounded like another stupid law at first. Imagine beings coming from the sky...almost laughable. But you are my second set in the last two years, and my reward for killing the first group makes me long for your deaths."

"Attack!" Tanya cried. They all knew it meant their foe was soon to attack, so they lunged into action, catching their opponents off guard.

IIa.

Lian was still slightly to Tanya's left when she screamed. He knew what he needed to do for the team, although it scared him to death. He ran and lunged directly in between the two beasts at the eight and ten o'clock positions, feeling one tear at his foot as he was in mid-air. He tucked as he landed and rolled perfectly into an upright stance. Lian followed his momentum through into a sprint away from the group.

He hoped that the two beasts were chasing him, but was too afraid to turn his head and look. He relaxed his body and focused on dodging through the many shrubs and trees in his path. Many uncoordinated crashes and yelps sounded behind him as his pursuers tried to follow his arduous path.

After he was nearly exhausted, Lian headed straight for a large tree. When he was right on the tree he stopped and whipped around to face his attackers. The two beasts were closer than he thought and lunged in the air at him as he turned. Lian let his fear overtake him and disappeared from sight.

One of the beasts smacked into the tree as the other pancaked its friend. They snarled and snapped at each other before sniffing the group in an attempt to locate their prey.

Lian sat up in the tree trying to catch his breath. He had correctly guessed that his fear would make him disappear, but then amazed himself at his ability to shimmy up the tree. He knew that his outfit, which repelled all odors, helped keep him hidden from the hairy, wolf-like creatures who surely had superb senses of smell. However, now he was stuck. He was confident he could kill one of them while invisible, but then he'd reappear and be quickly devoured by the other.

As he sat stymied as to what to do, the two creatures turned around and started back to the others. Lian had a crazy idea. He reached into one of his pouches, fumbled around, and threw one small piece of mojuila toward the ground. While the object was still in the air, the two beasts spun around and charged toward it. When they realized there was only one piece, they clawed, bit, and tore at each other until only one battered and bruised beast remained. It almost appeared to smile as it swallowed the mojuila.

The ecstasy was short-lived. Lian's knife blade penetrated the base of its skull and skewered its small brainstem.

IIb.

Matt spun to face the hideous creature at six o'clock. At the same time he threw his bola*. It was a weapon Gabe had made it for him using three heavy balls connected by cords. When it found its target, the balls would cause the cords to ensnare the opponent. The beast took only two short strides before its legs were wrapped up and it crashed to the ground at Matt's feet.

"Amazing! It worked!" cried Matt in his familiar, young shriek. Then he stopped, confused. He couldn't kill the beast but knew it would eventually free itself if he didn't act. As the animal clawed at its tangled feet, Matt did the unthinkable and touched it. He exhaled and felt himself reach inside its simple brain. As he inhaled, he pulled into himself all the mana and life force from the beast that he could gather without killing it.

He felt neither sickness nor the expected attack from the creature. He opened his eyes and saw before him a snoring half-wolf* creature.

Matt felt fully reinvigorated. He turned around just in time to see Dillon point his sword toward Matt. A bolt of lightning shot out and struck him squarely in the chest, knocking him unconscious before stopping his heart.

IIc.

Tanya felt there would be no attack from Lian's side, so she charged quickly toward the large wolf-thing at the four o'clock position, with Gabe following her lead. The beast swung at her with the curved sword in its left paw and tried to bite Gabe. She avoided it with ease, and Gabe blocked its huge canines without much effort. They exchanged a few futile attacks until she remembered what Dillon had said about the chess game.

Tanya pretended to swing and miss wildly with her right sword, exposing her right shoulder. The beast took the bait and swung its claw at where her shoulder should have been. It instead met Gabe's katana at full force, the hundred-folded sword slicing through its muscular arm like butter. The beast howled, but Tanya was not done. She swayed backward like the rolling tide and then crashed forward, thrusting her sword with all of her might into its exposed flank. Her sword sank halfway through its body; then she quickly rolled back into a defensive posture.

Gabe took over next, skewering the creature before sliding back. He had performed a perfect sideways slash, opening up the beast's chest and slicing its heart. It dropped to the ground, wracked with spasms.

They both turned around and saw Matt being struck by a lightning bolt. When they wheeled around further, they saw two Dillons. One Dillon was standing with his sword drawn, and the other was lying on the ground.

IId.

Dillon estimated it would take the man at least three seconds to reach him. He inhaled and quickly drew the water energy into him, then shot his right leg and right arm toward the beast at two o'clock. From his fingertips and thumb, five long icicles exploded forward, propelled by the heat generated from his creation of the frozen water. They traveled faster than any thrown weapon could have, giving the creature no time to react. They pierced its body cleanly before the aeroheating from their travel melted them into harmless water and steam.

The beast laughed and took one step forward before the blood shot out of its five new orifices. The icicles had ripped through its heart. It fell dead to the ground.

Dillon redirected himself toward the man, drawing his sword to prepare for an attack. He was surprised to see that the man had not moved. He had drawn his weapon, which looked less like a sword and more like a long rod.

"Very impressive, mage, but you should know that lighting always wins out over water." Mankin finally showed an evil smile, and Dillon felt the mana gathering to the man right before the lightning bolt shot out from the rod and arced perfectly to Dillon's sword. A searing pain jolted Dillon's arm as the electricity went through the sword and into his body. His heart stopped and his entire body shut down.

III.

Man, I really need stop having these near-death experiences. Dillon was floating over his body. He looked down and knew this wasn't a time to explore. Dillon gathered healing energy around him and noticed that he could see the energy being pulled into him from miles away. He was able to make his heart beat again, but stopped there when he saw his attacker stoop down and touch his unconscious body. In less than a second the man morphed and looked exactly like Dillon.

Dillon was still staring when the fake Dillon shot a lightning bolt at Matt just as he turned around. Matt's face showed confusion as he was thrown backward from the impact. Dillon didn't see Matt hit the ground. He was looking at the energy the man had gathered around him.

In the astral plane, Dillon could clearly see the energy lines going into the man. He noticed that the energy wasn't the pure form Dillon brought toward himself, but was a combination of small strings coming from different pure colors of mana.

"Hey guys, he was a changeling, but I knocked him unconscious," said Mankin in a voice and with mannerisms that perfectly replicated Dillon's.

Gabe and Tanya just stared at him.

The fake Dillon took a step toward them and kept talking. "Quick, we have to see if Matt is okay and find out what happened to Lian."

Dillon could tell that Mankin was still gathering more mana. He was going to strike again.

Dillon knew he must act. He relaxed and tried to draw the energy away from the fake Dillon. The lines wavered and started to stray. Dillon kept his focus and was soon able to redirect about half of the energy into himself. He could do no more.

Mankin looked around, trying to hide his confusion. Something was wrong with his power. It wasn't drawing in nearly as fast as normal. He had to stall for more time.

He turned his back on his two soon-to-be victims and went over to the warrior he had just fried. He pretended to try to help him. Just another minute and he would be ready to attack.

Everything was much clearer in the astral plane on this planet, and Dillon watched Gabe's and Tanya's expressions as they tried to figure out what to do. There was no way they would confront Mankin without any sign of aggression from him. Dillon realized that the man was ready to attack and watched, helpless, as he methodically turned around and pointed his rod at Gabe and Tanya. Energy rushed through Mankin's meridian system and into his arm. Dillon saw it transform into electricity as two lightning bolts shot out from the rod.

Gabe and Tanya saw Dillon turn toward them and point. Tanya knew an attack was coming and pushed Gabe out of the way. She didn't realize that the lightning would still head straight to them because of all the metal they were carrying.

The two deadly bolts arced toward them.

They were about to strike when two metal poles appeared out of the ground before them. Both lightning bolts hit the poles and were grounded.

"Hello, Mankin. It's a pleasure to run into you again."

Everyone that was conscious turned around to see a thin, elf-like being dressed in wondrous green robes and holding a simple, beautiful, green staff.

"Arlar*! What in the world do you think you're doing? In the name of Mungoth I claim these other-worlders as mine. Mine to dispose of. Now get out of here or else you will feel the full wrath of my power!" It was clear that Mankin had lost his cool since he was spitting as much as he was yelling.

Arlar stared right at were Dillon's astral projection was and smiled. "Normally I would agree that it is none of my affair, Mankin, but I am intrigued by this group of young travelers. Intrigued enough that I would even ignore the mighty power of you and your lord Mungoth."

Mankin smiled, "Do you think you can easily dispose of me? You know, Arlar, that we are almost equal in power and you have only a fifty percent chance of living. Furthermore, if I don't return to my outpost within a week and signal that everything is okay then you will be found out by Mungoth and destroyed."

"Well, I am a bit selfish and admit that I do value my life. How about a wager then?" Arlar waited for a response from the changeling.

"A wager? Go ahead."

"You against the female warrior. If you agree then you must first reveal how to light the signal to Mungoth's minions. That way if you die we can make sure we are left in obscurity for a while.

"Now, if you defeat her then I will help you kill the rest of them and even provide a wagon for you to carry them back to your outpost."

Gabe and Tanya watched, perplexed, unsure of whether Arlar was friend or foe.

"Fair enough. How do I know the others won't interfere?" Mankin asked.

"Before you reveal the information for the signal you may touch her and change into her. That way none of them will know who is who."

"Agreed," Mankin snarled.

Arlar turned toward Tanya. "I'm afraid you do not have a choice, Tanya. Let him touch you and then prepare for battle. If you do not obey, I will be forced to aid him in your death." Arlar's voice had lost its light-heartedness.

Tanya thought this was all crazy, but she was confident that she could win. She just needed to remember to set up her opponent and strike when she created an opening. She stepped toward Mankin and let him touch her. She felt the energy shoot out from his fingers and watched him quickly assume her form and her possessions.

The false Tanya stepped back and then spoke, "You must light the rocket with the yellow ribbon."

"How do we know that he isn't lying?" asked Gabe.

"He's telling the truth. I can read his aura." Lian stepped out of the foliage, a little disheveled but with no apparent injuries.

"Ok, let's begin," said Arlar.

Mankin lunged at Tanya, who knew the attack was coming. She easily avoided it but had to continue ducking and dodging an onslaught of attacks. Then she realized they were not meant to injure, but to confuse the others as to who was who.

His attacks became more exacting, with a deadly precision that she often barely avoided. She found it hard to pick an opening or set him up for a mistake. Mankin, Tanya realized, was an expert swordsman who wielded his two short swords far better than she could ever hope to.

Suddenly Tanya felt two strikes coming at her. Mankin had set her up so that she could only avoid one of them. She parried the one that felt like sure death, causing her to step into the path of the other sword. It caught her squarely in the arm, nicking the edge of her metallic arm band and cutting down to the bone. She gasped and collapsed to both knees from the pain.

Mankin knew he had the female warrior in an unbeatable position. He was amazed when she avoided the death blow, but was happy to see his other sword slice into her arm. His energy had returned and was now at full force. He took one step back and pointed his sword at her, forcing the mana down his arm and out to the sword.

Something went terribly wrong again. The mana just disappeared, leaving him confused and exposed for a brief second. It was just enough time for the female warrior to lunge forward and, with the sword she held in her good arm, cut cleanly through both of his legs. Then a knife hit him in the jugular while another embedded perfectly between two bones of his spine. Mankin fell to the ground, unmoving.

This would have killed a normal man, but he was a changeling and only needed time to readjust his body's organs. He felt two swords attack him as he pretended to be dead and calmly fixed his body. He gloated, knowing it was only a matter of time before he killed her and the knife-thrower.

Then Mankin felt the one thing he feared. Fire began to burn his flesh. His eyes snapped open and he howled and screamed until his body was fully ablaze, then exploded into ashes.

"You never said we couldn't help her, right?" Lian had put away his set of matches, closed the pouch of oil, and was looking cautiously at Arlar.

"You heard my words correctly. Now let's fix your friends and get underground since your leader's mana trail can be seen by a blind man on another continent." Arlar walked over to Matt's body, bent down, and touched him. "Interesting. He restarted his heart and has almost completely healed himself while unconscious. I certainly cannot say that I have seen that before." Arlar concentrated, and in less than ten seconds Matt's eyes opened.

Dillon watched as a large figure in green light walked up to his body and touched it. He felt himself being wrenched back to the normal plane. When he opened his groggy eyes he saw Arlar, averaged-sized, standing before him with a smile.

"Now, let's grab the wounded and get underground." A large hole with steps leading down appeared in the middle of the open grassy area. Arlar easily picked up Matt in one arm and Dillon in the other and carried them down the steps. Gabe looked at the others, shrugged, and followed. They must have gone down two hundred steps before entering a tunnel that was about eight feet wide and had a soft, green glow emanating from its walls. They walked along for about an hour until the tunnel led to an expansive and brightly lit cavern.

"Welcome to my home!" exclaimed Arlar, who gently laid Matt and Dillon down onto two plush pillows. "Now, I have to get to Mankin's outpost to set off the rocket, but I will be back before morning."

They all watched in amazement as Arlar began to change before their eyes. He grew taller, his face elongated, and scales appeared on his skin. They watched until before them stood a twelve-foot-long, green dragon. "That should keep your conversations and your minds going while I'm gone." He made a laughing-type snort before darting out another tunnel in the cavern.

IV.

"Wow, a real green dragon! Although, a lot smaller than I imagined." Lian was just as excited as he had been when he first identified the ogres.

"Yeah, real neat. Let's get out of here. That thing tried to get us killed out there." Tanya was angry at Arlar, but didn't even look like she'd been in a fight. She hadn't noticed that her once-serious wound had all but disappeared.

"Well, he healed you, so that must be worth something. Anyway, he was able to see me in the astral plane and knew I was working to stop Mankin's energy. I admit it would have been nice for him to take on Mankin. But maybe he couldn't interfere directly." Dillon really thought that the dragon was just having fun. He started to practice moving his limbs, which were finally responding after the electrical surge.

"Anyway," he continued, "we don't know how to get back to the surface and have nowhere to go. Why don't we just sit down and eat what he left us?" They all stared at the beautiful, if not strange, arrangement of food on the stone table. Exotic smells danced into their noses, reminding them that it had been a while since they tasted anything more than dried, packaged meals. Dillon pretended to be excited as he grabbed some unknown meat and ate it. He was glad to find out that it didn't taste too bad.

"Uh, Dillon?" questioned Lian, "That kind of looks like the stuff at a Chinese herbal shop."

Dillon looked up at Lian with a horrible expression on his face, until Lian started laughing. Still chuckling, Lian walked over to the table and started to eat. Only then did the others dig in, finally realizing just how famished they were from the short yet grueling battle.

After all had eaten, Dillon again asked each one to recount their individual part in the fight. The strategy of attack had been almost perfect, if not for his assumption that Mankin was wielding a sword instead of a lightning rod. Unfortunately, it appeared that no new powers had manifested. Dillon really had no idea what to do next, so he told them about the astral plane, seeing the mana flow, and being able to steal Mankin's energy.

"So if you can actually help defend us from magical attacks in this astral plane, then why not go there all the time?" asked Matt.

"Well, first, I can only get there when I'm either asleep or almost dead. Second, my body is helpless when I'm astral. So, sorry, but I'm not too keen on watching myself become chopped liver," said Dillon.

"Hey, I get knocked out every darn time we get in a fight and I seem to do all right." Matt had his sense of humor back, even though he was rubbing the imaginary bump on the back of his head from the ogre attack. He was able to heal his body, but the mental trauma was hard to shake off.

Lian stood up as he picked his fingernails with a knife and spoke, "Guys, I know I was excited about the green dragon, but do you remember what green dragons are known for? Are green dragons known to be friendly? Heck no, they are deceitful and like to toy with their prey. I say we try to find a way out of here before he comes back and decides who's the appetizer and who's the main course."

"You haven't much meat on your body, so I'm guessing you'd be the toothpick he'd use to clean his teeth." Tanya smiled at Lian as she spoke, who responded by picking his teeth with his knife.

"Nope, we're staying here and resting. If he wanted to kill us he could have when we were much weaker. At some point you have to trust someone or something. I choose now." With that Dillon took off his backpack, laid it on the floor and rested his head on it in order to "sleep."

Dillon's words seemed final, and no one really wanted to venture out on his or her own. Eventually they all fell asleep, even Matt who was feeling a bit claustrophobic.

V.

Dillon opened his eyes to find the old, elvish man with the green cap and staff studying him.

"Hi, Arlar. How was your trip?"

"Wow, you are simply amazing, Dillon." Arlar walked in a semi-circle around Dillon, still studying him. "I am barely old enough to remember the time when the ancient mages walked on Igypkt. They were able to call forth vast amounts of energy and perform amazing feats that are now only in books of legends. However, they pale in comparison to your abilities."

"How so?"

"On Igypkt, there are two ways beings draw forth mana. For magical creatures it is an innate ability that can be powerful, yet limited in breadth. Humanoids figured out a way to call the energy to them by gathering incantations and powerful artifacts. However, all of you have an innate ability to gather at least one form of pure mana, which I have never seen a humanoid do on Igypkt." Arlar paused and turned his head, "Your gift, Dillon, is even more unusual since you are a beacon for all energy. It is also why it is a good thing we got you underground."

"I don't understand," replied Dillon.

Arlar used his staff to draw a circle about three feet in diameter and tossed dozens of pebbles into the circle. "Let's say this circle is my world. The grains of sand represent everyone who has some type of mana, and those pebbles represent those of us who possess the most powerful of magical abilities. Strong mana users can sense each other when close enough and can even see the ripples of energy drawing to those nearby." Arlar then picked up a rock about the size of his fist and dropped it in the circle. "This is you, Dillon. If we hadn't brought you down into the bowels of my lair, you would have dozens of search parties hunting you down at this very minute."

"Uhm, exactly how far underground are we?" Matt's stammering voice was barely above a whisper.

"Matt, your claustrophobia is going to get the best of you one day. Please go walk through the green door with the white rose on it. It will make you feel better, and later on we'll work on that weakness." Arlar motioned toward the door to help Matt along.

"Yeah, it's a freezer room so he can eat you later—" Lian's voice turned into a shriek as Arlar, who had quickly transformed back into a dragon, pinned him to the ground. Arlar was hissing as saliva dripped from his pointed fangs and hit the ground next to Lian's neck. The wet pool hissed on the ground.

"I am here because I know of your quest and believe in it. But all of you need not live in order to help me," snarled Arlar. Just as suddenly as Arlar had changed, Lian was freed and Arlar again stood in human form next to Dillon. "As I was saying, you will continue to draw a lot of unwanted attention if you do not learn how to control and mask your abilities. Dripping water off of your fingertips is merely a small patch that prevents you from exploding."

"I know, but how do I learn how to control it, and why do you want to help us?" Dillon hadn't even flinched at Arlar's reaction to Lian. He thought it was a good lesson for his cocky friend.

"Learning to control the energy you have at your disposal takes discipline and practice, which I can teach you." Arlar finally turned his attention to the others, even smiling at the unhappy Lian. "Now, why do I want to help you? Simple: I grow weary of this new ruler of Igypkt and fear he has gained enough power to do some serious harm to all that live. You, like the others from the stars that preceded you, clearly have a mission to remove him. But, unlike the others, you are the only ones to make it through their first day on our planet. So far you have the best chance to finish the task at hand."

"So, you think this Mungoth guy is the one that we also seek. Where does he live? We were told that he is to the east, and probably in the city of Ladean. But if you are right about the others not making it very far, then I'm thinking that the ones who sent us on this mission really have no idea where he is." Dillon thought it was funny that traveling away from where they'd thought Cahlar was might have actually been the best decision he'd made so far.

"Wait a second. Mungoth sounds a lot like Moon God. That would have to be Cahlar since he is from the Moon." Gabe smiled at his ability to solve the riddle.

"Well, it sounds like you are a very bright group; however, finding him and answering your other questions will not be as easy. I'm fairly certain that he is not on Kalansi, but more than that I do not know. It is said that Mungoth had a powerful spell cast over his lair, and that all who leave it forget where it is."

"So how are we to find it, then?" asked Dillon.

"I only know of one who can answer your question. You must ask The Fallen One*. It is said that he has been around since before mana entered our lives. He keeps track of the past and watches the future. His power is unrivaled...or *was* unrivaled. However, he is also cursed and must answer any question that is asked of him." From Arlar's tone they could tell it was not going to be easy.

"Where is this Fallen One?" Dillon had a feeling he wasn't going to like the answer.

"Follow me." Arlar walked through the green door with the white rose. They all followed and were amazed to see that they were now in a luscious, green, underground arboretum with hundreds of small sounds from the living creatures that inhabited it. They also saw Matt lying in the middle of the large room with his eyes closed.

"Isn't this just great?" Matt's smile seemed to be permanently etched on his face.

"It's just an illusion," remarked Lian, speaking for the first time since Arlar had chastised him.

"Yes, but a beautifully intricate one that I often enjoy in order to help me forget that I live in a cave." Arlar walked over to the near wall and swept his hand across it, causing the overgrown vines to move out of

107

the way. Behind the vines was a detailed map[#] of Igypkt, with Kalansi and two other vast continents displayed.

"I have spent many centuries flying over Igypkt and making this map." Arlar touched a spot near the bottom of the Kalansi continent and then touched another spot near the middle. "This is where we are, and this is where The Fallen One lives. The distance is great, and Kalansi is a harsh land. However, that part is the least of your worries. The Fallen One is nearly immortal and keeps an army of undead surrounding him and his desert so that he is not disturbed. You cannot reach him on land."

"Oh, great!" Lian scoffed. "Battle an army of undead. Sorry, that doesn't sound too promising. Are you sure there isn't someone else that offers answers for a small service fee? Do you have a library with internet service?" Lian stopped his rant and took a step back as soon as Arlar glared at him.

"What are these red circles?" A refreshed Matt had rejoined them and was now staring at almost a dozen dots on the map.

"Those are the spots were others like you have landed and this one in the center of Cureio[*], the capital of Kalansi, is perhaps the most well known. The flying ship still sits in the center of the city for all to see." Arlar touched the map and a blue dot marked their landing spot. "And this is where you landed."

Dillon looked away from the map and took a couple slow steps away from the group. He sat down and stared at what appeared to be a blade of grass. "I wonder how long we have been groomed for this mission."

"What do you mean?" asked Gabe.

"What are the odds that the five of us, all possessing unusual chi ability, would wind up living in the middle of the Mojave Desert and become best friends? Tanya, your parents moved from Los Angeles because they inherited an estate from a cousin who was accidentally killed at work. Gabe, your Mom was helped by an inheritance from an unknown uncle that allowed you to move out of the inner city. Lian, your Dad was suddenly reassigned to Edwards Air Force Base in the Mojave Desert after twenty years at Tinker Air Force Base in Florida." Dillon then looked over at Matt, "Matt, why did you move to the Antelope Valley?"

Matt looked down at the grass and softly rubbed it with his feet. "My dad always said he was abducted by aliens and that they told him they would leave him alone if he moved to the Mojave Desert. He's a little strange so I thought he just didn't want me to know the real reason. I guess he must have been telling the truth."

"Our friendships and our entire lives have been controlled by the Mulshins?" Tanya's voice was deeply angered.

"Worse yet, I fear that they had no problem killing people or letting others kill people to ensure we were together." Dillon's last statement caused all of them to remain quiet for a long time until Arlar spoke up.

"I don't understand a lot of what you are talking about, but I have to ask a question. Do your friendships feel any less or have you a desire to change your life?" Arlar waited a minute to give them time to think. "I thought not. You see, your lives together may have been set up, but you control who you are and who your true friends are. Even more importantly, you control your destiny."

It was amazing how quickly their emotions changed from shock and fury to happiness, and all with a few words from a stranger.

"Now back to the map. I said you cannot reach The Fallen One from the desert, but everything I have read says that in order to reach The Fallen One you must find the entrance to the bowels of Igypkt. My tunnels once lead me to a portal that teleported me to a stairwell. That stairwell appeared to go down forever, and the dark mana emanating from the place was the largest I've ever felt. It must be the entrance." As Arlar spoke, the map transformed from a relief of Igypkt into a series of tunnels and caves. "I have not been through many of these tunnels for decades, but I promise that I will get you safely to the portal. After that, it is all up to you."

"What about this training you mentioned for me? How long will it take?" Dillon was more eager to learn how to control his mana than running into a lair to be torn apart by undead.

"Actually, all of you need training and quite a lot of it. So let us see if my hunches are correct. Tanya, turn your back to me please." Arlar's voice was soft but commanding. As soon as Tanya turned around he flung a rock at her as fast as he could. She had already stepped aside before he had finished his release.

"Lian, come over here and hold this pebble. Come on, I won't bite today." Arlar's humor wasn't rubbing off on Lian, but he did step forward. "Now I want you to relax your mind and throw the pebble at Tanya whenever you are already."

Lian cleared his mind and slowed his breathing until it appeared that he was a statue. He pretended he was a spider on the wall, waiting for his prey to cross his path. With an amazing suddenness he struck, throwing the pebble toward the middle of Tanya's should blades. Tanya moved, but was somewhat surprised by the attack as it managed to nick her tricep.

"Both of you are very impressive, but can use a lot of work. Tanya, you can sense the energy that others direct toward you but are only focused on very aggressive attackers. You will need to learn how to sense even someone only watching you and how that simple look can be the setting up of an enemy's attack days before it happens."

"Great, just like a game of chess. I hate chess!" Tanya was smiling, now having further reinforcement of Dillon's criticism.

"Lian, you are not just a thief. You have the traits of an assassin and you know of your ability to become truly invisible, which is one of the hardest abilities of all to learn and master. However, you also can shield your mind from others; a simpler but equally powerful talent. I will teach you to walk in the shadows and even become unnoticed in daytime crowds. You will also need to learn how to detect and dispel magical traps."

"Why would you want to help me?"

"Your ethics are questionable, but your loyalty to your friends is unequaled. I do not hate you; I just do not like you that much." Arlar turned his head away from Lian. "Matt, you will need to learn how to truly heal. Also, while you cannot harm living things without dire consequences, you can ask any living thing for help. Some will listen, some will not, but regardless you need to learn how to ask."

"Gabe, what can you do? There is a gold energy emanating from you that I must admit I do not understand."

Gabe pulled out his vibe sword and, exhaling calmly, turned on the switch. The cutting edge shimmered and grew the usual couple of inches in height.

Arlar stepped back and was shocked enough to unconsciously start to transform back to a dragon. He caught himself mid-transformation and returned to his human shape. He mumbled something under his breath that only Lian caught, but then spoke-up quickly, "I will not pretend to comprehend what you can do. I have never seen anyone that can draw the golden mana*. However, I do know that I can help you channel your mana to work this tool you brought with you. Now, it's time to get to work. Each of you will be separated and must train with me for a week. Then I will lead you to The Fallen One."

"How'r you going to train us all at the same time?" asked Tanya, whereupon Arlar separated into six identical humans.

"You counted one too many." Lian still somewhat held his wit in check, although now it was because he was wondering why Arlar called Gabe his "liege."

"Now, you can't expect my complete undivided attention, can you?" All the Arlars laughed, which created an unnerving echo. "Well, it's time to start." Each Arlar and one adventurer walked through a newly appearing door and into a different room.

VIa.

"Dillon, I must admit I don't understand where you are from or how humanoids like yourself can naturally gather mana. Regardless, I will train you all to the best of my ability." Arlar stepped back a few paces, holding his eyebrows in a furrowed position. "Now, show me how you gather and direct your mana."

Without hesitating, Dillon inhaled as he swept his arms from his sides up into a wide circle above his head while shifting his right foot out to shoulder length distance. He then stepped forward and pushed both hands in front of him with a rapid exhale.

"Now do that thing where you create those fast moving icicles." Arlar requested. He watched as Dillon concentrated and flung them off his hands at the wall.

Dillon looked over at Arlar who was staring right through him. After a few more seconds Dillon broke the silence. "And?"

"Oh, sorry." Arlar walked up to him. "You draw in every spectrum of mana possible and only use the type that you need and can use. The fix is simple: you will create a mental shield around you that constantly pushes away the mana, and then we'll work to draw in only the type of mana you need. The process itself will take all week because of how far and wide you attract mana. Let us get started."

VIb.

"Hi Tanya, it is truly a pleasure to meet a warrior princess." Arlar bowed deep, dropping his eyes to the ground.

Tanya giggled in reply.

"As your journey continues it will be you who protects your friends. You see, shortly you will all be strong enough to withstand most direct attacks that Igypkt can offer. It will be the sneak attacks that can take out your friends. A sneak attack requires more planning and surveying than a normal attack. The type of mana that will be directed at you will still have the same intent as an attack, but it will be a hundred times weaker. We need to attune you to this, and train you how to constantly keep your sensing at the highest level."

"Ok, but how do I do that?" As Tanya questioned Arlar the large room transformed into a busy medieval street, with hundreds of people from all walks of life. "Is it an illusion?"

"Yes, but real enough that you will be able to sense things that happen. Over the next week we will go over hundreds of scenarios, varying the intensity, intent, and complexity of those trying to harm or spy on you and your friends."

Tanya smiled inside. She had intensity, she had focus, and she loved a challenge.

VIc.

"For you, Matt, I have three things we will work on. First, you need to learn how to summon and talk with animals and plants. You will not use words like humanoid mages, but use the intent of your mana. You will start with the basic mana colors and as you become more adept you will be able to intertwine them into various shades and hues to make more complex requests and demands. Second, we will work on how you heal beings while also protecting yourself from the non-physical things you draw out."

"I am definitely on board with that!" Matt exclaimed, still remembering what happened when he tried to heal Dillon. "And what's the third thing?"

"To accept that you are a healer, and that your purpose in life now is to re-establish that which is good."

Matt huffed out a breath, which evoked a smile from Arlar.

VId.

"So, I'm sorry we got off on the wrong foot. Can you forgive me?" Lian was scared to death of Arlar and it showed.

"We did not get off on the wrong foot, as you say. I see who you are. I know you are driven by self-interests, a bloodlust, and a drug addiction." Arlar looked him squarely in eyes, unflinching. "Am I wrong?"

Lian did not avoid the eye contact and his apologetic demeanor quickly changed. "Nope. You pretty much summed me up. So, let's get started."

"Both walking in shadows and becoming lost in crowds start with your intent. You will send out various types of mana that cause living things to either avoid you or not be interested in you. For example, you can send out to others that you are an insect or that you have a contagious disease. That tends to tell people's subconscious to step away." Arlar had picked a spider off the wall and was staring at it while he spoke. "The next part is using the energy of your surroundings to blend in. You will take that energy and materialize it around you to mask your body. When walking in shadows you merely bring the darkness around you. However, becoming invisible in broad daylight requires the use of all mana colors."

Arlar placed the spider on the ground as he continued his lecture. It scurried away from Arlar and toward Lian, who quickly stepped to the side to avoid the little arachnid. "Magical traps are a different thing altogether. A trap is the creation of a web to snare one's opponent, rapidly unleashing the pent-up spell. You will learn how to sense such a trap, how to see its magical lines, and how to unweave it so it dissipates harmlessly back from where it came." While Arlar spoke he created a tight web of energy between his hands, winding it up and letting it slowly dissipate."

"Are we going to start?" Lian was impatient.

"We already have Lian," Arlar snorted and pointed to his feet.

Lian looked down to see that his feet were wrapped in some type of blue, glowing material that was levitating him above a large pool of fuming liquid.

VIe.

"Gabe, your energy is very rare indeed. In fact, I believe it is usually only seen with deities. However, there may be another explanation. In ancient books it is referred to as the mana that transforms lower energy to higher energy. I believe you are using your talent to transform mana into useful energy for the tools you brought with you." Arlar's voice was very serious.

"You said that my energy is rare, but how rare?" Gabe now understood how he made his vibe sword work.

"Maybe one in a million humanoids would have such energy. But remember what I said before. Humanoids cannot draw the energy naturally like you and your friends. They would need spells, which I don't believe even exist for golden energy. In your case I will teach you to draw the golden mana to you, but it won't be easy. Gold mana is found as flakes or small pieces of sand within other mana. It will take a lot to draw forth, and there will never been a large supply."

Gabe couldn't hide his excitement. "Kind of like gold on Earth."

VII.

On the eighth day they were finally released from their rooms and allowed to see each other again. They all cheered and hugged as if they had won a soccer tournament. Then they stared in awe at the feast Arlar had created for them. At the table they talked about what each had learned while working with Arlar. They laughed at each mistake then oohed and awed whenever one of them showed off a new ability. After many hours they had eaten their fill and the conversation had all but ended. Arlar came into the room and sat down with them.

"Arlar, has Cureio undergone any dramatic changes in the last ten years?"

"Why yes, Dillon. From what I have heard, it has changed quite a bit. All of the lower class citizens recently became indentured and the men of the families must join the army to prevent imprisonment of their families. They are fed and rewarded for reporting those that plot against the queen of the city. In fact, all citizens must worship the ruler of the city, but that part seems to be standard practice among humans."

"Interesting. Well, it's time now for us to take the next step of our quest." Dillon's words were not well-received since no one wanted to go and fight the undead. "Matt and I will go and speak to The Fallen One, while the rest of you will travel to Cureio."

"What? Didn't you learn in our role-playing games to never split up? Someone always dies. What could possibly cause you to make such a stupid decision?" Matt's outburst wasn't the only one, simply the loudest.

Dillon decided that now wasn't the time to be a harsh commander. Guylen had once told him that his closest allies needed to be able to speak freely. "There are three reasons. First, I talked with Arlar and a lot of the tunnels are inhabited with beings we don't want to meet. We will need to travel faster than our legs can carry us and only two of us can fit on Arlar's back.

Second, I believe that one of the three Mulshins we are looking for is ruling Cureio since the only spaceship still around, besides ours, lies openly in the center of the city. Arlar's recent words of new changes only confirmed my suspicion. I need you to go and scout out the city, explore the spaceship, and learn about this ruler of Cureio. When Matt and I are finished we will meet you in the city and will need to know all the information you have gathered."

"And thirdly, you're afraid that we'll die if we go with you." Pain was evident in Tanya's voice.

"No I'm not afraid you will die. I know you will die." Dillon let his words sink in before continuing. "Remember, The Fallen One is cursed to answer anyone who can get to him. You may feel compelled to ask questions that he does not want answered and therefore will ensure you can't ask. I'm sorry but I will not let that happen." Dillon was assuming that if The Fallen One could see the future he would know Dillon was coming and what he wanted to know. His thought process must have appeared flawed to his friends, but somehow he knew it was right.

Lian chimed in as he walked in-between Dillon and Tanya, "Hey, we've been stuck down here in this meat locker for a week. I say it's time for us to go to a city and indulge a little."

"Now, let's gather our stuff and be ready to leave in one hour." Dillon stood up and headed back to his room. When he got there he looked at the plain, cold room that had served as his training center for a week. He had learned when and how to draw in his energy, but still had a hard time being able to draw in the different types of mana other than what worked best for water. Arlar had told him it would come with time and practice. As a surprise Arlar had also taught him how to travel into the astral plane without requiring him to fall asleep or incur a major injury. It took a while with deep meditation, but it was a big step for him.

Dillon picked up his belongings and walked over to a moisture-ridden wall. He touched the cold stone and performed a simple breath count until he was completely at peace. He could then feel the underground stream that was only meters behind the wall. He pulled in the energy from all around him until his body felt like it would explode. He then gathered and used the moisture from the stone wall and focused it into a very small but strong water stream emanating from his fingertip. It smoothly blasted away at the rock wall and within ten minutes he had reached the underground river. The waterspout made a smooth arc to the ground and trickled its way to the far end of the room. Dillon followed it and then again smoothly blasted a larger hole in the rock floor until he hit a small cavern leading to another part of the underground river. He stepped back and made sure the little stream worked, surprised at how much effort he had needed to complete the task.

Arlar had told him that he could carve through rock at an amazing speed, but could only do so in large chunks. He had always wanted a small stream but would have flooded the whole cave if he had tried it himself. It wasn't much but he was sure that Arlar could now use this room to create a real miniature forest.

When Dillon stepped out of the room, the rest of the group was ready to go. "Ok, let's move out. Matt and I should meet up with you in Cureio within two months. If we don't show up then you have a choice of either continuing the journey or blending in and enjoying a new life on Igypkt. Trying to find Matt and me would be foolish, unless you also want to become undead."

Arlar walked out of his main chamber as he spoke, "Remember, Lian, that you must follow the tunnel that continuously leads upward. After about two to three days you should hit a dead end. You will have to use these exploding balls to blast a hole through the rock face. After that you just follow the path until you see the big city."

"You sure it won't explode while it's on me?" Lian asked because he was sure Arlar wouldn't mind him being blown to bits.

"I would never dream of doing that. The blast could hurt Gabe or Tanya." Arlar smiled and gave Lian a wink.

While saying their goodbyes, Dillon pulled Lian aside. "Thanks for agreeing to split up, without asking why."

"As Arlar said, my friendship is unequalled. However, I expect an answer when you come back." Lian gave him a healthy backslap before turning away.

"If I come back alive." Dillon stated seriously, causing Lian to look back. They stared at each other for an extra minute, acknowledging a deeper understanding of what Dillon expected of Lian if he didn't return.

Arlar transformed himself back into a dragon, and flattened out the scales closest to his front legs. Dillon and Matt stepped onto his bent leg and climbed up his back. "Keep your heads low and your eyes alert, you two. We'll be traveling pretty fast, but there are underground dwellers that still may try to attack us." Without allowing any more time for sad goodbyes, Arlar leapt into motion and charged down one of the caves with amazing speed.

Chapter 8
A Life Worth Giving

I.

Matt was surprised at how fast Arlar could move and change directions without upending his passengers. It allowed him to focus on his breathing and keep his claustrophobia at bay, in spite of rushing through a very small tunnel in pitch darkness. After what Matt guessed to be two hours of traveling at a blistering pace, Arlar turned his head toward them and howled, "Goblins ahead."

Just then they charged into a large room filled with spongy, glowing fungi and a number of small, hideous creatures. They were thin with scrunched-up faces and long pointy ears. Their bodies were speckled with dark blotches, tumors, and boils. They all shrieked and dodged Arlar as he charged for the other end of the room. They were clearly more intent on getting out of the way of the speeding dragon than trying to attack them. Arlar opened his mouth as he leapt over the largest goblin, striking him with a stream of lime green fluid. Matt turned around in time to see the goblin writhe and scream in pain as his body started to melt. The whole sight, though quick, caused his stomach to try and release what little food was inside.

"Now why did you do that?" Matt screamed loud enough to overcome the ruckus they were just leaving behind.

"If I didn't, they would come down the tunnel to my lair and try to kill me. They wouldn't succeed, but it would be annoying. This way they will mind their own business." That was the end of any conversation for a long while.

Cave upon cave came and went as Matt and Dillon lost track of time in the darkness, but they guessed it was past nightfall. Although things had been uneventful, both were starting to get saddle sore.

"When are we going to stop for the night?" asked Matt. "I need to sleep."

"We can't stop. There are ancient, powerful creatures in this section of tunnels that can sense intruders. If we stop we could have a very difficult fight on our hands." Arlar glanced back and saw their exhaustion. "I'll slow down a little so you can sleep."

Arlar reduced his speed by half, creating a softer and more rhythmic ride that soon caused Matt and Dillon to close their eyes.

Dillon floated next to his body, looking down at a sleeping Matt on top of Arlar's brilliantly green form. He was no longer constrained by his inability to see in the darkness, and the astral plane enabled him to peer beyond the limits of the tunnel they were in. Dillon was amazed by the abundance of passageways and caves all around them and the number of creatures inhabiting the underworld of Igypkt. Occasionally he would see and feel a creature possessing huge amounts of mana and watch as it sensed their presence and tried to track them down through another tunnel. However, their speed combined with the complex interweaving of caves was enough to dissuade them all. All but one.

Dillon had learned to recognize the eerie sense of his astral nemesis, which he had always fled from. But tonight was different; he decided it was time to confront his fear.

Dillon ripped his sword from its sheath as he quickly spun around. The Sword of Baillen* was a mana-channeling weapon that could permanently harm or kill anything in the astral plane. It had been a lucky find for Dillon, as astral weapons were very rare.

He easily parried the fangs of the giant gray bat he had come to know all too well. The creature flapped its wings to rise up and swung at him again with its leg. Dillon met the appendage with the full force of his sword but, unlike his previous parries, he drew the red fire energy from around him and released it through the weapon. He severed the leg in half on contact, raising a piercing shriek.

Startled, it quickly spun around and flew into the astral fog; but Dillon willed himself to follow and matched its blistering pace. Dillon relaxed his mind and pressed forward at the same time, and noticed that he was actually gaining on the flapping beast. His sword was still glowing with red energy, which he continued to feed as he moved closer to the bat. He prepared to strike the rear of its elongated abdomen just as it spun around and opened its large fangs.

Oh crap! Since he was in the astral plane there was no such thing as momentum and Dillon surprised himself by stopping on a dime. The lunging fangs just missed his neck. Dillon smiled with even more confidence as he thrust the glowing sword through one of its fiery eyes. He pulled down as the creature reared up, causing the blade to rip all the way through its jaw. The bat's shriek was so loud that it vibrated through Dillon's form, and caused him to recoil a few feet.

"Imposs-ibllle! You cannot destroyyyy meee."

Dillon was shocked to hear it speak, but also in no mood for a conversation. He moved forward, easily parrying* the weakened attacks from its two swords. When he saw the perfect opening, he jumped upward with the sword in both hands and dropped down through the creature, letting his weapon carve the path. He expected an explosion or something, but instead watched the anticlimactic ending as the bat's body melted and faded away into the fog. Dillon smiled to no one in particular and willed himself back to his body.

"No one has ever killed a daughter of Shiva before. You are pretty impressive, Dillon." Although he could not see, he knew that Arlar's head was turned around and looking at him.

"I've been told that before." Dillon smiled and winked at Arlar.

"Well, time to wake up Matt. Hold on."

Just then they plunged straight down and Dillon felt his stomach leap up into his throat.

"Ahhhhhh!" Matt awoke upon hearing the shriek from his own throat. The rapid fall prevented him from regaining his composure. He felt the tunnel walls closing in on him. His chest muscles constricted and he started to wheeze for air, although the tunnel had plenty.

Arlar opened his wings as the tunnel widened and glided in for a landing. It would have been a beautiful touchdown, if not for Matt's incessant screaming. Once on the ground, Arlar spoke out in a deep, commanding voice "Asal, mundath, keel da' vundar!"

Dillon covered his eyes as a bright light appeared above their heads. Matt stopped screaming but was still hyperventilating. Dillon touched Matt's back and sent calming blue energy through his arm until Matt relaxed and regained his breath.

"Thanks."

"No problem. Wow, look at size of this cave." Dillon wasn't really in awe but was attempting to save Matt from an embarrassing situation. The oval room was about the diameter of two football fields and rose to almost one hundred feet at its center. There were several eroded boulders strewn about the floor and a small stream trickling through the cave. Dillon noticed that the walls were not smooth stone as he first thought, but rather a vast expanse of intricately carved hieroglyphics. He started to walk over to one of the walls when Arlar, still in his dragon form, stopped him.

"Wait a minute." Arlar hissed and quickly spat four balls of acid out of his mouth. Each landed perfectly behind some of the boulders. Strange howls arose and quickly disappeared.

"What made that noise?" asked Matt, who had now regained his composure.

"They are goluns*, descendents of goblins who thousands of years ago ventured into the bowels of Igypkt to rule their own world. They built vast caves such as the one we are in and became a force to be reckoned with. Then the goblins grew jealous and sealed off many of their caves. With no food source, most of the golun civilizations were decimated." Arlar spoke as he casually checked behind the boulders that now contained pools of fleshy acid.

"If they're the last, then why did you kill them? Helping a race into extinction isn't exactly kind." Matt's constant sympathy alarmed even him. *It must be this darn path I'm forced to walk.*

Arlar shrugged his shoulders. "They are hideous creatures and wanted to eat us. Next time I will leave one for you to talk to."

Dillon had made it over to one of the walls and was carefully examining the rock carvings. After a short while he placed his right hand on the wall and felt a pounding energy driving against his hand. He pulled away quickly and turned to Arlar.

"Yes, there is great magic in these walls," said Arlar. "The goluns had many powerful earth mages. Only they knew how to unlock the carvings, which gather and store energy. Even the ancient mages dared not walk here when the goluns were at the height of their power."

Dillon placed his right hand back on the wall, closing his eyes and breathing slowly. He could easily feel the strong pounding and the yellow mana that was somehow just out of reach. *Strange how it sounds like it is living, almost like a heartbeat. In fact, exactly like a heartbeat.* Dillon had an idea. He used his breath count to further relax his body and slow down his own heartbeat. He then focused on matching his heartbeat to the beat of the walls.

Once they were synchronized he could feel how alive the walls were. With each beat it sent its power into him, and with each heartbeat he sent it back. The ebb and flow was comforting and powerful. Dillon felt as if he could merge with the wall and decided to try this with each heartbeat that pushed out at the wall. After about five minute he stopped, opened his eyes, and pulled his hands away. Both Arlar and Matt were watching him.

"Oh man, you just put your handprints into the wall! How'd you do that?" Matt was not as giddy as Lian could be but was close.

"I don't know. I just felt the power and sort of merged with it."

Arlar went up to the wall and looked, without touching. "Well, you didn't unleash the energy the way the goluns have done, but you found a different way to draw their power. As with your ability to control water, you drew out the purest earth mana and used it to will the rock to move out of your way."

Dillon remembered how difficult it had been to carve the hole in one of Arlar's caves to create a waterspout. But what he had just done required no effort and little time. He again went to the wall and touched it with both hands.

This time he first practiced moving the normal storage of his chi from his lowest chakra up to his solar plexus, where earth movements began. He controlled his breathing and grounded his feet, drawing strength and power from below him. He made his thoughts earthen and solid, and felt at one with the ground before he even turned his attention to the walls.

Again he slowed his breathing to match his heartbeat to the beat of the walls. Then he willed the beat of the walls to speed up, faster and faster. He felt the pounding through his whole body, and enjoyed it.

He heard loud crashes all around him as if the walls themselves were coming down.

"Dillon!" This time the shriek was from Arlar. Dillon pulled away from the wall and looked around. The room was now littered with dozens of man-sized boulders.

"What were you trying to do? Kill us?"

Dillon had never seen Arlar so distraught. Matt stood motionless with his mouth hanging open as far as his tendons and muscles would allow.

"Uh, sorry." Dillon looked at the walls and was sad to see that he had ruined some of the hieroglyphics.

"Well, I need to sleep for a while. You two stand guard for a few hours." Arlar stretched out; yawned wide exposing his long, sharp teeth; and plopped down on a smooth section of the rock-riddled floor.

II.

The small creature sat as still as the earth itself; hidden in a small tunnel high atop the dome, it watched as its fellow warriors were destroyed by the dragon. Well, w*atch* was not quite the correct word, since it relied on smell and the vibrations of the rock to tell what was happening. It would report the massacre back to their king. Regardless, the dragon would be gone soon enough and peace would return.

He started to leave but stopped when he sensed the human changing the regular rhythm of the mana stored in the stone walls. He then felt the human will the rock to move and form around his hands.

The golun could not believe what was happening. Only the most powerful of his race could summon forth and control the energy in the rocks. Shock turned into horror as the human unleashed the power of the earth that had been trapped inside the walls—untouched for hundreds of years. The ever-increasing vibrations caused fissures to form and cracked off large chunks of stone, sending them crashing to the ground.

As soon it was over the golun scampered away. The earth-mover had to be stopped, or what was left of their entire race could be destroyed.

III.

The trio endured another uneventful day of swift riding, followed by Matt dozing off around what must have been nightfall. Arlar had said they were going to travel over seven hundred miles through the winding tunnels in just two days, and now neither Matt nor Dillon doubted him.

Of course Dillon was not asleep, but was hovering in the astral plane. He was semi-aware of his surroundings and could feel more strongly the power of the earth around him. The energy became more intense as they neared another cave. They swiftly broke into the expansive room, whereupon Dillon felt a rush of earthen energy all around them. He quickly willed himself back to his body.

"Watch out!" Dillon cried as he felt the ground rapidly rise up in front of the charging Arlar. Arlar had the ability to carve through rocks, but not at the speed he was traveling. He instead jumped up into the air as fast as he could and almost cleared the stone wall that had suddenly appeared before them.

Almost. His chest smacked into the unyielding barrier and all could hear the bones snapping within the dragon. Arlar's body stopped as if impaled on a spear.

Arlar had jumped high enough so that, when Matt and Dillon were thrown off of his back, they were easily launched over the wall. Matt awoke flying through the air and was still relaxed enough to only received bumps and bruises as he skidded across the stone floor. As he began to regain his wits, he sensed the evil beings all around him and lay motionless, feigning unconsciousness.

Dillon found himself flying through the air again, but this time it felt more like his days of surfing rather than being hit by a car. He exhaled, curled up his body and rolled as he hit the ground. After more than six summersaults he popped up onto his feet and spun around so he could face his opponent. Instead Dillon was enveloped by the blackness that left him in a defenseless state.

Pebbles began to rain down on Dillon. A small rock smacked him in the shoulder with enough force to drop him to the ground. This was actually a good thing because shortly after a man-sized boulder whizzed over his head. *It must be more goluns*, Dillon thought as he felt one of them unleash the power within the rocks.

"Dillon, they are pure evil. I can feel it within all of them. They kill for fun. They want to kill us." Matt whispered the words so that their attackers would not know he was conscious.

I guess one of their earth mages does live, but I need to see him to fight him. "Arlar, I need light and fast." Dillon was now running blindly forward and kept tripping over rocks. Although he had started to learn how to become one with the earth, he still didn't have a natural grasp of his new abilities. He only knew that he needed to touch a wall in order to draw from the golun hieroglyphics. "Arlar!" He began to fear that Arlar was dead from the impact until he heard the deep, raspy voice.

"Asal, mundath, keel da' vundar!" The room burst into light. Dillon shielded his eyes, hoping he wouldn't be stoned to death before he adjusted to the brightness. He kept dodging flying rocks, and after a few seconds was finally able to look around at a not-so-pretty picture.

The cave was easily five times larger than the one where they had recently rested, and the floor was barren except for the new stone wall and the rocks that were being hurled at them. Intricate hieroglyphics rose the entire height of the walls until they merged with a ceiling that was completely covered in thousands of goluns, who clung to the nooks and perched inside concaves.

The odd creatures appeared similar to a wiry goblin, except for their faces. Where their eyes would have been, there were inward spirals, like a hypnosis spinning wheel, leading to small holes. Dillon surmised that these orifices enabled something akin to echolocation, the way a bat used its ears.

"Stop now or your friends will die!" The ground rumbled out the words. Dillon stopped about four feet from the wall. He turned around in time to see the stone floor rise up into two tombs that encased both Matt and Arlar.

The ground rumbled again, bringing forth words as if voiced by a deep-throated sailor with a mouthful of marbles. "You have entered our kingdom unwelcomed and awoken the earth. Your friends will go free if you agree to die."

Dillon was not listening to the words, but instead was feeling the earth around him and trying to figure out which golun was speaking among the mass of moving bodies that clung to the upper wall and ceiling. Dillon stopped using his eyes and instead let the earth point him in the right direction. His body felt the pulses until he finally honed in on the one that moved the earth and stared directly at him. "You would spare them just to get to me. Why?"

There was a pause as the king sensed that Dillon had spotted him. "You can move the earth, but not yet as good as I. You need to die before you are powerful enough to destroy my people."

"Too late!" Dillon sprang at the wall and gripped onto two larger hieroglyphs. He instantly felt the beat of the stones and the power that lay inside them. Dillon started to relax and become one with the stone, but then sensed the leader also trying to control the energy. The rhythm in the stone shook violently between the two wrestlers, as each tried to grasp the power within the rocks.

Both could hear the deep pounding within the rock, resounding like a drum in their souls. Dillon started to gain the upper hand. He knew that the leader controlled the power through incantations, not innate ability. He could not react fast enough to keep up with Dillon.

"Attack him!" The ground rumbled but the voice was now shaky and strained. Dillon felt the pain of rocks smacking against his body and knew he needed to get away fast before one broke his bones. Two goluns grabbed a large rock and threw it directly at him just as Dillon walked into the wall.

All the screaming, jostling, and high pitch yells by the goluns stopped. They were awestruck. They all had the ability to feel the earth and knew he was now inside the wall. The leader too was stunned.

Dillon used the few precious seconds to wrestle complete control of the power in the rocks—the power that was now a part of him. He was the earth and the earth was him. He felt it aching to escape the thousands of years of imprisonment by the goluns. It pounded Dillon, demanding to be released.

Dillon could now feel every golun on the wall. He tracked the leader as he scurried around for a hiding place. Dillon was sure that if he didn't act fast then the king, who was more experienced, would wrestle back control of the earth's energy.

Dillon took some of the mana he now controlled, drew it in tight like a spring. Upon Dillon's command it uncoiled from behind a piece of the hieroglyphics.

A dagger-sharp rock cracked off and launched straight at the leader. The impact snapped the king's head backward and embedded the stone into his head, killing him instantly.

The earth sang out in joy.

Without thinking, Dillon sped up the rhythm of the rocks until they vibrated with an incredible force. All of the hieroglyphics shattered, releasing the earth's power and sending thousands of screaming goluns crashing to their deaths. Those close to the ground landed safely, but were crushed by falling bodies or broken hieroglyphics.

In less than a minute the room had become a silent, open tomb.

Dillon still felt the rush of energy within him and focused the power to open the top of the stone enclosure that the goluns had built around his companions, hoping it had not become their casket. He stepped back out of the wall and released his control of the earth, allowing it to slowly dissipate. Not a single golun breathed, but he desperately hoped his friends had not been awarded with the same fate.

Matt climbed out of the five-foot-high stone tomb and just stared at the carnage all around him. He had heard the rumbling and muffled screams but had been too panicked in the small enclosure to understand.

Now that he was out, he was stunned. Yeah, he had wanted their evil wiped out. He had even wished them to die horribly. But he still felt the pain from the loss of so many lives.

"Matt, get over here quick!" Matt was startled back into action by Dillon's voice coming from the open tomb were Arlar had been trapped. He ran over and jumped to the top and looked inside. Dillon was sitting in a large pool of blood. He was holding Arlar's long, green head and looking at the ribs that protruded from his thick scales. Arlar's eyes were closed and his breathing arrived in inconsistent gulps.

Matt knew that he hadn't much time before Arlar died. He jumped into the tomb, splattering Dillon with Arlar's blood, and crouched over the bones. "Dillon, before I can try and heal him we need to get his ribs back inside his body." Dillon gently placed Arlar's head on the ground as he spoke to Matt.

"I need you to grab under the scales and lift with me," directed Matt.

Dillon reached down and, with some difficulty, was able to lift the natural armor plating high enough to slip his fingers underneath. He then looked over at Matt who also had his hands under the plates.

"We need to lift on three. One, two—three!"

Both of them grunted from the effort and felt the scales scraping past the bones. When they had completely lifted the armor plating over the bones, Matt told him to push forward before releasing to prevent the bones from going back through the same hole. Dillon then stepped back to allow Matt to work his magic. Arlar's bones were still not set right and caused the plating to bulge out grotesquely.

Matt knelt down and placed his hands on Arlar's chest. He slowed his breathing by slowly counting to eight as he inhaled and followed this with an eight count on the exhale in one continuous cycle. He did this for about two minutes and then doubled his inhale and exhale count to sixteen.

After another two minutes, he began to take in blue and green energy during his inhale and store it in his first and seventh chakra, followed by an exhale up his spine with no release of energy. Matt could feel the power of the energy he had gathered pulsing through his body and surprised himself when he was able to further store the energy in his second through sixth chakras.

With his eyes closed, Matt looked at Arlar through the mana emanating from his hands. He could feel the massive trauma his body had suffered from the sudden impact of hitting the wall. To his amazement, he could even sense his soul slipping away. As he looked deeper inside Arlar, he saw that one of the rib bones had broken off and punctured Arlar's lungs, filling them with blood. This was where he needed to work first.

Matt exhaled and moved the energy he had gathered into Arlar's body. He constricted some of Arlar's muscles and even veins in a careful pattern to move the bone along and force it out of the lungs to where it belonged, the way a snake swallowed prey and moved it to its stomach. Matt repeated the constrictions to push the blood out of Arlar's lungs. He then drew in more energy and pushed it through Arlar's body, healing the complex webbing of lungs.

Sweat dripped off Matt's body as he moved on to the next step. Arlar's body had given up its autonomous repair of the damage. Matt had to force his non-responsive body into action. He drove the dragon's cells to start healing, compelled his body to create more red blood cells, willed the heart to keep beating. Once Arlar's body began to respond, Matt mended the numerous fractured bones and other damages.

Matt finally stepped away when he felt there was no more he could do, unaware that more than four hours had elapsed. To his dismay, Arlar's breathing was still shallow. He showed no improvement.

"I fixed everything I could understand, but he lost a lot of blood and his brain was deprived of oxygen for a while. I just don't know if he'll make it." Matt staggered to the top of the short wall before turning around to speak. "I need to sleep." He then stumbled down the other side, out of Dillon's sight. He was too exhausted to stay awake and also couldn't bear to be present if Arlar passed away. He simply couldn't face that.

Dillon climbed out of the earthen tomb and surveyed the area. The light Arlar created was dim, but still illuminated the room enough to see what he had done. The golun bodies were stacked two to three deep. Many had been impacted by huge shards of hieroglyphics. Dillon's nose caught the stench of death that had started to fill the room, forcing him to put his sleeve over his nose and mouth.

His arm blocked the pungency and caught the tears that had fallen from his eyes. How easily he had just killed thousands of lives overwhelmed him. But there was more. Somehow he knew it was just the beginning of the carnage he would leave in a trail behind him. He slumped down against the wall and closed his eyes for a minute.

****

"Hi Dillon, how are you doing?"

Dillon looked up to see the familiar white light in the astral plane.

"Hi Guylen. I guess I'm okay. How did you find me on this planet?"

"We knew where you had gone, but to get here took time." Guylen seemed to study Dillon's soul. "I know you are saddened by the loss of life, and what you will do in the future. However, you have chosen a path of change, and change comes with a price."

"I have come to grips with my role in changing the future. But how can you expect me to nonchalantly accept that I have killed, and will kill so many?"

"I would be worried if you weren't concerned about it. Thousands upon thousands will die, Dillon, but billions will be saved when you ensure their future."

"Guylen. You always come here to inspire me and train me. Are you allowed to help me?" Dillon sensed a smile on the white being's face.

"Go toward the light and know you must create even more light." A chuckle rang out from Guylen as he left. Dillon awoke to a brightly lit cavern. He knew what that meant and jumped up and into Arlar's resting place. The dragon's eyes were open and he winked, even though it was obvious that he was far from feeling well. Matt was grinning next to him.

"You made it! How are you feeling?" asked Dillon.

"Good enough to breathe. But I'm in no condition to go anywhere. The good news is that you are only a few hundred feet from the portal."

"What? We're there already?" Dillon was surprised at their speed of arrival, but flustered by what seemed like impending doom.

"Yes. The tunnel is on the opposite side from where we entered the cavern. It leads right to the portal. I am guessing The Fallen One paid the goluns handsomely to protect this entrance."

"But what about you?" asked Matt, wondering if Arlar could defend himself if discovered. His eyes had closed again.

"I can do no more, and this would have been the end of my journey with you anyway. I will stay here and recover until I am good enough to walk. Then I will go back to enjoying the life I lead before we met." Arlar opened his eyes, "It was a true pleasure to help you in your quest. I know you will fix what is broken."

IV.

There was no point in procrastinating. Dillon thanked Arlar and then jumped back over the wall, forced to again look upon the mass of rotting corpses strewn about the floor. He knew they were evil and wanted to kill him and his friends, but only because he entered their home. Invaded their home and then turned it into a mass grave. This was still hard to accept.

Dillon covered his mouth and nose as he carefully picked his way through the bodies and rocks, with Matt following closely behind. As they neared the opposite end of the cave they noticed a large boulder that shielded another tunnel exit from view, which would have gone unnoticed to anyone farther than a few meters from it. They proceeded into the man-sized, winding tunnel and walked a couple hundred feet until darkness was behind them and a faint glowing light lay before. They walked another hundred feet until they rounded a bend and were faced with what could only be described as a dark, whirling vortex.

White light was leaping out of the vortex in various patterns, only to be pulled back in. The spinning blackness bubbled and pulsed like a boiling caldron of oil. The vortex was suspended above a ten-foot-deep pit from which numerous metal spikes protruded. More spikes bordered the portal above and all around, even attached to the sides of the walls where they stood. Bones of various creatures and humanoids were impaled on the spikes in grotesque positions as if they had been thrown at a very high speed.

The entire place was devoid of any sound.

"So what do we do now?" Matt's words, although only a few feet from Dillon's ears, disappeared quickly and were almost missed.

"It seems like the vortex absorbs anything that comes near it." Dillon yelled and noticed that there was no echo. His words were quickly drowned out by emptiness.

"So what do we do now?" Matt repeated in a louder voice, although the sound again barely reached Dillon.

"Jump in."

"What? Don't the impaled bodies on the walls and ground worry you? If we miss we're sure to become their close friends."

"My guess is that the bones are from those that came from the other side."

"How sure are you? And what makes you think there aren't the same spikes on the other side?" Matt still wasn't convinced and gasped as he saw Dillon leap forward, stop in midair, and then become drawn into the portal. He looked around and only then realized he was alone in a small cave that seemed to be closing in on him.

"Any place is better than this." Matt closed his eyes and jumped into the swirling black cauldron.

V.

Matt felt nothing and opened his eyes, expecting to be headed toward a large spike. Instead he found himself floating in blackness. Just as he was ready to try and move, he felt as if he was on a turbulent airplane ride that rapidly dropped out of the sky and then twisted upside down. Bright light blinded him as his feet landed on solid ground for a brief moment before he skipped and skidded across a smooth stone floor. His stomach churned and he threw up as he tried to jump to a stand and prepare for attackers. What he saw was Dillon standing in front of a similar pile of liquid, wiping his mouth.

"Kind of like having the stomach flu and being thrown off a roller coaster, huh?" Dillon turned away from the wall they had skidded toward and looked back at the portal from which they'd been thrown. It was next to two other similar portals. The walls of the room had been worked to a smooth finish and had a number of unwavering torches spread out to brighten the area. The torches were surely magical as there was no blackness or soot from their burning. The room itself had two tunnels leading out.

"Yeah, but that sinking feeling in my stomach has been replaced by a stronger one all over my body. Dillon, I have become more in tune with living things since being on this planet, and life is completely absent here."

"Then I guess it's time to go greet death." Dillon grabbed a torch off the wall and drew his sword as he spoke. He turned to Matt, smiled, and strode toward the tunnel on the right.

In less than fifteen feet the tunnel opened up onto the side of a spiral stone staircase that was carved out of the walls of a thirty-foot-wide tower. The four-foot-wide stairs left a large, empty space in the middle that went up and down into darkness farther than Dillon could see. He was sure it went on for miles in both directions. Matt stepped next to him and kicked a small stone off the stair they were standing on and watched it plunge into the darkness.

"Don't bother counting. I'm sure it goes down a long way. Besides, we are going up."

"Up? But remember Arlar telling us that everything he read said that in order to reach The Fallen One, you must find the entrance to the bowels of Igypkt."

"Yes, and we found the entrance. It never said to follow it. Besides, let's just assume it doesn't go all the way to the bowels of Igypkt, but comes close. What about air? At some point there wouldn't be enough air flow for us to function. I say let's head up, and if I'm wrong then we can always try going downward." Dillon also remembered that Guylen had told him to follow the light. The only way he could imagine seeing a light was by going up.

"But we both know that The Fallen One is a vampire, right?" Matt asked. He wasn't completely convinced that Dillon knew what he was doing.

"Right."

"Then why would he get close to the surface where the sun could roast him alive?" asked Matt.

"Because no one would look for him there. Tell you what. If I'm wrong I'll buy you dinner at Domingo's when we get back home."

"Yeah, real funny. Like any of us expect to go back to Earth." Matt decided not to argue. Going deeper into the planet would only further irritate his claustrophobia. At least with Dillon's choice, he would finally be able to get out into open space, even if it was to quickly die.

Dillon looked up, sighed and started to ascend the mountain of stairs. After a few hours of climbing, his quadriceps felt on fire, and with each new step they felt like they would burst and send him plummeting to his death. He finally just plopped down against the wall, exhausted. After calming himself and drawing in some energy, he peered up at Matt, who looked like he hadn't walked more than a mile downhill.

"How are you doing so well?"

"You forget, before I was forced to be this nature-loving pacifist I trained to be a warrior. Just because I have to hug trees doesn't mean I'm going to turn back into a fat Friar Tuck. Also, I'm able to speed up the oxygen uptake from my hemoglobin and facilitate transport to my muscles and thus reduce lactic acid build-up." Matt smiled at Dillon.

"What? Well, I need a break to regain my energy. Do we have anything left to eat?"

"I've got some hard yellow berries. They don't taste great, but don't rot fast either. I also have some garla root* that is a good protein supplement." Matt was fumbling around in his backpack for more, but this was all he could find.

Dillon bit into one of the hard berries and tried to swallow the foul-tasting fruit. "You've got to stop taking this nature thing so seriously. I'd eat some moldy bread if you had it."

"Hey Dillon, look up ahead. I think I see an alcove or something." Matt picked up his staff and started bounding up the stairs. About ten steps from the alcove he nearly tripped as the stair he stepped on sunk slightly.

Matt stopped and looked down at the step, catching a glimpse of a bright flash of white light shooting out from the alcove. He was then overcome with a sickening feeling of death and slowly lifted his head to see the hulking, rotting corpses coming down to greet him.

Dillon jumped up and charged after Matt with his sword in hand. "I'm on my way, hold on."

"No Dillon. These I can fight. They are an abomination and need to be destroyed." Rage welled up inside Matt as he charged toward the soul-trapped corpses. He somehow knew that they were the living dead and that he could destroy them.

The first zombie was about six feet tall and missing half of its head. A large axe was still stuck in its neck where its head had been split. Maggots were crawling all over its body and landing on the ground as chunks of rotting flesh were shaken loose. As Matt neared the zombie, it grabbed the axe with its right hand and pulled it out of its body, ready to attack.

Matt stepped within striking distance of the zombie and let it take the first swing. The zombie was slow and clumsy. Matt didn't block it but stepped forward to avoid the attack. He braced his back against the wall and swung, forcing the staff head strongly into the off-balance zombie. It teetered on the edge of the stair with its one eye looking right at Matt.

"Thaaannkk yoooouuu." The zombie slowly rumbled the words and then fell off the stair and into the darkness.

Matt had no time to think about the compliment since a smaller and more agile zombie leaped forward to replace the first one. Almost all of its flesh was still attached, but it was green and rotting. It looked elvish and held a short knife in one hand.

Matt struck at the zombie. It leapt in the air above his head and stuck to the wall just beyond his reach. The knife whipped out of its hand toward Matt's throat, but lodged into his staff instead. Matt wanted to smile, but a large, rotting wolf had already taken the place of the vacated step in front of him. Its three-inch fangs snapped at his legs and midsection.

"Matt, you're out-flanked. Drop back so I can help!"

Matt ignored Dillon and instead stuck the head of his staff into the wolf's mouth to hold it at bay. He took a deep calm breath, gathering healing green energy. He shot his right arm up toward the hanging zombie, exhaled, and focused the healing energy toward it. The creature screamed as the green energy struck it, causing it to fall off the wall and tumble into the darkness. Matt then twisted his staff out of the wolf's mouth, spun it in his hands and struck downward on the creature's head. There was a loud crack as the staff went through the bone and drove the wolf's head into the stone. Matt kicked the limp animal off the staircase and then turned to Dillon.

"Sorry, but it may have been my only chance to fight."

Dillon smiled and put his hands up in a defensive position, "No argument from me." They laughed and started to climb the stairs again, passing the alcove with caution.

"I wonder why there weren't more? In all honesty it didn't seem like a strong set of guards to stop anyone from getting through."

"My guess is that they only serve to catch anyone or anything that wasn't meant to come through the portal." Dillon thoughts jumped as he retraced the battle in his head.

"Hey Matt, what did that creature mumble to you as it fell?"

"It said thank you. I think its soul was trapped in the body and forced to protect this area. By destroying the body then its soul could be freed." Matt stopped and looked around, not feeling well. "We must be close to where we want to go. It's almost as if I can sense hundreds of creatures racked with pain. As if trapped between life and death. I sure hope we don't have to battle them all. I'm up for a fight, but not one that big."

Dillon put his sword back in his scabbard and replied, "We won't be fighting if we get to him first. He must answer the questions we ask, although I would like to know why."

VI.

The Great Mage threw open the doors of the main chamber and basked in the heat emanating from the lava pit. He barely glanced at the ten-foot, muscular demon holding a flaming sword that matched the sparks crackling from its red body. Jialin* had no time for pleasantries and strode straight up to the being relaxing on the metal throne.

"Yes, Jialin? I assume it must be urgent?"

"It is, my Lord. A series of strange events have occurred on Kalansi. By themselves they are mere flickers of a steady flame, but together they hint at something greater."

"Go on."

Jialin stared at the soft, human-like thing standing before him. He had once dreamed of ruling, but found out that he had no talent for politics or planning. He had then assumed he would serve a powerful king, but instead found himself aiding an outsider whose powers were invisible to the naked eye. However, he had seen Cahlar in action and knew that no single being was a match for him.

"More than a month ago your soaring scouts noticed that a mana field the size of a mountain was moving west of the desert into the woods leading toward Cureio. They say it then disappeared into the forest. The soarers* are as dumb as they are fast, so we took it to be a mistake. However, yesterday the golun king sent word that a human mage who moves the earth was in their tunnels. He said the mage unlocked the secrets of their power and was headed right toward them. But again, the goluns are not very trustworthy and barely smarter than the soarers."

"Interesting. Any reports of fire from the sky?"

"I thought the same things, my Lord, but upon checking the sentry logs there was nothing. However, when I looked further there was mention that Mankin had sent up a rocket, but followed it with an 'all clear' one shortly thereafter." Jialin knew this wasn't good news.

The wind snapped loudly as Cahlar stood faster than even the demon could track. A smile crept across his face as he spoke, "So, one has finally made it through my web. The Mulshins are either finally getting smart or lucky. Diabold*, open the entrance to The Knowledge Chamber. It's time I visited The Fallen One."

"You are going yourself, Master? But, I always go for you," stated Jialin.

135

"Jialin, my life and vision for my empire is being threatened. Besides, I want you to have your first taste of power. You will assume leadership while I am gone."

Jialin bowed, "Thank you, my lord."

Cahlar looked over at Diabold who was walking down the stairs and into the lava below. His skin hissed and crackled with each step until he was completely submerged. Deep, guttural incantations emanated from within the lava followed by the formation of a twenty-foot, rectangular hole. Diabold stepped out of the lava and into the hole. He bent down and lifted a two-ton rock to reveal the entrance to a large cavern. Cahlar jumped up high into the air, hit the ceiling, and sprang off of it as he transformed himself into a wedge. He used all the momentum he created to dart down through the air pocket inside the lava and into the cavern, traveling fast enough to not melt. He reformed into a human shape as he hit the ground and looked up at Diabold. "If he gets too full of himself, kill him!" Diabold smiled and nodded as he placed the rock back over the hole.

Cahlar stared across the cavern at three circles of different colors of pure light that spun wildly on the wall. Only two things had truly amazed him since he had come back to Igypkt. One was the ability to teleport by walking through the spinning colors; the other was The Fallen One's ability to predict the future. If the reports were true, the third would be the human that may have the power to destroy him. He cursed himself for never asking The Fallen One if an Earthling would unseat him and his power. Of course, he killed all those that came from the sky, but never really thought they could harm him. Although upset, he maintained his calm and casual façade as he stepped through the boiling black surface of the vortex.

VII.

They walked another forty minutes up the stairs until they reached a simple door on the wooden ceiling above their heads. Dillon grabbed the handle and opened it as he continued to walk up the steps and into the room, followed by Matt. The room had a dim gray lighting emanating from the roof, so he threw the torch back down the underground tower before looking around.

The room was maybe thirty feet in diameter, with no furnishings other than a metal pentagon in the middle of the floor. On it stood a tall and very thin man, dressed in loose fitting brown pants and an oversized black shirt.

"Dillon and Matt. Nice to finally meet you. I see that your journey wasn't too eventful." The voice was melodically soft, almost seeming to be both comforting and uncaring.

Dillon stared at the vampire's face, immediately noticing that his mouth did not move with the words and that his eyes were completely white.

"If you know our names, then you can read our minds and know why we are here." Dillon had stepped forward to make the statement.

"No, you are wrong. I know your names because I know almost everything that happens on Igypkt." The Fallen One glided off the pentagon and pointed back toward it. "Relax and look through where I stood."

Dillon calmed his nervous breathing and looked at the empty area where The Fallen One pointed and then past it. He started to shift his focus to his third eye and noticed the massive white mana field coming out of the ground and stopping about seven feet above it.

"Now look deeper into the light and you will see that it is composed of millions upon millions of smaller, multi-colored strands. They are mana cords for each living and non-living thing on Igypkt. They are pulled to the core of the planet were I gather them and bring them up to me."

"How does that let you know the answers to the questions we ask? Can you see the future?" Dillon was confused and intrigued.

"No, I can only answer questions and predict the future based on the probability of occurrences from the interactions of the strands. For example, when you take a step on a blade of grass, one of your mana strands interacts with it, which then interacts with those grass strands around it. Those grass strands interact with the insects on the grass and so on. As you take each step I can see what strands are impacted and can tell which direction you are likely going. I can also look at where you have been, what you have done, and then predict where you are going and why you are going there."

"Why do you do this, and why are you called The Fallen One?"

"Both questions have one answer. I was born before the beginning of the mana age. At that time our planet was at the peak of its technological revolution, and we were exploring the stars, looking for others to share in our existence. We directed almost all our resources and attention away from our own planet and its happenings until one day we noticed that our technological systems were failing. We soon discovered that it was a result of mana, a form of energy we had completely missed in our scientific studies. Further research helped us understand mana and how it affected technology; but we also discovered that our planet had entered a long and enduring mana field. As you surely could guess, it would and did destroy all technology on Igypkt.

"A small number of our people left the planet to continue exploring the stars, while most stayed behind. As the elected ruler of Igypkt, I also stayed and was determined to discover a way to merge mana and technology. I delved into studying what mana was and why it wreaked havoc with logic-based systems. Unfortunately, I became side-tracked with a discovery of how one could harness the mana.

"I was able to modify a virus to absorb mana into one's body. I introduced the virus into my own body so that I could gather mana. It worked, and I was soon able to gather and control mana like no one that lived on Igypkt, but I lost my desire to direct it into technology. I let the virus consume me until I became what I am now: the first true vampire. I cannot handle sunlight, silver, or garlic because the virus cannot survive them. I need fresh blood because the virus feeds off mine. I was a prisoner of my own design.

"I became enraged and filled with the desire to hurt others. I hunted out anyone or anything I could find and infected them, while also replenishing the blood my body craved. I did not believe in the spiritual side then, but soon became an icon of evil for the tens of thousands I infected and all of their loved ones. I found that those I infected would do my bidding and I soon realized that I had trapped their souls, and tied them to my evil ways.

"Eventually my rage subsided and I fell back to wanting to help Igypkt thrive. But I had cursed myself through my actions and fallen from grace in the eyes of my own people. The only way I could now help was through watching and advising others. I again studied how mana worked and how it flowed. I learned all that I could about it until I was able to gather the mana strands to myself and observe how they delicately interwove or separated as time progressed. With the knowledge I could answer the questions of those that made it to me. That is, as long as it helped my planet."

"What about the Mulshins? Are they telling us the truth? What do they really want?"

"You have no time for these answers. Ask me your most important question now." Something had startled The Fallen One, who drifted back into the pentagon.

"How do we reach Cahlar and the other two Mulshins?"

"Great wording of your question, Dillon. If you had asked where Cahlar was, then I could have told you as of this moment, but it would not help your cause. To reach Cahlar follow your friends, board the floating city, and travel to Ishtan. From there find the bowl of life, then drown your sorrows. The other two Mulshins are shadows of their former selves and not worth your worry."

Dillon's hands started to sweat and his heart was pounding. Something didn't feel right and he had a strong hunch as to what it was.

"It is now time, Dillon. You know what to do and must do it quickly," demanded The Fallen One.

Dillon gathered in the blue energy from all around him, especially from the energy source that The Fallen One was standing within. The mana drew to him faster than his own thoughts could command. He raised his hands and felt the oxygen and moisture being sucked from the air. Two massive water fountains sprang forth from his hands and struck the stone ceiling with such force that it exploded outward, revealing a beautiful, sunny day—a shining day that was quickly spoiled by the view of hundreds of undead flying around the top of the tower.

Dillon had a thought and was barely able to gasp out his final question to The Fallen One, who had already caught fire from the sun's rays. "Is there good and evil?"

"Don't be a fool, Dillon. Of course there is."

Matt looked over at The Fallen One, as he gulped for oxygen that was depleted by Dillon's spell. His white eyes revealed nothing as the flames engulfed his body. The silence of his passing was a paradox beside the tens of thousands of screams around Igypkt as the trapped souls ripped themselves from their undead bodies. The ground started to rumble and shake, and the floor of the tower began to give way.

Matt sprinted and took off, using his staff to launch himself to the top of the now roofless wall. Once on top, he was surprised to see that the tower was only a tower from the inside and a one-story, round hut from the outside. He turned around and reached down an arm in time to catch Dillon's hand and pull him up to the wall. They both jumped off and started running as the tower and ground behind them collapsed.

They ran past rotting corpses of dragons, trolls, giants, humanoids, and animals whose souls had been freed. Then a shrill cry came from the expanding sinkhole that was so powerful they both fell down and covered their ears. It quickly passed and they were left on the ground looking back at the heaps of corpses and the large pit where The Fallen One had died.

"Why the heck did you do that?" Matt was furious and also exhausted from their sprint.

Dillon stood up to survey the large new crater. "I had to. Cahlar had entered through another portal and was going to reach us shortly. Even if we had gotten away he would have been able to ask everything about us, including how to find and destroy us."

"But you killed The Fallen One."

"I couldn't have if he didn't want me to. In fact I think he forced me to do it. I can only assume he had predicted that the future of Igypkt was safer in our hands than in Cahlar's. He gave his own life to ensure it went down the path he wanted."

"Oh." It was all Matt could muster until the obvious hit him. "Wait, we are running from the very thing we are trying to track down? Why?"

"I was wondering when you would ask that since this seems counterintuitive, but it's very simple. We all saw on the moon just how fast and powerful the Mulshins are. Even as a team, we are no match for a single Mulshin. At least not on their terms. We need to grow in our abilities, learn about this planet and..."

"...then attack him." Matt finished his sentence.

"No. We need to find out his weaknesses and then develop the best strategy to get the mana-converting device. We may be able to trick him out of it or maybe even something else, but if we have to attack him then we only have a chance of winning if we do it on our terms."

Dillon thought about their next step. "Now we need to meet up with our friends, find out what they've learned, and board this floating city. Getting there is going to take a long time. If Arlar's map[#] was correct, then we are almost two thousand miles away from Cureio."

Matt stared at the sky, and in a matter of seconds a large raven appeared in the distance, flew toward them, and landed on his shoulder. He softly rubbed its feathers and then fed it the last of the hard berries before it flew off.

Dillon chuckled as he spoke, "What are you, a beast master now? Did you talk to that raven?"

Matt laughed at the thought, "Talked to the bird? No. I think it could sense I wouldn't harm it and it took advantage of me. Now, I did learn that ravens aren't very nice though." Matt was trying to brush off the white dropping that the raven had left splattered on his shoulder.

"Let's head due west."

"Through the desert, are you insane?"

"Listen. I'm sure Cahlar didn't die in that collapse. He now is aware that we're on Igypkt, and he's going to send everything he can at us once he recovers. He's got to know we are heading to the big city and would take a direct route to get there or get to the sea and travel by boat. If I remember Arlar's map correctly, there's a huge bay on the other side of the desert. We'll go to a coastal town and, instead of traveling by the sea, we'll travel from town to town until we get to Cureio. It'll take twice as long, but we have a much better chance of making it there alive." Dillon still didn't know if it was the best choice, but his logic usually helped people to agree.

"Yeah, but the desert?" Matt wondered how they could make it.

"I figure the biggest problem in the desert is dehydration, and you don't have to worry about that." Dillon raised his right hand, pointed his finger at Matt, and shot him with a short burst of water.

As he walked away he thought, *Creating water from the air is becoming almost second hand, pun fully intended.*

VIIIa.

Cahlar braced himself to exit the portal, somehow overlooking the two pools of fresh vomit glistening on the ground. He continued his attempt to figure out how the portal worked. If it was a wormhole to another part of Igypkt, then how could a carbon-based life form enter and pass through it without every cell being ripped apart?

The science riddle started to anger him, so he focused his thoughts on another enigma as he ascended the long stairway. The Fallen One had claimed that he had trapped souls within the dead bodies of those he had infected, turning them into zombies, skeletons, and even vampires. Cahlar didn't believe it, but had seen many of the creatures himself. It had to be a virus that kept the nearly rotting creatures from dying. That would explain the zombies and maybe even the vampires, but not the walking skeletons he had seen many times. What could they be?

Cahlar pondered this issue as he easily overextended his legs to stride up the staircase four steps at a time. He began to pass the alcove, but stopped when he noticed that the three zombie guards were not there. He quickly surmised what had happened and darted up the staircase at a speed most humanoids could barely see.

His thoughts raced even faster than his legs. *If it was the Earthling then how did they find the secret entrance? What would The Fallen One reveal to them?* He needed to get to the top fast.

Cahlar forced himself to a sudden stop when he heard thousands of screams echoing from above. The tower shuttered. The cracking of rocks filled the air. He knew he couldn't make it to the top or return to the portal, so he raced back toward the alcove.

Huge rocks and pieces of the stone staircase started to rebound off the walls and stairs around him. Cahlar's excitement rose with the challenge, and his megalomaniacal smile split his face nearly in half.

Within forty feet of his destination the staircase gave way. He stretched his legs out to three times their normal length and with all his strength pushed off from the wall, launching himself at the alcove. He elongated his arms an extra three feet to catch the edge of the alcove, and he smiled again. Just as he began to pull himself up, a boulder struck the alcove ledge.

The alcove collapsed. The stones plummeted down the hole, with Cahlar following in the wake. He let out a shrill scream of frustration (not fear), which was quickly lost in the massive avalanche.

VIIIb.

Jialin and Diabold looked at each other at the same time. They both felt the shift in balance as thousands of souls were released from their prison. Jialin had learned to feel the tainting of mana by good and evil, and discerned that something big had happened. Diabold's internal reaction was more serious since he fed off evil. The release of the imprisoned souls lessened his power. He didn't tell Jialin, and he wouldn't tell Cahlar either; they both would easily figure out he was so much more than a lesser demon whom Jialin had conjured and trapped.

"I guess The Gallen War* is ready to begin," remarked Jialin.

"Maybe, but it might be best if I ask my true liege."

"How rare, Diabold. A good thought from you. You may go, but remember you are still bound by me," Jialin chided.

"Yes, Master." Diabold hid his anger from the puny human. He knew he would have the last laugh. He walked into the lava pit and let its flow carry him through an underground portal and to the plane where he ruled. It was time for him to start planning for The Gallen War.

VIIIc.

Sileya* paused from reaping the wheat field and wiped the perspiration away from her brow. A one-person farm was hard work, but she had to grow enough crops to both eat and trade for needed supplies. It had taken her years to become self-sustaining, and this year she would be able to help some of the new families.

Many of the local farmers and fisherman in the small coastal town had become her friends. Last spring they had even given her three chickens as a sign of her acceptance into their community. She treated them as if they were made of gold, and worked even harder to lend a hand whenever possible.

She lifted the scythe to cut more wheat, but dropped it when the exhilaration hit her. Countless trapped souls were being released from their magical bindings, and she felt each one. The ecstasy was more powerful than anything she had known in her very long life. Sileya sunk to her knees and thanked *The Unity* * for this sign while tears ran down her face and onto the ground. After a few short minutes she got up and walked back to her hut. Beautiful golden flowers sprang forth from where her tears had struck the ground.

Inside the hut, Sileya first washed her face in the stone water basin and then dropped her dusty work robe to cleanse herself, revealing her stunning beauty. Her olive skin had been darkened by the many hours she spent outside each day, but no wrinkles or blemishes marked her face. She released her light brunette hair, which fell down past her defined shoulders. It captured the breeze just enough to move in a mesmerizing pattern. Time could not easily age her body, even as her mind could not shed centuries of sad memories.

Sileya slowly knelt down, opened a dirt-covered trap door in the floor, and brought out a wrapped traveling robe. She unfolded it on top of the wobbly table she had made herself, revealing a simple golden chain attached to a large, colorless diamond. She put on both the chain and the robe before leaving the hut.

It was time to find out who was restoring balance on Igypkt, and if The Gallen War was to begin.

Chapter 9
The Woman's Change

I.

Gabe, Tanya, and Lian casually walked along the slowly ascending tunnel. Gabe guessed that they would arrive in the big city many weeks ahead of Dillon and Matt, and saw little need to rush to Cureio for their scouting mission, especially considering that Dillon had really sent them to the city for their own safety. Gabe didn't question Dillon's motives anymore, but knew that once they arrived in Cureio he would do more than just sit around and wait for the duo's return.

Gabe looked down at his glowing vibe sword, which he was using as their light source. Through continuous practice, he was able to draw enough golden mana for the blade to emanate to the size of a long knife. Not where he wanted to be, but now he could use it in a fight. Back on the Moon, however, Gabe had learned that close combat with the vibe sword required a completely different fighting style than did a normal metal sword in hand. The vibe sword would effortlessly cut through any weapon it contacted, causing both pieces to continue the path toward him if he wasn't careful.

"So, if Dillon is killed by The Fallen One, what do we do?" Lian asked.

"Lian, why'd you even think that?" snapped Tanya. She had stopped and turned around to look at him as her words echoed off the tunnel walls.

"Hey, come on. It's not like we're living back in the A.V.*. We actually have to worry about death and dying here," retorted Lian.

"It is actually a good question, Tanya. If any of us die, I think Dillon can and will go on. If he dies, then we will need to figure out if we can complete our mission. We might have to accept the fact that we simply are not powerful enough to continue." Gabe had also stopped and turned around. "I personally believe we will just have to blend into Igypkt's society. Why, what do you want to do, Lian?"

"I don't know and don't care. I was just bored and wanted to create conversation." Lian laughed at himself.

Tanya smacked him over the head before turning around and following Gabe again. Lian giggled, pleased that he had evoked a reaction.

Many more hours passed in silence as they walked inside the dark and rank smelling tunnel. The only sound besides their footsteps was the frequent splat of a water droplet giving in to gravity. Suddenly, Gabe held up his hand, signaling them to stop.

"What's wrong? I don't sense an attack." Tanya still drew her swords as she whispered. She breathed softly and reached out with her senses to see if she could feel any threats, but nothing alarmed her.

"Arlar said that the tunnel would continue all the way to the top without entering any caverns; however, there is a cavern ahead of us which may mean someone or something is inside."

"Maybe Arlar just forgot." Lian's voice was soft as he slid up against the wall. "He *is* rather old, and Alzheimer's could explain a lot about him."

"No. The cave is new. I made it." They all snapped to a defensive stance and readied their weapons as the deep voice resonated off the walls around them. None of them could detect the voice's origin because the sound bounced around. Gabe motioned for Tanya to join him at the cavern entrance, with Lian positioning himself four feet behind them and facing in the opposite direction.

"Don't worry. I won't hurt you. Well, as long as you don't hurt me."

"Holy cow! A talking stone head! Cool." Lian's excited voice reverberated off the walls.

Gabe turned toward Lian and followed his eyes down to the ground between them. A gray head a little higher than their knees was looking at Lian.

"I do talk with my head. But I am more than a head." The gray creature slowly rose out of the brown stone until his head and shoulders disappeared into the rock at the top of the tunnel, about seven feet high.

The creature was easily over nine feet tall and had the muscular frame of a basketball player on steroids. Its stomach was large in proportion to its lean frame.

"Yes, Lian, a stone giant." Gabe smiled since he'd beaten Lian to his self-appointed job of identifying creatures on Igypkt.

The stone giant then sank a couple of feet back into the ground so that his head reappeared. "Someone should have made these tunnels bigger. How do they expect me to talk and walk at the same time?"

"Uhm, excuse me? You built this cavern?" Tanya was still weary of an attack from this gentle-seeming giant, but did not sense any impending doom.

"I built it, and it's mine. You can relax inside or go through to the other side," Was the reply, although the happy look on its face suggested he wanted them to stay.

"Well, we do have plenty of time on our hands. Do you mind if we stay for a little while? I hope we will not be a burden?" replied Gabe.

"I would like that." A smile appeared on the giant's face as he walked past them and into his cavern.

"What's your name?" asked Tanya.

"A giant's name is full of low rumblings and groans, but my humanoid friends call me Ghost*. I think because I am lighter in color than most of my race." Ghost smiled at Tanya and then reached down to the ground, where he started gathering and molding the stone as if it were clay. In a few short minutes he'd formed a chair, followed by two more. "Please have a seat."

"Do you have anything to drink, like maybe water?" asked Lian.

"Oh, no. Water is bad for stone giants. It melts us."

"Oh, really?" Lian deliberately pulled his leather-skin water bottle from his waist, and uncapped it while he took a big swig. Ghost leaned back slightly at the sight. Lian then stood up and, to the horror of his comrades, spit the fluid onto the stone giant's face.

Ghost clutched his face and fell to the ground, letting out a low, rumbling scream. He rolled back and forth while moaning loudly.

"Lian, why did you do that?" yelled Tanya as she rushed to Ghost's side, apologizing for Lian's behavior. She hoped he wasn't permanently injured, and also that he wasn't mad enough to attack them. Her sixth sense still hadn't sent her any warning.

"Oh, I'm ruined forever. Why? Why did you hurt me?"

"We're really sorry, Ghost. Is there anything we can do?" Tanya's soft side poured out. While she apologized, Gabe stepped between Ghost and Lian. He also looked around to see if there were others who might come to Ghost's aid.

"My face is ruined forever! What will I do?" Ghost stopped rolling on the ground. "Please do me one favor?"

"Anything, just let me know how I can help." Tanya was bent over Ghost, holding his large stone head in her hands.

"Tell me, how bad is it?" Ghost pulled his long, gray hands away from his face.

Confusion racked Tanya's mind when she saw only the giant's big smile.

"There's nothing wrong? You sure you're hurt?" Tanya was still looking for damage. Ghost and Lian laughed loudly.

"You losers!" she screamed as she let Ghost's head smack the floor. Tanya jumped up and charged toward Lian, who already was running behind a large, stone table for protection.

"How could you two plan this? You never even saw each other before." Gabe asked, although he thought the trick funny.

"I could tell he was lying about the water. His aura changed and was beaming bright. Besides, one jokester can always sense another."

Ghost had stood up and was walking over to Lian, still chuckling at the joke he had played with his new friend.

When he got close, Lian smacked him on the stomach. "Hey, what's up with your stomach? It doesn't seem proportional."

Ghost was confused at Lian's big word, but then smiled as he figured out what Lian was asking. "Oh, it's how I store my rocks." Ghost reached right through his skin and pulled out a handful of smooth pebbles, each about the size of a human eye. With his other hand he pulled out two larger rocks about the size of his fist.

Ghost's stomach was now normal in size and shape. He then placed all but one pebble back inside his stomach as he looked across the cavern. He wound up his arm and threw the pebble against the wall with such force that it exploded, leaving a nice scar across the rock face.

"Wow, now that's a fastball!" Tanya was amazed. She figured that the strength of the throw had to be some part of his magical ability.

"Ghost, I want to know what brought you to these tunnels and made you want to make this your home." Gabe thought it strange that Ghost would pick such a secluded place. He seemed very sociable.

"I was told to leave Cureio." Ghost's face and demeanor became like the stone he was made of. He sat down in his own large, ornately carved chair and looked off into the distance.

"Why were you removed?" Gabe's voice was gentle and almost seemed to apologize for asking.

"We all were kicked out. All magical beings. It started many years ago. They first told us that only humanoids could live in Cureio. We were given places in the underground levels. They weren't as nice as our houses from before. Lots complained or left, but it didn't bother me; a rock is a rock. Then they forced all of us out a few months ago." Ghost looked directly into Gabe's eyes. "There was a big battle. The humanoids weren't nice. I decided to go far away."

"I am sorry, Ghost." Gabe was sincere and looked over at Tanya, who had found it hard to sit still and was now practicing her sword techniques. Lian was listening but picking his nails with his knife again.

"It's not your fault. There are good people and bad people. Cureio's leader Jalouw* is bad," replied Ghost.

"Do you know much about the leader?" This is what Gabe had wanted to ask before, but he had waited for an opening.

"She took over many years ago. She seemed nice. Then the round piece of metal fell out of the sky. She stopped leaving her tower. We never saw her again. We only knew she was alive because of her mean rules. To not bow down before royalty meant death. To bump into a noble by accident got you in jail. Before I left she enlisted every man into her army. If you didn't go she put your family in jail until you did. She made a big army. I didn't understand this. We had no enemies. Sometimes I still watch the city and am sad."

"Hmmm. What about that piece of metal that fell out of the sky? Was it big?" Gabe was excited but again tried his best to appear somber.

"Oh yes, very big. It came from the sun and was on fire. It flew across the sky and bounced all around the top level of the city. It landed in front of the mages's tower, right across from Jalouw's tower. I was selling gems and saw everything. I ran to where it landed and saw the metal open up."

Ghost shook his head as he spoke again, "They didn't have a chance. The city mages sent fireballs into the hole. We heard horrible screaming. The fireballs kept going in. Jalouw yelled from her tower not to stop. Many mages passed out from using all their mana. When it was over the soldiers dragged four burnt heads out. They put them on poles around the piece of metal."

Tanya had stopped practicing, and Lian had walked over and sat down next to Ghost. They all knew that could easily have been themselves.

"Is the piece of metal still there, Ghost?" Gabe now had much of the information that Dillon had asked for, but he knew that they still needed to get inside the ship and learn all they could. Learning more about Jalouw was not going to be easy.

"Yes, it's still there. Jalouw said it was a warning to anyone that came to destroy her. She has guards and a magical shield around it. If anyone gets too close, they are killed."

"How easy is it to get into the city?" Tanya switched the subject because Ghost looked very sad.

"The city? All cave entrances from below are sealed off. Whistling hounds* roam the passages. The sea ports are only for dropping off goods. You can only enter through the front gate."

"What about scaling the wall?" Lian didn't like the idea of just walking through the front door and being roasted alive.

"The city is surrounded by a moat. The walls are over a hundred feet high."

"What? One hundred feet high? No way! How big is this city?" Lian had done a lot of reading on ancient villages and knew it was hard to support a massive city without rapid transport of produce and supplies.

"Twenty-three stories. There are ten above ground and thirteen below. It's expensive to live at the top and free below ground. The lower levels aren't for the weak." Ghost stopped and looked at them all. "Why are you going there?"

Gabe decided honesty seemed best with Ghost. "We came from the sky just like those that were killed in Cureio. We need to get in there, see the flying piece of metal, and learn about Jalouw."

"Wow, from the sky?" Ghost just stared at them in amazement. He couldn't think of anything to say.

"Well, we should probably be going now, Ghost. Thanks for the help." When Gabe got up to start packing, Ghost finally spoke again.

"Can I go with you? Not into the city but up to it. I can help with going through the caves. I know a way to get real close. It's safer than above ground."

150

"That would be great!" exclaimed Lian as the other two nodded their agreement.

II.

Gabe, Tanya, and Lian benefited greatly from the addition of Ghost. There were a number of new caves and many foul beasts that had found the tunnels and now called them home. Ghost, however, was familiar with almost all the new passages and helped them either avoid or sneak past the inhabitants.

Lian seemed to enjoy Ghost's company the most. The two could often be heard laughing and snorting at each other's bad jokes and warped ideas. Both Tanya and Gabe noticed that Lian's mood had become less dark and more light-hearted with each day that passed, and they had been in the tunnels for many days.

"Hey guys, did you notice that it's slowly been getting warmer in here?" asked Tanya.

"Tanya's right, and it also reeks of sulfur." Gabe slowed his steps as he started to round a bend.

"Yeah, I noticed, but I thought it was just Tanya. Did you ever start using deodorant?" Lian snickered, noticed Ghost's smile even though he had no idea what deodorant was, and then started to laugh.

"Suck on some more mojuila." Tanya kept walking without looking at Lian, but knew she had hit a nerve.

"Oh no." That was all Gabe said when he finished turning the corner. He was now standing on a brightly lit ledge about ten feet wide. Gabe shielded his eyes and stared downward as sweat beaded off his chin. Roughly two hundred feet below him was a river of molten lava. Gabe looked to the other side, nearly eighty feet away, where another ledge provided an entrance to the continuation of their tunnel.

"How are we going to get across?" Lian stepped back from the ledge and checked out the walls to see if he could shimmy over to the other side.

Tanya stepped closer to the ledge as she spoke. "If we can just get one of us across, then we can use a rope to have the others climb over. What about having Ghost go around to the other side and we throw a line to him?" She reached into a pouch on her belt and pulled out a very thin rope provided by the Mulshins. Although it only weighed a few ounces, it was a hundred feet long and could easily hold their combined weight.

"No problem." Ghost started to walk into the stone wall of the tunnel.

"Wait." Lian's word wasn't very strong. He was lost in thought as he looked at the cavern walls. "Guys, look at all the pits in the walls."

"Yeah, I see them, Lian, but it makes no sense for you to risk losing your life scaling across when Ghost can easily go through the rock to the other side and help." Gabe wondered if Lian didn't trust Ghost to hold the line.

"I'm not sure any of us want to go across. Take a look at some of those larger pits." Lian pointed to a couple that were about ten inches in diameter. "You see how the edges around the rock have been melted? It's like whatever caused the holes was also very hot."

"Something like a lava rock being throw up here from below?" Tanya took a step back. She felt a slight sense of foreboding that she had missed earlier.

"Exactly." Lian turned around to face Ghost, whose head and neck were sticking out of the rock at chest height. "Ghost, can I have a small rock please?"

"Sure." One of Ghost's long hands extended out of the wall holding a rock the size of a tennis ball.

"Well, let's see if I'm right." Lian stepped near the edge of the ledge, aimed, and threw the rock to the other side. They heard a series of thuds as it landed on the other side. "Hmmm. False alarm I guess."

"Something still doesn't seem right." Tanya was concentrating and could sense the mana strings coming from below. She'd felt her sense for danger perked up just a little when Lian launched the rock across the gap.

"Ghost, can you make a rock about twenty pounds?" Ghost nodded as Tanya reached into her traveling pack and pulled out her sleeping bag. He laid the rock on the sleeping bag, and Tanya wrapped it around the center of the rock to try and make it look like a person with a cape.

"Can you gently throw it to the other side?" Tanya hoped she was wrong and that she wouldn't be without her sleeping bag for too long.

Gabe and Lian were staring at each other, both impressed by how Tanya was not only stepping up, but using her brain.

"That's easy." Ghost picked up the rock and walked out onto the ledge. He hefted it into his right hand and, without much effort, lobbed it into the air.

Tanya's body tensed as darkness swept over her. "Fall back!" She screamed at the top of her lungs. Gabe and Lian knew to listen and had already started peddling backward as a slew of fiery missiles flew up toward the flying rock. At least three hit their target. The others slammed into the sides of the cavern walls, spraying molten lava in every direction. All of them yelped in pain as small lava streaks hit their hands and faces, while others fell harmlessly off their protective clothing.

"Wow! That would not have been fun." Gabe was crouched down and grimacing as he poured water on the burnt skin of his left hand. Tanya was holding her hand up to her neck, and Lian was clasping a cloth to his cheek bone. Ghost had also come back. He seemed uninjured.

"Is everyone ok?" Gabe asked.

"Hurt, but much better than being burnt toast. What's down there?" Tanya dressed the wound on her neck as she talked. Lian was on his stomach and had scooted to the edge of the ledge. He was looking directly into the lava.

"That's not just lava down there." Lian's voice rose in excitement. "Wow, I actually see fire elementals* swimming in the lava. And by the looks of it, there are lots of them." Lian looked back with a smile on his bleeding face. He had again identified a new class of creatures. He scooted back to the group and sat down next to Ghost's head and shoulders, as the rest of his body was in the stone.

"Great, now how to we get across?" Tanya spoke as she finished dressing her wound and started on Lian's.

Ghost piped up. "I could dig a tunnel, but this is very hard rock. It would take many days."

"Fall back!" Tanya barked. She rolled away from the ledge with speed. Gabe and Lian followed suit just as a fist-sized lava rock landed where they had been.

Lian stared back at the chunk of cooling lava. "We don't have time to wait for a tunnel," he said. "There is no possible way they could have thrown at that angle unless they were climbing up toward us."

Gabe was reaching into his pack that Lian had retrieved from the ship. "Got it!"

"Got what?" Tanya asked as she drew both her swords and faced the cavern entrance.

Gabe put a metallic band around his wrist. "A projectile resistor." He closed his eyes and drew deep, controlled breaths into the pit of his stomach, feeling the energy quickly build inside him. After a few cycles of inhaling and exhaling, the golden mana ball churning in his stomach was large enough to use. Gabe inhaled one more time and followed it with a long exhale that focused the energy down his arm. To his pleasant surprise the wristband lit up.

"Wow!" Lian was amazed that Gabe could make it work. "But what happens when they're close enough and don't need to throw things at us?"

"Not what I was worried about. We are going to use it to stop our momentum when Ghost throws us across to the other side." He touched the metallic screen to get the proper dimensions. "And done!" Gabe pushed one last button and watched as a six foot by three foot shield of translucent yellow light appeared in front of him. He continued to control his breathing to ensure that the wristband would keep working.

The projectile resistor wristband worked by densifying the molecules in the air to stop flying or falling objects. It would also slow down a running opponent. The versatile shield could be set up to be as thin and hard as a metal plate or soft and thick like a pillow. The denser the air, the harder it was for things to get through. Gabe had programmed it to be soft, hoping that it would work on both sides of the shield.

"Incoming!" Tanya's voice was a warning siren. Gabe turned toward the ledge with his wristband facing the same direction. A fiery arm appeared from below the ledge and flung a dripping lava rock at them. Gabe closed his eyes as the molten rock slammed into the yellow resistor shield. The heat hit his face as he opened his eyes and saw the solidifying rock at his feet.

"How are we supposed to fight that?" Lian cried as the tall, fiery apparition climbed onto the ledge. The tall creature looked completely unnatural, as if a bonfire had grown legs and arms. It grinned as flames flickered out of its sharp mouth.

A basketball-sized boulder whizzed by Gabe, striking the fire elemental in the chest and launching it off the ledge and back down into the lava pit.

"Like that." Ghost smiled at Lian and started to mold another rock.

"Our time is almost up. Ghost, I need you to throw me to the other side at the rock face right above the tunnel entrance. It has to be hard and fast so the elementals don't have time to throw more lava rocks. Can you..." He didn't have time to finish his sentence as Ghost grabbed him by the waist and launched him like a rocket straight to the other side.

Gabe barely had a second to straighten his body out and face the wristband toward the wall as he struck it. His body hit the yellow shield fast. Gabe felt as if he had landed against a big air mattress. He fell down to the ledge, tucked, rolled twice, and spun around to face his friends who were still on the other side. To his horror he saw that dozens of the elementals were scaling the wall and had almost reached the ledge.

"Hurry!" Gabe screamed. He then remembered that he didn't tell Ghost to throw the others at him instead of the wall above. He only hoped that Ghost was smarter than he thought.

Sensing the urgency in Gabe's voice, Ghost grabbed Tanya and Lian and awkwardly threw them both at the same time. They flew across the cavern end-over-end, straight toward Gabe. They hit the shield at the same time and fell to the tunnel floor with Tanya landing on top of Lian.

Ghost looked at the fire elementals now on the ledge. "Sorry I can't rock your world," he laughed while sinking rapidly into the wall amid an onslaught of lava rocks.

Without an adversary, some of the fire elementals had turned around and were now climbing toward the newly reformed group. They gained on the friends at an amazing speed, moving at the pace of a fast walk. Gabe estimated that in less than ten seconds they would be on their ledge. Meanwhile, the ones on the other ledge had turned around and were preparing to launch new missiles at the group.

"There's no harm in running, I always say. Do you think we can outrun them?" Lian pushed Tanya off him. "Ugh! Man you're heavy!" He stood up behind Gabe just as the first round of lava rocks hit the translucent shield. The shield sputtered and disappeared.

"Sorry guys, I am zapped. I guess it is time to test our legs." Gabe was exhausted but knew it was time to retreat at full speed.

They charged down the tunnel and had only traveled about fifty feet when they heard a rumble behind them. Trembling vibrations followed and coursed up their legs. They heard rocks falling, but none dared to look back—hoping instead that they could outrun whatever was coming after them.

In a matter of seconds the ground was pitching and rolling so much that they lost their footing and fell as the tunnel behind them collapsed. By now their martial arts training was so instinctual that they each immediately tucked and rolled back to a kneeling position.

"What was that?" Tanya exclaimed as she stood back up, unharmed. She drew her swords just in case the elementals figured out a way around or through the collapsed tunnel.

"I don't know, but I'm sure glad I'm not claustrophobic. Collapsing tunnels is the last thing any of us want to dwell on." Lian's voice was a little edgy and completely lacked sarcasm.

They stood in blackness for a short while until Gabe found what he needed in his backpack and lit a torch. He simply didn't have any mana or mental strength left to use his vibe sword.

"Creating tunnels is hard work; destroying them is easy." Ghost's head appeared from above, and Lian laughed loudly in relief.

"True friends are found in times of crisis," Gabe said. "Thank you, Ghost. Now we should start moving just in case they figure out another way to get to us." Gabe started down the tunnel with the others following.

He smiled at the recollection of his initial mistrust of the giant; he had been prepared to use his vibe sword at the first sign of aggression.

When it came down to it, they had trusted Ghost to save their lives, and he did.

III.

Cahlar sat back in his throne, still seething from the missed opportunity to thwart the Mulshins' latest attempt to overthrow him. He slammed his fists into the metal throne. All within earshot heard the ringing and the groan of the metal yielding under the impact. How could they think these Earth children could beat him? Time and time again they were all quickly killed, and yet more always appeared, and more would continue to die.

Cahlar's skittish eyes darted past his advisors, servants and the guards standing in the room as he contemplated the situation. He now knew where his enemy was and that they must travel to Cureio if they hoped to leave Kalansi and come after the devices he possessed. Of course, his surprise in Cureio would not only stop them but be the initiation of his plan to be the first ruler of two planets.

But he wasn't going to wait for them to fall into his snare. Being passive with enemies was a quick way to die. He needed to lay out a plan to capture them before they could fully use their powers. It would not be easy with them on another continent where long distance communication was done by gunpowder-fueled rockets and mindless birds.

Cahlar stood up and walked out of the room and into his library. He'd stared at the map[#] of Kalansi etched into the wall as soon as he heard of his new visitors. Now that they'd passed The Fallen One, there was a high probability that they would either take the direct path to Cureio or try to get to the ocean and board a sailing vessel headed to the city. He needed to get to them fast.

In all but the most dire circumstances, he needed at least a month to mobilize his search and destroy parties. But then again, this was a dire time.

"General Trailerton*?" Cahlar kept his eyes on the map as a figure stepped out of the shadows from a far corner of the room.

"Yes, my lord?" The voice had a deep-throttled, yet hollow-whisper to it that seemed unworldly.

"While I admit I don't understood nor completely believe your ability, I do need your services. You and your riders must set off to Kalansi. I require you to find the otherworlders, then notify all that have my allegiance of their location, and pass along my orders to destroy them. Also, you must ensure Cureio is at the highest of alerts. Only then will you attack."

"My lord, once we find them it will be oh-so-easy to destroy their souls and leave their unmoving bodies for the ground crawlers to consume."

"No!" Cahlar screamed and whipped around so fast that the general only saw him once he stopped. "It will be my way or…" Cahlar held up the ring on his finger and tapped the white stone within it, "…I'll crush this rock and you and your astral riders with it."

"Yes, my lord. We will leave immediately." The general's body faded into transparency until all that was left was a wisp of silvery-black smoke.

Cahlar looked down and gently rubbed the metal device tucked within his chest. He smiled as he realized it was time to recharge its power source.

IV.

On the ninth day of travel, Gabe, Tanya, Lian, and Ghost woke up and spent almost half the day walking along a straight, gradually ascending tunnel. Lian and Ghost positioned themselves in the middle of the group and were again laughing at each other's bad jokes when Gabe stopped and held up his hand for them to be quiet.

"What's wrong?" Lian whispered as he slowly stepped sideways and pressed up against the wall. He carefully pulled out a knife and strained to see in front of Gabe. Tanya was behind them and, as she didn't sense any threat, did not draw her weapons. However, she headed Gabe's signal. She knew that she was still learning to detect danger and was well aware that this planet was one giant death trap. They had to act as a team and trust each other's strengths.

"It seems that our tunnel has been blocked." Gabe spoke in a low whisper as he reached out and started to feel the area in front of him. "This is strange. It *looks* like a big boulder in our path, but it is more like paper mâché that someone has painted." Gabe grabbed a little of the fake rock and crumbled it in his hand. He dug his index finger farther into the material, quickly penetrating to the other side. He decided it was best not to focus his energy flow into the vibe sword, which left them in darkness. When he pulled his finger out of the hole, a weak light emanated through from the other side.

Gabe crouched down to look through the small opening. On the other side was a round cavern about forty feet in diameter. The ground he stood on was six or so feet higher than the cavern floor, where there was another exit at his two o'clock. On the other side of the cave was a metal cage that imprisoned a beautiful, semi-naked young woman covering up part of her body with a torn robe. She sat inside, her face puffy from crying and her legs and arms punctuated by bruises.

"So how much you think they'll give us for her?" A crackling voice spoke freely to Gabe's left, just out of sight. Gabe used his finger to quietly dig a wider hole before peering back in. The speaker, a light-skinned man, was dressed in chain-link body armor and had a long sword at his side. He had a scraggly beard but otherwise lacked any real sign of being a battle-hardened warrior.

"Her kin will need to pay us in jewels. I'm sure they have plenty acquired from eager journeyman who had been away from civilization a little too long." The new speaker was a stout, robed man with many scars on his hands and face. He walked with the aid of a crude, wooden staff.

"Not only didn't we have to pay, but we also will *get paid* for our fun." Another fighter-type commented as he and two others sat at a table and laughed.

Gabe turned back and whispered to them, "There are four men in the cave. A tough-looking leader, a mage-type, and two grunts. They are holding a woman hostage. She's been beaten and, well…she looks pretty demoralized."

Fire raged within Tanya's belly. She knew what Gabe had wanted to say and found it hard to calm herself down. "We must free her no matter why she's been captured." Tanya was shaking and then noticed she had goose bumps on the back of her neck. She disregarded the discussion that Lian and Gabe started to have and tried to sense what was making her skin constrict.

Suddenly she knew that someone was behind her. They were aiming a weapon right at the back of her neck.

V.

Slask* had been quietly perched in the tunnel above the intruders for a few minutes. He was a skilled assassin who could remain still for hours without any physical or mental drain. He and the others had known there would be at least one recovery attempt from the wood nymph* clan before negotiations would begin. They hadn't expected it to come from the tunnels, but he had seen the finger dig a small hole in the mud that sealed their emergency exit. After signaling the others, he scaled the wall out of sight and climbed into a tunnel above them. He'd waited at a small hole connecting the two tunnels, right behind his prey.

Carefully and with muscle-straining smoothness, Slask had lowered his head, upper body, and arms down through the hole. He always covered one eye with a patch so he wouldn't have to worry about night blindness, and after removing it he could easily see the three figures crouched near the mud wall. The one peering through the hole looked like a fighter, and pressed up against the side of the curved tunnel was a novice shadow walker. Slask's eyes then trained in on the intimidating, tall warrior closest to him. She not only looked ready to fight but gave off an aura of power and extreme confidence. She would be his first victim.

Still hanging upside down, Slask braced his right arm against the edge of the hole and used his left arm to quietly draw a small pipe from his inside shirt pocket. The veins on his neck stood proudly out from the sheer strain of his position. Slask couldn't help but let a smile trace over his lips as he prepared the blowtube. She wouldn't even know what hit her. She would be unconscious in seconds, and dead in a matter of minutes. The other two would be easy pickings for the rest of their crew.

The blowtube was pursed between Slask's lips and aimed right at the exposed back of her neck. Slask relaxed, waiting for his opportunity. Time was not important; perfection was.

With a simple puff of air the feather-shafted needle sped through the air and hit its victim. She flinched, then placed her hand on the wall and slumped down to the ground. Her bow and quill of arrows fell gently in front of her. Slask pulled himself back into the hole, expecting some sort of commotion. He was surprised to only hear the remaining two continue to talk about an assault plan.

The fools. They must have been really cheap mercenaries. The wood nymphs clearly had placed little value on the trapped young female. He changed his mind and decided he might as well take out another one. Slask prepared his blowgun again and lowered his head through the hole. He gasped inward, almost sucking the needle into his own mouth, as he found himself staring into the eyes of the supposedly fallen female warrior. Her bow's string had already snapped back from her hand as she laid on the ground.

Not so inexperienced, was Slask's last thought as the arrow pierced the bulging artery in his neck. His body fell to the floor, and his small sword rung out against a displaced rock.

"Good shot, Tanya. Let's go!" Gabe screamed as he thrust his entire body through the seal. The dried mud and cloth shattered like a window. Gabe intended for his yell to shock his opponents and give his team time enough to take the advantage. He tucked his body for the landing and rolled right toward the wizard.

Tanya burst through the hole with a higher scream, launching herself in the direction of the grizzled warrior. She landed on her feet, absorbing the full impact of the fall with her legs. She took only one step before her whole body stopped. Tanya couldn't see Gabe, but she hoped he wasn't frozen like her.

"Ah, is this the best they could send? A few young and extremely stupid kids trying to make a name for themselves."

Tanya cringed as she felt one of the kidnappers grab and spin her toward the voice. It was the voice of the mage, who was talking to Gabe but now turned his attention to Tanya. He walked toward her with hunger in his eyes.

"I admit it is pretty nice for them to send another woman as I have grown tired of the nymph. You will be a nice distraction as we wait for the ransom to arrive." The mage stepped up to her and was within striking distance when he staggered. Just then Lian appeared on his back with a knife slashing toward the mage's throat—for a sure fatal blow.

Lian's knife stopped no more than an inch from the mage's throat. Suspended on the mage's back, Lian looked perplexed. The mage tucked and spun, and Lian was unceremoniously thrown to the ground.

Tanya saw the warrior step forward, and upon closer inspection he didn't appear to fit into his armor. In fact, it was now clear that the warrior was the one voicing out the incantations that froze them. "Very impressive, my children, but not good enough. You may have killed one of my bandits, but you assumed that our clothes gave away what we did." The fake warrior pulled out a knife and walked toward Gabe. "A true illusion indeed, ending with a well-written tragedy. Death is soon to be your—ahhh!"

Tanya heard the low whistling and barely saw the basketball-sized rock hit the real mage in the head. The force of the blow was so strong that his body did a complete flip in the air before thudding to the ground. The rock kept traveling and bounced off an ornate hanging on the cave wall. Tanya felt her muscle control come back as she watched all the decorations in the room disappear. The chains and cage trapping the young woman vaporized.

The two lesser bandits rushed out of the cave upon seeing their leader so easily disposed.

"Just as I thought! He was an illusionist." Lian had jumped back up to his feet and was looking at the two thugs running out of the cave. "This world is amazing!"

Tanya glared at the fake-mage in front of her, clad in flowing robes. He had drawn his sword and the lust in his eyes had been replaced with a crazy, thirsting glare.

"He's mine!" Tanya's procured her two swords so fast they appeared to fly into her hands. Anger boiled within her, but she didn't let it cloud her vision. She controlled herself—and waited.

"Young wench. Even if they kills me after, I'll make sure your blood forever stains the floor of this cave." The warrior lunged forward before he finished his sentence. Tanya diverted his sword to the side with ease and stepped a few feet away. He flew by her but not carelessly, as he kept himself protected. It was clear that the old warrior had a wealth of experience and trickery.

While he was impressed with her first defense, he knew he would soon run his sword through Tanya. He screamed and swung at her, expecting her to block the sword so he could kick her in the midsection and topple her over the chair right behind her. He felt her block and—pleased that the female warrior had fallen for the trap—lifted his leg up and kicked. Pain seared through his leather-clad foot as it slid through Tanya's other sword.

Tanya saw the amazement in her enemy's eyes when her sword impaled his foot. As he pulled back she knew it wouldn't be the end. He was simply too tough. Limping, he came at her again with both hands on his sword. He faked a lunge to her left side, and Tanya stepped back. He followed the gesture with a small sweep of his sword to her opposite arm, using his good leg for power. She dropped her sword low and hit his handle flush. He screamed as all the fingers on his left hand were sliced off right below the knuckle, falling to the floor.

"Come on! You have one good hand left. Fight like a man, you bastard!" Tears streamed down her cheeks as she yelled. She had held back long enough.

Her attacker was awestruck. He never imagined he would be dismantled so easily by such a youngster. Let alone a woman. He almost admired her—almost. He had one trick left.

With a loud grunt he struck downward onto Tanya's head, knowing she would need both swords to block such a powerful attack. As the sword descended, the thumb of his fingerless hand pressed a small knob on the butt of the handle. The long blade sprung off and left a tiny knife blade. The grizzled warrior smiled; Tanya was in the wrong position to block this blade. His arm swung down to her chest and lunged forward, but only a bloody stump pushed against her. The agony hit at the same time his knife-hand dropped to the floor behind Tanya.

Tanya heard the scream and stepped back to watch her victim whimper in pain as he slumped down onto one knee. She had sensed the onslaught and set up her two swords into a V-block* closer than usual to her attacker. His wrist hit the V with precision, severing it cleanly. She had broken him; there was little left to do.

Tanya stepped forward and placed his neck between the V of her swords. "I don't know just how much pain you've caused others in your lifetime, but I do know that at least one will be avenged." Her tears still flowed as she looked down at him, seeing blood starting to bead under both swords.

"No, you are not worth such an honorable death." She looked up at the nymph behind him as she pulled the swords away. She did not see the warrior-thief's smile, nor the way it stopped dead as her sword plunged into his stomach and sliced sideways then down. Without looking at him she pulled the sword out and walked toward the young lady. Gabe had turned away, but Lian watched the man fall sideways, writhing as his insides streamed out onto the earthen floor.

Tanya knelt by the woman, expecting to comfort her. But when she looked in the nymph's eyes, she saw a passionate wisdom far beyond the apparent age of her flesh. Tanya melted into her arms and sobbed. The woman's embrace was soothing, and she whispered to Tanya in a melodic voice. "Don't feel sad for me, my child. My beauty is a gift and a curse. But no matter what happens to my body, my spirit will never surrender."

She held Tanya for a few more minutes as Gabe, Lian, and Ghost talked.

"So how did you know that he was a fake mage?" Gabe wanted to take his mind off the death lying about his feet.

"Uhm, I didn't. When I saw Tanya barely deflect that needle by twitching to make it bounce off her sword, I knew these guys were good." Lian gave one of his casual smiles. "Sorry to disappoint you, but I wasn't going to rush into battle. Instead I climbed up into the hole and scurried to the other entrance.

"When I got there I saw the supposed mage guy doing all the talking while the fighter guy was straining real hard just standing there. I didn't know what to think, so I told Ghost to be prepared in case I went after the wrong guy. I decided to attack the one getting too fresh with Tanya."

"Yeah," Ghost smiled, "and when I saw him freeze Lian, I knew there were two mages so I helped." Nobody had the heart to tell Ghost that there was only one mage.

"I didn't know if Ghost would do it, so I was working on the freeze spell we were under. It was a mental illusion, a trick on our brains. If you asked your arm to move, it wouldn't; if you told your legs to run, they wouldn't. Our brains were sending the wrong signals. The key was to ask the opposite. You tell your legs to stop and you could move them. I had just figured it out when Ghost went bowling for bad guys." Lian was smiling but not laughing. He was concerned about Tanya.

"Hey guys, we're about four days from the city," she interrupted. "There's nothing here, so I say we push on. Nallene* agrees with Ghost. She says we should stay in the tunnel. It will lead us right to the city." Tanya's eyes were dry and she looked incredibly calm. Next to her stood the nymph, now clothed in an old robe, holding her hand. In spite of the baggy gown, the three men couldn't help but stare at her lustfully.

"I want to thank you all for what you have done. I have been a prisoner here for a short time, but I know my people miss me. I cannot offer you riches but promise that if you need me or my people, we will be here for you. Only ask the trees for our help." She thanked the men with a kiss on the cheek and then hugged Tanya. Nallene looked into her eyes. "What is your name?"

Tanya hesitated and looked into the woman's deep blue eyes. Her world spun. She found herself as a little child on the dusty and downtrodden Indian reservation where she'd been born, where her Mom and Dad had given her a name that she hadn't remembered until this moment. "It's Taima*, and it means the crash of thunder."

Nallene smiled, wiped a single tear from her own eye, and touched Tanya's face with the same hand. "Where there is rain, thunder will follow." She smiled one last time before she turned and left the cavern.

Tanya looked around the room, seeing the two dead bodies and blood on the floor. She felt no remorse for what she had done. She wasn't sadistic, yet she now yearned to be the warrior that brought the thunder. She knew that her fate was to be played out on the battlefield.

"Let's go. And from now on, call me Taima," she barked out as she made her way to the tunnel entrance on the other side of the cavern.

Lian glanced over at Gabe, but even he knew this was no time to joke. They both looked once more in the direction of where the wood nymph had disappeared before rushing to catch up with Taima and Ghost.

VI.

Each one of the team, except Ghost, spent the waking hours of their walk through the dark and cramped tunnels reflecting on their recent battle. Here the rules of society were dictated by the local powerhouse and run by the most aggressive and evil beings.

"I wonder if there will ever be a time on this planet when good is the norm," Gabe spoke aloud but intended the words for his own reflection.

"Yes, fairly soon." The confidence in Taima's voice surprised Gabe and Lian.

"Yeah, when and how?" responded Gabe.

"First you should ask *who* will make this world full of good. That's us. Then you can ask how. That is for us to figure out. Everything we have done has been a reaction. If we keep it up, we will make a mistake. Then it will be over. So we need to start planning many steps ahead. We need to start imposing our will on our enemies."

"Holy crap! That was insightful. Guess my chess lessons are paying off. Much to my shock."

Gabe half-expected Taima to lash out at Lian.

Taima's smile was true. "Well, since I've been here I've grown. How about you, Lian?"

Lian diverted the jab with comedy. "Nope. Still the same height I started at. I have to admit you do look more and more like an Amazon woman, though."

Gabe stopped walking. "Okay, okay, you two. Can we step back to what Tany—uhm I mean...Taima said? How do we plan? I believe in us, in our abilities. I even believe we can take on the Mulshins that have brought dictatorship and oppression as their homecoming presents. But we have journeyed nearly halfway through the underbelly of this continent and have seen evil stacked ten-fold upon good. That wretchedness has thrived for thousands of years and will still infest Igypkt's soul when we are back home nestled in the warmth of our own society. How can five aliens change the very fabric of a nation, a continent, or a world?"

Gabe's speech moved them all.

"I don't know yet," Taima answered. "But we have to figure out how. We have to do it. They need us." Her plea was strong, but Gabe's doubt still wrapped around the others.

"Wow, you say things good, Gabe." Ghost didn't even hear Taima's response.

"No kidding. That was impressive." Lian wondered if he could use his own words to twist anything to his benefit.

"Yeah, impressively pathetic," Taima scoffed. She turned back around and trudged forward again. The others quietly followed.

Walking for many hours eased the tension. They had all become so accustomed to the cramped, dim tunnels over the course of almost two weeks that none noticed the changes around them. Suddenly Taima skidded as if on ice, then caught herself.

"Watch out," Taima's voice broke the epic silence. "The ceiling is dripping and the floor has some slippery plant on it."

"Wait." Lian stooped down to the ground. "This is lichen*, and it needs sunlight to survive. We must be close to the exit!" Lian's voice rose to a near scream at the thought of fresh air.

They quickened their pace until the passage narrowed to less than two feet high, preventing further travel. The tunnel became even smaller, leading right up to a hole the size of a fist—where natural light was

entering. It appeared that the tunnel had collapsed long ago and some small creature had burrowed its way to the surface. The group couldn't contain their excitement.

"Thank goodness we have Ghost with us. Ghost, can you widen this?" Gabe didn't even want to think what could have happened if they couldn't get through on their own. He didn't think the mini-bombs that Arlar gave Lian were powerful enough to blow through so many feet of rock.

"Yes." Ghost walked into the rock and began his excavation work. Within an hour the hole had become wide enough for them to crawl out.

Gabe was the first one to squeeze to the surface, not waiting for Ghost to move away from the entrance. Taima breathed deeply as she crawled out, relying on her feel to ensure no attack was coming. Lian was the last one, snaking his way out with extreme caution.

"Ouch. I hope no one attacks us, because it is so bright that my eyes want to stay shut!" Gabe covered his eyes. Lian and Taima were forced to do the same.

It took many minutes for them to be able to see anything at all. When they did, they saw that they were standing underneath an ample tree, halfway down a hill and facing a mostly-obscured city. Not far to the left was a well-travelled road where a few wagons and travelers passed. Fortunately, the friends were hidden behind the tree.

"Is that really it over there?" Lian pointed through the foliage.

"I think so, but it is really hard to see." Based on what Gabe had learned from Ghost, he knew it would be awe-inspiring.

"Yes, it's the city." Ghost's head was sticking up from the ground, just as when they first met him.

Lian turned around with a sad smile on his face. "This is as far as you go, my friend?"

"Yes. They will kill me if I get closer. I'm sorry." Ghost's expression mirrored Lian's.

"No reason to be sorry. Without you we couldn't have gotten here." Lian tried to cheer up his friend, despite his own sadness.

"Thanks for trusting us when we did not trust you. I assure you that if you ever need help, we will rush to your side."

Taima nodded her agreement to Gabe's words and bowed down.

Ghost merely nodded before sinking back into the earth.

Chapter 10
Appendages

I.

Dillon and Matt had scarcely sifted through the desert for a half day, yet the searing climate was already causing them to discuss turning around. When they started, Dillon had wanted to travel thirty miles a day. He figured they could easily cross the shortest distance through the desert in under five days, since dehydration would not be an issue. However, he had failed to account for the large hills covered with a fine dust that made them wonder if quicksand would be easier to traverse.

At the top of the next hill Matt looked ahead and, as he expected, only saw miles and miles of rolling desert. He looked behind himself, saw the downward slopes of the mountain range from where they had started, and let out a sigh.

"Sorry to be a pain, Dillon, but I could really use more water." Matt may have been in great shape, but this wasteland sapped all of his energy.

"Sure thing. Are you okay?" Dillon opened an empty water bladder and buried it halfway in the sand. He then took out his sword and held the point over the top.

"Not really. Since I've been on this planet I've been able to draw upon the energy of the living things around me. That's why I haven't tired. But there's nothing to help me here…nothing. This place is absent of all life."

"Do you wonder how Gabe, Tanya, and Lian are doing?" Dillon stopped his preparations and scanned the horizon to the west.

"Yeah, every minute that I'm not thinking about water, heat, and if we are going to survive."

Dillon ignored the complaint. "I left them on their own to infiltrate a foreign city that we know nothing about by traveling through dangerous tunnels where they may not...." Dillon's voice trailed off into a thought that Matt could complete on his own.

"You may be our leader, but we all chose to come here knowing we could die. End of discussion as far as I'm concerned." Matt smiled as he continued. "But one thing I don't understand. Why did you tell them they couldn't come along with you because it was too dangerous, and then you bring me? Am I expendable?"

"Pretty much. You're our weakest link. You can't even fight without getting sick. I figured if I could afford to lose anyone it would be you." Dillon let a strong smile crack across his face as Matt laughed. "Honestly though, I was too afraid to do it on my own. I'm still a teenager no matter what people think my future holds." Dillon still didn't tell Matt the whole truth.

Dillon closed his eyes and steadied his breathing. Drawing the mana to him was now easy and fast. He gathered it to below his belly until he had enough. He directed the ball of energy down his left arm to his hand holding the sword and poured it into the chemical equation he knew so well. After less than a minute he had filled the bladder with refreshing, cool water. Something tickled the hairs on his neck.

"What's wrong?" Matt asked as he took a swig of the water.

"Something wasn't quite right when I created the water, but I don't know what."

Matt stopped and looked behind him. "Did you notice that we aren't walking in a straight line?"

Dillon looked back again and confirmed Matt's words. Suddenly it hit him, "That's what was bugging me. When I drew the mana in, a lot more came from the northeast than from anywhere else. I imagine that when we were walking we were drawn toward that, whatever it is."

"And you want to go right toward it, don't you?" asked Matt.

"Of course. I think we may have found a natural area for mana concentration." Dillon smiled, cleared his mind as he stood up, and let emptiness lead his footsteps.

II.

After six more days of following Dillon in his relentless pursuit of the energy source, Matt was almost to the point of pure exhaustion. Not to say that Matt couldn't feel the mana, but he definitely wasn't driven to it.

Nothing. Nothing but hills and hills of sand with the burning sun slowly sucking the life out of me. I feel no life around me nor even death. Well, soon enough I will feel my own if we have to walk one more mile in this blazing heat. Matt's thoughts had been one after another of withheld complaints coupled with a fear that he may not be able to make it out of the desert alive. He now looked only forty feet in front of him, keeping his focus on Dillon. *How is he doing it? We've both had nothing but water and small bits of dried food. But he's marching as if he doesn't even notice the searing heat or the sand that has chaffed every part of my body.*

"Dillon, stop. Please stop. How much farther do we have? I'm sorry, but I just need a long break." Matt dropped to his knees, using his staff to keep his body from falling forward.

Dillon turned around and looked down at Matt. "I think just another day and we should be to the city."

Man, he looks more like a 30-year old man than 18. The things he's been through in such a short time and the weight on his shoulders have really changed him. And here I am being selfish and complaining about a little walk. Heck, at least I'm not unconscious as usual.

"Sorry, Dillon. Just give me a minute and I'll be ready."

Dillon smiled and chuckled as he spoke, "Matt, can't you feel it?"

"Oh wait. I feel something. It's coming to me. Yeah, Here it comes. It's the...it's the...it's the heat!" Matt grimaced as he realized he was a little too sarcastic.

"No. We are standing on top of the mana source." Dillon spread his arms and raised his head to the sky as he took in an incredibly deep breath.

Hmmm. Yeah I can feel it, but it doesn't seem to be some overwhelming energy that completely fills me up.

Holy cow!

"Uh, Dillon, any particular reason why you are glowing?"

Dillon barely heard Matt as he reveled in and played with the power emanating from beneath his feet. He pulled in the mana from below, rolled it around in his belly and let it stream out of his crown chakra. There was more than even he could gather. He finally looked over at Matt, whose jaw was wide open.

"It's amazing, but we're not quite at the source. In fact, I think we're standing on a really big hill and it's somewhere below us."

Matt stepped closer to Dillon and turned slowly in a complete circle. He could see that they were maybe a few hundred feet higher than their surroundings, but that the hill sloped slowly over a couple miles so it would have been hard to notice until they were near the top. The dry, hot wind, which had been blowing on him for days, picked up and shot more sand into his eyes.

Matt didn't wipe them; in fact he faced the direction of the wind and thought while Dillon continued to soak in the energy from beneath him.

"Dillon. Don't you find it strange that this whole time the wind has been blowing from the northwest and yet it's a dry heat?"

"What do you mean?" Dillon slowly replied without opening his eyes.

"Well, the mountains are to the east and normally what creates a desert is the wind blowing from the other side of the mountains. As the air rises to climb over the mountain, it can't hold as much moisture and dumps it. As it comes over the other side it soaks up all the moisture, thus creating the desert. The whole time we've been traveling, the wind has been blowing from the ocean through the desert toward the mountains. This place should be a tropical rainforest, but it's not. It's just not natural."

Matt turned to look at Dillon for a response and almost screamed as two hands shot out of the sand and grabbed Dillon's feet. The hands were long and drawn out with black, piercing nails at the end of its ten-inch fingers. The mottled-gray arms were slightly exposed, revealing fiery veins that protruded from its skin like geysers of lava were about to spring forth.

An unnatural fear raced through Matt's body as he watched the twisted hands wrap tightly around Dillon's legs. Dillon barely had time to look down before he was sucked underneath the sand.

Matt's fear had frozen his legs in place, while his head shot in every direction looking for the impending attack. He sensed no life-force, not even the undead, but somehow he knew it didn't matter. There had to be more of them. Just then powerful hands shot upward and grabbed his own legs. As soon as they touched him, his legs became numb. He started to raise his staff to attack, but it was too late. Darkness engulfed his eyes as sand raced into his nose and mouth.

III.

Cahlar took a deep breath through his nose, smelling the rancid air emanating from behind the door. The moans of pain on the other side only excited him more, but he attempted to control his desire to rip open the door and torture those inside.

Cahlar told his body and mind to calm down and even felt himself regaining his composure until he heard an agonized scream. He was like a child on Christmas day, standing before a large, gift-wrapped present. The scream was his affirmation that he could open his gift. He giggled as he thrust the door aside and charged in, to the horror of those inside.

The dark cavern was a cylinder almost thirty feet long that housed nearly two dozen haggard and bloody humans chained to the walls. The captives tried to shrink back into the shadows, hoping to avoid their tormentor's interest.

Cahlar soaked it all in before turning to the seven-foot-tall, dark, elfin woman completely clothed in red leather.

"How are my pets today?"

"Barely living, as you requested, my lord." The joy in her voice was enough to send shivers down anyone's spine.

Cahlar elongated his smile to cross from ear to ear, showing off sharp, jagged teeth he had just transformed for this event. "Which one should I choose today?" More screams echoed off the walls of the barren room as drool slipped down Cahlar's chin.

Cahlar walked over to a cowering man, wrenching the man's arm out and holding the hand inches from his razor teeth. Cahlar waited for a scream, but the man only looked him in the eyes. Frustrated, Cahlar bit off the man's thumb, exhilarated by the blood spattering against his face. The man moaned, but refused to scream.

"Make sure he is healed enough to have that thumb torn off again. Maybe next time he'll beg for mercy." Cahlar walked out of the room and shut the door. He looked down at his chest, allowing his body to expel the metal case. He gently massaged the front until a small compartment opened up, revealing a blackened toe. Cahlar slowly pulled it out and replaced it with the freshly cut thumb, before resealing the compartment. Even in the short time of the exchange, he could feel his computer-based network start to feed errors into his body. He knew it would take hours to fix the damage caused by the seconds without protection from the mana field.

    The rotted toe rolled to a stop against the door as Cahlar woozily walked up the stone staircase.

Chapter 11
The Sands of Time

I.

Matt kept his eyes tightly closed as he was dragged down through the sand of the desert. The speed of descent made his skin feel like sandpaper was scraping it smooth. Initially he struggled to slow down, but the sharp claws wrapped around his legs were too strong, and Matt decided to save his energy for a later opportunity to escape—at least he hoped there'd be one. The claws would have sliced through his skin if not for the special protective clothing he wore.

Matt tried to occupy his mind with small things in order to avoid the horrifying feeling—now a reality—of being unable to breathe. He sucked in a mouthful of sand and was lucky that the descent only lasted for tens of seconds, even though it felt like forever.

His surroundings turned from sand to air as Matt was thrown onto a smooth, hard, hot surface. He rolled a few times before landing on all fours. Matt coughed out all the wet sand in his mouth as he jumped up into a defensive stance, expecting the creature that pulled him under to attack.

Instead he looked up in time to see it caught in a mini dust devil that sand-blasted the flesh from its body. The creature howled in pain until there was nothing left but a pile of claws and bones, lying only feet away from another similar pile.

From the reddish glow at the far end of the room Matt saw Dillon pointing his finger at the heap , but paying almost no attention to it. Instead he was looking at one of four book stands spaced evenly around a depressed area about nine feet wide in the center of the room. In front of each platform was an arrow carved into the marble floor, pointing toward the center to the carving of a square about a foot long. Dillon's face appeared intensely focused as he traced over something on the stand with his right hand.

"How on Earth did you do that?" Matt saw that Dillon was oozing blood from every part of his exposed skin after their underground travel.

"We're not on Earth." Dillon smiled but still didn't look up. "Actually, the same way you are unconsciously healing yourself from the sand scraping we took on the way down. The mana here is so high that it's like we have an endless amount of power."

Only after Dillon spoke did Matt realize he had completely healed himself. "Okay, but how did you sandblast those creatures?"

"Chemistry 101. I used the mana to superheat the air. Since pressure and volume are directly proportional to temperature, I was able to increase the pressure of the air around the sand to create mini-vortices. I then uniformly directed the heat around the sand, causing it turn in any direction I wanted. I don't think I could have done it normally, but here it's very easy."

Matt looked back over at the two piles on the ground before hearing muffled groans from the far side of the expansive room. The hairs on his neck stood up and he could no longer appreciate the incredible beauty of the pure white marble that made up the room. He couldn't help noticing that halfway down the room was a thick, yellowish, web-like mass cast from one wall to the other. Behind it were reddish shadows writhing and striking at the obstacle.

"Uh, Dillon. What was that noise, what is that stuff, and what's behind it?" Matt almost stammered, but again Dillon's response was robotic.

"I think those things causing the noise are demons. Behind them is a mass of lava causing the red glow. I was able to use the sulfur in the lava to create the rubbery web. Did you know that elemental sulfur typically appears in rings of six or eight? When heated to high temperatures, these rings break up and form longer chains like a polymer. If you rapidly cool them, they form a rubbery material." Dillon smiled again without looking up as he walked to the center square and traced it with his hand. "I pulled the sulfur chains from the lava and splashed it across the middle of the room and used my yin energy to cool it and form the rubbery blockage. Unfortunately, it will slowly convert back to the sulfur rings and become brittle. Hopefully I'll have enough time to figure out what this place is before they break through."

Matt's curiosity overcame his fear and he walked over to Dillon. He touched him on the back to heal his wounds, but was careful not to take in any of his energy. Since the last time he'd done that he'd almost died, in this place he imagined he would explode into millions of tiny pieces.

With one breath and in less than a second Dillon was healed. Matt was now amazed at this mana hot spot.

Matt looked at the ruins on each stand. The Mulshins had taught them to read the common dialect of Igypkt, but it only helped a little. "Something about four books and unity. Also, it says something about fishing or boating."

"Yeah, but look at the lines on the floor in front of each stand. They are different lengths, but when you add them up they equal the diameter of the square. I wonder if it means..."

Dillon's words were stopped short as the ground started to shake and rumble.

II.

Galgalor*, overseer of the Baylan Wastes*, was basking on his throne inside the lava stream when he felt the disturbance. Someone had not only tried to cross his lands, but had dared to challenge him by coming to the desecrated ruins of the Fishing Station. Diabold himself had given him this land, the tasking to keep others out, and his name. This trifecta advanced him to being one of the most powerful lesser demons. He was also responsible for weaving the web of deceit called The Gallen War, which pitted humans against magical creatures. The Fishing Station's power was one of only a few mana sources strong enough to allow his magical lie to spread over the entire planet.

Galgalor's chair rose from the reddish-orange stream with a low rumbling sound. His throne and portly eight-foot frame dripped thick pieces of cooling lava as he stood up and looked across the hundreds of writhing demons stretched across the floor. He noticed the new obstruction thrown across the room and thought it was interesting, but not as much as the human who'd created it. It would be fun to bring the mage to his knees, begging for death from unbearable pain.

As he walked forward, Galgalor's long talons protruding from his four legs tore into those beneath him. Their screams brought him as much pleasure as their retaliation. Countless claws and fangs drove into his legs and midsection, ripping chunks of flesh from his body. He grabbed a long arm that had stabbed into his torso and ripped the limb off. As he lumbered forward, he straightened the arm and picked at the four sharp talons on its front. It was a suitable weapon.

Galgalor stepped up to the yellow obstruction, grabbed it with his free hand, and brushed it aside. Flames dripped from the melting web. He laughed deeply at the two small humans in front on him. Energy emanated from them, but they were just children. Soon to die.

"Oh my god, Dillon! This planet is a deathtrap. What do we do?" Matt was shocked that he hadn't wet his pants.

"Dillon? Yes, what will you do? Might I suggest you both start screaming so when the pain starts you can move right into begging for death? It won't help you, but it will make me very happy." Galgalor's voice was deep and commanding. He had stopped about twenty feet from the pair. It was so much fun to toy with humans, and he knew that his appearance was what scared them the most. His four obese legs wrapped around him like a spider's, seeming to barely keep his massive stomach from crushing them. His torso and arms looked human but his mouth split his face sideways, with multiple oversized fangs protruding and bending back inward to pierce his own skin. The three eyes spaced evenly across the front of his face literally sucked in the horror of his victims.

"What is this *unity* thing, and what was this place for?"

The one named Dillon spoke calmly while the other hid behind him. Galgalor opened his mouth wide but whispered in a guttural tone, "Don't you wish you knew? But you see, this is my domain, and you do not ask the questions. Or are you too arrogant to realize that? Maybe I need to help you." Galgalor jumped forward with lightning speed to within ten feet. He lunged out with his enormous arm that held his newly acquired weapon. The four claws pierced the man called Dillon in the shoulder.

Galgalor expected a reaction or counter attack but only heard a slight grunt. No matter, the poison in the claws would kill him in a few seconds.

However, his face bunched up when he saw the wound healing and the young man just staring at him. "Ah, so you can heal pretty fast. However, I bet you will not be able to recover from me tearing your body apart and feeding it to my minions." His laughter echoed in the large room.

"No thanks. I prefer a skewering," Dillon retorted calmly.

Another low yet short rumbling filled the air followed by mini-explosions going off all around Galgalor's feet. Galgalor barely had enough time to looked down and watch as dozens upon dozens of marble knives penetrated his corpulent body and shot out the other side. He closed his eyes and howled in pain, his voice rising in force with each wound he suffered.

Finally, nearly spent and with all his weight being born by the marble stalagmites that had lifted him a foot off the ground, Galgalor felt no new pain. He opened his eyes and saw the young mage walking slowly toward him. There was no fear in his eyes, and as he neared the demon's suspended body the marble floor buckled and created steps upon which he climbed to come face-to-face with Galgalor.

"What is your purpose here, beside to bring pain and suffering to those on this planet?" The mage's voice was cold but lacked anger.

Galgalor gathered as much strength as he could and used it to form his sideways smile before he spoke, "Pain and suffering is all that is needed. I can still bring you that." Galgalor could hear his hundreds clawing their way toward their master, driving themselves as fast as they could to try and make a meal of the two intruders. Speed above ground was not a gift they possessed.

III.

Dillon stared into the three eyes of the massive demon perched before him. There had to be a reason for its posting, but he knew there was no way he could make it talk. Pain was something it enjoyed, and Dillon didn't have time to think of a trick. Not with the frightening yet slow army of demons headed toward himself and Matt.

"Dillon, how do we get out of here?" Matt had stood up to an early comer in the mass heading their way. It swung at him, but he used his staff to deflect the attack. Without thinking he spun his staff around and struck down on the head of the creature with all his might. The loud cracking sound was quickly interrupted by Matt's scream.

"Yee hah! I can attack demons without getting sick." Matt went to step forward and meet the oncoming assault, but Dillon had jumped off his staircase, grabbed Matt by the shoulder, and pushed him toward the sand-filled hole from where they had entered.

"Dillon, it's blocked, and those demons are getting faster for some reason." Matt was swinging his staff and hitting two to three of them at a time. However, they kept pressing forward on the sandy floor and didn't seem to mind Matt's blows.

"Not for long." Dillon raised his hand, touched the center of the sand, and heated the air—starting inward and expanding it out. His mana poured out quickly, creating a large hole up to the surface with a solid sand staircase for them to climb.

Dillon started to take a step forward but stopped as over the wrasps of the demons he heard Galgalor bellow at them. "I'll see to it that you will feel my pain ten times over!"

Dillon turned and while still holding the sand grains in place he spat in the direction of Galgalor. However, it was not merely a gesture. The spittle split into three parts and with a sound like a gunshot they broke the speed of sound. Each, now a frozen drop, hit their targets. Galgalor screamed as all three of his eyes exploded from the impact.

"Now let's go." Dillon and Matt raced up the stairs inside the sand tunnel. As Dillon controlled the earth, yellow mana flowed into and out of him at a speed he never thought possible.

Halfway up the sand stairs they looked behind them and saw that the very slow demons had started to enter the tunnel. They didn't attempt to climb the stairs, and instead dozens at time were rapidly sucked into the sand.

Now three quarters of the way up, Matt barely dodged a claw that shot out of the wall at his head. Dillon caught another on his boot that came through the stairs.

"Matt, they're incredibly fast in the sand." Dillon had drawn his sword and was dodging and parrying dozens of arms lunging out at him.

"Yeah, I kind of figured that out. What do we do when we get to the top?" Matt's words were choppy as he climbed the stairs while warding off the poisonous claws. "They're still gonna be after us." Unknown to Galgalor, he had already been touching Dillon when the claw had first stabbed him, so Matt had been able to nullify the poison. However, the poison was powerful and a couple more hits would be too much for him to neutralize.

"I have an idea. I sure hope it works. Just follow my lead." Dillon stumbled and nearly fell from a strike to his knee. He took a few more clumsy steps to the top and jumped up high in the air. Matt didn't know why, but did the same and was surprised to land on a flat surface a foot above the sand.

"Hold on to me," ordered Dillon as he dropped his effort on the tunnel and allowed it to collapse while he shaped his sand platform into an oval board. "Surf's up, dude!" Dillon stepped out from the weight of his future, and morphed back into his true age.

The mana field around them was still strong, enabling Dillon to maintain the shape of his board while he superheated the air molecules at different points underneath them. They took off immediately and topped more than twenty miles per hour over the sand dunes. But the demons were just as fast and continued to claw at them from the sand below. Every once in a while a demon would leap completely out of the sand and lunge at them.

"Why don't you go higher?" Matt was barely able to hold on and fight off their assailants at the same time.

"The mana field is getting weaker. If we go higher we may find ourselves dropping out of the air when I lose this extra ability." Sweat poured down Dillon's face as he tried to focus on doing way too many things at once. Controlling the board and the air under it, staying on the board, and fighting the demons was getting harder and harder the farther they retreated.

Suddenly he sensed that some of the demons had gotten ahead of them and were preparing for an ambush. He redirected the board, like cutting across a wave, toward a high hill and pushed their speed up to nearly thirty miles per hour. They hit the top of the hill just as Dillon lost all the extra mana. The board dispersed into a fine sand, leaving Matt and Dillon hurtling through the air. Their yells lasted a few seconds as gravity won out and whisked them onto the down slope. Dillon exhaled as he hit the ground, rolled several times and ended standing on his feet with his sword pointed downward. Matt was successful at rolling, but again landed on all fours before he jumped up with his staff in hand.

Dillon and Matt stared anxiously at the ground, waiting for claws or whole bodies to burst out of the sand. They slowly walked backward for more than five minutes before they let down their guard.

Dillon finally looked at Matt who started performing a really bad moon walk. He laughed and shook his head, which helped erase the aged look on his face that he had acquired all too quickly. "That was the best ride I've ever had. All these years I've had my parents take me to Huntington Beach to surf when I could have just ridden the sand."

"Yeah, but I much prefer water in my shorts than sand." They both laughed and looked around at the endless hills.

"Wow. The effect of having so much mana was so strange. I wasn't afraid of anything and was sure nothing could hurt me. But now that we are out of that place, thinking of that demon scares me to death."

"Hey, Dillon?"

"Yes, Matt?"

"If those were demons down there, then where are the angels?" Matt recalled Dillon's question of The Fallen One pertaining to good and evil.

"We have a long way to go, so let me tell you a story," Dillon smiled at Matt's puzzled look.

As they walked west Dillon went on to explain the glowing being he saw in the astral plane, and the thousands of battles that angel-like creatures had fought to protect him when he was young. He believed that there were angels in that plane, and talking with Matt further solidified this belief. However, as he recounted different battles, he realized he couldn't close the loop on the question.

"I guess what I'm saying is that there are angels, I just don't know if any of them are present on this planet. We haven't seen a single one nor even heard mention of them."

Matt thought for a second. "Well, if what you say is true then there must be angels everywhere, and I'm sure they will appear when things are truly dire."

Dillon believed in angels, but wasn't so inclined to think that they would come. Everything that had already happened on this planet seemed pretty dire.

IV.

Salas* sprawled over a large rock to the west of the city of Cohvan*, staring at the ship setting sail hours after sunset. It was rare for a ship to depart at night, as few could navigate through the treacherous rocks in the cove. He smiled at the knowledge of what precious cargo this vessel carried under the cover of darkness. He knew because the frightening General Trailerton had informed him of his newest targets and their location less than a week ago. A week was not a long to prepare, but it was enough for a well-honed team like his.

Salas's spies, wizards, archers, and warriors had infiltrated the mid-sized fishing town and its surroundings less than a day ago. They quickly spread out and assimilated, so he was sure that none of the locals knew they were all part of the same small army—an army specially created to search out and destroy those that had fallen from the skies onto Kalansi. The most recent visitors were aboard the ship trying to leave. *Trying* was the key word.

Salas slowly looked around the cove. Pride swelled in his chest as he knew where each one of his men was posted. They were ready to attack, but not until he gave the signal. He was a patient man who always analyzed the situation before he acted, and he was waiting for one more piece of information before allowing the onslaught to begin.

After a few short seconds he heard the very quiet efforts of his most trusted advisor scaling the large black rock. Salas turned to see the cloaked humanoid finish climbing and deftly crawl over to him. His slanted eyes glowed in the night, betraying his cat-like being. "Major Salas, Sir. I have seen with my own eyes the two outlanders boarding the ship that is now in the cove. I also stayed to ensure they did not get back off or jump overboard near the docks."

They both knew that no one would be foolish enough to plunge into the waters without being close to shore. The baby serpents swarming the sea were too small to attack a small boat, but still large enough to bite off a limb.

"Excellent, Lieutenant Lynn*. It's time." Major Salas stood up and stared intently at the ship. It was too bad that all aboard would be lost, but none could claim ignorance. All knew that heading out to sea at night meant their cargo was wanted.

He looked at the ship one last time as it neared the center of the cove. He thought it strange that it was now steering east, opposite Cureio, as it would take three times as long to get to Mungoth.

"Major Salas, look! Next to the ship on the port side!" Lieutenant Lynn's night vision easily spotted the small boat and two passengers, while it took Salas a couple of seconds to pick out the bobbing little vessel. Once again Salas basked in how his patience was paying off. If he had acted any sooner he would have destroyed the ship and the outlander would have escaped under the cloak of chaos.

"Lieutenant, signal for groups one and five to follow my lead, groups two and seven to sail out and capture the vessel, and for the rest to hold their positions." Communication without words was one of his army's strongest assets, facilitated by his trusted lieutenant's innate gift.

Lieutenant Lynn stood up and raised his hands to the stars. His incantation sounded more like purring than an invocation of magic, but Salas felt the mana gathering and whirling around the rock. With one last word, a complex pattern of colored lights shot forth and illuminated the entire cove. Salas hefted his spear in his right hand and took aim at the small boat that was now a good hundred feet from the ship and almost a half mile from his vantage point. He took one step forward and hurled the heavy spear into the cove.

Anyone who didn't know him would have laughed at the attempt to throw his spear more than three hundred feet, but shortly after it left his hand the spear erupted into flames and accelerated toward it target with the apparent speed of a streaking meteor. In only a few seconds it struck the little boat, shattering the spear into hundreds of flaming splinters that set the boat on fire. This was followed by no less than twenty flaming arrows striking the two figures on the boat, causing them to fall to the floor. Lastly, Group Five launched twenty small black objects that hit the vessel, causing mini-explosions that shredded it apart. No one watching would have believed the distance the airborne weapons had travelled. Magic was a wonderful thing.

Salas still held his original spear in his hand as he stared out at the now calm waters. The small boat was destroyed, the ship had stopped and raised a white flag, and two of his ships were headed toward it. If the outlanders had been aboard the rowboat and somehow survived, then the young serpents would have already started their relentless attack. If it was a trick and they were still aboard the small ship, they would be found and everyone aboard killed. His chest stuck outward as he thought of the new promotion he would soon accept.

V.

Dillon and Matt dragged their dripping wet bodies out of the water and sat on the sandy beach. They both turned and faced the bay, watching the two young serpents speed away.

"Poor, misunderstood creatures. They're just really hungry all the time and you can't blame them since they have to grow over a hundred feet in a few short years," commented Matt. It had all started one night while he was looking across the harbor. One had come close to shore and Matt could sense that it was only looking for food. Getting the serpents to help them was not as hard as holding on while riding on their backs for what must have been thirty miles. "That was a great plan, Dillon, although a little scary. Who knew that we would be able to survive an attack from one of Cahlar's death armies?"

"Yeah, and without anyone having to perish. However, I'm more concerned about those creatures that gave us away. They seem to live in both the astral and normal planes. I'm sure we have everyone fooled, but they could find us again and probably will." Dillon was reflecting on his encounters with them over the last week. Every night when he "slept" he could see them in the distance. They would follow him, but never seemed to want to do anything else. In fact, when he tried to get close they would back away. He realized that as long as he couldn't avoid them or attack them they would be able to find him again and again. The only option he could think of right now was to keep moving. It definitely wasn't a long-term solution, but it was the best he had.

After about ten minutes, their Mulshin clothes were completely dry and they were ready to start walking.

"So which way should we go?" Matt's words echoed what Dillon was asking himself.

"I haven't a clue. How about we head inland a little bit and find a road. We still have weeks, maybe even a month, until we get to Cureio if we now don't use the coastline." The recent attack had changed Dillon's plans. There was no sense in staying along the coast where two strangers might be tied to the attack at Cohvan.

"Sounds good to me. Although I'd really like to find an In-N-Out and get a nice, fresh hamburger."

"Matt!" Dillon's tone was strong and serious enough to make Matt turn around. "If you're gonna wish for In-N-Out then it has to be a Double-Double. Get it right." They both started laughing as they headed inland, thinking about their favorite So Cal burger joint.

It took a little over an hour to find the coastal road. When they had finally stepped onto the hard-packed path, the sun was starting to rise and they could see that they were right at a fork in the road. The path indeed proceeded in the expected northwest and southeast directions, following the coastline. The other went southwest and appeared to bisect beautiful rolling grasslands and another vast desert.

Dillon tried to justify his guess. "If we take the southwest fork, it might lead us straight to Cureio. Maybe along the way we can figure out what the four books with the *unity* thing means and why fishing or boating is so important. Also, why those four lines added up to make a square. It might help just to ask people on the way."

"I think that may not be such a good idea." The fluidic voice that startled both of them could be traced to a figure gliding toward them from the easterly trail. The voice was feminine, but staring into the rising sun made it hard to tell anything else about the stranger.

"Hello. Might I ask your name, my lady?" Dillon's response shocked Matt. Aside from Arlar, every new being they had met attacked them. Now they were wary of any new visitor. This time, though, Dillon was acting a little too friendly.

"Pardon me?" The carrier of the voice was now out of the direct sunlight and Matt saw a stunningly beautiful woman in simple traveling clothes.

"Sorry. I merely asked your name. Mine is Dillon, and this here is my friend Matt. We are travelers headed to Cureio. Would you care to join us?"

"Excuse me?" The lady seemed shocked but a slight smile was starting to appear on her face.

"What?" Matt was both astounded and confused.

"Yeah, well, we are traveling that way, and you seem alone. I mean walking by yourself, so you could walk with me. Uh, I mean us." Dillon was stepping on his own words but just couldn't stop. There was something about her that made him forget the weight on his shoulders and all the pain he had experienced over the last ten months.

"Thank you for the offer. It's very flattering, but I travel alone." Sileya was amused at the cute boy's offer and his obvious crush. More importantly she needed to know what they knew about the Fishing Station. "Now, I apologize for listening in on your conversation but I also have heard about *The Unity* and four books. I thought it was hearsay. Do you have proof?"

"Well, we don't know much more than what we saw. In fact, we actually didn't see the books but the stands—"

Sileya interrupted. "Impossible. You could not have seen the Fishing Station. No one has been there for hundreds of years." Her demeanor was less composed now.

Dillon felt the energy crackling around the woman and instinctively allowed his own energy-gathering to start. He saw the woman's deep blue eyes widen at what he was doing.

"What manner of demons are you?" Sileya prepared for battle, as she could only believe that was what they were. Very few knew of the Fishing Station, let alone what was inside. The demons had made sure that no one could even come close. This demon's power was immense, and it could very well mean the end of her very long journey in this life.

Dillon's adoration floundered as soon as he saw that a misunderstanding was surely going to beget a fight, and a fight with someone whose power was more than any he had felt. He remembered Arlar's teachings of mage battles but feared this woman might easily win due to his inexperience.

"Wohohoah! Wait a minute." Matt stepped between them before he had time to think of how stupid it was. "First, I assure you we are not demons. Second, we have no reason to lie. Even if we knew who you were, why would we be so open about what we are doing? Wouldn't we want to gain your trust and then attack you when you didn't expect it? So please believe us when I tell you that we went through the desert and were pulled into the sand by demons and dropped into a huge underground room. It was there that we found the four book stands and the ruins we were talking about. Why are you so eager to attack us?"

No one moved as they all tried to asses each other's intent.

VI.

The molten lava in the far corner of the Fishing Station danced like sun spots flaring out as they tried to escape their parent star. A fiery spray shot out and struck many of the sluggish demons sprawled over the floor, with howls of pain flooding the room. Even though they were very slow, they seemed to almost scurry to the sides of the room, hoping to not be the way of what was coming.

Diabold rose from the lava in an even grander entrance than Galgalor's when the intruders had entered. The molten liquid flamed and smoked off his muscular body. Diabold took a step onto the rock floor, letting the lava flow down around his leg, forming archaic symbols on top of some of the slowest moving demons, who screamed in horror. His other foot rose out of the lava and stepped beyond the rock to the marble floor, causing it to strain under his weight and power.

"Galgalor!" Diabold surveyed his surroundings. He was on his way back to Cahlar's lair when he sensed the cries for help from one of his more powerful servants. Normally he would ignore it, but Galgalor held the deceit spell for all of Igypkt, and the loss would ruin his plan.

He moved his head slowly in the direction of the low murmurs far across the room. At first he only saw numerous marble outcroppings from the floor. He then felt that someone had dissolved the spell that kept the marble smooth and age-resistant. Difficult, but not impossible. He was shocked when he stepped further away from the lava and observed Galgalor suspended just above the floor by stalagmites that pierced his obese frame. Diabold strolled across the room and walked up behind the contorted figure.

"Master...Master...Help me. The human intruders. I tried to stop them, but one's mana was more powerful than I have ever felt on Igypkt." Galgalor moaned after pushing out the breathful of words. "Please free me...Master!"

Diabold raked his sharp claws against a few of the stalagmites holding Galgalor up, barely listening to the words that his minion gasped. He reached out with his mind and noticed that mana still flowed all around the marble, but he could not understand why. He grabbed onto one of the thicker columns and snapped it between the ground and Galgalor's body. Diabold heard a rumbling and his unworldly speed barely gave him time to jump back before another stalagmite shot out from the ground and pierced Galgalor again, ending in a loud scream from the helpless demon.

For the first time since he'd met Cahlar, Diabold hesitated. Sure, there were many who could cast a permanent change spell. But there were no human mages left that could cast such a powerful continuation spell.

Diabold took another step toward the back of Galgalor, extending one of his powerful arms out and around the demon's head. His claws tightly grasped the bulbous chin and, with bone-crunching strength, turned Galgalor's head so he could stare deep into his eyes. Diabold yet again had to hesitate as he glared into the three festering, hollow orifices that once held confident eyes. "Did these intruders say anything of where they were from, my pitiful minion?"

"Noo!" Galgalor groaned as Diabold's claws ripped into his flesh. "The companion of the one who did this to me only said something about not being from this planet."

"Did you tell them anything about the web of deceit?" Diabold had lost his temper; his energy lashed out in all directions around him and dust spewed forth from the marble cracking up and down the hall.

"No, Master, I promise. I said nothing. The spell is still intact and I still command it."

"But you were beaten by an outlander, and a young child at that. You do not deserve the post I have given you." Diabold felt no pity for Galgalor, only disgust. "Unfortunately I cannot kill you and assign another without severing the spell. It is a dilemma for me, as I fear you will break easily and tell all if the child comes back."

Diabold's hand still tightly gripped Galgalor's jaw. Without waiting for a response, Diabold ripped open Galgalor's mouth and with his other hand grasped the writhing tongue. He pulled with all of his might, enjoying the sounds of the muscles popping and the wails from Galgalor. He held the detached, two-foot tongue up high, admiring his work. "This should ensure you will not betray me nor foul my plan." Diabold extracted his claws from the blood soaked jaw, letting Galgalor sink back onto the stalactites that suspended his slumped mass. He turned away to walk back to the lava pit, deep in thought. This boy had the power of an ancient mage even without any training. His perfectly laid plan could easily be destroyed if the outlander was allowed to live.

Halfway to the boiling pool he realized he was still holding the thrashing tongue and tossed it to the side of the room. It solidified before hitting the ground, bouncing across the floor like a rock before resting against the wall. A great artifact, The Tongue of Galgalor, had been created.

VII.

"The Fishing Station was taken over by demons hundreds of years ago, and the surrounding rich farmlands were turned into a desert of despair, with sand dunes covering the once beautiful city of Ahmarn*. Since the demon takeover, no one has ever survived a crossing through the desert, let alone seen the Fishing Station and lived to tell about it." Sileya hadn't been back to the Fishing Station since they were forced to abandon it, but she knew it was still a source of great evil. She was not going to easily let her guard down in front of these two simple travelers. "How else would you know about the marbled halls and what lies inside unless you were one of them?"

Sileya held the mana around her. She did not need to chant out loud to cast a spell, as hundreds of years of training allowed her to merely mumble most spells. As a true lifegiver*, she could even bring back the dead, or destroy the undead and demons.

"Although I do not wish to challenge you, I must ask one question." Dillon pressed. "How do you know what it looks like if no one has entered for hundreds of years?"

Matt thought that Dillon's words were still too nice for a woman so close to killing them. Suddenly Matt recognized Dillon's crush and almost started laughing.

"I was there when the demons broke through the hall and swarmed up from the lava stream." Sileya began to tire of holding back so much energy, but she noticed that the one named Dillon seemed to have no trouble at all. In fact he was still gaining mana.

"Wait. That would make you hundreds of years old. From Arlar to The Fallen One to you. How do you all stay alive for so long?" Matt was the one that spoke. His recognition of her true age evoked slight disgust; Dillon had a crush on a great-great-great grandma. Of course, she was very pretty.

"You know Arlar and The Fallen One?" Sileya's conviction that these two were demons began to waiver. Now she was confused.

"Yes, Arlar helped us when we first...uhm...arrived on Igypkt. He also took us to The Fallen one, which may have even cost him his own life. We destroyed The Fallen One, but I think he wanted us to." Dillon didn't want to go into all the details of their expedition. He couldn't imagine that telling her they were from outer space would really help matters.

"You were the one that destroyed The Fallen One and released the trapped souls?" Sileya lost her concentration and the spell's energy snapped away from her like an over-stretched rubber band. "You've started The Gallen War. Yet you are so young. You do realize you must also end the war?"

Dillon slumped forward as if all weight had returned to his shoulders. He lowered his head slightly and rubbed his eyes with his right hand. "War? No, I don't want people to die. We're here to save my people from being oppressed or even completely wiped out by others."

"But how will you do that without fighting?" Dillon's innocent expression caused Sileya's last defense to crumble. She took a couple of steps toward the young man.

Dillon's blue eyes caught Sileya's. "I don't know, but if there's a way I'm going to find it. This Gallen War, whatever it is. Well, I didn't plan on starting it, but if it ties into my quest then I guess we must understand what we've gotten ourselves into.

"The Gallen War is a battle for supremacy between humans and magical creatures. When magical creatures first came into being, they worked for humans and there was peace. Over time they resented their jobs and wanted to become equals. It was difficult to find a common ground, but we came close just as both sides prepared for the largest war our planet had ever known. Battle lines were drawn on each continent in case an agreement could not be reached. Just as troops marched toward each other, a treaty was signed, and minds bent on destruction were turned toward rejoicing and friendship. Everyone was happy and the festivities lasted late into the night.

"However, it was a just a ploy. Paseath*, the leader of the magical creatures, had planned all along to ignore the agreement and in the middle of the night started his slaughter. His armies killed men, women, children—most of them sleeping peacefully after a long night of celebration. Humankind barely survived and almost became slaves to the magical creatures. But Raslya*, the last great human mage, fought back the magical creatures and freed the humans at the cost of his own life. Small wars raged for nearly a century, and always to a stalemate. Eventually an unspoken truce came about, but we have not forgotten the treachery. The humans have been waiting for the sign, as stated in the prophecy, that The Gallen War would start anew and all the evil magical creatures would be destroyed. The death of The Fallen One launched the prophecy into motion."

Matt and Dillon had intently listened to Sileya and let their guard down as the story ended.

"Wow, that's a pretty nice tale, but what does Gallen mean?" Matt asked. "I don't get it. Also, are you telling us that everything was fine when the magical creatures were your slaves? Last time I checked slavery wasn't a good thing." Matt waited for a response, but only saw Sileya's very confused eyes staring back at them.

"Sileya, are you saying that all humans are good and that every single magical creature is evil?"

Sileya looked over at Dillon and nodded yes very slowly.

"If that's the case, then Arlar is evil?"

Sileya's face became even more scrunched. Anger started to show in between the forced wrinkles appearing on her face. "Yes, it has to be, but..." Sileya was becoming angrier by the second, and Dillon feared her next move, whatever it might be.

"Sileya, sorry we got off our original conversation. Are you heading to Cureio as we are?" Dillon tried again. "Surely three travelers will be a safer group than two, and quite honestly we don't know the way."

Sileya was still lost in her confusion. "Huh, well uh, yes, that sounds like a good idea now that I know you are not demons."

"I admit that we do have to get there fairly fast, so we won't be resting very much."

"That's not a problem at all. We can make it there in about two weeks," replied Sileya. She seemed to be at ease again as she allowed the conversation to wash away from her mind. However, Dillon knew there was something there and intended to push again along the way to Cureio.

"Two weeks? How?" Matt couldn't wait to reunite with Gabe, Tanya, and Lian.

Chapter 12
The Soulless City

I.

Gabe, Taima, and Lian all stood around for a while after Ghost had sunk back into the ground. Their eyes were now fully adjusted to the light shooting through the dense foliage and they had no excuses for not pressing onward.

"Well, I think it may be time to see if anyone is expecting us. We should creep closer to the road and step out when the coast is clear." Gabe was surprised to find himself excited to get back into a city. He hadn't realized just how much he missed the hustle and bustle of street life.

Lian was the first to move, with swiftness that seemed to contradict his silence as he headed for the road. Less than three feet from the thoroughfare he froze in his tracks as a group of heavily armed men with red clothing walked right in front of him. Lian was nearly in plain sight of the guards, and Gabe and Taima thought he would surely be noticed. Much to Taima and Gabe's surprise they didn't even glance his way as they passed by, laughing and jabbing each other about some lady from the previous night.

Lian twisted his head sideways and winked at Gabe and Taima before the guards were out of sight. He turned back to the road and, after a few minutes, motioned for them to come forward. Together they stepped out onto the thoroughfare and turned toward the city. In unison they stopped and stared.

"Wow!" Taima's word said it all. The city was a distance off and colossal in height, shaped in a nearly perfect circle about a mile wide, with a massive bridge that rose all the way to the gateway for the top level of the city. It was awe-inspiring enough to stop anyone, but what really caught their eyes were the reflections of yellow, orange, and white lights emanating from the city walls. A soft array of swirling colors and shapes danced throughout the entire mammoth structure. It fascinated and entranced the three travelers.

"Now why would anyone want an entire city that looks like that?" Gabe couldn't believe it was just for fun; there had to be a reason.

"Maybe it's a big signal for the aliens in outer space to see. Since we are headed for it, I'd say it worked." Lian laughed at his own joke and was joined by the other two.

They heard a cart coming from behind them and started down the hill. The red-clad guards were easily a half-mile ahead of them now, and it was clear that only a few people were traveling the road today.

"As much as I would like to get into Cureio, I say we first head to one of those villages outside the city and stay a night or two just to gather information." Gabe said.

"I agree, as long as we get to sleep in a real bed. I'm tired of lying on rock floors. I miss my sleeping bag." Taima's words made them all realize how long it had been since they had enjoyed a comfortable place to sleep.

The road they were on was about as wide as a four-lane highway, and a deceptively long distance from the impossibly steep bridge that appeared to provide the only entrance to Cureio. After a half hour, they finally reached the first outcroppings of houses and farmlands surrounding the city base. Shortly after that, they came upon a massive wooden, three-story building with lots of noise and music emanating from within.

"Either we found an inn for the night, or it's just the local Catholic choir tryouts." Lian smiled, but this time the others ignored him.

"Hey, did you notice there aren't any men working the fields or walking on the roads?" They all looked around and saw that Taima's observation held true.

"Why Taima, I must admit I personally have no interest in finding a suitor, unlike yourself. But now that you mention it, the odds are stacked in my favor." Lian took a step to the side as Taima glared at him.

"Stacked in your favor? Funny, I didn't know this was a village of the blind and tasteless." Taima smiled back at him and waited to see what he would do.

"I think you are correct, Taima. Looks like Ghost was right about people being forced into the army." Gabe looked around and saw many red dots surrounding the base of the city, the bridge, and all around the top level. "Maybe there is a war going on."

"Or a war to come, since I'd hope that the women and children would be brought within the city before it started." Taima looked around calmly and heightened her sense for danger. Nothing alarmed her.

Gabe shrugged his shoulders and strode up to the tavern. He calmly opened the door and walked in, expecting a dark large room, a ruckus of people, and filth. Instead he entered a brightly lit hall, with clean tables and employees all wearing a standard gray and white uniform. The loud music was coming from an unmanned band clashed with the calmness of the place.

A rather short, stocky man at the door greeted him warmly.

"Welcome to the *Flying Fishermen's* Hotel and Restaurant seated a short distance outside of the marvelous city of Cureio. My name is Sheimda*. What can I do for you, sir?" questioned the doorman.

Taima and Lian entered the building as Gabe spoke. "Do you have a suite with two separate rooms?"

"Most certainly. Would you like one with running water, sir?"

"Are you kidding me?" Taima squealed at the suggestion.

"How much is it?" The place looked way too nice for them to be able to afford. All they had was the money from the ogres who attacked them the first day.

"Two sill, and well worth it." The doorman's demeanor suggested that this was a bargain.

"Thanks, but do you have anything cheaper?" Gabe tried not to guffaw at the price, which was twenty times more than a normal room.

"Certainly. We have bunk beds and no water for…" The doorman stopped as Taima grabbed Gabe and spun him around.

"Gabe. After what we've been through I would kill for running water and a nice room to sleep in. Two sill is a bargain for my happiness."

"It does come with complimentary food and drink, sir. I'm sure your lady friend will be very happy."

"Excuse me? No, no, no. She will have one of the rooms and we will sleep in the other." The man must have assumed they were together, not because of their similar skin color but because of their bickering.

"Oh, I see. Well, no matter." The doorman winked at Gabe and Lian.

193

"Ew! That's not cool!" Lian spoke out.

"Relax, Lian," replied Gabe. "It was a simple misunderstanding, but does it matter anyway? Step into the twenty first century."

"More like the ten thousandth century on this planet." Lian took a step back while the other two laughed.

The doorman stood by until the laughter died down, held out his hand for the money, and then escorted them up to the third level hallway before stopping at a large door.

"Your room, sirs and madam. Food will be up within the hour." He had barely opened the door halfway before Taima charged by him.

"I call dibs on the shower!" Taima yelled as she ran into the first side room she saw and slammed the door. Within a few seconds the door slowly opened and she sheepishly peered out at the doorman. He subtly nodded his head in the other direction, and Taima strolled over to where he had motioned and shut the door behind her.

"The closet?" Gabe asked. The doorman slowly nodded yes. Gabe and Lian chuckled as they shut the door behind them and gazed upon their plush room.

II.

A couple hours later they were draped over the chairs in the living area, filled with great food and a little alcohol.

"Now that was surely the best food I have ever had." Gabe patted his belly and grinned.

"Yeah, that was better than anything I've ever eaten on Earth. Hard to believe we had to travel across the stars just to get some good food." They laughed and continued on carefree, recounting their mission and what had happened so far. As the night darkened, they all came back to the same thought.

"I wonder how Matt and Dillon are doing?" This time it was Taima who asked the question.

"There is no way for us to know, but I am sure they are fine. Remember how the ogres called him an ancient mage? He not only has the power, but he is also learning how to use it at a very fast pace. Heck, by the time he gets to Cureio even Mungoth will be no match for him." Gabe meant his words to be excessive, but he noticed how both Lian and Taima's features froze.

"Well, all that food and drink made me tired. I'll see you tomorrow." Taima stood up, stretched, and walked to her room.

"Me too. See ya in the morning, Taima." Lian casually strolled off to the other room and out of sight.

What did I say? Guess I hit a nerve. Oh well, at least the food and drink were good. Gabe stared upward at the small beam at the top of the ceiling, with no particular thoughts on his mind.

He tensed up as he heard the whistling of objects flying through the air. He didn't even need to move his eyes; a small knife and an arrow struck opposite sides of the very small beam he'd been staring at. "What the..." was all he got out as the timbered beam screamed and fell from the ceiling. Gabe barely rolled off his chair before the beam crashed through it. He spun around in time to see the fallen structure grow arms and legs. Its wicked eyes whipped frantically back and forth between the three.

"Incoming!" Taima's voice prepared them all as the creature's arms whipped outward. From each one a large wooden spike flew out as fast as an arrow. Taima easily side-stepped the one directed at her, but Lian misjudged the speed of the other and caught it on the right side of his chest. He grunted from the pain and looked down at the spike that was now embedded a good inch into his ribcage.

Taima saw the wooden creature turn to look at its only escape path. "The window!" she cried. The creature was closer to the window than any of them.

Gabe had been observing the creature while searching through his belt pack. Just as he saw the creature turn and run for the window, he found what he wanted. He slipped his hand through the loop and flicked the yo-yo like device like at the wooden creature. The air crackled as an electric web flew forth with a thin trail leading out from Gabe's hand. Gabe braced his feet on a heavy chair, ensnared his prey in midair, and pulled back strongly.

The creature howled in pain as electricity seared it, raising smoke and the smell of burnt wood. It thrashed and flailed as Gabe braced himself, his arms holding the chord taut. He focused his breathing, sent his gold mana into the loop strap around his wrist, and watched the electricity crackle all around the web.

"If you stop moving, the web will not hurt you!" Gabe grunted out at the creature. It ignored his words.

"Take cover!" Taima flipped the dining table over in front of her, Lian ducked behind the bedroom door, and Gabe jumped into the chair.

The explosion rocked the inn as thousands of splinters embedded into everything in the room. Gabe felt his device retract back into his palm. No one moved.

Gabe's voice was the only sound as wood dust settled all around them. "Everyone okay?"

"Is it gone?" grunted Lian from between the door and wall. He snaked his head out and looked at the other side of the door, which had a number of nasty wood spikes stuck in it.

"Yeah, I think that was its last-ditch effort. Whatever it was." Taima was already out from behind the table, staring at the empty space the creature had occupied.

"More importantly now is to find out who sent it." Gabe could not believe that someone already knew they were here.

"I'm going to find out." Lian strode toward the window and opened it up.

"Lian!" Taima yelled out as she went after him.

Lian had one foot on the window sill as he turned around. Taima looked into his eyes and then down at his chest. Lian looked down and remembered the stake lodged between his ribs.

"Oh." Lian grasped it and yanked it out without thought. "Ahh!" He staggered back off the window sill and braced himself against a post.

"Are you okay, Lian? I think you need to lie down." Gabe walked forward and put his hand on Lian's shoulder.

"No. I'm okay. I guess that's what you get from watching too much TV. I thought it wouldn't hurt." He smiled and started toward the window again.

"You cannot possibly think you are going out there," Gabe said.

"It's a mere flesh wound. Mind over matter." Lian's voice grew distant as he didn't even break stride.

Taima stuck her head out the third floor window after him, but saw nothing. She turned back to Gabe and shrugged. "What do we do now, Gabe?"

"Get out of here fast and find another empty room. I really do not think anyone was after us, but I am not willing to bet my life on it." Gabe stopped to think and looked around. "Funny how no one has come to check out what happened."

They went into the hallway, and as the door shut a smile crept across the flames in the fireplace. The smile and a flickering face were carried out by the steps of two small, red feet. The creature, no more than a foot high, ran toward the window, jumped out, and softly hit the ground. Its light danced and flickered as it ran down the street and into a dilapidated hut.

III.

Sheimda strode confidently up the steep incline of the bridge leading to Cureio's power-level. His small stature made him appear weak, while his baggy clothes masked a powerful frame honed from decades of intense martial arts training. Not just the doorman for the *Flying Fishermen* Hotel, Sheimda was also the bouncer who kept the peace.

Halfway up he approached the first set of four guards standing at attention. Sheimda huffed at the guards and showed the etched sign on his palm. The small, winged boat floated up to just below his fingers before sinking back down.

"Sheimda, we all know who you are, and there's no reason to flaunt it. Besides, you're merely a novice *Flying Fishermen*." One of the guards glared at him as he spoke.

Sheimda said nothing and kept walking up the bridge, showing his palm all the way to the top entrance. In front of the massive steel gates were a dozen large guards on horses. If anyone or anything unwelcome tried to run up the bridge, they would charge down in a line and knock the attacker into the serpent-filled moat. Even a giant would have a hard time standing its ground against the galloping horses.

Sheimda knew that the gate was rarely opened at night. But there was another way in. He looked up above the gate, "Lower the bucket!" He waited as a large wooden container was reeled down, and he stared back at the wizard eyeing him from above. Once through the hole he was amazed to see the room filled with the queen's special troops. "What's going on, wizard?"

"*I* will ask the questions, Sheimda. What is your business?" The bald Lifmin* glared at the short doorman.

"Just one of my usual runs. You know I'm required to report on a regular basis."

Lifmin glared at Sheimda, but received no more words. "Very well, but you cannot return until the gates open in the morning."

"Fine." Sheimda strode through the open stone door, down the stairs, and onto the busy streets of Cureio. The city's open, upper level never slept, but was known to become more dangerous as it was engulfed

197

by darkness. He weaved in and out of the traffic before dodging into a side alley. Sheimda was very aware of his surroundings and feared little, even when he heard the small noise off to his right. He merely turned his head in that direction, not noticing the noose slipping around his neck until it was too late. The black-clad, wiry shadow holding the other end of the noose jumped from the rooftop, past a protruding joist, and to the ground.

Sheimda felt the constriction of the unusually thin, steel-like rope at the same time it lifted him off his feet and propelled him into a darker alley on his left. His muscular neck prevented his spine from snapping, but he now hung a few feet off the ground, grasping at the noose as it cut into his skin. Time ticked away and his vision began to shrink to nothing. Just when he thought it was over, his feet touched the ground and the noose loosened enough to allow him to gasp for breath.

"What was that thing in your hotel that attacked the travelers?" The voice had a low growl to it and labored breath.

Sheimda felt the noose start to tighten again and it was all he needed to share everything. "It was a demon ear. It is conjured from the pits of Hell as a spy."

"Who conjured it?"

Sheimda coughed and gulped more air before he spoke. "The *Flying Fishermen* of course. You're not from around here are you?"

"Shut up! Why were you going to them?" The voice gasped itself, as if it couldn't get enough air.

"Just to inform them that new travelers were coming. That's all." Sheimda's eyes widened as the figure glided toward him.

"Please don't kill me. I promise I won't say a word to anyone." Water filled Sheimda's eyes, their arrogance now completely erased.

"I accept your promise." The man's hand shot out and snapped the doorman's neck in a split second. The dark figure gathered his noose and swiftly climbed back on top of the roof. He turned back around and sighed, exposing a half melted faced to Sheimda's now blank eyes.

IV.

The window quietly opened on the second floor of the inn. The black-clad man crawled into the room while eyeing the two figures asleep on opposite couches. He slowly drew a knife from his belt as he crept between them. He thrust the knife downward, striking the apple on the table with a thud. Both Taima and Gabe looked over and smiled.

"Welcome back, Lian. What did you learn?" Gabe noticed that Lian grimaced as he sat down on the chair.

"Not much. The doorman had snuck out just when I was leaving. He walked right up to the castle gates and they let him in," responded Lian.

"Not good. Why didn't you stop him?" Gabe knew there was more, but let Lian play him.

"I wanted to follow him into the city."

"You went into the city? What was it like?" Lian had caught Taima's attention.

"It had walls and streets and lots of people." Lian smiled as Taima stuck out her tongue.

"Well, what about the doorman?" Gabe was tiring of Lian's toying now.

"He won't be telling anyone anything?" Lian took a bite of the apple and grimaced again as the pain shot through his ribs.

"You killed him? Lian, this isn't a game! What if he had a family? We're not murderers!" Taima had stood up and was glaring down at Lian.

"I didn't kill him. Someone else did. Someone clad all in black just like me. I was too far away to hear the conversation, but he killed the doorman fast. I lost him on the rooftops. It was as if he disappeared." Lian threw the core of the apple out the window, again forgetting his injury until it was too late.

"You need to get that looked at." Taima had changed her anger to caring as she looked at Lian.

"I did. Why do you think I was gone half the night? But the man said it would take a few days before it felt better." Lian lifted his shirt to show the patch with a yellowish liquid oozing out its sides. "It turns out that healers like Matt are very rare."

"I hate to say it, but I think we need to get out of this inn. As soon as they find Sheimda's body the guards will be all over this place." Gabe really wanted to sleep on the comfortable couch. He hadn't even thought of asking Lian how he had found them in the new room they had snuck into.

"They won't find it tonight. I hid the body. I wanted to sleep at least a few hours before we moved out." Lian went over to the somewhat worn bed in the corner, lay down gingerly, and closed his eyes.

"Okay, but come tomorrow I think we need to split up for a couple days and gather as much information as we can before entering the city."

Gabe saw that Taima's eyes were also closed. "I will take the first two-hour watch and then Taima the second since we both already slept for a while."

V.

Gabe stood near an alley and watched the bustling crowd outside the city walls. Over the last couple days the number of travelers had increased nearly ten-fold and, with the upcoming events, was expected to explode in less than another week. He held onto the large burlap bag draped over his shoulder and nodded at the bearded old man who limped his way into the alley. Gabe casually looked around for a while, then turned and followed him. After about seventy feet he turned left into a narrower alley and smiled at the tall woman smiling back at him.

"Glad to see you both," commented Gabe as he went up and hugged Taima. Lian stepped out of a small shadow, still pulling the animal-hair beard off his face. "So what did you learn, Lian and Taima?"

As Dillon had trained them, they each recounted their last couple of days exploring before Gabe summed up everything. "The floating city of Nalistat* is set to arrive sometime in the next couple of weeks, and will then be heading to Ishtan. I sure hope Dillon gets here to tell us where to go, since it's only docked for a week. Also, the city is run not only by the queen, but by the *Flying Fishermen* and the Colors of Cureio*. The Colors of Cureio are clans whose rulership is passed on through the eldest child. If there are no living family members, then an open contest is held to see who will inherent the clan.

"We also know that the queen of Cureio resides in the Great Southern Tower, while the city mages of the *Flying Fishermen* hold the Great Northern Tower. Near the Great Southern Tower is the spaceship that I presume came from the Mulshins. It is surrounded by a powerful protection spell in addition to guards who patrol it around the clock.

"Lastly, there are only humanoids left in the city, even down to the lowest levels. The queen is paranoid and has set up ruthless rules. Almost everything is punishable by death...on the spot."

"You did forget one thing," Lian chimed in. "The city walls shimmer because they are magical and allow sunlight to pass directly through. The dancing colors and patterns are caused by the small amount that doesn't get through and bounces around and back out."

"Really? So the lower levels all get real sunlight? That's cool." Taima liked the idea.

"So how are we going to get in?" Lian asked.

Gabe smiled and opened his bag. "It turns out that the Purple Clan's leader, one of the Colors of Cureio, is not long for this world. He has no children and an open contest will soon be held to name his successor. I am going to vie for that title."

"No way. Well, that's great for you, but what about us?" Lian started to help pull things out of the bag and noticed only one robe and several small jewelry items with a strange insignia on them.

"Taima will be my bodyguard, and you will be my trusted advisor." Gabe put the robe on and some of the jewelry. "This jewelry all bears the sign of my house."

"Bodyguard? I can live with that." Taima donned some metal bracelets and a large necklace.

"Advisor? But I don't see any regal outfit," Lian asked. "Oh wait. You mean spy-like advisor?" Gabe nodded and Lian smiled.

"Sounds good. When do we go?" Taima looked around carefully, but sensed no danger.

"Now."

VI.

Lian's head poked out of the alley without the notice of a single passerby. He waited until the tide of people was at its busiest before he motioned for them to step out. They smoothly blended into the crowd and headed toward the Cureio proper. As they exited the last small village, they only needed to walk a few hundred feet until they were waiting in line at the bottom of the city ramp. The ramp itself seemed even more massive than when they first saw it.

Their eyes were those of tourists while their hearts raced fast with the knowledge that they would soon walk right into the mouth of the enemy.

A voice yelled out in the front of the line as if it had repeated the words thousands of times. "Only humanoids are allowed within the city walls. Any non-humanoids that are captured will be punished by death, as those who are its companions. The city guards are the law. Disobedience, defiance, or hostile acts are punishable by death. Stealing, fighting, but not adultery are punishable by death."

Another guard chimed in, "Ensure the harness is securely attached to your body at all times while on the ramp. Failure to do so could result in death from falling. If you survive the fall, you will be eaten alive by the serpents in the moat. Please do not feed the serpents. They are wild creatures."

The line moved quickly. It was apparent that most of the visitors were frequent travelers up the bridge. Horses, oxen-like creatures, carriages, and people were quickly attached to and pulled up by the massive chain. Lian stared at the enormous metal wheel at the top and the bottom, which moved the chain.

"I wonder what makes the metal wheels turn?" Lian's curiosity got the best of him.

"Magic of course." The words were sarcastically mouthed by a young boy behind him.

Lian turned his head around and spoke, "Well, aren't you a know-it-all?"

"Lian!" Taima hit Lian in the chest. Lian turned around to say something, but noticed it was their turn in line. They each grabbed a smaller metal chain that hung off the main chain, trying not to look like newbies as they wrapped them around their waists. Luckily, each chain end snapped smoothly in place and pulled them quickly past the dozen guards at the front of the ramp.

As they were walked up the bridge, their increasing vantage point made it hard not to be amazed. In back of them lay the huge, depressed bowl of small villages and farmlands. Three quarters of the way up they could easily see the massive forest that ran along the entire western coast.

"It would be nearly impossible to attack this city by surprise." Lian had turned completely around and was walking backward.

"At least not from this side. I do wonder what is accessible on the sea side." Gabe was looking ahead as they approached the top. He tried to remain calm as he stared at the two dozen guards in front of them.

"Prepare to unbuckle and walk quickly to the gate. Failure to do so may result in being fed to the serpents." The speaking guard seemed to take pleasure in his words.

When they reached the top they each grabbed the buckle and quickly opened it. Then they stepped into the line for entrance through the gated-wall and onto the top level of the city.

"You three, over here!" The same soldier that was barking orders pointed at the trio.

The tension in the three must have been easy for even a blind man to see.

Gabe pointed to his chest, "Us?"

"Yes, you three! You think I'm an idiot? It was easy to see that you've never been to Cureio before. State your business!"

Gabe swallowed hard but took the few steps toward the guards as ordered. He puffed up his chest as he spoke. "I am here to compete for leadership of the Purple House. This is my bodyguard and my information specialist." Gabe successfully came off aloof and way more confident that he felt.

"Bodyguard? Her? You mean bed maiden." The guards all started to laugh. Gabe sweated, expecting Taima to draw her swords and start a fight. Instead he saw her cross her arms and smile.

"I doubt you've bedded anything more than your own mother. And I'm sure your fighting skills are as bad as she says your love-making is." Taima kept her arms crossed, careful not to be perceived as initiating any act of aggression.

The guard whose manhood had been insulted drew his sword. Taima dropped one foot back, bringing her body into a defensive posture. That was as far as she dared go since she knew that drawing her swords would invoke an immediate attack by hundreds of soldiers and many mages. One more move and their journey would surely end before they even entered the gates of the incredible city.

"Wait!" Gabe had to act fast. "I said I am here to vie for rulership of the Purple House. Are you purposely trying to undermine the open and free competition that has been promised? Has the lure of a few extra coins corrupted those charged with protecting the city? Do you fail to see that physical protection is only a part of the oath you all swore? You are the enforcers of the law, but you must also set the standards that those within the city adhere to. It is not easy to walk such a straight line. However, it is a challenge that must be taken. Else the walls of this once great city will be nothing but a hollow shell. If you attack us, you are no better than the thugs and murderers that live in the shadows. Now please let us pass."

The mana flowed from him and rode on the sound waves he cast forth. Everyone within earshot was mesmerized by the emotions that Gabe had woven through them.

From the row of soldiers, one stepped forth. He was tall, muscular, and exuded confidence. The soldier did not walk up to Gabe, but to Taima. He slowly took off his helmet, revealing long-flowing, blond hair and a perfectly trimmed goatee. His brown eyes looked right into hers as he spoke. "Your friend speaks eloquently even as he attacks our integrity. Regardless, it leaves me in a difficult situation. If I let you go, then I failed at my job of both protecting the people of this city and obeying the orders of my liege. If I lock you up, and your friend speaks the truth, then I am interfering with the affairs of the Purple House. Your friend may have no clue of how vicious and unfair the weeks ahead will be for him, but that will not begin here."

Taima couldn't help but smile. "What do you propose?"

The guards' leader smiled back as he spoke. "Simple. If you are a bodyguard for royalty, then you should be able to beat my soldier." He pointed at his soldier with the drawn sword before he spoke again. "However, the rules of my liege are clear. If you take up arms against any of his soldiers then you are to be killed."

"So I must defeat him without using a weapon? I suppose that I also must not kill him?" Taima enjoyed the exchange.

"Nor permanently injure."

"Sir, I cannot attack a defenseless woman." The soldier's anger had dissipated.

"Then how did you bed your mom? Did she let you?" Taima was sure they would be jailed if the solider didn't attack her.

The troops were all laughing, including the leader. The insulted soldier screamed and lunged at Taima, attempting to run her through with his sword. Taima stepped sideways and forward while delivering a straight ridge hand strike to her opponent's throat. She dropped her left arm onto his sword arm while her right hand twisted his shield to the side. He was still gasping for air when she brought her left knee straight up into his groin with all her might. He lifted a foot off the ground and came down with a thud. It was over in seconds.

Taima looked up to the leader. "Do I need to continue?"

"No, I think that's enough. You may proceed."

From above a trap door opened and a wrinkled, bald head appeared. "No, they cannot proceed. They must be interrogated, Kailman*!"

Kailman looked up at the little man. "Wizard. You have been around many years and surely wisdom has forced itself upon you. Are you telling me that the people we are looking for would walk right up to the front gate, pretend to be in the most public of contests, then take on one of my men?" Kailman looked at his men, who all started to chuckle.

"Well, uhmm, no?" The wizard stammered, not realizing how Kailman was using public confrontation to undermine the wizard's powerful position.

"Very well." Kailman put back on his helmet and turned toward the crowd. "The ramp is now jammed, so let's get back to work!"

The guards, who had formed a defensive line, stepped aside to allow the alien trio to pass. Taima smiled at the back of Kailman, wishing she didn't have to leave just yet.

Lian had not said a word the entire time, and no one would remember that he was even part of the group. It was just as he wanted.

VII.

Forty paces through the gates and the city was everything Gabe had hoped it would be. The hustle and bustle clearly disoriented Taima and Lian, but to him it was like a complex symphony—one that he could read and maybe even direct.[#]

"So, what do we do now?" Lian spoke as he looked nervously about, noticing the two towers as his only points of reference."

"Well, let me see," replied Gabe. "There appear to be water holes to the east and west, and the marketplace must be to the north. We should go to the north and get something to eat first."

"How do you know that?" Lian responded.

"By the people and what they are carrying." Gabe smiled, looked up at the sky, and then looked down, noticing that the floor was emanating the same colors and patterns as the outer walls. "After that we will get our bearings and then sign me up for the competition."

"You're not really going through with it?" Taima thought Gabe had been using the contest as a ploy for them to get inside the city walls.

"To be honest I did not think so at first, but look around at the people," Gabe said. "The city appears to be under military rule and preparing for a large assault." Lian finally noticed all the soldiers marching down the streets and how the people quickly moved away from them. He also saw the posted signs that demanded each family enlist their firstborn son in the city guard, just as Ghost had told them.

"And?" was Lian's response.

"And, we need to figure out what is going on and be in the best possible position to execute whatever plan Dillon has in mind." Gabe didn't tell them that the competition and potential to rule one of the city's most powerful clans was simply too tempting for him to pass up.

VIII.

It was a challenge for Lian and Taima to navigate through all the people that had flooded the city streets. They kept bumping into or being bumped into by the crowds. Lian, who didn't seem able to dodge anyone, was frustrated at how clumsy he was in the city.

After ten minutes Gabe stopped and turned around. "Well, here is the marketplace. Although I'm sure neither of you can buy anything."

"Why's that?" Taima spoke up.

"Where are your purses of money?" Gabe laughed as both checked their persons and realized they had been pilfered.

"You knew it was going to happen and you let it?" Lian was miffed.

"No, I took the coins out when we were getting ready to enter the castle. Just in case. You need to realize we are in a new and no less dangerous environment. We all have to be careful."

Gabe's lecture was not well received. "I think saying that before we entered the city would have been just as effective." Lian responded.

"No, I doubt you would have listened to me." Gabe handed back their money and the extra purse with Lian's mojuila. Lian ripped it out of his hand and snarled. Gabe ignored him.

"Guys, it seems we're being followed but I don't sense any immediate danger. They must be a number of paces behind us." Taima relaxed her body as she spoke.

"Yes. The non-uniformed guards have been following us since we left the gate. I am sure they are just ensuring that we are going to register for the Purple House contest." Gabe looked around as he spoke. "Mmm. Those places to our right smell great. I say we go over there and eat first."

They entered the heart of the marketplace and were soon overloaded with great smells of food and hot drinks. Gabe picked out a somewhat busy outdoor restaurant and asked to be seated. They ate and relaxed for over two hours, talking about nothing important as they took in the new scenery. While the people inside the city were all humanoids, they were diverse in shapes, sizes, and colors. When they were ready to leave, Gabe asked the young waiter for directions to the Purple House.

"You're going to sign up for the contest?" The boy's eyes widened with excitement.

"Yes, I am." Gabe smiled as he responded.

"Wow, and if you win then you can lead the Purple House against the evil Nalistatians*? That would be so cool." The boy's voice rose with excitement.

"Why would we want to do that?" Gabe's words reflected what they all were immediately thinking. If the Nalistatians were defeated, then how would they leave this continent if they needed to?

"The Nalistatians are evil and are coming to attack. They must be defeated if we are to win The Gallen War." The boy saw the looks on their faces and was confused. "You don't believe in The Gallen War."

"No, no, we do. I assure you of that." Gabe had to think quickly. "I am just trying to figure out how we can defeat the non-humanoids on other continents if we cannot get to them. What do you think?"

"I dunno?" The boy seemed appeased and turned to go wait on another customer.

When he was out of earshot Taima spoke out. "Damn! That's their master plan. If they defeat the Nalistatians then we're trapped. I'm betting that we have to get on the floating city to find Cahlar."

"Then it is really important that we get immersed in the politics of the city. The only way I think we can do that is to win the Purple House contest. It is time to go see what it will take." Gabe rose to leave as he spoke.

IX.

Gabe casually led them along the busy streets and corridors of the crowded city, stopping once in a while to ask for directions. In less than a half hour they stood before a three-story, ornate building decorated with purple banners and cloths. The structure was nestled in front of a crystal clear, small lake with a stream that flowed through the city wall and cascaded into the moat below. No less than twenty guards clad in purple stood at attention along the pathway to the large, open doors.

"I thought it would be bigger." Lian guessed it wasn't much more than five thousand square feet.

"What do we do now?" Taima asked.

Gabe answered by walking between the guards and up to the open doors. Taima and Lian followed. They entered an unimpressive holding room with four more purple guards protecting two doors on the other side of the room. Directly between them and the doors was a wooden desk whose rich, dark wood seemed to have wisps of purple traveling along its crevasses. Behind the desk sat a thin, young man picking at his fingernails with a small file.

Gabe walked up to the desk and waited for a response. The man did not acknowledge his presence, even after Gabe cleared his throat. Finally Gabe lost his patience and spoke. "I am here to compete for the soon-to-be-vacated spot as the Purple House lead."

The file dropped to the table as the man assessed Gabe. "You can talk, eh? Well, you have gotten farther than most. Now, if you can write your name I might really be excited." He opened a drawer of the desk and extracted a piece of paper, a bottle of ink, and a pen.

Lian and Taima looked at each other with the same thought. They had learned to speak and read what they had been told was an old Earth dialect, but had skipped learning how to write due to time constraints.

Gabe smiled, wetted the pen and rapidly wrote his full name. The man behind the table became more interested and, by the time Gabe finished, had leaned completely out of his chair and into Gabe's personal space.

"My name is Jearn* and may I say it is a true pleasure to welcome you to the contest for ownership of the Purple House." Jearn extended his hand as he spoke.

Gabe ignored the hand and merely nodded his head. "How many have registered for the contest?"

"You are number nineteen and I'm sure one of the last to enter. Demanding simple writing skills as an entry criteria is difficult enough, but then letting an entrant know that the chance of survival is less than fifty percent really reduces the size of the field." Jearn opened another drawer on the cabinet and pulled out a metallic purple band.

"Fifty percent?" Gabe didn't like the odds.

"Well, it's not only from the challenges but also the competition that occurs outside the Purple House." Jearn held up the seamless purple band and, as if in a magic show, snapped it over Gabe's wrist.

"Such as accidental deaths, sicknesses, assassination attempts, kidnappings?" Lian's quick response evoked quizzical looks from everyone in the room. "What?" Lian asked the group.

"Good guess." Jearn stood up and walked around to Gabe who was still trying to figure out how the band had made it onto his wrist. "The bracelet will not come off until you are either dead or lose in the competition. It will be a clear sign to all that you are be protected by the city and house guards...to the best of their abilities."

"What do I do next? Do I stay here?" Gabe thought it was too easy.

Jearn laughed as he replied, "You definitely are new around here. Why would we want you here? I don't want to get caught in an assassination attempt. However, you can stay at any inn within the city walls for free. You will be treated very well, even if you must be buried."

Jearn handed Gabe a thick book and a piece of paper. Gabe stood still, staring at Jearn with determination to outwait the man.

"Very well. The book is a historical writing about the city and the Purple House. You need to have read it for your first test. The paper describes the ten tests that have been chosen by the Purple House lord to determine who will be his successor. Grading for each test will either be by points or elimination." Jearn motioned to the exit, refocused on his nail file, and sat back down at his desk.

Gabe shrugged his shoulders and they all left the building.

"That's strange." Taima was looking at the guards.

"What?" Lian responded.

"The guards all have shields now and seem prepared for something." Taima started to feel a little uneasy. A few steps more and they were beyond the guards. "What happened to all the people?" The street was much less crowded than before.

"Watch out!" Taima's siren was all they needed. Gabe and Lain tucked and rolled as Taima's swords ripped from their scabbards, forming an X that clanked as a small knife ricocheted off them.

Lian was barely out of his roll when his return volley spun through the air toward the figure he had just spotted on the rooftop. The assassin was already gone.

The three formed a rough circle with their backs facing inward and awaited another attack. However, Taima felt nothing coming and sheathed her swords. The guards hadn't moved, but a cheer went up from within the shops around them.

Jearn's head popped out from the building with a shocked looked on his face. "You aren't as green as I thought you were. Imagine that." He then disappeared back inside the building.

X.

Gabe plopped down into a seat in the room of the luxury inn that he had picked from the slew of recommendations. Apparently it was an honor to host a house competitor. He looked at the parchment Jearn had provided.

Competitive Events

I.   Written Exam on the History of Igypkt and the Purple House
        Day 1, Morning   Location: Purple House
        Points: Elimination, 70% to Pass

II.   Archery
        Day 1, Afternoon   Location: Arena
        Points: 100 pts to winner – 10 per placement thereafter

III.   Long Distance Run
        Day 1, Evening   Location: Arena
        Points: 100 pts to winner – 10 per placement thereafter

IV.   Kondit's Puzzle*
        Day 2, Morning   Location: Arena
        Points: 100 pts to winner – 10 per placement thereafter

V.   Martial Arts Tournament (Savarail*—Full Contact)
        Day 2, Afternoon   Location: Arena
        Points: 100 pts to winner – 10 per placement thereafter

VI.   Martial Arts Tournament (Savarail—Forms)
        Day 2, Evening   Location: Arena
        Points: 100 pts to winner – 10 per placement thereafter

VII.   Accounting & Strategy (dollars & politics)
        Day 3, Morning   Location: Purple House
        Points: 100 pts to winner – 10 per placement thereafter

VIII.   Endurance (standing in sun, no food or drink)
        Day 3, Afternoon   Location: Arena
        Points: 100 pts to winner – 10 per placement thereafter

IX.   Fulcrum
        Day 3, Evening   Location: Arena
        Points: 50 pts for winning team

X.   Political Speech on Current Political Issue
        Day 3, Night   Location: Arena
        Points: 100 pts – 1st place, 50 pts – 2nd place, 25 pts – 3rd place

"Wow, this does not look as easy as I thought it would be. How am I going to train to win all these events?" pondered Gabe.

"You don't have to win all the events. You just need to earn more points than everyone else by the end," Taima pointed out as she grabbed the paper from Gabe. "This is just like a decathlon. It's all about strategy. You can't burn yourself out on an event you know you can't win."

"I can easily put together a probability matrix based on your strengths and determine—" Lian's words dropped off as they heard shouting and yelling from the street below.

They all headed to the window as Gabe tapped on his wristband shield, setting it to the dimensions of the opening to stop any possible projectiles.

When they looked down, they saw no less than a dozen foot soldiers, four armor-clad horsemen, and a robed man standing around a blue, muscular, bird-like being who was bound in ropes and chains. The birdman was tossing and turning as he tried to break free. They could hear the incantations of the robed man and feel the mana release. The bound creature's head started to sway and the tension in his powerful frame disappeared. A stack of papers in his claws dropped to the ground as he slumped against the door entrance.

"Now take him quickly and place him in the cage. We finally caught the author of the underground paper, and the leader of the resistance party!" shrieked the voice of the bald, well-groomed mage.

Gabe's anger rose up through his heart and into his throat. He realized that this prisoner was going to be put to death just because he was different. Gabe's hand reached for his vibe sword, but was stopped by the grip of another.

He stared at Taima, demanding an explanation with his glare.

"Gabe, not now. There are too many of them for us to take out and you know it. Also, even if we somehow win, we will blow our mission before Dillon arrives in the city." Taima felt strange being the rational one.

"But, it's not...not." Gabe couldn't finish his sentence.

"It's not fair because he looks different? I know. I also know that sacrifices must be made to win the war. We may soon be trying to stop an entire racial clash, but not yet. Not now." Taima herself was in pain at the thought of what was going to happen. The longer they had stayed in the city, the more they had learned about The Gallen War and how wrong it was. However, they couldn't expose themselves to their enemy yet.

Gabe shrugged off her arm and stormed out of the room. He slammed the door behind him then stopped, trying to collect himself. When he finally did, he strolled into the now quiet street, eying the stack of papers the creature had dropped. Without caring who saw him, he picked them up and walked back into the hotel.

He would fight back.

XI.

Lian walked into the familiar tavern on the sixth level of Cureio. It was a members-only club, but it didn't need a guard at the entrance. If you weren't invited, you would quickly find yourself in a coffin.

The lights were low and the mood was quiet. Lian slowly looked around, then headed to the bar. The bartender needed only to glance at him before nodding in the direction of the back door. Lian tried to relax. He grasped the handle of the door, opened it, and stepped into the dark alley. He immediately noticed a large man nestled in the shadows, smoking a cigar-like object.

"How much you need?" His guttural voice asked.

"Five lots." Lian's hands shook madly as he held out the money. The man surely took the trembling for drug use.

The man stepped forward enough for Lian to see the tracks of scars peppering his rotund face. He switched the money for the contraband, revealing a hand missing two digits. "Five lots is enough to kill a man if he isn't careful."

Lian didn't answer or look up as he pocketed the mojuila.

"Good luck, kid. You'll need it." The man laughed as he walked away.

Lian heard the door open behind him. From his previous survey of the bar and the weight of the footsteps, he knew what two men had come out. Without turning around, Lian spoke. "You two didn't think that I would notice you sitting in the back of the room next to the staircase?"

The skinnier of the two replied as Lian slowly turned around. "We don't much care. You seem to have a lot of money and some mojuila. It's good enough reason to empty your stomach." Both men pulled out their knives as Lian finally turned around.

The one talking was holding his knife like an ice pick, while the shorter and more stout thug held his with the knife butt facing out. The stout guy he would have to watch out for, and take on last.

Lian shifted his body slightly to the side of the novice, causing him to swing with a downward strike. Lian blocked the man's attack and wrapped his other hand around the arm, locking the knife behind the man's back and throwing him off balance. Lian shifted the novice to the side to act as a shield from the other attacker.

He had kept his blocking fist tight but now flung it open, releasing a spray of pepper extract into the other attacker's face. This bought him enough time to pull down on the novice's trapped hand and lift up the elbow. The man screamed in pain as his shoulder dislocated. Lian dropped him to the ground and barely dodged a knife swipe by the other.

Lian then remembered that his chi didn't just have to be used for magical powers. He waited for another haphazard swing and blocked the arm with his wrist. This time he exhaled and shot out chi from his wrist. The man howled as both bones in his forearm shattered and his skin burned. The knife dropped to the ground.

Lian didn't stop there. He grabbed the man's broken arm and twisted it in the wrong direction.

"Ahhhh, please stop. I beg you. Please!" The man whimpered.

"You both work for me now. Is that clear?" Lian applied more pressure.

"Yes. Yes. Please. Anything you want," he moaned.

Lian let go and bounded between the shadows after his next victim. It took less than a minute to find the fat man with the two missing fingers. He was smoking again and relaxing against a dark wall.

Lian quietly scaled the rocky wall and positioned himself right over the man. He reached into one of his belt pouches and pulled out a thin chord. He controlled his breathing to try to undo his nervousness, then waited for the perfect moment.

The chord wrapped around the fat man's neck at the same time he was hit by Lian's weight on his back. Surprised at the attack, he grunted and instinctively reached with both hands for the noose. While wrapped on his back, Lian stomped the inside of the man's knee, causing him to fall sideways. Lian grimaced as he hit the ground but didn't let go. His jujitsu training kicked in and enabled him to handle the weight and strength of the larger man.

"Do you want to die tonight?" Lian whispered in his ear. The man didn't respond, but kept struggling to escape.

Lian gripped even tighter on the noose as he spoke. "You have one more chance to answer me, fat man. Do you want to die tonight?"

The man realized there was no escape and shook his head no.

"You work for me now. Do you understand?" Lian had not given up his tight grip. The man nodded frantically in agreement. Just when his eyes started to roll up into his head was when Lian let go and kicked him off himself. The man rolled, gasping for air.

"Now, who do you work for?" Lian asked.

It was going to be a long and dangerous night.

XII.

"Gabe, I've been thinking." Taima commented as they walked down the street.

"About what?" Gabe asked.

"I'm your bodyguard and supposed to protect you at all times. But to do that I really need to intimidate people. We want people to know not to mess with you." Taima was looking straight ahead as she spoke.

"Ok." Gabe didn't like where this was headed. When Taima became verbose, it was never good for him. "What are you trying to say?"

"There's an attack coming and I need you to cower so my reputation can grow." Taima had let her hands casually drop to her sides, next to her swords.

"Not cool, Taima, not cool." Gabe was venting, but understood what she meant.

"It's only one person and he's coming up behind you. I think he intends to use some type of poison weapon. His intent is not to cause a scene, but to do something more subtle." Taima tried to appear calm as she pulled the would-be-attacker's mana toward her. The more she focused on it, the more information she gleaned.

"On my count roll forward and to the right." Taima dropped her voice so only Gabe could hear. "Three, two, one."

Gabe tucked and rolled forward as a hand swiped out toward him. Taima dropped a foot backward as she drew her swords with the flat of the blade resting against her forearms. She spun and shifted her body, catching the hand against her metal sword with an upward block.

Taima looked at the hand first, noting that its fingernails were covered in metal with a tar-like liquid on them. She then looked into the surprised eyes of the female attacker as she thrust her hand straight at the woman's face. The butt of her sword made a sickening sound as it crushed the woman's nose.

The attacker's eyes were blinded by the tearing from her broken nose. She put her hands up in a defensive posture, but Taima surprised her with a left leg sweep, sending her to the ground. Taima ended with a sword against the woman's neck.

It was over so quickly that people in the streets only noticed the attack after the woman had landed on the ground. Screams erupted all around them as guards quickly encircled Taima and Gabe.

Gabe stood up and flashed his purple bracelet. "Thank you for your quick arrival. It was yet another assassination attempt thwarted by my ever-ready bodyguard."

The lead city guard stepped forward. "Yes, I can see that she has everything under control. I must admit that I am impressed that she did it again without any permanent harm to her victim."

Taima blushed as she realized it was Kailman, the lead guard from the main gate.

"What do you mean, no permanent harm? My nose is broken!" The female assassin whined, but also tried to nip Taima's leg with her poisoned claws. Taima had easily sensed it and kicked her in the face before she could finish the strike. The woman screamed again, much to the amusement of Kailman.

"We are sorry for the attack and will make sure that the assassin is processed to the full extent of the law." Kailman motioned his men into action while he bowed to Gabe, and even deeper to Taima.

"I'd prefer if she were not executed as I don't believe that killing will solve anything," replied Gabe.

Kailman gave him a half shrug in response.

"If there is anything else I can do, please let me know." Kailman followed his men who were carrying off the flailing woman.

"Is your reputation increased now?" Gabe asked, but he received no response. "Taima!"

"What? Uhm, yeah. Whatever." Taima pulled back to her immediate surroundings.

"Taima, I need to go into this bookstore for a while. Please wait outside." Gabe opened the rickety door and closed it behind him. He nodded to the store owner and slowly walked to a back corner with a stairwell leading down.

The stairs creaked as he stepped on them, which he knew served notice to the watchers below. Gabe continued down two flights to a room containing thousands of books in various states of organization. He ducked behind one larger stack of books and tapped on the floor with his foot. A heavy, stone trapdoor opened up with more stairs leading into a dark hole.

Gabe could now hear the distant sound of hand-powered printing presses at work. An immense, furry hand reached out to help him down the ladder.

XIII.

The only light in the hotel room came from the full moon outside. Gabe looked over at Lian as he pulled the black mask down over his face. "Are you both ready?" he asked.

Taima nodded and also covered her face, feeling the excitement of the night's mission rushing through her veins.

Lian opened the door to their room and carefully peered out. No one was in the hall. He motioned for the other two to follow as he rounded the corner to the back of the hotel. At the end of the hallway was a barred, open window. Lian firmly grabbed the vertical bars and pulled them off the ledge of the window. Gabe and Taima could see that he had dislodged them earlier.

Lian looked below before gracefully slinging himself out of the window and down to the first floor alley. With some help, Taima and Gabe followed suit. They spent the next half hour following Lian as he weaved in and out of the shadows of the alleys.

Ahead of them was the open area of the city where the object from the sky had come to rest. Surrounding it was a three-foot-high wooden fence, with four higher wooden poles on the barrier equidistant from each other.

Gabe squinted at the poles, confirming Ghost's story of where the blackened skulls from those within the spaceship now resided. His stomach churned at the thought of the kids trapped in the ship's cabin, roasted alive by the fireballs.

Lian's hand pulled Gabe back into the shadows as a guard squinted and peered down the alleyway before turning back to his station.

"How do we get past those guards?" asked Gabe.

Lian put his hand up to his lips to hush him. A few more seconds ticked by before Lian motioned for them to start heading toward the ship. Gabe looked at Taima and they both shrugged. This was Lian's specialty, or so they hoped.

As they crept forward, Gabe saw that there were four guards positioned around the fence, alert but clearly bored.

A large explosion to the northwest assaulted their ears. The guards all took a few steps in the direction of the noise, then stopped. Clearly they had been given a single order with harsh consequences for disobeying.

Another explosion went off; close enough this time for the guards to see the flash. All four charged away from their assignment and into the chaos of the streets.

"Arlar's gift?" Taima asked. Lian nodded in affirmation.

The torch lights around the open yard went out, and Lian sprang into action. He charged to the fence and stopped short right before touching it.

"Is it trapped?" asked Gabe. Lian was clearly focused on something else.

Lian relaxed his body and slowed down his breathing. He pulled mana into his belly and let it ride up his spine and out his third eye chakra. Soon he could see the thin lines of the magical trap. Lian kept his breathing under control and carefully unraveled the lines with his hands until nothing was left. He let out a heavy sigh of relief, took another deep breath, and leapt over the fence. He turned and gave a cocky wink, but this time it was really a façade. He was scared to death. This was his first time disarming a magical trap since Arlar had taught him.

Gabe and Taima jumped over the fence and followed him to the hatch of the ship. The hull was blackened from the fireball assault, but upon closer inspection they could see that it was only surface damage and still easy to open. Lian looked around before darting inside. Once Gabe and Taima had entered, he partially shut the lid and tapped Gabe in the pitch darkness.

In a short time Gabe's vibe sword glowed a good two feet in length, lighting up the entire cabin. Their eyes were greeted by a room uncannily similar to the one they had arrived in themselves—except this one smelled and looked of charred material. All the sleeping compartment doors were open, and inside they saw the burnt flesh and bones of the space travelers. Most likely kids their own age, from their own planet. Lian motioned them to one compartment that was empty.

"Maybe there were only four kids on the mission. I find it hard to believe anyone could survive what happened inside here." Gabe's voice was shaky.

Lian looked over to the single vertical compartment that was the latrine. He stood up and walked over to it, but couldn't pull the door open. "Gabe, come over here with your sword."

Gabe walked over, placed the vibe sword in the seam of the compartment, and pulled downward. He cut through the latch, and the door popped slightly ajar.

"Good job, Jedi knight." Lian commented.

Taima pulled the door completely open so they could all look inside.

"It's only partially burnt, as if someone yanked the door shut as a fireball exploded in here." Lian said.

"Yeah, but then how did the person get out after that? Look at the lock on the door. It clearly had been fused shut from the heat." Gabe knew the vibe sword left a clean edge when it cut through metal. He could see the melted parts of the broken lock and was sure it wasn't from him.

"I dunno? But I really think that the guy who killed the innkeeper is our fifth Earthling. It would also explain the burnt face I saw." Lian wondered if he was watching them right now.

"Gabe, what else do we need to do in here?" Taima felt they had already spent way too much time in the creepy cabin.

"We should do a quick once over of the ship to see if there is anything else and then get out of here. Remember to not look for the obvious, but see if there is something hidden." Gabe spoke but couldn't imagine how anything could have survived the fireball attack.

They all looked around for a while, but everything was burnt to a crisp.

"Look at this?" Lian whispered from the latrine. They all gathered around the door and stared down at the now open toilet. Lian reached down and pulled out a parchment that was slightly burnt around the edges. It was a picture of five smiling teenagers, flashing fake gang signs.

"Man, we must've looked as eager as they did before we left." Taima remarked.

"Those eyes. They're the ones I saw." Lian started to point but paused as he heard something outside. "The guards are back."

"Back, what are we going to do?" Taima's voice started to raise, but Gabe quickly hushed her.

"No problem. We just have to stay in here until tomorrow night. I already set up some help in case this happened." Lian commented back.

"Tomorrow night? You want me to stay in this tomb with dead bodies until tomorrow night? I'm gonna kill you, Lian." Taima managed to keep her voice to a whisper.

They heard another explosion that seemed just around the corner, followed by Lian laughing. Taima realized that he had played her and started slapping him on the back. "Not funny, Lian."

Lian dodged her attacks by charging to the exit. He peered outside before leaping out and rolling as he hit the ground.

****

Gabe breathed a sigh of relief as he plopped down on the couch in their room. They were all exhausted from the night's activities.

"So what do we do now? Do we try and track down this half-burnt kid?" Taima asked.

"He would be a man by now." Gabe wanted to just relax and unwind. However, as their temporary leader he knew he was being asked to provide direction. "Well, we are learning about the city, have explored the spaceship, and Lian's network has told us everything we care to know about Cureio's Mulshin ruler. I think the odds of finding our fellow Earthling is slim. He has the advantage of time and knowledge of the city. I say we continue with preparations for the Purple House challenge, learn more about the impending attack on the Nalistatians, and wait for Dillon and Matt to get back."

"Wouldn't that mean our whole foray into the spaceship was a waste?" Lian retorted.

"This is not a role-playing game, Lian. Not everything is going to fall into our laps." Gabe closed his eyes as he finished speaking.

No one said a word, but all privately hoped that they would see Dillon and Matt again. And soon.

Chapter 13
A Quick, Long Journey

I.

The trip to Cureio with Sileya started off strangely for Dillon and Matt. They noticed that with each step they took it seemed that they had taken many more, as if they were on an escalator. Dillon started watching his footsteps and noticed they were actually about four steps apart. When he asked Sileya about it, she smiled and said it was a simple traveling spell and not to worry. Also, as the trio walked along he noticed that no one bothered them at all or even seemed to acknowledge their existence.

"Sileya, how come no one seems to pay attention to us?" Matt spoke what Dillon was thinking.

"A simple avoidance spell. No need to be distracted by vagrants looking for a quick meal."

The day turned to dusk and Dillon sat down to think about their hiking rate. They were moving at a relatively fast pace, but the path wasn't straight or easy to walk on in many areas. This would normally have equated to about three miles per hour. Due to the longer days they had over ten hours of full-time hiking, which meant they could go thirty miles a day on the road to Cureio. Now, with Sileya's traveling spell, they were moving about four times their normal pace and had covered around one hundred twenty miles in one day! If they kept up this pace then they would be to the city in about fifteen days.

Before they arrived at the city, Dillon needed to figure out the truth behind The Gallen War and why Sileya's story didn't make sense. He hoped he could get the answers from Sileya without making her leave. He was sure they would need her help in an unknown city, where they were probably expected.

After an uneventful night, the trio repacked their belongings and started off toward Cureio. Silence was there companion for many hours until Dillon decided to start his verbal attack.

"Sileya, before The Fallen One was destroyed I had asked him if there was good and evil." He hesitated to let Sileya bring herself into the conversation.

"He is good at twisting words, but what did he say?"

"He said something like, 'Don't be silly Dillon, of course there is.' Then he smiled and disappeared in a rather gruesome way."

"Mmmm," was all Sileya muttered.

"Do you think there is a good and evil?" Dillon reached down and pulled a blade of grass from the ground to play with, but his mind was sharply focused on her reaction. He almost missed the blade due to the traveling spell.

"Of course I do. Good is not easy to define and thus has many levels, depending on the context of your question. For example, a lone farmer might define good as how she treats her family, the land, her neighbors, and those that she comes in contact with. She would hold those values as part of one having good morals and thus those who try and destroy those values as being evil. You see, evil is always the opposite of good." The discussion did not seem to upset Sileya at all as she continued her thoughts out loud. "Now a mayor of that town might have a different view of good for himself versus what is good for his town."

"What do you mean?" asked Matt. "Isn't that conflicting?"

"In a way yes, but in another way no. Let us take a man who is pious and for his whole life has willingly given away all his earthly belongings to those that need it, and in addition will not fight any who attack him. He is seen as a wise and even-tempered man so one day his town elects him mayor. As such they entrust him with both the survival of the town and their own individual livelihoods. Now the mayor is in a dilemma. If he leads them down his own path of no personal belongings he will surely lead all of the town people to poverty. Also, if he takes his pacifist approach to running the town he is in charge of, they will surely be taken advantage of by neighboring towns."

"What is he to do then?" Dillon placed the blade of grass in his mouth and stared blankly forward.

"It is not a simple choice, and therefore not a simple thing to answer. For the *Flying Fishermen*, whose duty is to protect the people, we have very strict personal morals but we chose a democracy of sorts to determine which values are good for Kalansi. We also asked the people to tell us what they viewed as moral goodness for their society. We then swore to uphold those values as laws and to protect them and their people to ensure order.

"Those things that were opposite of this good became evil. It is our job to wipe out the worst of the evil and to help guide the people through the other evil that abounds." Sileya swelled with pride that she'd taught these young men the values of the *Flying Fishermen*. They had been to the sacred place, and there was no reason to hide who she was.

"Were the books created before magical creatures were around?" Dillon figured it was time to up the ante.

"No, in fact the leaders of the magical creatures helped create the laws. They even..." Sileya's voice trailed off as confusion played in her mind.

"Hey do either of you want a reed of grass to chew on? It helps pass the time." Dillon quickly snatched a couple pieces and offered them to Sileya and Matt.

Matt grabbed one but stared at Dillon, trying to figure out what he was doing. Dillon just smiled and started walking again without talking, allowing the others to follow. For lunch Sileya provided dried meat and fresh fruit while they continued to walk to save time. After another hour, Dillon spoke up again.

"Oh, I almost forgot about our last conversation on good and evil. Sileya, did your order write down these laws? Was that what those four pedestals were for?"

Sileya thought nothing of it as she answered. "Yes, well at least one of them. There were four sacred books and together they were called the *Unity*. They are *The History of Igypkt, The Foundation of Mana, The Life of a Flying Fishermen* and *The Gallen War*. The *Flying Fishermen* outlines how the laws came about for the land, how they are set up, and how we are to protect all that live on Kalansi.

"Now the one for The Gallen War. I assume it details what you told us about how the war came about and how one will come to finish the war?"

"That is correct, Dillon." Sileya kept her eyes open as they entered a dangerous section of their journey between the north and south deserts.

Raiders knew there was only one path for travelers to follow, and many potential ambush sites. Her avoidance spell would help them, but the smarter and more-determined bandits could not be charmed.

"So, if this battle is between humankind and magical creatures, then one can assume there will be humans on one side and magical creatures on the other with no crossing over?"

"Yes, Dillon. That seems rather obvious."

"Sorry, I'm just a little slow. Now on the wholly human side I can also assume that those troops came from towns and cities that only have humans? Do these cities themselves have laws to outline good and bad behavior?

"Yes, in fact all cities are required to have them. Part of the *Flying Fishermen's* job is to visit the cities and ensure the rules are being obeyed."

"Good. Now what happens if a human breaks a law?" Dillon had cast his fishing line, and was reeling Sileya in.

"It depends on the severity of the act they committed. They may have to repay, lose their property, or even serve time in a jail." Sileya was amazed that these young ones hadn't been taught the simple rules of living in a society.

"Ah, so there are jails for those that commit the most evil of acts such as murder and rape?" Dillon cautiously watched Sileya's eyes to make sure she didn't become angry.

"Yes, because in fact there are always some who are incapable of living within the constraints of society and there are always those who are inherently evil."

"So for magical beings and their society, which of course is purely evil, there must also be outliers that are good. Then The Gallen War is not about good versus evil, but one of discrimination. Fighting those who are different from us. In fact I could be fighting a good magical creature like Arlar when my ally to the right of me could be a human convicted of murder!" Dillon's voice had risen in crescendo fashion, ending with him almost yelling at Sileya. "You in fact are supporting the murder of innocent beings simply because of how they were born!"

"No. No. Nooo!" Sileya dropped to her knees for the second time in as many months as tears rolled down her face. "We cannot kill the innocent no matter what their race." All three felt a sound like the snapping of a rubber band and both Dillon and Sileya saw a thin chord of mana emanating from Sileya's forehead that quickly disappeared in a wisp of smoke.

Dillon and Matt looked at the ground surrounding Sileya. To their amazement they saw a perfect white lily grow forth where each tear hit the earth. By the time Sileya stood up and looked at them she was centered in a pool of white beauty.

"Thank you, Dillon. I clearly mistook your appearance to represent naivety. You are wise beyond your years and saved me from making a terrible mistake. I don't remember everything, but I do know that there is no such thing as The Gallen War. It is The Fallen War, and *The Unity* resides within the city of Cureio where the *Flying Fishermen* now live. It is there that I will find the truth."

II.

Galgalor no longer enjoyed the skin-tearing grasps and bites from his slow-moving minions that surrounded his new throne of pain. They knew no recourse would come from their suspended master and dug deeper every day into his bleeding flesh, which now festered between the bloated maggots. He had not even attempted to move in days, sulking in his despair.

In an instant Galgalor felt the snapping of one of the strings from his intricate web of lies and moaned as loud as one could without a tongue. He knew it was only one string, but a web is only as strong as its weakest thread. Diabold would not be happy.

III.

General Trailerton and his riders glided through the astral plane in a rush to track down the power source he had sensed only days before. Salas's confidence glowed in his own belief that he had destroyed the two outlanders, but the general was not convinced. He did not want to be the one to report their deaths to Mungoth without proof, especially when his existence was wrapped around the finger of the unforgiving ruler.

As he drifted in closer, he could see three figures about forty feet from the well-traveled road. He popped into the normal plane to survey the situation. Unlike most, he and his ghost trackers could quickly traverse through one plane and into the other. They could also see between the planes, but their vision was blurry when doing this.

The General noted that the muscular monk was pacing the campsite while the other two slept. Stepping out of the astral plane allowed him to confirm that the two men were the ones he wanted, but he did not know the third. A risk, but one he felt worth taking on. Last time he had done what Mungoth wanted and notified others of the outlander's existence. They had failed. Now his patience was gone and it was time for him to seize the moment and then demand his freedom.

He yearned to charge in, but first he needed to reward Salas for his mistake. The General reached into the mind of his weakest rider and ordered him to go dispose of Salas and place Captain Lynn in charge of the Kalansi assassination army.

General Trailerton motioned for the others to surround the three victims. In the astral plane they would go unnoticed and could easily ambush the trio without much effort. He watched while his sytraks* moved into action, but then hesitated. Something gnawed at him, and his wealth of experiences told him to hold off.

The General again surveyed his surroundings. There were several ruins in this area of the astral plane. A run down hut with no roof stood to his far left; off to the right a set of stairs ran up nearly twenty feet and led to nowhere; and a number of very large stones were strewn about the landscape.

IV.

"I do hope that you are merely wishing to warm yourself by our fire."

The General spun around and looked at the top of the stairs, seeing a young man in his early twenties who appeared to wear nothing more than leather armor with no visible weapons. But appearances could be deceiving. General Trailerton stared into Dillon's eyes and did not like what he saw.

"So you knew we were coming, outlander. I must admit that I am caught by surprise. But surely you realize that I and my sytraks are not tied to a single plane. We still have the upper hand." The General and his seven riders moved several paces toward Dillon's motionless body and his worldly friends.

Dillon took his first look at the creatures under his hunter's direction. The sytraks appeared humanoid with dull-black bodies covered in short, silver-tipped fur. Their hairy faces were mostly normal except for the long snouts they used for tracking. Their arms ended in double, six-inch long blades that curved sharply back around and up to their wrists. The blades were curved backward from the way normal claws protruded, and would be extremely dangerous from a simple back-handed slap. An eerie, red-orange glow emanated from them.

"Really?" Dillon sent a mana surge to Sileya and Matt while calling forth his astral weapons. General Trailerton and his riders stopped and watched with some surprise as the famous Sword of Baillen appeared in Dillon's left hand and the Lost Rider Shield covered his right. But this was nothing compared to their shock when Dillon whistled and six massive, snow-white wolves gracefully leapt out from behind the large rocks in the astral plane. Their landing placed them perfectly in front of the seven sytraks, impeding their path toward Dillon's body and friends.

"The Wolves of Destiny* obey no one, young Dillon. Hythea* and his pack have wasted centuries trying to defeat me and will risk your life if it means they can kill one of my sytraks." General Trailerton was buying time with his words while weighing his options. He was taken aback by Dillon's confident appearance and downright scared to see the wolves. He no longer had the upper hand, but if he could get to the worldly body of the outlander then his mission would be complete. He knew of Cahlar's grand plan but only cared about his own benefit. The sooner he killed the outlander, the sooner he would regain his freedom.

Upon surveying the surroundings again, Trailerton realized he had made another error in his rush to attack. The outlander's body was nestled against a massive tree in the natural world and was also completely within a large rock in the astral plane. Only a few parts of his body were exposed.

Hythea interrupted his thoughts. "You are correct, Trailerton, in that we obey no one. However, Dillon is an equal and his fight is worthy of our allegiance. You show that you lack the wisdom that comes with the passage of time." The glowing white fur of the largest wolf shook with the snarling voice. "It is true that in the beginning our purpose was to destroy all sytraks in order to help restore the balance of good and evil. However, we are as you said, the Wolves of Destiny, and our purpose now is to ensure that you do not destroy the destiny of this warrior. He alone holds the key to shifting the balance of power to good." Hythea knew that in order to aid Dillon they needed to bite and lock onto the sytraks. When a Wolf of Destiny had a sytrak in its grasp then the sytrak could not travel between planes. "You will not be allowed to retreat. It is your time to die, even if we all must die with you."

V.

Both Matt and Sileya felt the surge of mana that Dillon sent. It was the signal that the battle would begin.

"How can I fight when I can't even see them coming?" Matt questioned as he yet again felt useless in battle.

"Get as close to Dillon's left side as possible and I'll take the front and right sides. We need not worry about his back or from below as the sytraks can't materialize into a space that is already occupied. Let's hope the Wolves of Destiny got the message and also decided it was worth their while to come. Without them it will be a short battle." Sileya chanted out loud and four more arms appeared around her torso.

"That's pretty neat, but what about weapons?" Somehow she still looked beautiful, even with six arms.

"No need. If I touch them it will feel like a sword slicing into their very soul. They are bringers of death, and I am a cultivator of life."

Matt's eyes kept shifting around as he imagined shadows popping up. "This is like waiting for a shot by the doctor."

Then the barrage began.

VI.

Dillon was pleased that he had caught the plane-shifter off guard, but was also strategically leery since the Wolves of Destiny had only arrived minutes before the others. His body was the weakness and his enemy knew it. Dillon didn't know if Matt and Sileya could stop the attacks if Trailerton or his troop were able to get close. In the astral plane, things could move as quickly as the speed of thought, but Dillon wasn't sure how fast they could materialize in and out of planes.

General Trailerton and his seven sytraks were in a fighting wing formation; with two sytraks to each of his sides and three more about five paces behind to cover their backs. Dillon was on the set of stairs to their north. With the hut to the enemies' south, the enemy was forced to head straight into the wolves to get to Dillon's body. He calmly watched the General, waiting for his move.

An unseen signal launched the enemy down the path Dillon expected. All charged forward except for Trailerton, who instead flew in the direction of the hut while two small swords appeared in his hands. As Hythea and his wolves charged to greet the sytraks, Dillon realized

Trailerton's plan and admired his tactic. Trailerton had a one-man advantage and was letting his soldiers fully engage the enemy so he could circle around and get to Dillon's body.

Dillon flew off the stairs, circling around in an opposite pattern to Trailerton, while barking out for the last wolf to stay back and wait for an enemy to break through. The narrowing field, he felt, would allow the wolves to compensate for their fewer numbers.

Trailerton countered, and without any verbal communication two sytraks switched their course and trailed Dillon. Dillon was still headed to his body, but was too close to one of the wolves, who was on the outside and had not yet engaged. If Dillon continued past the wolf, he would leave it trying to fight off two sytraks at once. Dillon stopped and spun around in time to use his shield to block one of the sytrak attacks on the wolf. The shield looked small, but its magical power extended its block an extra foot in every direction.

Hythea engaged two of the sytraks to prevent a head-on assault to Dillon's body. He was the only wolf that was clearly faster than the sytraks.

The battle was on.

Dillon heard teeth and blades crashing against each other as he parried the sytrak's blades with his own weapons. While sytraks were much faster than the wolves, the wolves appeared more cunning and set up openings on the sytraks with fake attacks.

Dillon side-stepped one of the glowing knife-hands, positioning him to see a flash of light near the hut. It was followed by an immediate yelp. He blocked another attack and turned just enough to see the injured wolf stagger. Its face was burnt black and its snout caved in. Dillon knew it was a magical attack, even though he had not yet learned how to use magic in the astral plane. Trailerton whipped by the wobbly wolf, leaving the finishing blow to the sytraks.

Dillon struggled with the speed of his sytraks, barely blocking the multiple attacks. He heard an unnatural growl that was cut short as powerful canines ripped the throat out of a sytrak. Hythea let out a bone-chilling howl to show his pleasure. As the pack leader it was fitting he record the first enemy casualty.

But the sytrak who had dealt the deathblow to the injured wolf was now following the General. Dillon remembered his own teachings of teamwork, parried his sytrak's attack and then lunged forward at the sytrak on the wolf next to him. His sword found its mark, with its magical power honing in on the enemy's weakest spot and critically wounding it. He had little time to revel in his hit as he heard an incantation. Trailerton had charged upon the wolf that Dillon had ordered to stay back. The wolf was not afraid, and appeared poised to strike when suddenly Trailerton's shadowy form dissipated from the wolf's view. Another hollow yelp filled the astral plane as Trailerton appeared behind the wolf, dealing a deathblow to its neck. Trailerton was now only a thought away from Dillon's body.

  Dillon screamed in frustration and grief as he timed his attacks on the sytrak to occur exactly when the wolf beside him attacked. The sytrak blocked his own attacks but left an opening that the wolf quickly took advantage of. The wolf's canines penetrated the sytrak's ear hole and opposite eye, closing with bone-crushing force. Dillon spun around in time to see Trailerton exit the astral plane, with his two small swords poised to attack.

VIIa.

The battle in the astral plane had been going on for some time, but on Igypkt only a second passed before Trailerton appeared in front of Dillon's body. His two-sword attack came swiftly. Sileya was barely able to deflect them with her four extra arms, which were as hard as stone and sent sparks flying when they hit the swords. Trailerton disappeared again and reappeared to Sileya's left as Matt shouted a warning. Sileya adjusted quickly enough to catch one sword, but the other sliced into Dillon's left quadricep. Trailerton disappeared and appeared again next to Matt. Matt blocked one swing, but he couldn't stop the other that hit Dillon's right shoulder.

  In and out he popped another dozen times, leaving Matt and Sileya exhausted and Dillon's body covered in blood.

  "This isn't working, Sileya; what do we do? He's going to die!" Matt worried, even though the rapid attacks had stopped.

  "Relax." Was all that Sileya said. Matt felt her words and calmed himself just as a black-gray creature appeared out of thin air with its glowing, knife-like hands striking down at Dillon.

  Even in his surprise, Matt was able to deflect both hands. Sileya lunged forward, her hands spinning in every direction. One just caught the disappearing creature. A shriek rang out as the misty form crackled and hissed, then fell to ashes on the trampled grass.

They repositioned themselves and waited.

VIIb.

Dillon and the wolf at his side charged toward Trailerton and the sytrak near Dillon's body. They watched as Trailerton rapidly dissolved in and out of the astral plane. Fresh blood dripped off his swords.

Dillon had learned to hide his astral chord but could feel the energy in it waning. He finally reached Trailerton, but not before he had disappeared at least a dozen times. When the General was at last forced to turn around to greet Dillon, he did it with a calmly-wicked grin carved into his stone-cold face.

Trailerton's smile disappeared when Hythea upended one of his warriors and crushed its spine in his teeth. Trailerton was now at the disadvantage and knew it, with only the sytrak next to him and one more well behind him—who would soon be engaged by Hythea and two other wolves. If he was going to perish, he decided, he would make sure the outlander went with him. He mentally commanded the sytrak next to him to attack Dillon's body as he moved to engage Dillon and the wolf in the astral plane. The sytrak disappeared and screamed as it immediately met its death.

Dillon smiled at Trailerton's shocked expression. "Nothing like having a high priestess on one's side, eh?" Dillon knew that Trailerton would not surrender and wasted no more words on the doomed spirit.

Trailerton swung madly at them, amid the shriek of the last sytrak being destroyed by the wolves. Soon there would be Hythea and three more canines against him. Dillon knew Trailerton was distressed and watched for any last acts of desperation.

Trailerton started to dissolve into the normal plane, the evil smile yet again crossing his face.

Dillon's mind raced. What would Trailerton do? Would he defeat Matt and Sileya? What could Dillon do?

Dillon heard a growl and watched Trailerton's smile leave yet again. Hythea had somehow appeared behind the General and was locked securely on his neck, keeping him in the astral plane. "Don't you think I would have also learned a few tricks myself over the centuries?" Hythea's voice was raspy, his grip tight.

Dillon took full advantage of the opportunity and lunged his sword through the General's body. He followed with a wide-sweeping attack that cut General Trailerton in half. The two pieces fell to the ground. The wolves surrounded the prey that they had been hunting for centuries, growling and snapping their teeth as Hythea raised his head and let out a powerful howl that threw the gray mist backward for hundreds of feet.

Dillon looked away as the wolves ripped apart the astral body, filling their bellies and souls.

VIII.

Cahlar watched from his throne as Diabold removed the one-ton rock from its location underneath the parted lava flow. Cahlar was stymied again as he tried to figure out what Diabold was. A demon is what he was told, but surely not the beings from the planes of Hell in human religion. That would be impossible. However, it seemed as if Diabold was more than he let on and could easily crush Jialin if he was so inclined.

Jialin started his incantation and slowly raised up the travelers coming through the portals while protecting them from the surrounding lava. The stone lid and flowing lava ensured that no one coming through the portal could surprise the paranoid Cahlar.

Cahlar was in a good mood and greeted each one with a slight bow. He gestured for them to walk into the meeting room to his right. In turn he was greeted with very deep bows fitting of his title as Overlord.

Jialin ensured that everyone was seated in the large room before motioning for Diabold to shut the door and wait on the other side. Cahlar took the seat at the head of the table and looked at the seven feudal lords he had originally chosen to rule Igypkt after The Gallen War. Four of them were powerful human mages from Ishtan and Kalansi; two were chieftain shapeshifters* from Malafand*; and the last was a blue-green humanoid with gills and fins from Nalistat.#

"Thank you all for coming to this emergency meeting. The web for The Gallen War is stronger than ever, and soon we will see a battle that weakens the most powerful humans and creatures on Igypkt. We will gather our army to swiftly take reign of the devastated world, whereupon you will all gain the lands that you were promised." Cahlar paused, then slowly rose from his chair. "However, like all well-laid plans, an anomaly has occurred that we must quickly resolve."

"Anomaly?" The huge bear-shifter did not like Cahlar's indirect words.

231

"Yes, anomaly. It seems that the Mulshins I told you about have landed another spacecraft on Igypkt. This time the aliens not only survived the first day, but are headed to Cureio as we speak."

"Survived? No, he has done more than survive, Cahlar. He defeated your sentries, took out the powerful doppelganger* Mankin, and even destroyed The Fallen One. The rumor of his magical ability is said to equal and possibly surpass that of the great mages!" spoke Qwazlo*, the mage who could see into the past. His words had drawn the whole table into a verbal frenzy. The noise in the room was deafening, but Cahlar did not try to squelch it.

Finally, Danekro* the great bear-shifter growled out. "What are you going to do, Cahlar?"

"Do? I have already done something. My largest and best assassination troop already engaged them in Cohvan, on Kalansi. I should receive word shortly from General Trailerton that they succeeded, or that he finished them off himself." Cahlar looked around at his disgruntled subordinates. "But, I have also decided that it is time to put an end to these alien invasions."

"How, Cahlar? They come from the sky, just like you." Dovern* the doppelganger* spoke up. They had all seen Cahlar's powers and had no doubt that he was something of a deity.

"No, Dovern. They come from their home planet called Earth, and it is to their home planet that we must travel and conquer." Cahlar barely hesitated before he continued. "Their planet is not like yours, as they do not yet have mana-casting humanoids or magical creatures. Earth is only starting to gain mana, and it will be a long time before any can challenge your powers. Some of you will rule the alien's home world as near demigods. Under my supreme authority, of course."

"How does that stop the Mulshins?" asked Kaieesh* the Nalistatian.

Cahlar had to think fast, as he didn't want to reveal his true plan. "Simple. With us ruling both planets, the Mulshins will not be able to recruit Earthlings to attack us. We will recruit the Earthlings to attack them. But first we must get there."

Cahlar really needed them on Earth to help find the between-world portal that had so far eluded him on Igypkt. With the portal, not only would he be able rule two planets, but he would have a way to avoid the Mulshin attacks. This was especially important as the Mulshins became more and more desperate to get his mana-converting device. If he could hold them off long enough, they would be forced to leave the Earthling's solar system for good. He would win. Cahlar smiled as he brought his thoughts back to the moment.

The grumbling rose again. Many of them were nervous at the thought of traveling to another world, but the sounds died down in a matter of minutes. Ruling a planet full of non-magical beings was too enticing for any of them to pass up.

"How will we get there?" It was Dovern again who spoke.

"That is where I need your help. We will travel in the alien's spaceship, but we need to bring it to Ishtan." Cahlar ignored the predictable gasps. Except for the watchful flyers, traveling through the air was out of the question on Igypkt—let alone through the sky. Cahlar also did not tell them that he would not travel with them, and instead would come up with an excuse at the last minute to stay behind. For now, Igypkt was the only place where the Mulshins could not reach him.

"Near demigods? I do like the sound of that," stated the human, Niefa*, who was still relishing in Cahlar's earlier statement. Niefa was a master creationist who bred powerful, magical abominations and unleashed them on Igypkt for fun. He could only imagine the havoc he could wreck on this new world.

"Let's focus on the problem, Niefa. We need to find a way to quickly bring this massive structure to us. Any ideas?" Cahlar was stymied again, and he hated being stymied. It truly disturbed him.

"Very few creatures on Igypkt can travel in air, and nothing can cross the dangerous seas except the island of Nalistat," reasoned Kaieesh, the blue-green creature. "Niefa could create a creature that could carry the starship on land, but nothing by sea or air. Also, it is way too big to fit through a portal." Kaieesh logically went through the problem as he scratched the scar on his right shoulder. "Our only solution is for Niefa to bring it to a portal on Kalansi, and then for those who are going to this 'Earth' to travel through the portal."

"The portal to The Fallen One is nearly inaccessible. That leaves only the hidden one in Cureio." Cahlar could not understand how he had missed such an obvious solution, but he tried not to look surprised or impressed by something he should have already considered.

"I have just the new creature to move the ship." Niefa said.

The conversation went on for another hour as they planned out the details of the spaceship's move and which of them would be traveling to Earth.

"Thank you again for coming," Cahlar concluded. "As a reminder, we must ensure that Cureio stops any outlanders from entering the city and that Nalistat does not leave for the open seas ever again. Is that clear?" Cahlar stared at the doppelganger and the bluish-green humanoid, who both nodded affirmation. Cahlar stood up and walked to the door, signaling the end of their meeting.

Dovern bowed as she walked buy, allowing her body to transform into the female Mulshin who was all too familiar to Cahlar. It was meant to unnerve him, but it did not. Cahlar had no guilt in killing, even if it was his lifelong colleague and conspirator. In fact, it actually excited him.

Cahlar smiled as the last of his guests were lowered into the portal cave. He still had no worries of someone coming through the portal unannounced. The probability of an attack from there was nearly negligible.

Once they were all gone, he laughed out loud as he thought about his new plan. He would soon be the ruler of two magical worlds, with only a child in his way.

Cahlar heard a cracking noise amid his laughter and looked down at the ring on his finger. The glow had been replaced by a dull, fractured stone. He directed his quizzical gaze to Jialin. Cahlar enjoyed the power he had in these magical lands, but he understood so little about the place.

"I fear the General has been dispatched, my lord." Jialin shrunk back slightly as he saw Cahlar's body start to literally bubble with rage.

Cahlar could not believe it. Another loss at the hands of the Earthlings hit his psyche deeply, fueling his paranoia while threatening his inflated ego. His mental state weakened by the millisecond, causing the nanobots in every cell to perform non-uniform actions. Lesions started to form on his skin while his insides melted. Cahlar's frustration and fear turned to anger. His eyes darted madly about, looking for anything to release his rage upon. His eyes locked on Diabold, only feet away.

With all the energy he could muster, he struck out both hands with enough force to shatter stone. However, his arms caved-in upon impact and did not even dent Diabold's chest. The crazed look in Cahlar's eyes went away as he looked up at the demon.

"Are you better now?" was all that Diabold said.

"Yes, yes. Much better. Thank you. Uhm...sorry." Cahlar had regained his composure, but was staring up at something that he now realized may be even more powerful than him.

"I have seeker demons* on the scent of your outlanders. I will tell them to speed up the chase." Diabold, uninjured by the attack, was still amazed at Cahlar's speed and power.

Jialin's face flushed as he too finally realized that Diabold was much more than he thought. The mana he summoned forth when Cahlar attacked had weakened Jialin's knees. Jialin bowed his head to the ground in the hopes of not being noticed.

IX.

Exhausted and mentally sore, Dillon bowed to the wounded leader and what was left of his pack before his form slowly evaporated out of the astral plane. He opened his eyes to see a sheepish-looking Matt staring down at him, while Sileya held his head in her two normal arms. He could feel a dozen wounds that should have been life threatening, but between Matt and Sileya, they were being healed by the minute.

"So, did you let those creatures get through just to try and prove who is a better healer?" His smile was infectious and a red rose sprang up and unfurled its petals between him and Sileya. Such a sign would normally have embarrassed all three, but after such a battle they were lost in the joy of just being alive.

In about another hour Dillon had almost forgotten that he had even a scratch, and he was sitting up eating more dried meat and some turnip-like vegetable. Matt and Sileya were exhausted from the healing and joined him in eating.

Sileya was the first to break the quiet. "So you two are really not from our world. Why are you here?" She studied and used the stars in her conjuring but never could have imagined that there were others living beyond her planet. Dillon and Matt had come from the same stars she revered, and she could not help but stare in awe.

"Ok, but by the time we're finished you will either think we're insane or that you are insane for believing us." Matt was excited to finally tell someone their whole story without having to worry about hysterical laughter or another death threat.

As they walked, Matt and Dillon took turns explaining their story while Sileya seemed to ask a question a minute, especially about Earth and the Mulshins. She took in everything, and before they knew it, more than six days had passed. Just as Dillon reached the point in the story where they had escaped the attack at Cohvan, they saw the Peaceful Gateway

Forest in the distance. The name seemed a little hollow; the last time they had been there, they were attacked by Mankin.

"So your mission involves seeing what happened to the other outsiders who landed in the city, reuniting with your friends, figuring out if the ruler is a Mulshin, and finally determining how to get to the ringleader who holds both the key to this 'electronic stabilizer' and your way home?" Sileya's tone didn't even contain a hint of disbelief.

"Yep, pretty simple for a bunch of teenagers raised in the over-crowded California school system." Matt's joke was lost on Sileya.

"We still have almost five full days until we arrive at the entrance to Cureio. With any luck we will get there well before anyone following us can warn the city or set a trap." As a giver of life, Sileya could also sense violent deaths for hundreds of miles. She could feel these tragedies increasing behind them and knew that those bringing the death would have caught up to them if not for her *Fleet of Foot* spell*.

Sileya quietly prayed that they would win the race to the city. Hopefully, she could save Dillon's life. Something inside her told her it was the right thing to do. Even if it meant her own life must end.

"It looks like we will be spending one more night in the open before we head into the forest," commented Dillon. Every night since he had awoken on Igypkt Dillon looked forward to seeing the stars. They cleared his mind and calmed his soul before he closed his eyes to drift into the astral plane. Normally when he arose in morning he was refreshed, but it had been more than a week since Dillon felt that way.

He knew why. He knew it was all because of the incredibly beautiful woman that shared their trail and rested each night only feet from his side. He also knew some of the same feelings were tied up inside Sileya. The rose had said it all. They were both, however, uncomfortably restrained. He, because he had never felt love before and didn't know what to do except ache. She, because she was one of the oldest humans on Igypkt and could not bring herself to accept the love of such a young man. Dillon could see her fighting it. Just one look in her eyes revealed everything, and he was sure she could see his struggle readily exposed in his own eyes.

He looked up again and sighed. The night signaled a newfound loneliness. He would do what he had done every night this last week: walk around the astral plane and pray for the sun to come up. The morning brought a chance to talk to her and, with it, a temporary calm.

Matt stepped out to the perimeter of their campsite and stared at the ground. He breathed in deeply and inhaled the beautiful scent of the greenery all around his feet. As he exhaled he encouraged it to grow, and watched like a proud father as a massive thicket silently surrounded the camp. Yet something was still bothering him. He looked over at Dillon and Sileya, able to see in their night routines the yearning they held at bay. At first he was repulsed since Sileya was so much older than Dillon. However, he had now watched them for days and could see that their souls were meant to be joined. They just needed a little help.

Matt looked down at the ground as he breathed deeply again, drawing the mana into his body. As he expelled it, the grass under his feet wriggled and writhed, moving him a few inches. He smiled.

X.

Dillon felt the rays of the morning sunshine tickling the exposed part of his neck and warming his back. He felt unusually refreshed and at peace. With his eyes still closed he breathed in and followed it with a slow, warm exhale. He then realized that his side facing away from the sun was also warm. His arm was wrapped around another person.

His eyes popped open at the same time and speed of Sileya's, as she too realized her backside was being embraced in a warmth and comfort she had long forgotten existed. They both just laid there as if frozen in place, stuck between wanting to stay and needing to move away.

"Breakfast is ready." Matt's voice broke the silence without touching the tension. He hadn't prepared anything for breakfast other than the usual berries he grew each morning, but he thought they might not move the whole day if he didn't speak.

Dillon removed his arm from around Sileya's waist and slowly pulled himself up into a seated position. Sileya then rose and hurried over to the fire, pretending to warm herself.

Matt walked over and handed Dillon some berries, somewhat disappointed that Dillon would not acknowledge the smirk on his face. Frustrated at being ignored, he turned to Sileya.

"So why is it called the Peaceful Gateway Forest? Who's at peace in there?"

Sileya continued to rub her hands near the fire as she spoke, letting the words help regain her composure. "The last great war was between the demigods and the great mages, with the final battle taking place on

Kalansi. Untold numbers lost their lives on the western side of the continent, and in their honor the city dwellers of Cureio spent years burying the fallen in a fledgling forest. Their bodies have provided the nutrients that turned it into the beautiful forest in front of us, and their souls still calm those that enter it."

Matt was trying to grasp a battle where so many lives were lost that a forest of this size could be created. It was horrifying.

"Sileya, from what I've learned so far, I assume the great mages were human. But what were the demigods?"

"Ironically they were the offspring between the great mages and magical creatures. You see, the mages had come into power over the course of thousands of years. They controlled the whole planet, and for the most part constantly worked to ensure the people and creatures under their rule were taken care of and that order was maintained.

"However, as one would expect some of them became bored with the mundane work of their day-to-day oversight. As history tells us, a small group was drinking heavily one night and decided to have a little fun. They set up a contest to see who could copulate with the most powerful of magical creatures. It was not an easy challenge for any of them, and each spent years mastering transformation spells before setting out on their ill-conceived mission. It was a short-lived game but one with long-lasting effects. Soon their half-breed children were born, and in many cases they possessed the innate magical abilities of their non-human parent coupled with the blood-line and mystical powers of a great mage. As they grew up some became more powerful than even Thoakeip*, the greatest ancient mage in the history of Igypkt."

They finished their berries and packed up their belongings. Sileya paused for a brief minute, closed her eyes, and quietly spoke the arcane words for the traveling spell. It was one of the hardest spells she had ever learned and required all her concentration. Her words beckoned the mana and gathered it from miles away, which flowed faster and faster around her until she summoned the final word. She felt dizzy for a moment as mana flowed both down her feet to the ground and up to the stars. She opened her eyes and motioned for the other two to start walking.

"So, the demigods decided to rule Igypkt and a battle ensued?" Matt thought the rest was obvious but wanted to make sure Sileya continued.

"Not exactly. Initially they were not hungry to rule. But the humans were amazed by their power and started to bring them gifts for favors. Soon they started worshiping the half-breeds and eventually placed them as demigods. The demigods couldn't help but become jaded by their power combined with the millions of followers. Soon they placed demands on those that worshipped them and those demands became more and more of a burden until the worshippers became oppressed. They couldn't appease the demigods' appetite and this made the demigods angry. They decided to punish them all.

"Of the demigods there were four who had become the leaders and planned to overthrow the mages and enslave all humanoids: Baleon*, son of the gryphon princess Leyacien*, who could not only fly but also control the winds he flew; Easnem*, the daughter of the great golden dragon Paslewo*, with the knowledge of all known magical spells; and Iwneik*, the daughter of the doppelganger Luseow*, who could instantly assume the shape and knowledge of any humanoid or creature he saw. Their power was unmatched and—"

"Wait, that's only three. What was the fourth?" Matt had stepped in front of Sileya, blocking her path.

Sileya looked at them both, gauging how much to say. She decided it couldn't hurt to tell the real story, especially if they were here to overthrow Cahlar and possibly lead The Fallen War.

"Ok, but it was decided a long time ago that the rest of the world should not know what I'm going to tell you. So please don't speak of this again." She didn't wait for an answer. "The last demigod was Death*."

"Death? So, who would Death's mom be? I would assume that Mrs. Death couldn't produce offspring." Matt's smiled infected Dillon, but Sileya tone became even more serious.

"Death was not its real name; it was a given name by the worshippers. You see, Thoakeip was one of those mages in on the original wager. The reason the bet didn't last was because Thoakeip made such a grave mistake that they disbanded. A mistake so bad that it cost him his life to fix." Sileya had continued walking and was staring at the ground as she spoke. "He was a kind man, but not without his own faults. His greatest weakness was what made him the greatest mage of all time; he was a fierce competitor and always had to win. For the bet he had figured out how to copulate with the Mist of Despair*, and their offspring was a creature in-between this world and the astral plane who could kill any in its path. The effects were powerful enough to even sicken the departed one's families."

"So Thoakeip couldn't face them head-on, so he must have had to figure out a way to weaken, disarm, or trick his opponent." Dillon was entranced by the story.

"Very good, Dillon. He chose trickery, betting that the overconfident demigods would think nothing could defeat them. Thoakeip had a message sent to each one of the four lead demigods challenging them to a contest of mana and magical ability. There were to be four challenges with two set up so that Thoakeip could easily win and two that he would lose. As expected there was a tie, and Thoakeip pretended to be irate and lose his temper. He challenged all four to the greatest magical feat ever.

"You see, Thoakeip and the four demigods were all able to create and transport themselves through Igypkt using teleportation holes. The same ones you went through to get to The Fallen One. However, his challenge was that they had to teleport to another world. A world that Thoakeip had studied for centuries in the astral plane and one he shared with the demigods." Sileya stopped as her voice started to shake.

"What's wrong?" Matt was so enthralled with the story that he didn't see the obvious.

"It's Earth, isn't it? They went to Earth." Dillon was stunned and had too many thoughts running through his head to even form a question.

"I think so, and I'm sorry if it was. The story passed to me was that to create such a portal was only possible by the creator itself becoming the portal. Thoakeip went first but failed. Death himself wanted to take the lead and created the portal out of its own body. But it was not foolish enough to trust Thoakeip. So when Thoakeip went through to verify his success, both Iwneik and Baleon went with him." Sileya looked at the two again as another tear rolled down her face. "I am really sorry."

"You mean they are still on Earth?" Matt blurted out.

"I don't know for sure; no one does. What I do know is that Thoakeip's plan would not have worked if Death wasn't subdued. However, Death did not know that Thoakeip had won over the golden dragon's daughter, Easnem. As soon as the three went through, Easnem cast a permanent stasis spell* on Death whose mana and magic was almost all being used on the portal spell. Death knew that if it changed back, it would lose the two other demigods forever, which caused it to hesitate just long enough to be trapped."

240

"But how come the others couldn't just come back, and what happened to the Death portal*?" Dillon thought this all sounded very bad for both planets.

"No one knew why, but they didn't come back. After what you have told me I think it could be because of the very low mana on Earth. Anyway, the final battle was fought between the remaining lesser demigods and the great mages. The demigods were defeated, but at the cost of countless lives, which created the forest we walk in. The Death Portal as you call it was hidden away and even I don't know its location. However, its disappearance did not happen immediately, and history told us that many magical creatures left Igypkt through it before the decision was made to conceal it."

"Please don't take offense at this, Sileya, but your planet has some pretty neat history." Matt knew he shouldn't have said it, but Sileya's half-smile showed him that she understood his intent.

They walked on quietly for a few more hours until Dillon spoke up.

"Sileya, were the demigods immortal? Such as having the ability to not age, just like yourself?"

"Well first, it is not that I do not age. Rather that I can slow down the passage of time as it relates to my body. The demigods were far more powerful than me and I imagine they also could do the same, and probably better."

"So I assume from your answer that it is another magic mastery using mana. If that's the case, then what about with weaker mana fields?" Dillon was very afraid of the answer.

"Hmm. I never thought about that. I have travelled through areas with strong mana and lived in places where it is much lower." Sileya's voice stopped as she thought for a while. "Still, in those weaker places, I have not noticed the difference in this ability. The slowing of time's effect on the body requires incredible mastery but very little continuous effort. I would thus say it is not terribly changed."

"That isn't very good for my home if they're still around. Especially if Earth is moving into a mana field."

"Dillon. You really think they are still alive on Earth?" Matt spun his head toward Sileya as he continued. "How long ago was this war and the time they crossed over?"

"Somewhere around a couple thousand years ago, but I do not know exactly." Sileya answered.

"And how old are you?" Matt asked for an answer that Dillon had wanted to know all week, but was afraid to know.

Sileya hesitated, but only for the same reason Dillon had not asked. "Around eight hundred years, but I stopped counting a long time ago."

"Wowser! That means you are over forty times my age." Matt had clearly lost his focus.

"But more importantly it means that the demigods could be alive." Dillon answered, although he was thinking more of Sileya's age.

"I am saddened for what destruction they may have done if it was your planet, but I just cannot imagine they are still alive. The demigods were not reclusive, and you would have known if they were alive."

"I hope you are right, Sileya." However, Dillon had a gut-wrenching feeling that the demigods were still alive on Earth. Waiting and hoping for the mana to come back strong enough to either rule Earth or use the portal to get back to Igypkt.

For a while the news of the demigods and the revealing of Sileya's age really bothered him, but the farther he walked the more the thoughts slowly melted into the back of his mind. Just when they had almost completely receded, Dillon remembered a meditation his dad had taught him after a rough couple of weeks when nothing seemed to be going his way.

His dad had told him that one often holds onto the negative ten times longer than the positive, and we eventually fail to see all the good things that are happening. This forces the subconscious into a state of despair and depression that can be difficult to erase, even after our consciousness moves on. However, his Dad had said, the inner smile meditation^ was just the medicine needed to bring one's perspective back to a healthy state.

After doing the meditation technique just once, Dillon had had to admit that he did feel better. In fact, things had seemed to start going his way the moment he woke up the next day.

Dillon knew that if he tried to forget about the demigods and Sileya's age, they would continue to bother him until he had dealt with them. He wondered if he could do the inner smile while walking.

Dillon continued to keep pace with Sileya and Matt while concentrating on maintaining a steady breathing pattern. Unlike seated meditation, it was unwise to try and slow down one's breathing for faster-moving meditations. Instead, it was better to keep a consistent rhythm and maintain an active flow of oxygen. He counted his inward breath, and then exhaled the same count. He repeated this for nearly ten minutes before starting the inner smile.

On his next inhale, Dillon imagined a very small, pink ball perched at the very back of his tongue and slight above his throat. As he exhaled, he held onto the small ball to maintain its size. On the next inhale, he drew in one positive thought; in this case he pictured walking with his mom and dad along the California aqueduct. The warm thought collected in the back of his throat, making the pink ball slightly bigger. When he exhaled, Dillon again made sure to maintain the size of the ball.

He continued with thoughts of his friends, surfboarding, bringing home his report card, flying over the poppy fields with his dad, and much more. The pink ball was the size of an apple before he turned his attention to positive thoughts about the demigods and Sileya.

For the demigods, he knew they could do no damage without a mana field, and there was still time. It was much better to know that the future was in peril, and not that it had already happened.

For Sileya, age should not matter, especially on this planet. He thought about the color of her eyes, her beautiful neckline, and the lips he hoped to taste. Dillon held all of this at the back of his throat, and swallowed before inhaling. He allowed the warmth of the pink ball to slowly travel down to his stomach. On the next inhale he let the ball explode throughout his body, and instantly felt the calming energy relax him.

"What was that?" asked Matt as he stopped and stared at Dillon.

Sileya had turned around to also look at him.

"What's what?" Dillon responded slowly.

Sileya picked up where Matt left off. "The feeling as if my mother had just embraced me with a warm blanket on a cold night, kissed me on the cheek, and gently rubbed my back until I fell asleep."

"Oh, sorry. I was just doing a new meditation."

"Well, it was weird. Knock it off." Matt was clearly uncomfortable.

"I liked it." Sileya smiled and winked before she turned around and continued walking.

Dillon saw much more in that wink than just friendship. It reified his decision to be positive about Sileya. The meditation had done more than change his attitude; he had confronted his fears and neither bothered him now. The pink energy still pulsed outward with his heartbeat.

"I can still feel it, Dillon," commented Matt without looking back at him.

XI.

Dillon and Sileya woke up in the same position they had found themselves in the morning before. However, this time it was not Matt's doing. Somehow their fears and inhibition had been lessened, although neither was close to fully accepting their feelings. Sileya still rose up without comment and walked to the fire to eat berries provided by Matt, while Dillon subtly watched her.

The three wrapped up camp and proceeded to walk after Sileya had recast the traveling spell.

"How much longer before we are out of the forest?" asked Dillon. He longed to see the stars at night again.

"I think it will be about another hour or two." Sileya still had not thought of a plan for how to get into the city or how to confront those that she had abandoned so long ago.

"Ewww! Does anyone else smell that?" Matt's nose wrinkled in disgust, but he kept sniffing.

"I don't smell anything other than some strong flowers." Dillon thought they smelled good, kind of like honey.

"No, something under that. I don't know what it is, but it's coming from ahead and to the south slightly."

"I do not smell anything either." Sileya was sniffing also and was about to shrug her shoulders when she caught a mana strand of something not naturally found in the forest. "Wait, we need to go that way." She pointed and let Matt take the lead.

It took about ten more minutes of walking off the trail with Matt's constant remarks about the smell before Sileya stopped them. "Oh no. I smell it also, Matt."

"What is it, Sileya?" Matt felt like the answer was right at the tip of his tongue.

"Close your eyes and stop fighting it, Matt." Sileya felt he should get used to trusting his instincts. It was clear that he always pushed them away because they left him vulnerable, and they reflected a part of himself he still did not want to accept.

Matt listened and closed his eyes. He sniffed more, but still could not name the pungent odor.

"No, stop using your nose. Breathe in the energy."

"But I smell it," challenged Matt as he opened his eyes.

"Trust her, Matt." Dillon didn't know what was going on but could see Sileya was teaching Matt something.

Matt closed his eyes again and exhaled in frustration, but did follow it with a slow inhale. He let the breath bring in whatever energy was out there. After a few seconds he caught the thin trail leading to him. On his next inhale he pulled the dark mana trail closer and let it travel to where it wanted...his heart. On the next inhale he perceived in the distance the dark trail rushing at him faster than he could react. It hit him flush and he fell to the ground, overcome with the sickness he typically contracted after trying to harm a living being. He threw-up the berries he'd had for breakfast and continued to heave for another minute before looking up at Sileya and Dillon. Sileya nodded while Dillon looked like he understood somewhat, but not completely.

"Death. Lots of it..." Matt gasped while Sileya just nodded "...and someone innocent was just killed."

Sileya looked taken aback, while Dillon instinctively moved into a slightly more defensive posture.

"Are you sure, Matt?" Sileya asked.

Matt sprang forward and started running madly to the southwest. He only screamed out one sentence as he disappeared from sight.

"Another is going to be killed!"

Sileya dropped her traveling spell for them all as she and Dillon hastily followed. Both were rapidly gathering mana with a speed that caused their whole beings to glow and become blurry to even the non-mana trained eye.

Up ahead, obscured by a row of shrubs, they heard yells of anger along with some screams. Dillon and Sileya burst through the bushes, not sure what to expect. They took a brief second to gather in their surroundings. Dillon was amazed to not only see Matt swinging his staff to and fro, but also to see the plant life within the entire area swaying to his bidding.

There was a carriage trail coming from the west that ended right in front of two large trenches not far from Matt. Stopped at the end of the trail were two horse-drawn prisons. Inside the cages were seven tied up creatures with woven bags over their heads. All of them appeared to be quietly sleeping. Another humanoid prisoner lay on the ground in front of the trench with its canvas-covered head chained to a large and bloody tree stump.

Dillon and Sileya quickly turned their attention to the five uniformed men battling the plants that mercilessly attacked them. The vines grabbed feet, arms and necks; the shrubs threw thorny limbs in faces; and the trees crushed bone with each hit. It all stopped quickly as Matt swayed and fell to the ground at the same time Dillon and Sileya felt a rush of energy hit him. They both turned toward the bald, well-groomed man from whom the mana had come.

Each extended out an arm. From Dillon came a blast of water, meant to stun but not kill. Sileya's one-word chant called out a burst of wind also meant to subdue. They both hit the mage at the same time and flung him into the tree behind him hard; the cracking sound led them to believe the bald man was dead.

Dillon turned toward the five soldiers, who were struggling to just stand up. They all were eyeing Matt to decide if they wanted to attack.

"Stop now or you will die!" Dillon bellowed in the loudest voice he had ever used.

Initially the command was simple to obey; they could barely stand from the vegetation beating. However, the soldiers re-weighed their options as Matt began to stir and open his eyes.

"Now, we will not harm you if you put down your weapons." Dillon expected no compliance. He looked at the one he assumed was the leader and reached out a hand while exhaling. He 'grabbed' at the sword and started to rapidly vibrate the individual atoms that made it up. The vibrations were subtle to the soldier holding the weapon, but the intense heat it generated was not. He screamed in pain as he dropped the sword that still held some of his burnt flesh. Upon seeing this, the others dropped their weapons.

Matt had regained his senses and commanded the vines to wrap around and tie up the five men. Dillon stepped forward, "Why are you beheading these creatures? What have they done?"

The leader did not speak up, but another responded, with an unexpected venom in his voice. "They are just animals and their death means nothing. How dare you attack the queen's men. Who are you?" the man yelled.

Dillon's voice was on edge. "They are not animals. Now, what have they done wrong?"

The leader spoke up. "They were found inside the great city of Cureio. The law states that any non-humanoid creature shall not reside within the great city. If found, it will be captured and destroyed."

"Oh my God! Dillon." Matt spoke in both earnest and amazement.

"Just a second, Matt." Dillon kept his gaze on the soldier. "Who decreed this law?"

"Jalouw, of course. The same who will see to it that you are treated just as fairly for the crime you have committed." Dillon's heart seemed to both jump and sink. They finally knew for sure where one of the Mulshins was located, but it also meant they would soon be testing their wits against this powerful being.

"Dillon. These are open graves." Matt didn't seem to care about what the soldiers said and it took a second before his words sunk in. Dillon turned to the south and stared at the two ten-foot wide, parallel open trenches. After about forty feet in length the dirt had been replaced, creating a mound. These mounds went up over the hill and out of site.

Dillon took a deep slow breath and turned his whole body toward the south. He slowly started walking that direction, ignoring the thump of the awakening mage as Sileya's spell slammed him back into the tree.

"They did this, Sileya. They killed all these creatures just for being found within the city walls." Matt's voice rose with each word, anger and hatred filling his voice. The vines he controlled tightened on the soldiers like a snake constricting its prey, while he fought the mounting sickness wracking his body. The murderers would die shortly.

"Matt. I don't think you can blame them. It is surely The Gallen War spell." Sileya had covered his shoulder with her hand, helping calm Matt down. The men all gasped for breath as the vines lessened their grip. "Let me talk to them." Sileya stepped forward and began to whisper to the men.

Matt looked after Dillon, who was still walking alongside the western-most trench and was almost out of view. He then looked at the prisoners, who were all trying to break free of their bindings. He assumed that the mage must have had some kind of control over their minds. This would also explain how he fell asleep mid-battle.

Matt then noticed that the captive on the trunk had not moved. Its body was unclothed but covered in a light blue felt, very similar to feathers. Even through the covering he could see the bulging muscles on its six-foot-plus frame. Its arms ended in three large fingers that began as soft blue felt at the base and ended in a dull, black texture. They looked like clipped talons. Its legs ended strangely, with the back part similar to a hoof and the front mimicking a human foot—except again for the talon-like ends that were clipped off and bleeding. The creature's powerful stature was frightening, and Matt thought it best to wait until Dillon returned before setting it free.

The mage woke up again after a few more minutes, shaking his head from side to side. With the wave of Matt's staff, a tree limb thunked him on the head, sending him face-first into the leaf-covered ground.

Dillon returned almost a half-hour later, walking parallel to the eastern mound. He did not speak until he was right next to Sileya and Matt.

"The Gallen War?"

"Yes. They do not understand what they have done. They believe that they are ridding the city of evil." Sileya's always-confident voice was quivering, "Just like I believed before you two came along."

Dillon looked between Matt and Sileya. "I was so sure that the evil spell causing The Gallen War could be changed without loss of innocent life. Maybe it still can. I hope it still can. But if not, then it still must be fixed. And we must do it." Dillon shifted his gaze a little higher as he accepted the destiny that everyone had been saying was his.

"So what do we do with the soldiers, mage, and the creatures?" Matt looked over at the mage, who was starting to wake up again.

"I used a spell on the soldiers that erased their minds. They'll remember in a few weeks who they are and what happened, but by then we'll be long gone." Sileya turned toward the mage who was staring at his own hands and feet. "I think the mind-control mage has been knocked back into childhood."

Dillon turned his attention to the wagons and spoke up. "Prisoners, please listen up. We are going to free you, but in return we ask that you not attack us. The humanoids are under a spell that makes them think all magical creatures are evil, and we will work to change this. I promise you."

They walked to the first cart and Sileya used one of the soldier's keys to open the cage. They slowly untied each creature one at a time, leery of an attack. However, every one merely bowed and ran away.

When finished, they turned to the creature still chained to the stump. "Sorry that you had to wait so long, but I have a feeling you will require a little more effort from us."

As Dillon finished talking he saw the muscles on the creature's body bulge and writhe. He heard the groan from under the canvas mask and from the chains. To all their amazement, the chains started snapping until the creature was completely free. It stood up and ripped the canvas bag from its head, revealing a light blue, bird-like face with a bleeding beak that had recently been chopped down to almost nothing. In spite of this, its majestic appearance and royal aura were not dampened.

"And how are you three going to take on an entire city, continent, and then the world? Your swords, no matter how sharp, can only reach as far as your arms can swing." The statement was enunciated in perfect rhythm to establish dominance.

Impressed, Dillon saw before him a powerful ally he must win over. "While at some later day I trust you will see that my sword's path reaches the full length of my intent, I would rather argue with you on the point that a weapon is only one tool for battle. An extension of the warrior who must have an even stronger mastery of his words and strategy in order to win the day. I will use all the gifts I have been given and all the skills I have learned to unravel the evil that has been cast."

The creature's eyes pierced through Dillon's gaze before looking at Sileya, then Matt. "A simple, young outcast thinks he can step into a man's game of political intrigue? You will quickly be laid over the laps of giants and spanked before being sent home to suckle on your mother's breast."

"Wisdom is the son of time, but only useful when self-reflection holds his hand. If you are to be an aged one who believes his wisdom is best kept in the fear-locked corners of his mind then that is your choice. I will use what I have learned to act!"

The creature did not return the attack. He stared at Dillon for many seconds before the feathers on the side of his bloody beak raised up. It looked like either a smile or an invitation to dinner. "So, the words you spoke about fixing what is wrong came from the heart. How do you propose to repay the scores of lives recently cast into the bowels of this forest? Lives so easily cast aside by humanoids such as yourself."

Dillon again went with his gut feeling. It was no longer a mental joust, but a time to show need. "I honestly do not know yet. We have friends in the city and have to get to them and learn the strengths and weaknesses of our enemy before we decide on a course of action. We clearly need help."

"Yes you do. I will help you but only with my words, for I do not think you can win."

"That is more than enough. But first, do you mind if we fix that which our own kind did to you?"

"Thank you, but it was more than an axe that wounded me. Spells were cast so that they would never regrow."

Dillon looked over at Sileya and Matt, who both nodded. He turned back to the creature. "What is your name?"

"Wynhorn*."

"Wynhorn. Sileya and Matt can heal you if you let them."

Wynhorn looked at the powerful woman and the muscular lad. He slowly raised his head up and down once. They both went up to him and touched his shoulders. Matt closed his eyes and used his energy to feel inside of Wynhorn's body while Sileya worked to unravel the spell that stopped the cartilage growth. In only a few seconds she had thrown it aside, but held on to see how Matt worked. She was amazed at what he did and how he caused Wynhorn's body to heal and regrow at an amazing pace. While she could use spells to get a similar effect, she saw that Matt was using pure energy and shaping it to his will.

After a few moments, Matt opened his eyes, took a few steps back, and sat down on the ground to recover. Wynhorn did not look at or touch his re-grown beak or claws, but stared at the places on his body where his old scars had been. They too were gone, and he felt none of his usual aches and pains gathered from the battles he had been through.

"Amazing!" was the first word out of Wynhorn's now-beaked mouth. They all sat down, next to the gravesite, and listened to Wynhorn tell his tale. How the city had a beautiful past, both good and bad, but none as bad as when Jalouw took over. She had arrived in broad daylight, boldly stormed into the king's tower, and easily threw aside all the guards. Her speed and power was no match for anyone or anything on Kalansi, and she quickly dispatched the king and took control.

Wynhorn went on to describe how the nine great ruling casts where slowly being converted to mere puppets of the new queen. How many new, senseless laws were created with each bearing the penalty of death. He talked about his life within the city. How the ruling casts were family-run but competed for upon the natural death of its leader if he or she was heirless. How the Purple House was open for a new leader and how Wynhorn himself was favored to win the week-long contest and be declared its chief. Jalouw then mandated that all magical creatures be thrown out of the city. Wynhorn was ready to challenge the ruler and had already won over most of the city, until word of The Gallen War ripped through the continent. The hatred tore apart his own supporters and Wynhorn was forced to leave. He came back to run the underground uprising, but had been caught and wound up where they found him today.

"Wynhorn. Do you know anything about a metal object that landed in the city?"

"Yes, I was there when it came down. I, like many others, saw it open up and heard the screams of those inside as the mages threw fireball after fireball into the hole. We all saw how Jalouw screamed like a madwoman and had the four charred skulls dragged out and placed on stakes. Strangely enough, that seemed to be the point when her maniacal lust for complete control sharply rose."

"You said only four bodies were pulled out? Not five?" Dillon was a little excited.

"No, just four. I was in the sky watching. I'm sure of it."

"In the sky? You can fly? How, if you don't have wings?" Matt hadn't seen many flying magical creatures, and Sileya had said they were rare.

"Yes, my whole race can fly."

"Your race?" Dillon had found that such an open-ended question usually gave him more information than he could have dreamed from a pointed question. Too bad he hadn't learned it before he'd met The Fallen One.

"You do not know of my race? Nor of the continent of Malafand?"#

Sileya nodded, but Dillon and Matt just shrugged their shoulders.

"Really? What about the triad city of Dopplegange*, one of the three stops of the floating island?" Wynhorn received the shrugs again. "Where on Kalansi have you grown up?"

"Sorry, I am a simple young outcast." Dillon didn't smile, but on the inside he was aglow with laughter.

"Yes, very well. Although you clearly are not as educated as one might think, wisdom has aged you faster than your outward appearance would suggest." Wynhorn received yet another shrug from Dillon. He resigned to accepting Dillon's ignorance and began his history lesson. "There are three cities that are connected by the floating island of Nalistat. The one you are headed toward on Kalansi is the first and where the island was carved from. The second is the Great Emperor's city of Chinot* on the lush, tropical Ishtan. The last docking is at the city of Dopplegange on my homeland Malafand. Malafand is where all shapeshifters came from and where all but a handful remain.

"Scattered through my continent are majestic falcons, eagles, bears, deer, and the mighty bison. Also small but wise foxes, rabbits and frogs. Of course, one cannot forget the doppelgangers who control the city and the southern lands of Malafand."

"Are they all evil like Mankin was?" Matt knew he had a bad habit of interjecting, but even Dillon's stare didn't make him feel guilty.

"Mankin? Mankin is unique and very powerful for a doppelganger. Sure, he can shapeshift, but he also has the ability to control lightning. Or should I say *had*?" Wynhorn noticed Matt's used of the past tense and began to surmise that there was something special that this group of travelers may hold. Very special if they were able to kill Mankin. "Anyway, to answer your question, no. Doppelganger laws are strange and often thought of as benefiting those that thrive on evil. However, their unique ability to mimic all they touch yields a different mindset and a bizarre way of life. They do not value the lives of others lives since they can capture and hold a part of the soul of those they kill.

"Now, as I was saying before. Malafand has many kinds of shapeshifters, and for the most part we live in harmony, even with the doppelgangers. My home is in the great, snow-covered mountains of the north, where we fly on the winds with no known enemies or predators. As a race we ensure justice is upheld and that all respect the land we live off of."

"You said few left, so why did you leave?" Dillon thought that Wynhorn's voice yearned of home while his mannerisms betrayed a royal bloodline.

Wynhorn smiled. "Simple, I am an outcast. As much as I love to soar over the valleys and live with my siblings, I always yearned to see more. To be more. I felt alone on Malafand and boarded Nalistat when I was still young. I never regretted leaving, not until recently. That is to say when Cureio and all of Kalansi became a land steeped in racism."

"Oh no!" Sileya stood up and looked nervously to the west. "What's wrong" Dillon jumped to his feet and searched with his eyes, then his mana. Something was coming fast toward them and the feeling Dillon had was one of doom. "What is that?"

Sileya weighed their options as she spoke. "They are seeker demons. Each one has a single purpose, and that is to hunt and track down the being it thirsts for. I should have told you earlier, but didn't want to worry you about something you could not fight. Also, my traveling spell was assured to get us to the city and into the safety of the *Flying Fishermen* before the evil creatures caught up to us. However, this side step slowed us down enough for them to catch up."

"Ok, so I can kill demons without getting sick. It's just another insurmountable fight as I see it." Matt's words exuded his confidence from the previous battle in the desert.

"No. The prey cannot harm it, but it also cannot directly harm its prey. When a seeker demon finds its target, it will leap into the very soul of that being. All evil creatures who see that being will want the power trapped in the being's soul and will do anything to kill it. All creatures of good that see the being with think it is evil and will do everything in their power to destroy it." Sileya wondered if casting her traveling spell would allow them to run and reach the city in time.

"Can a creature that is not the target stop them, my lady?" Wynhorn's calm was not shared by the other travelers.

Sileya gazed at Wynhorn, realizing that he now knew who she was. "Possibly, but I've never seen or heard of one trying. It is still a powerful demon and can physically hurt any creature that is not the one it seeks. Death would seem inevitable to any that try to stop it."

"Well, having my head chained to a block of wood made me feel like death was inevitable. Maybe it was only a temporary delay. We will see. Now go and set right that which is horribly wrong." Wynhorn's muscular body rippled while he sprinted between the two trenches. He was changing quickly, and after running less than thirty feet the man-like creature was replaced by a beautiful, blue falcon nearly six feet long. On an incredible wingspan he soared out of the trees and up toward the sky.

"Wow!" Dillon stared in awe. "I guess he also changed his mind about only helping with words."

Sileya finished casting the traveling spell. "Now we must run. But stay on the path, because we will be moving so fast that the bushes and shrubs cannot be moved out of the way. If you run into one it will slice through your skin like knives."

The three sprinted and a fifteen-mile-per-hour dash became a sixty–mile-per-hour drag race. They couldn't keep it up for long, but when they slowed down to a strong jog it would still amount to nearly a thirty-miles–per-hour pace.

XII.

Wynhorn glided high above the trees. His eyes easily focused on the three demons racing through the wilderness. Unnatural blood seeped from the bodies of what only could be described as recently skinned bears. Their overly muscular frames heaved awkwardly as they crashed through the forest, leaving behind a trail of rotting vegetation.

The shapeshifter knew he would not come out of this encounter unscathed. However, he was a politician on Igypkt—a land where a politician must be battle-hardened. He took one last circle high above the seeker demons before folding in his wings and straightening his body for the faster-than-freefall descent. The wind rushed by him with such a howl that he could hear nothing else. His eyes remained focused on the neck of his prey. He counted the seconds until impact; perfect timing was the true weapon of his race.

The demons heard a slight crashing as Wynhorn broke through the tree line. With less than a second to react, the demons were not fast enough to defend his attack.

Wynhorn flared his wings wide open before impact and whipped one talon out at the creature's bloody neck. He did not stop there. In an instant he was a humanoid again, and the talon attack was replaced by a hardened foot-hoof. It smacked the back of the demon's neck with such a force that the sound of thunder cracked through the air. Wynhorn's attack drove its neck into the ground. His leg continued down with such force that, when it hit the ground, he could feel the sinews, tendons, muscles and bone all straining to near breaking points. The force would have shattered a human's leg, but Wynhorn's body was built for just such an attack. He sunk down into the ground to absorb some of the impact and then launched back into the air. He followed it with a summersault that landed him on a tree limb some fifteen feet in front of the three horrid demons.

The demon with the freshly broken neck rose and stared at its attacker. It looked even scarier with its head hanging nearly to the ground from the snapping of its spine.

From his higher vantage point, Wynhorn twitched his neck slightly. He had never seen a creature survive his fiercest attack.

"Leave us to our seek now!" The howling words echoed with the pain of a tortured soul.

"Well, you can speak I see. Although I must point out that your vocabulary is seriously limited. Maybe I can interest you in a more challenging war of words. Well, at least challenging for you." Wynhorn was trying to stall, and his words were the best way he knew how. He had thought himself a safe distance until each sprung upward around him. Their speed and power prevented his retreat.

They were too much.

Each one dug a claw into his body. *I guess death was inevitable*, was his last thought as he was pulled down from the tree.

XIII.

Dillon, Matt, and Sileya's sprint ended after only a few minutes, but it was followed by hours of running at a pace that left them all longing to stop. Still, Dillon was amazed at how far he could now push himself after never running more than a half hour on Earth. His body had become almost perfectly honed for physical exertion, as was his mind. He calculated that in a just few hours they had gained almost a day of travel.

"We must stop running now or we'll attract attention," gulped Sileya. She slowed to a walk and let go of the traveling spell.

"Who will know we are coming? All I see is a big hill in front of us." Matt wasn't gasping for air like the others, but walking allowed him to focus his running energy elsewhere.

"You'll see in a minute." Sileya was still amazed by the site of Cureio, even after all the times she'd seen it.

Dillon and Matt climbed up the gentle slope of the tree-covered hill and stopped when they reach its apex. Only thirty feet high, it was dwarfed by the stone wall of the circular city that was thrust more than one hundred feet straight upward from the surrounding flatlands.[#] Fourteen large archways at varying heights on the lower part of the wall had been sealed. The only visible entryway was a massive stone bridge leading up and over a forty-foot-wide moat. The bridge went straight to the top of the city at an angle that seemed nearly impossible to walk up without sliding back down. Wagon after wagon of travelers were being pulled up or pushed down the slope by a large chain.

Dillon stared out over the expanse with no words to capture what his eyes beheld. They had paused long enough that others were now passing them, all humanoid.

Matt was amazed. This was a role-player's dreamland. An ancient city with all the sights and sounds of medieval times he could have only seen in movies on Earth. "So this place isn't just one vast, desolate wasteland. That city must be home to hundreds of thousands of people, and I'll bet the surrounding farmlands have nearly the same amount. Cool!"

After a while they pulled their eyes away from the city and surveyed the farmlands and mini-villages surrounding the outer reaches of the walls, noticing how they were all abuzz with activity.

"There's not a single non-humanoid in sight. Wynhorn was right." Dillon looked back at the top of the bridge and could see red-cloaked guards everywhere. "Also, it looks like they are waiting for us."

"More likely they are all getting ready for Nalistat to dock," Sileya reasoned. "When the island docks, goods are traded from the other two continents. Also, the massive purple rugs on the sides of the gate entrance signal that the throne of the mighty Purple House will soon be vacant. Such an open leadership position is a large, week-long event. When you combine the two then you get a city bursting at the seams with people and activities. It is a perfect time for us to enter." Sileya started walking forward.

"What's with the strange reflection off the castle walls?" Matt queried.

"It allows light into the lower levels of the castle." Sileya thought nothing of it, but Dillon and Matt were stunned at the implications. Natural lighting passing through solid walls could help solve their world's energy crisis.

"How do you think we should enter? Grab some coverings from one of the villages and buy a cart with stuff to sell?" Dillon said, but he thought it sounded too simple.

"Exactly what I was thinking," Sileya responded. "You must have done this before."

"Only around a table during the weekends." His reply left Sileya with a confused expression.

Chapter 14
The Gathering

I.

"I really thought we were going to just walk right up and through the gate." Matt muttered as the immense chain pulled them up the steep bridge.

"Really? You are gullible, but so cute," commented Sileya, whose backhanded compliment stupefied Matt. She adjusted the small bundle in her hands as Matt walked next to the large oxen-like creature that was called a moalan*.

"Okay, we are almost there. Are you ready, Matt?" Dillon whispered.

"No. No I'm not, but what choice do I have?" Matt patted the moalan as he spoke. "Sorry, friend, but we need your help."

****

The soldiers at the entrance to Cureio had been on high alert for a week now, with nothing exciting to report. Thousands were entering the city every day, and inspecting them all for a few non-descript outlanders was draining. They had only been told that the criminals were barely men, most likely with no scars and having perfect teeth.

The soldiers heard a commotion about halfway down the bridge, and several of them moved in the general direction to see what was happening. They caught a glimpse of a moalan that had been spooked. The powerful creature whipped its neck to the side, snapping the smaller chain that was attached to the giant moving chain. It spun around wildly, trying to find an escape. A stunned, stocky man stood right in its path, and with a slight nudge the massive creature sent him tumbling off the bridge. The soldiers watched as the creature's back feet then slipped off the bridge. It snorted as it lost its balance and started to roll. A woman clutching her baby was clipped by the moalan, sending all three off the bridge and plummeting into the water. A young man screamed in horror and jumped after the woman and baby.

The soldiers knew it would only be seconds before the sea serpents arrived. Many on the bridge averted their eyes, but all the soldiers stepped closer to the edge to peer at the only exciting thing to happen in a long time.

The massive coils of the sea serpents appeared just as the woman surfaced and screamed wildly. She was pulled under while a six foot head erupted out the water, holding half of the moalan in its many rows of teeth. More serpents arrived, and the water turned into a bubbling cauldron of teeth and blood.

It was over quickly and the happy soldiers started to yell for people to move faster and make up the lost time.

"See I warned you all. Keep moving I say, but do you listen? No. Maybe now you will heed my words." A single soldier continued his lecture to the incoming traders.

II.

In the pitch darkness a splash was made, followed by a mad gasp for air. Two quieter and less panicked splashes shortly followed. One could hear a mumbled incantation and a dim light appeared in the small alcove.

Dillon pulled himself onto the ledge and reached out to help Sileya. Matt appeared to levitate out of the water, until one could see the serpent body that was lifting him. The beauty of its green scales glistening as the water flowed off of them was starkly contrasted by the piercing black eyes and dozens of saber-like teeth thrust outward from its gaping mouth. The massive head stared at him as he softly jumped next to Dillon and Sileya. Matt turned back to the serpent and gently patted it and tapped its snout. The creature cooed and sunk back into the water. As soon as the serpent was gone, Matt spun around to complain. "Are you sure that was the only way to get into the city? Fall fifty feet into the water, then swim twenty feet straight down into a small hole under the bridge and swim another twenty feet up? We could have died."

"But we didn't, did we? All because of you. Thank you, Matt." Sileya put on her best act and smiled at Matt. Matt stammered and stopped his whining.

"Sileya, can you bring your light over here? I think I found our entrance." Dillon had climbed a few steps and was stretching his arm out, holding onto something out of the light's reach.

Sileya walked over and pointed the magical light up toward where Dillon had climbed. They all saw the thick steel bars blocking the entrance into a black hole about five feet up the wall.

"Holy cow. I think we're stuck in this cramped, smelly place unless you have some magical spell for this, Sileya." Matt exclaimed as Sileya shook her head no. His claustrophobia started to sink in.

"Hmmm. I think I have an idea." Dillon started to slow his breathing and pulled in the energy around him. Sileya and Matt watched as water started to drip off his fingers while he held the steel bars. After nearly ten minutes Dillon pulled his hands back and said one simple word. "Done."

"Wow, you turned the bars reddish-orange, Dillon. Hey, how about something a little brighter to liven up the room? It's a little drab in here." Matt didn't understand why Dillon was just smiling at him, and he also didn't realize that his own harsh words stemmed from his claustrophobia.

Dillon didn't take his eyes off Matt as he pulled out his ninjato and started hitting the bars with the butt of the handle.

Matt watched as red-orange flakes started flying everywhere. "Oh, oh oh!" Matt exclaimed as he finally realized what Dillon had done. "You oxidized the iron bars using the water and your mana. Awesome!"

The two colored bars broke free and made a solid thud as they landed on the stone floor. "You cannot create light, but you can do that?" Sileya asked.

Dillon raised his palms upward and formed a sheepish smile. He knew the chemical equation for the oxidation of iron, but not one for emitting light. He turned to look at the dark hole. "So where does this take us?"

"To the seventh level. A little dangerous, but we can handle it." Sileya gracefully jumped up, caught one of the remaining bars, and pulled herself into the hole with one smooth motion.

They were all so pleased with the success of their plan that none of them thought about the amount of mana Dillon had gathered and released to destroy the bars.

All around the city the most powerful mages stopped in their tracks and stared into nothingness. An ancient mage had arrived.

III.

Sileya had successfully guided them past the whistling hounds and up seven levels of the city in only a couple of hours. She finished with warning them about thieves as they stepped out into the afternoon light. Matt and Dillon stopped to watch the hustle and bustle of a medieval-like city packed to the hilt due to the two upcoming events.

Dillon looked over at Matt and said, "You know, we never talked about how to find each other when we arrived at the city. This could be more difficult than finding a needle in a haystack, especially if they are hiding on a lower level."

"Why would a needle be in a haystack?" Sileya ignored their laughter as she realized it was another saying from their planet. Instead, she proceeded to walk swiftly through the crowds.

Dillon and Matt struggled to keep up with her, bouncing off people and barely dodging large moalan and their carts. Before they knew it, they were standing in front of the Great Northern Tower.[#]

Dillon and Matt froze and tried to figure why Sileya was walking right up to the front door.

"Excuse me ma'am, what do you think you're doing?" asked one the four guards in front of the massive wooden doors.

"Going to the library of course. It's still open to the public, isn't it?" Sileya innocently asked.

"It hasn't been open to the public for years. Why do you want in there?" The guard gripped his sword tighter as he spoke.

"Really? I'm so sorry, young man. I am from the farmlands southwest of Cohvan. When I was younger my grandmother brought me here to read stories. Since I'm in town to barter with the Nalistatians, I thought I would visit the library for sentimental reasons." Sileya's voice sounded sincere.

"Well you can't and I'm sorry." The guard himself almost sounded sincere, but then resumed staring straight ahead.

Sileya replaced her innocent smile with a look of dejection and walked away.

All three missed the skinny, one-legged man leaning against a shop wall, intently watching them.

IV.

"Hey, aren't we just retracing our steps?" Matt asked.

"We are going back down the lower levels. I need to read the book of The Fallen War to see what must be set straight." Sileya said as she walked.

"I also want to know about the lines we found in front of each bookstand when we ran into the demons. Sileya, are there any sentences underlined in each of the four books?" Dillon had a hunch it was something big, but just didn't know what.

"I do not remember, but we can check." Sileya glided down the stairs to the second level, turned, and continued down to the third level where the stairs ended. The lower level supports and houses prevented her from walking in the same direction to the Tower as she had on the city's top level. Dillon and Matt were completely lost and had to trust her memory.

"Are we there now?" Dillon asked when Sileya stopped.

"No. We are close though." She said and then walked into the open door of a small gift shop. Dillon and Matt followed her lead, pretending to browse through the merchandise as they headed farther and farther into the back of the store.

When no one was looking, Sileya opened a back storage room door and they all scurried through it, quickly closing it behind them. She touched the ground in the far corner and mumbled an incantation, but nothing happened.

"What's wrong?" asked Dillon.

"Nothing," stated Sileya as she sat down and lowered her legs right through the solid floor. She then dropped out of sight.

Dillon decided to go next and carefully lowered himself down, followed by Matt. Once through the floor they were surprised to find themselves in a three-foot wide passage with some light coming through the long wooden wall in front of them. The wall was actually the back of a bookshelf from where the light emanated.

"Where are we?" Dillon asked.

Sileya immediately shushed him. She pointed at the holes from where the light was emanating. Dillon peered through one and saw a small library on the other side. A young, tall man was sitting at a table reading an old book as thick as one's head.

Sileya sat down and motioned for the others to do the same. Dillon and Matt both went into a full-lotus position and meditated.

After many hours they heard the rustling of a lock followed by the shutting of a metal door. Sileya stood up and went back to the bookshelf. She grabbed the lower part of the shelf and pulled it backward, causing the whole piece to detach from the shelf. She then shimmied under the remaining part of the bookshelf to the other side.

"How come the whole thing doesn't just open? Wouldn't it be easier?" Matt asked as he barely squeezed through.

"It would be too easy for anyone to spot. I made the opening a long time ago for when I wanted to get out into the city unseen." Sileya reflected on her years as leader of the *Flying Fishermen* and the loneliness that often trapped her.

"Sileya. Who was that man? He controlled a large amount of mana." Dillon assumed he was like Sileya, appearing much younger than he was.

"Fihneum*. He was second in charge of the *Flying Fishermen* until I lost the city of Ahmarn to the demons. Then he assumed command. He's a good man, but is extremely arrogant." Sileya was looking around the room and then pointed to one of the shelves. "Here they are."

"Just like that? I would've thought they would be harder for us to find." Dillon commented.

"Don't be fooled. This section of the library is three levels deep, each with a series of magical seals that only a few know how to unlock." Sileya pulled down the thinnest of the four books; it was *The Fallen War*. "This is going to take a while."

"That's okay. Matt and I will look in the other books for any words that are underlined." Dillon pulled down *The History of Igypkt*, *The Foundation of Mana*, and *The Life of a Flying Fishermen*.

Hours passed without any excitement. Sileya quietly read while Dillon and Matt exchanged yawns as they slowly flipped through thousands of pages.

Matt turned the last page of his book and gently shut it. "Nothing, Dillon."

Dillon shut his book also. He felt like there was merit to his hunch, but he couldn't even find the first piece to this puzzle. Exhausted, he looked over at Sileya, who was only halfway through her book. He laid his head down on the table and closed his eyes.

Dillon expected to go to the astral plane, but something tugged at him. He saw the four books in his mind, spinning around and around. They started spinning so fast that the letters in the titles were disappearing.

Dillon snapped his head up, startling Matt and Sileya.

"Do you have a writing utensil?" Dillon asked. Sileya handed him the scriber that had been on the table. Dillon had no paper so he wrote the names of the books onto the table. He then crossed out each letter that was a duplicate until he was left with only twelve letters. He sounded the strange word out loud with no result.

Matt just yawned again, and Sileya went back to her reading.

Dillon had another thought about the length of the lines. He arranged the books in increasing order by size, then repeated his crossing out of the letters. He took a deep breath and spoke the order of letters aloud, "Wpkudtyr."

Sileya let go of her book and jumped back as it lifted into the air along with the other three books. They started to spin slowly, picking up speed until the wind was strong enough to whip their hair and clothing all about.

"What's happening, Dillon?" shouted Matt.

"I have no idea!" Dillon screamed back as he shielded his eyes.

A bright flash of light shot out from the center of the books. They stopped spinning, and each book opened up and floated gently down to the table. Dillon stepped forward and looked at the open book in front of him. On the pages before him, a sentence was now underlined. He looked over and saw the same for each of the other three books.

"A restless city is where he began the journey." Dillon read the first line aloud from *The Fallen War*, then one from each of the others, beginning with the smallest book and ending with the largest. "Is it a coincidence that the three continents are equidistant in travel? With blue mana gathering one can feel like he is drowning in sixty feet of water. A *Flying Fishermen* casts his net before sunrise in order to feel fulfilled."

After Dillon read the words, the underlining disappeared and the books shut themselves.

"How did you know to do that, Dillon?" Sileya knew a magical incantation when she heard one, and the one Dillon spoke was very old.

"I dunno. It came to me when my eyes were closed, but I have no idea what it meant or what the sentences mean..." Dillon was perplexed. "That made a lot of noise. Shouldn't we be leaving?"

"No one could hear what happened down here. I need another few minutes to finish reading before we leave." Sileya cautiously opened *The Fallen War* to where she left off. As she finished she looked at Dillon in amazement.

Dillon didn't like the expression on her face and asked Sileya, "Does it say I'm going to do something?"

"The book talks about the future war between good and evil, as we all know. It says that the battle between good and evil must be fought, or else the demons will gain their foothold on Igypkt. It tells of how an outlander must fight for others so that his people will not be destroyed." Sileya stopped, looking deeply into Dillon's eyes. He said nothing so she continued. "Lastly, it says that even if the outlander succeeds, his own lands will be oppressed."

"The Mulshins?" Matt asked.

Dillon was surprisingly light-hearted as he spoke. "It could be anything, Matt. The Mulshins, demons, Igypktians, even the IRS. Who knows? We can't worry about it right now. All I know is that we need to find our friends and together figure out what needs to be done. Let's go." With that he slid back under the bookcase.

V.

"I am starving. How about we get some food once we are topside?" Dillon was worried but just didn't see what he could do at the moment. Everywhere he went he was told how he was going to do this or save that. Right now he just wanted to eat and find his friends.

They all stepped onto the top level of Cureio and immediately noticed that something was wrong. The place was quiet and only a few people were in the area. Those few were about two dozen mages and what seemed like an army of guards dressed in red.

"By the order of the *Flying Fishermen* and the queen of Cureio, I demand you to lay down your weapons and beg you to not even think about using magic." A loud, commanding voice came from one of the cloaked mages.

"How did they know we were here?" Matt asked.

Dillon's mind raced backward. "The steel bars. I wasn't thinking about the mana I was drawing."

Sileya stepped forward slowly and spoke, "Fihneum. These two are here to help us. The Gallen War is a fake. It is The Fallen War. Surely you know this. I saw you in the library reading the book. Let them go."

"Sileya? I did not expect you back. However, I don't know what you are rambling on about. This Fallen War you speak of must be a joke. As you said yourself, I was reading of The Gallen War earlier today." Fihneum turned his gaze toward Dillon. "This outlander mage must be turned over to the queen. He has aided and abetted countless magical creatures. I have my orders."

Fihneum raised his right arm, showing a stump where his hand had once been.

"Wait! Wait! Wait I say," came a voice from behind the guards. "Fihneum, what are you doing? Good thing I got here in time. This ancient mage could wipe you from existence if you aren't careful."

Dillon thought the man looked familiar and then remembered that he was the mage in the forest who had cast the sleeping spell on Matt and the magical creatures. But there was no way he could have recovered from his head thumping so fast and travelled back to the city before them.

"Is that so?" Fihneum replied.

"Yes, you fool. I will take these three into my custody for personal beheading by the queen." As the old man spoke, a moalan-drawn cage with ten guards charged into view.

The old man walked closer to the three prisoners. Dillon looked into his eyes and recognized a cockiness that could only belong to one person. The man raised his hands, chanted in a low voice, and mana poured out. Dillon's head nodded and he slumped to the ground, followed by Matt and Sileya. The guards picked them up and placed them in the cage.

"Good job, Fihneum. I'll tell the queen of your cooperation in this matter." The old man and the special guards took off into the darkness.

The mage next to Fihneum looked at the departing group. "Strangest spell I've ever seen cast."

"Really? I have used that one before, Elzer*. Maybe your studies need some more work." Fihneum turned and walked away.

265

VI.

The moalan-drawn cart and guards rushed through the streets toward the Great Southern Tower, scattering people who otherwise would have been trampled. The bald man looked down at his sleeping captives. "Brace yourselves, and stay close."

The old man pulled back on the left reign of the speeding moalan, forcing the creature to turn sharply down a side street. The speed was too fast for the cart and its left wheels lifted off the ground. Instead of trying to correct his mistake the old man tugged even harder on the reign. The right wooden wheels couldn't handle all the weight and shattered, sending the cart, cage and driver skidding along the street before slamming into a grain and barley stand. The cage shattered on impact with the stand, freeing the amazingly coherent captives.

The queen's personal guards ran to and fro in a panic, yelling out orders as they searched for their escaped prisoners. The large sergeant of the guard ordered them to spread out, pointing to various areas with a hand that was clearly missing two fingers.

Dillon, Matt, and Sileya followed the agile old wizard through shops, back alleys, and empty rooms. He finally stopped next to a very solid door and tapped a rhythmic code. The door opened and they dodged inside, up a flight of stairs, and into a nice hotel room.

The two dark-skinned occupants jumped up into a fighting stance, but then quickly laughed with delight. Sileya watched as hugs were shared and joy overflowed the room.

"You made it back! How did you find us?" Taima squealed, letting her feminine side take over.

"Don't give us any credit. It was all Lian." Dillon slapped Lian on the back. "How did you find us, Lian?"

"Easy. When I heard the gossip of someone using great amounts of mana in the city, I figured it had to be you. Since we knew you were coming, I had some associates watching the towers around the clock. Once they saw you and also saw the mages setting a trap, then I decided it was time to act." Lian was pulling off his disguise as he spoke.

"Some associates? Who are your associates?" Matt asked.

"You don't want to know," Taima grumbled.

"Hello. I apologize that we ignored you in all of our excitement." Gabe extended a hand toward Sileya.

"My name is Sileya. You must be Gabe, and you must be Tanya." Sileya shook Gabe's hand and gave Taima a big hug.

"It's Taima, but no big deal." Taima gave her a healthy embrace.

"What? Taima? I didn't know we could change names on this quest. You know, I always wanted to be named Jackson. It has such a strong sound, don't you think?" Matt smiled at Taima who only replied by hugging him.

"Sorry to shorten our welcoming," Dillon interjected, "but I think Lian just gave us an opportunity to overthrow the queen if we act tonight."

"Really? We confirmed that the queen is the Mulshin named Jalouw," replied Gabe.

Dillon nodded.

"I thought we were avoiding a direct confrontation with them. What did I miss?" Gabe was stupefied and scared.

"One thing. We are going to surprise Jalouw, and if we set it up correctly we should be able to at least incapacitate her and get the mana-converting device without a fight." Dillon sat down on one of the wooden chairs. "We need to catch up quickly."

Dillon and Matt recounted their travels, with Sileya speaking up to add information from when their journeys merged. The other three were amazed at their encounters, and even horrified when they found out that real demons existed.

Dillon had neared the end of the story where they had fought at the massive gravesite when Gabe stopped him.

"The blue creature, Wynhorn. You mean to tell me that he is alive?" Gabe was clearly excited.

"I didn't say his name, but yes he's alive. Or at least he was. The seeker demons may have killed him. Why?" Dillon asked.

"He was the one we saw captured outside this very window by the old wizard that Lian mimicked to rescue you. He was the leader of the resistance here in Cureio." Gabe couldn't wait to tell others of Wynhorn's survival.

"The old wizard was also the one we found preparing to kill him and other magical creatures," Dillon added. "However, after a few too many lumps on the head he is surely walking aimlessly through the forest now. That's why we saw through Lian's disguise so quickly." Dillon continued talking, wrapping up their findings within the Great Northern Tower's library and the magic of the books he had uncovered.

Dillon then asked Gabe, Taima, and Lian to recount their story. The other trio reciprocated their amazement at what the group had gone through and what they had found. Dillon stopped them only when they talked about the spaceship. He asked to see the picture.

"So what do you know about the ruler of Cureio?" Dillon asked.

Gabe puffed up his chest as he answered, "Not much, except that he's as psychotic as Mungoth. He, I mean she, started the massive killings of magical creatures and was responsible for the increase in indentured troops for the city. It is clear that she wants to execute a surprise attack on Nalistat, and to do it she must gain a majority of votes from the House Colors and *Flying Fishermen*. She controls three of the House Colors and thinks she has a stranglehold on the *Fishermen*. Also, she has bribed many of the competitors for the Purple House challenge. If one of them wins then, when combined with The Gallen War deceit, she is all but guaranteed voting consensus to attack Nalistat."

"Her hold on the *Flying Fishermen* is weak. Fihneum could have stopped us since he must have known Lian was a fraud," Sileya analyzed. "My guess is he knows The Gallen War for what it is, but the rest of the clan is caught by the spell. He will be with us." Sileya saw the look on Dillon's face and subtly shook her head no. Dillon had no idea how long it had been since she had loved another, and how long it would be before she loved any man but him.

"Also, one of the competitors for the Purple House can never be bribed." Lian smiled as he looked at Gabe.

Both Matt and Dillon raised their eyebrows as Gabe's cheeks reddened in embarrassment. "I figured it was the best way to understand what was happening in the city and...and to try and stop the senseless slaughtering of innocent lives."

Dillon nodded his head as he spoke. "Agreed, and that's why we are going to take on Cureio's leader, even if I was told by The Fallen One that she is not part of our mission anymore. The way I see it is that we must take out Jalouw, Gabe needs to win the Purple House, and Sileya must bring the *Flying Fishermen* back to their senses. If we can do all of this then we can disperse the army, prevent an attack on the Nalistatians, and leave us a way to Ishtan with no innocent lives lost."

"But what about the evil spell that is pitting humanoids against magical creatures?" Matt asked.

"Sorry, Matt. I haven't figured out how we can stop it. We broke Sileya of the spell through logic and reasoning over many days. I don't know how we can do that for an entire continent or world." Dillon looked over at Lian as he continued. "So, what do you know about Jalouw and her fortifications?"

Lian sauntered over to the couch and plopped down. "Everything."

VII.

Jalouw sat on the golden throne in the great hall, listening to the updates of the recent events. The outlander with the powers of an ancient mage had entered the city and had been captured. Then the foolish wizard and his troops had let them escape.

"Where is Lifmin? He better have a good explanation!" shouted Jalouw.

The soldier cowered as he spoke, "Your highness, we could not find him after the cart crashed. We think the outlanders are holding him hostage."

"Then bring the soldiers to me that caused this mess. They will pay!" Jalouw screamed in a high pitch as the soldier jumped up and charged out of the room.

Jalouw sat quietly for some time. She was surprised that the young kids had made it this far, but was not too worried. She could see no way that a small band of humans would be able to stop a full assault on Nalistat. The Nalistatians were the only ones capable of making the floating island move, and soon they would be wiped from existence.

****

The door to the throne room flung open as a soldier charged forward. He took a knee at the bottom of the steps and bowed.

"You may proceed," Jalouw remarked after some time.

"Ma'am, we have all of the soldiers who let the prisoners escape." The soldier was shaking.

"Very well. Let them in so I may see them grovel for their lives." Jalouw needed to set an example for her troops, especially as they approached the war with the Nalistatians. She of course would not let any of them live another day, but the groveling both set an example and gratified her.

The soldier sprinted back out the far door, and within a minute both parts of the double doors opened slowly. Eight soldiers walked forward in two rows, with their leader in front. All held their heads down.

Jalouw stood up from her throne and made her way to the top of the three steps of her raised stage. She looked at the group with a quizzical expression. This was a strange assortment of soldiers, with varying body types and builds. She quickly brushed away the thought. "So, you let the captives get away. What do you have to say for yourselves?"

The leader stepped forward, took off his helmet and bowed. His flowing hair was recognizable even to Jalouw, who relaxed a little. "Kailman? You led these men?"

"Yes, my lady, and I take full responsibility for the loss of the prisoners," Kailman replied as he stared the queen straight in the eyes.

Dillon scanned the area while keeping his head lowered. The extravagant room was roughly forty feet long and thirty feet wide. Lining the walls were large and ornate rugs, embroidered with hulking Egyptian-looking deities that almost seemed to jump out of the fabric. He took note of the two guards at the entrance, two at the bottom of the stairs leading up to the throne in front of them, and one at each door opposite the throne on the raised platform.

Dillon surmised that they should be able to get off one volley of attacks before having to engage the real soldiers. His plan had a good chance of working, but he had seen the Mulshins in action on the Moon. Their speed was unbelievable, and a surprise attack was the only hope they had at catching Jalouw off guard. Hope and luck.

"You know the punishment is death, Kailman. How do you answer?" Jalouw waited for the begging. She would enjoy this.

"I will gladly take my place next to the innocent beings we have all killed due to your lies and deception!" Kailman's voice rose at the end, signaling the attack.

The robes of the fake soldiers dropped, revealing their weapons. In one fell swoop bows were strung, knives and shuriken readied and spears aimed. Dillon cast and fired a circle of ice bullets around Jalouw to prevent her escape as all the projectiles flew. Each hit their mark before she had time to react. The impacts flung her backward into the throne, her body sagging heavily into the plush red seat.

Kailman and Lian's two henchmen in the rear had not attacked Jalouw. Upon Kailman's command they had instead ripped their swords from their sheaths and charged at Jalouw's guards before they had a chance to call for reinforcements. Sileya too was assigned to subdue and used two wind gusts that caught the guards on the platform, lifting and slamming them into the wall. They both fell unconscious onto the ground.

Kailman did not want to kill his own men. He had smacked one of the two guards near the steps in the mouth with the flat of his sword, then dodged the other's sword as he punched him in the throat. When he had turned sideways he could see that the two guards at the main entrance were already asleep on the floor with the eight-fingered brute and skinny thief high-eighting each other.

Dillon almost couldn't believe how easy it had been. He raced up the steps to the body of Jalouw. His Mulshin instructor had explained to him that they kept precious possessions in their chest cavity, and that it was the most likely place to find the mana-converting device.

Dillon clasped his ninjato with both hands, aiming the point of the blade at the base of Jalouw's neck. He paused for a brief second, spooked by the lifeless figure that still looked human. He took a deep breath and thrust inward and down, splicing open the clothing and body. Blood raced out and his stomach churned, while the stench only added to his desire to vomit. Dillon almost stopped but then heard his ninjato screech against metal. As he finished his cut he saw a black object about three inches in diameter exactly where he thought it would be. He reached inside the warm innards, grabbed the device, and pulled. He stared at his blood-covered hand, and almost gagged from the stench of the filleted body.

Dillon whipped around and raised the trophy high over his head. "We got it! We got it!"

The others started to cheer. They stopped as the lighting dimmed and the room began to blacken.

"The tapestries!" screamed Dillon as the eclectic set of Egyptian deities he had loved to read about came to life and stretched out of their two-dimensional trappings. He could name them all as they stepped onto the floor: Anubis* the jackal-headed god of mummification, Isis* the goddess of Magic, Monthu* the falcon-headed god of war, and Sekhmet* the lioness-headed goddess of war.

Dillon was horrified, but still he ran to help as the nine-foot-tall creatures engaged his friends.

VIIIa.

"Sileya! Shift to the right and help Lian with Isis," Dillon shouted as he and Kailman stepped up to confront the insanely-muscular Monthu. The behemoth* held a scimitar* in one hand and a long spear in the other, attacking Dillon and Kailman at the same time. The speed of the scimitar was fast; Kailman's small shield barely blocked it, but the scimitar's power shattered the shield's wooden top.

Monthu thrust his spear at Dillon's chest. Dillon stepped to the side, but Monthu flicked his wrist and caught Dillon off guard, swinging the butt of the spear up to catch Dillon under the chin. Dillon's jaw smacked shut and the flesh split open. The spear butt continued upward, forcing Dillon's head back and compromising his balance.

Kailman saw Dillon lurch backward and stepped in front of him to block the scimitar aimed at his chest. The blow was too powerful, so he redirected the attack and grunted, then spun full circle to use his momentum for his own sword strike*. The sword broke in half when it hit the stone-hard leg of the war god. Kailman could not believe his family heirloom was no more.

Kailman had given Dillon enough time to regain his balance. Dillon grabbed a leather flask on his belt, uncorked it and sprayed the liquid all over Monthu. He spread out his arms and breathed in deeply, feeling the mana fly to him as fast as he could take it in. The equation for combustion of the alcohol with oxygen formed in his mind. The room's darkness briefly twitched brighter, right before Dillon exhaled and released his energy into the equation:

$$CH_3CH_2OH + 3O_2 \rightarrow 2CO_2 + 3H_2O$$

Flames erupted on Monthu with an explosive force that was impossible for a simple match to cause.

As the fire cleared, Dillon was staring at an unburnt falcon head. Monthu used his spear like a staff and smacked Dillon in the shoulder, snapping his collarbone and driving him to the ground. His scimitar sliced through what remained of Kailman's shield with enough energy that it struck bone. Kailman grunted from the pain, but didn't miss a step. He thrust his large knife at the deity.

VIIIb.

Sileya heard Dillon's first warning and turned in time to see what looked like the ancient deities coming alive. She was sure they weren't real gods, but their sheer size was still enough to invoke fear in anyone. As she prepared for the falcon-headed apparition, she heard Dillon's direction for her to help Lian. Sileya stepped sideways and in front of Lian, only to stare up at the eyes of the goddess known as the matron of nature and magic, Isis. Sileya prayed that she was not real.

Lian's knees shook as the giant creature directed her intentions on him. He could only imagine impending death if it got closer to him. Then he heard Dillon's directions, Sileya and the skinny henchman stepped in front to protect him, and Lian gave a quick sigh of relief. As Sileya began to chant, Lian wanted to sneak around their attacker but tripped over his own foot and fell heavily to the granite floor. He heard a pop and felt a searing pain behind his knee cap.

Sileya saw Lian fall out of the corner of her eye. She continued to chant, gathering the energy around her before finishing the spell. Sileya felt her body expand, and within a few seconds was the same size as Isis, along with four extra arms holding short swords. Isis did not attack. Sileya raised her arms to swing but then stopped as she heard a voice in her head.

Sileya, I am the matron protector. If you attack me, your unborn child will not live.

Sileya could not believe the creature knew what she had suspected but had been trying to ignore. She dropped all the swords and just stared at the deity.

The skinny henchman was the only one eager to attack Isis. He lunged forward and, gripping with both hands, swung his sword with all his might. It hit Isis in the upper leg, driving in a few inches before stopping. The henchman smiled at first, but then screamed as he watched his arms slowly turn to stone.

Isis pulled out her attacker's sword, causing his stoned arms to sheer from their sockets. The man screamed as blood squirted out, then collapsed unconscious to the ground.

Lian struggled to get up with his ruptured knee. Fear soaked his body as he saw Sileya freeze in place while his assassin was cracked apart.

This isn't going good, Lian thought.

VIIIc.

Taima heard Dillon's shout. She was shocked she hadn't sensed the impending attack. She turned and faced the towering lioness-headed divinity, who was readying a bow and staying near her tapestry. A flaming arrow magically appeared and shot toward Taima at lightning speed. Taima for some reason had no idea where it was going to strike, and relied on her athletic ability to barely dodge it. Another arrow flew at her, which she narrowly deflected with her left sword. Without her sixth sense working, she regrouped quickly and now was studying her attacker's motions.

"Fatman. Barricade the entrance so no one can come in," Taima yelled at the henchman. He spun around and followed her direction.

Taima side-stepped another arrow and then remembered that part of their team was behind her. She was afraid that her friends were being struck in the back. She smacked down another flaming arrow, then glanced backward. There were no arrows behind her. It was as if they had disappeared once they went past her.

She decided that dodging arrows would eventually be her downfall and charged the war goddess. After a half-dozen steps she was close enough to see its huge fangs and razor-sharp claws. *Maybe staying back would have been smarter*, she thought.

Her scimitars blocked and parried the attacks, until one claw snuck through and sliced the back of her right hand. Taima felt a strange tingling sensation and watched her flesh start to rot, forcing her to drop her sword. The pain rose exponentially as the disease tracked up her arm.

"Just great!" She shouted, "How can I block all these attacks now?" Taima kept her focus even through the intense pain.

One of the lioness claws swiped at her disabled side, now exposed. Taima started to grimace, but instead of the worst she heard a clang. The eight-fingered henchman had returned and blocked the attack.

She was ready to smile, but that was when she heard the garbled scream of the skinny henchman.

VIIId.

Matt and Gabe had spun to their tapestry when they heard Dillon's yell. Both had studied Egyptian mythology and recognized the rotting jackal-head of Anubis, the god of mummification.

"Hey, I think its head is undead and I can strike it!" Matt was excited, until he thought about what he was fighting.

Gabe already had his vibe sword in one hand and reached into his pocket to grab his electric webbing device.

Anubis was upon them in a mere second, and Gabe flung the blue web over his jackal head. He was surprised to not hear the hissing of burning flesh as he pulled it taught. Anubis reached for the webbing around his head, which left an opening for Gabe. Gabe thrust his vibe sword at Anubus's flailing arm and caught it flush. It only bounced off.

Matt swung at its leg with his staff, but his outcome was the same as Gabe's. He thought it strange that Gabe's tech weapons, though working, didn't affect their opponent.

Anubis attacked Gabe with his two-stick flail*. Gabe blocked it with his vibe sword, expecting to cut the wooden stick in half. It only bounced off again and, to his perplexity, he felt the force of the impact. In his moment of hesitation the flail smacked solid against his side. His ribs cracked like a whip. The pain was consuming.

Matt didn't understand what was happening. Then he felt Dillon release a spell and saw how everything flickered ever so slightly. Even the creatures.

IX.

"They're holograms!" Matt yelled out at the top of his lungs. He wanted to scream out that they were illusions, but that would notify whomever had cast the spell. No one on this planet would know what a hologram was.

Dillon cursed under his breath as everything started to make sense. He blocked another attack with his only good arm and looked at their state of despair. He had to do something but didn't know where their attacker was hiding. He tried to convince himself that the creature in front of him wasn't real, but almost took a spear to the ribs. As he side-stepped the attack he caught the glimmer of the throne.

"Lian, you still have any of those presents Arlar gave you? If so, I'd place it behind the power seat." The spear of Monthu swiped at Dillon's feet, knocking him to the ground. The scimitar came at him, but Kailman again blocked it with his knife.

Lian reached into his pouch and pulled out the last remaining ball. He couldn't stand, so he hoped his aim was good enough. He threw it up and over the throne and braced for the impact by covering his head and spreading out as close to the floor as possible.

The ball barely cleared the back of the chair, but it was enough. Everyone saw the bright flash, then the explosion and shock wave that ripped through the room.

Closest to the blast were Kailman, Dillon, Matt, and Gabe. They were thrown nearly ten feet backward and were stunned. The rest were knocked to the ground, but still retained their full senses.

Dillon was conscious, yet his arms and legs wouldn't respond. He couldn't hear, but he could look around. All the Egyptian deities had disappeared and the room was bright again. He strained his head to look toward the explosion and saw Taima and Sileya rush by him. They charged up the stairs with their weapons drawn. Taima made it behind the burning throne first and swung her scimitars into full motion, followed by Sileya's strikes on the stunned body. When they were sure the job was done, they turned back to their wounded friends.

Sileya came back to Dillon, while Taima crouched over and helped the dazed Kailman sit upright. Lian and the eight-fingered henchman were checking on Gabe and Matt.

Dillon started to relax as Sileya began her healing chant. He was dejected that the Mulshin mana device was only an illusion, and looked at his blood-soaked hands in disappointment.

Blood-soaked? His mind was jarred awake with fear. Dillon tried to stand up, while Sileya resisted. It took all of the physical energy he had left to escape her grasp and force his barely responsive body to the stairs. He heard a muffled voice pleading with him, but he didn't have time to stop or try to speak. He felt a hand on his shoulder as someone tried to pull him back. He managed to raise his elbow up in a circular motion—a wind Hoshin move—dislodging the grip.

Dillon made it to the stairs but couldn't raise his legs high enough to climb them. He let his feet run into the first step, tripping himself and launching his body forward. At the same time he lifted his open alcohol flask in front of him. The flask also flew forward, clearing the stairs and rolling to the side of the throne. That was the last he saw while falling, before his head smacked into the top step. He was still conscious, but barely, and felt the new, warm blood trickle down his eyebrow and drip off his cheek.

****

Lian hobbled over to help Gabe and Matt. For some reason his knee still wouldn't move, even though he now knew this was all an illusion. He saw Gabe unconscious and Matt moaning, but alive. Then he heard Sileya begging Dillon to stay on the ground and telling him the magician was dead. Her pleas grew louder, forcing Lian to look up.

Worried, he watched Dillon shuffle forward, shake off Sileya's grasp and reach the stairs. Unable to climb them, Dillon fell head-long onto the stairs and lost an open flask. The flask spilled a liquid all over the floor and came to a stop next to the burning throne. In an instant the spilled liquid caught fire. *Alcohol*, Lian realized.

An unworldly scream cried out, followed by a bright flash.

Déjà Vu hit Lian as he realized that the mage was a doppelganger. It all made sense now. She could look and act like the Mulshin ruler but also survive their first surprise attack. Lian had the feeling they all would have been dead if Dillon hadn't remembered Mankin and figured it out. The doppelganger Jalouw would have recovered while they attended to their wounded. They would have been in no shape to fight her again.

Gabe started to come around just as they heard pounding on the main entrance doors. "Your highness, what is going on in there?"

Lian limped back to the bag he had carried into the room and dropped on the ground before their fight. He yelled out in his best Jalouw imitation, "I'm coming. Hold your horses."

"Ma'am, we're going to break down the door," responded the voice on the other side.

"If you so much as put a scratch on my door I'll have you hung by the very fingers you pick your nose with!" Lian retorted as he pulled open the bag, and threw on new clothes, a hairpiece, and some make-up.

The door crashed open and a massive soldier charged in, easily holding a two-handed sword in his right arm. "Sorry, but for your own safety we had to come in. Uhm. Are you ok?"

Nearly a dozen more soldiers charged in as Lian readied himself to respond.

"Okay? No I'm not okay, and as you can see neither is anyone else in his room. An assassin disguised himself as one of the soldiers I was planning on reprimanding and set off a bomb. Luckily, Kailman and his troops showed their true allegiance and sacrificed themselves to save my life. Now help them all to my quarters before I decide to kill all of you for letting an assassin into my tower. And for destroying my doors!"

Lian turned around and limped back toward the throne. He had figured out that the limp was a result of his body swelling in reaction to an imaginary injury.

He tried not to smile as he made his way up the stairs and to the smoldering throne. He couldn't believe they had fallen for the ill-prepped disguise. He hadn't even had time to finish the make-up.

Lian looked down at the throne, which had been slightly dislodged from the explosion. There was a small gap, with a dulled, silver object inside. He reached down, grabbed what felt like a neck-chain, and pulled out the octangular device. It was about four inches in diameter and had been smashed, making it easier to identify the Mulshin electronics. A small door on one side was ajar. Lian opened it, revealing a rotted finger bone.

Lian wasn't at all dejected with the knowledge that only two devices were left, but he knew the others would be devastated. They needed it to get home.

X.

Dillon stared out the Southern Tower's only window, nearly eighty feet above the city's streets. The brilliant orange sun was now rising, bouncing its bright rays off the calm ocean. He rubbed his thumb across the octangular object that dangled from his neck.

A hand touched him gently on the shoulder.

"Everyone is up and recovering now except for Lian's skinny henchman. He died from the mental trauma of watching his arms being ripped off. Even though it was not real, the effect of such an illusion spell can be powerful." Sileya looked at what Dillon was wearing. "The doppelganger absorbed your thoughts when you reached inside her to grab the fake object. She used this to turn our worst fears against ourselves. The deities were always part of her plan, since they were on the tapestries. The key was how she used our fears through them."

After no response she asked, "What are you thinking, Dillon?"

Dillon continued to stare in the distance as he spoke. "So many things. Cahlar clearly killed his own Mulshin friend and left a doppelganger in charge. He must have also killed his other friend, but why? Also, why did this Mulshin device have a rotting finger in it? What does it mean?"

Sileya had no answers so she just rubbed his shoulder as he continued. "How can we stop this Gallen War? And what of the arrival of the floating city? I just don't know if our plan will prevent an attack on the Nalistatians. If we can't stop the attack, we won't be able to reach the only device that will let us get back home. What if just one thing goes wrong?"

"I don't know, but I do know that we can only try. I have to admit that so far it has all worked out. Not always as planned, but your leadership has made the difference." Sileya kissed his shoulder and walked away, giving him time to himself. She also needed time to think. To think about what the illusionist had forced her to realize. She could no longer pretend that a child wasn't growing inside her.

****

Dillon was still gazing out the window as the city woke up. *The streets are starting to fill with people. Innocent people who have been tricked to hate and kill others simply because they were born different. It's not right to harm them, but I don't know how we can stop the war without many dying on each side.*

Dillon's thoughts turned toward their experiences on Igypkt so far. *Why was I chosen to lead? I've only managed to place my friends in danger, nearly killing them at every turn. How can I be expected to save this planet, get us all home, and save Earth? I'm less than a year removed from being that kid riding on a skateboard. I sure wish Guylen had been around the last week.*

The immense burden and uncertainty were too much. Dillon's eyes moistened as his thoughts ran from worrying about the dangers of Gabe's Purple House challenge in two days to hoping his parents were coping with his disappearance, especially his mom. He had no idea what to do. Or even where to begin.

Dillon saw something small appear on the horizon of the endless ocean. It must be Nalistat, which meant it would be docking very soon. It also meant that the planned slaughter of the floating islanders was imminent, unless he and his friends did something to stop it. He looked down again and saw the now-gleaming spaceship directly in his view.

Dillon wiped the moisture from his eyes and stood tall. He may not be a perfect leader, but he was going to do everything in his power to ensure that no more innocent lives were lost. He didn't care how idealistic that sounded. It was a goal he must strive for in order to remain true to himself, in order to preserve hope, in order to survive.

Once Dillon realized what he needed to do, it all fell into place. It was time to go to Matt and finally get healed from his injuries so he could help Gabe reach his potential.

"Hey Gabe, I sure hope you like the color purple!" Dillon screamed toward the open door as he went to rejoin his friends.

Dr. Shawn Phillips spent most of his pre-adult life living in small farming communities in southern Michigan before moving to Holland, Michigan to pursue a degree in chemistry at Hope College. He then moved to California in 1992 to obtain his graduate degree in chemistry. He has spent more than a decade conducting and directing rocket propulsion research at the historic Rocket Research Site, located on Edwards Air Force Base. He holds a third degree blackbelt in Hoshinroshiryu and a green belt in Songahm Tae Kwon Do. He has two children, whom he joyfully raises with his wife, Yvonne Campos. They currently live among the beautiful desert hills of Palmdale, California.

A Must-Use Online Reader's Guide

Index & Timeline
www.dillonsdream.com/index.html

Glossary
(new words denoted by * in the novel)
www.dillonsdream.com/glossary.html

Maps
(map use denoted by # in the novel)
www.dillonsdream.com/maps.html

Meditations
(step-by-step meditations denoted by ^ in the novel)
www.dillonsdream.com/meditations.html

Educational
(literature circle questions, project ideas, research related questions, resource links, etc.)
www.dillonsdream.com/educational.html

Blog Room
www.dillonsdream.com/blog.html

Artist Corner
www.dillonsdream.com/artists.html

Dr. Shawn Phillips'
DILLON'S DREAM: WATER & EARTH

Qty	ISBN	Title	Price/Unit
___	9780982644638	Dillon's Dream: Water & Earth (paperback)	14.99
___		Dillon's Dream: Water & Earth Supplemental	4.99

Available wherever you buy books online, or use this order form

YBCoyote Press, 5654 Bienveneda Terrace, Palmdale, CA 93551

Please send me the quantity of books I have numerated above. I am enclosing a check or money order for $_____ (please add $2.50 /unit to cover shipping and handling).

Name_____ **Age**_____

Mailing Address_____

City_____**State/Zip**_____

Please allow two to four weeks for delivery. Offer good in the U.S. only (not Canada or Mexico). Prices subject to change.
You are welcome to send any questions to: info@ybcoyotepress.com
Or order from/visit our website at www.ybcoyotepress.com (including e-book)

Dr. Shawn Phillips'
DILLON'S DREAM: WATER & EARTH

Qty	ISBN	Title	Price/Unit
___	9780982644638	Dillon's Dream: Water & Earth (paperback)	14.99
___		Dillon's Dream: Water & Earth Supplemental	4.99

Available wherever you buy books online, or use this order form

YBCoyote Press, 5654 Bienveneda Terrace, Palmdale, CA 93551

Please send me the quantity of books I have numerated above. I am enclosing a check or money order for $_____ (please add $2.50 /unit to cover shipping and handling).

Name_____ **Age**_____

Mailing Address_____

City_____**State/Zip**_____

Please allow two to four weeks for delivery. Offer good in the U.S. only (not Canada or Mexico). Prices subject to change.
You are welcome to send any questions to: info@ybcoyotepress.com
Or order from/visit our website at www.ybcoyotepress.com (including e-book)